The Spartan Chronicles

MY SPARTAN HELLION

NADIA AIDAN

My Spartan Hellion
ISBN # 978-1-78184-513-4
©Copyright Nadia Aidan 2012
Cover Art by Posh Gosh ©Copyright 2012
Interior text design by Claire Siemaszkiewicz
Total-E-Bound Publishing

Total-E-Bound Publishing books by Nadia Aidan:

Downing Brothers
Sleeping with the Enemy's Daughter
A Rebound Affair
Riding Red

Heroes and Harlots
A Madam into a Mistress

Revenge Never Dies
Masochist

On a Dare
Every Desire
A Wicked, Wild Three Day Affair
Undercovers
Mating Season
Sex Therapy
On a Whim
Even the Devil Needs Love

MY SPARTAN
HELLION

Dedication

This is dedicated to Heather Snow, Dianna Love Snell, Mary Buckham, my wonderful editor Stacey Birkel, and the amazing writers of Passionate Ink. Without all of you this book would never have been possible.

Chapter One

Bones shattered beneath her blade, the warm ooze of blood coating her hand as she twisted her wrist and plunged deep. The man fell clutching his chest, the bright glow of life fading from his eyes like waves retreating from the golden sands of the Aegean.

Lamia did not spare the fallen soldier her pity, or a measure of remorse. The steely glint of determination hardened her gaze and she whipped around, her sword slicing through the air, a deadly warning to the remaining Athenian soldiers to hold their ground. Three of their men lay dead, and those who still lived hesitated on the other end of her blade, their fear wafting so strongly through the air she could taste its bitter flavour upon her tongue.

A dull hum echoed in the distance, the tiny reverberations whispering through her, even as every muscle grew rigid with the sound. Her pounding heartbeat matched the even thud, as steady as the faint clip-clap of horses' hooves, the subtle quiver stirring the dirt beneath her bloodied feet.

The trembling of the earth grew, while a chilling silence descended upon the *agora* of Athens, which only moments before had bustled with a cacophony of clashing voices and the din of music.

Her gaze remained riveted on the Athenian soldiers who took several tentative steps backwards. They were retreating, the fear in their eyes heightening her own, and her blood turned cold as if ice water now raced through her veins.

Squinting against the bright glare of the sunlight, she scanned the golden horizon, curling her hand tighter around her sword when she caught her first glimpse of the blurry figures in the distance.

A curse trembled in her throat but she clamped her lips tight.

More soldiers — at least a dozen.

Nausea clawed its way into her belly, insistent and violent, forcing her to battle against the bone-chilling fear that wove its way through her body. She could never hope to defeat a dozen men, but neither would she simply lie down and await defeat.

She had survived this long...

A cloud of dust rose like a pre-dawn fog around the advancing soldiers, their sandalled feet stirring up the arid dirt with every step they took towards the public square. These were not Athenian soldiers. Their movements were too efficient, the even staccato of their marching feet far too precise.

Her lids shadowed narrowed eyes as the soldiers drew nearer. Their bronze armour shimmered beneath the rays of the mid-dawn sun, the reflective glare illuminating the flag that bore their distinct crest. *Spartans*. Her heart beat wildly as if trying to escape from her chest, the dull throb of fear coiling inside her once again.

They had sent Spartans to kill her and she would have laughed had her situation not been so dire, her fate so clearly sealed. She was nothing but a simple swordsmith of the *Meshwesh*. Yet Attalus had sent soldiers of the finest army the world had ever seen to dispatch her. That he thought she was a dangerous threat to be quickly and efficiently eliminated was clear.

The Spartan soldiers marched forward until they were no more than five body lengths away. Corinthian-style helmets obscured their faces, the ominous masks of sturdy iron revealing only their eyes—all focused, full of determination, and centred solely on her.

A lone soldier stepped away from the phalanx, and, even though he wore the crimson horse hair crest atop his helmet that proclaimed him as their leader, she would have known he was the one who commanded them by his long strides and the confidence of his gait. His powerful build drew riveted gazes, and authority clung to him, surrounded him, emanated from him, as if he owned the entire world.

"Put down your sword," he demanded when he stopped before her, the deep timbre of his voice resonating with unyielding strength. The arrogance of his tone told her he was used to having his commands instantly obeyed.

This dawn he would be disappointed.

She tightened her grip around the hilt of the sword, her bruised knuckles red and chafing beneath the harsh sun. Holding his gaze, she stubbornly shook her head.

"We do not wish to harm you. Simply put down your sword."

She did not trust his assurance that no harm would come to her. After all, Atallus had sent him. She twisted her head from side to side with another defiant shake.

With a certainty, she knew she was going to die, and had she been alone she would have cried at the injustice of it all. She'd done nothing to deserve death, while the one whose hands were forever stained red with blood would probably draw breath for many *annos*. She blinked at the tears that burned in her eyes as her breath came out in ragged pants, dragging through her lungs. She refused to cry, for she was not afraid to die…not if that was her fate…

The one who'd spoken, the one she'd decided was their leader, turned towards his men then and nodded. His silent command was enough—the phalanx retreated, leaving him standing there before her…alone.

Beneath her breast, her heart did a quick flutter then thundered, sending blood rushing furiously through her veins, filling her with equal measures of dread and determination as she waited.

He faced her again, his clear blue eyes intense as he unsheathed his sword and approached slowly, hovering just beyond her striking range. Gripping her weapon, she began to circle, her wary gaze darting back and forth as she tried to focus both on him and on the men standing behind him. She did not trust them not to attack if she should wound him.

Circling like two caged tigers, they regarded each other warily, watching, waiting for the other to attack.

"Drop your sword!" he shouted again.

"If you are going to kill me, then so be it. I refuse to go back to Attalus."

His gaze flickered and he stilled. "I will not send you back to him. You have my word."

She studied him with narrowed eyes, searching for just the tiniest kernel of deceit shadowed upon his face. He was trying to trick her. As soon as she relinquished her weapon he would strike and she would be dragged back to Atallus where he would beat her, rape her, do whatever else his perverted mind could conjure.

"I do not believe you."

"I speak the truth. You need only to put down your sword."

She wanted to believe him, trust his word that he spoke the truth, but she trusted no one. Lamia shook her head. "No."

His eyes turned grim, the pure crystalline orbs darkening until they were a stormy grey, and for but a moment she had the strangest of thoughts—that a man with such beautiful eyes would be the one to bring her the ugliness of a violent death.

"Then you leave me no choice." His voice was resolute, the finality of his words breaking through her thoughts and forcing her back to the present just in time.

The force of his first blow nearly knocked her to the ground when his sword crashed down heavily upon hers. Metal crunched against metal as she parried his attack. She jumped back, trying to gain her footing, the scorching earth burning the soles of her feet.

She stumbled, nearly falling to the ground when his knee struck her in the ribs. Holding her side, she gasped for air. Every single breath was like drawing in fire as it burned through her lungs, but she managed to stay on her feet despite the agony. Every muscle in her body spasmed from exertion, until even her bones ached, but she refused to surrender. He would have to kill her if he wanted to win this fight.

Her opponent charged towards her, his sword raised high in the air and with both hands she grasped her weapon tighter, deflecting his next blow with a hard shove. Her teeth rattled and the muscles in her arms grew weaker from exhaustion, his overpowering strength slowly wearing her down.

She grunted, pushing back another attack, and he stumbled, his eyes wide as if he could not believe she still had that much power left inside her. She seized the opening he'd given her and swiped at his chest.

But with expert skill, he dodged her sharp blade and she missed. Her failed attack left her exposed and her body off balance. He did not hesitate. His powerful hand slashed downwards. She tried to duck to the left, but was too slow, fatigue weighing down her limbs until they were sluggish.

Something hard slammed into her jaw, and she felt as if she'd clumsily hurled herself against a large boulder as the wind rushed out of her. She staggered then stumbled, her vision blurry. Lifting her hand to her lips, her fingertips came away stained with her blood.

Then her world turned black, just before she collapsed in a heap to the ground.

* * * *

Thanos studied the sleeping woman, praying to the gods he had not seriously injured her. The physician had said she would be fine but that had been shortly past midday. Now it was dusk and yet she still remained motionless.

While she slept, he took his first real look at her. His gaze travelled the length of her body, drinking in the hills and valleys of her womanly figure. When he'd come upon her earlier, she had been filthy. Her abundant, sable locks had been a tangled, matted mess, her garments ripped and soiled, and her feet chafed with blisters.

With a slight grimace, he gently touched her swollen mouth. The blow to her lip had not helped, either.

Before leaving Athens, he'd hired a couple of slaves at the boarding house where he'd been staying to bathe and clothe her. He had not been able to tell then, but now as he gazed upon her washed form in clean garments, he could easily see she was a beauty. The rich sienna of her skin glowed beneath the burnished embers of the dying firelight as a gentle breeze from outside curled around them to carry her fragrant scent through the air.

A wisp of hair curled along her high forehead, and he brushed it back, grazing the soft tendrils with his fingers. Unlike the fierce woman he'd encountered in the *agora* earlier, in her sleep she was oddly vulnerable as her obsidian eyelashes rested against beautifully sculpted cheekbones. He should have pulled away — he should have folded his hand into his lap and waited until she woke. Thanos could not say what drew him — what compelled him to touch her — only that he could not seem to stop. Stroking a single finger across her cheek, his callused fingertip glided across the smooth silk of her skin. He then trailed it across the delicate flesh of her bare shoulder, before skimming down her arm.

The traditional Athenian *peplos* covered most of her sensual figure now, but the tattered clothing she'd worn in the square earlier had revealed ripe full breasts, a taut middle and rounded hips. A smile furled his lips as a wayward thought found purchase within the corners of his mind — that a figure as lovely as hers would be better suited by Spartan clothing.

The women of Sparta revelled in the magnificence of the feminine form. Unlike the women of Athens, Spartan women enjoyed displaying their beauty in revealing garments, sometimes even choosing to go nude at special occasions.

He started when she shifted beneath his fingertips, and, glancing up, his gaze settled upon her face. He stared in silence as she struggled to awaken, a low moan escaping her lips when she fought to prise her eyelids open.

"Take it easy," he whispered, resting a gentle but firm hand atop her shoulder.

She resisted his touch, her hand shooting out to push him away as she scrambled back against the sturdy wall of the tent, her ochre eyes flashing.

"Who are you?"

The hoarse croak of her voice didn't go unnoticed by him, and he frowned, worrying again of any lingering discomfort from his strike even as he answered her.

"I am General Thanos Aristaeus of Sparta," he offered in a gentle, hushed tone, not wanting to frighten her. "You should take it easy. You suffered a nasty blow."

She studied him with those lovely, piercing eyes of hers. And when they darkened, he knew she recognised him.

"You're the one who fought me," she stated, the accusation heavy in her voice.

"I apologise for striking you but it was the only way I could subdue you without hurting you. My intent was not to kill you —"

"Well, you should have. I will not be a slave to that madman."

He knew exactly of whom she spoke and he tamped down his rising fury towards Atallus for whatever ills he'd done to this woman, and he imagined there were many.

"And you shall not be." His voice was firm. He wanted to assure her she was now safe with him. "You are no longer his slave."

"How is that possible? If you do not plan to return me to Atallus, then why am I not dead?"

A good question — one he'd known would come the moment she awoke to discover she wasn't to be returned to Atallus. His small militia of Spartan soldiers had been in Athens for a fortnight, gathering information on the movements of the Roman army. He'd just concluded his meeting with Atallus, the pompous and arrogant governor of the city-state of Athens, when several Athenian soldiers had rushed in with the news that Atallus' newly acquired Berber slave girl had single-handedly killed three of his men and was trying to escape.

What could he possibly tell her? That he'd been intrigued? That in a moment of impulse he'd offered to purchase her from a very grateful and relieved Atallus? It seemed ludicrous, and yet it was the truth. As soon as his coins had settled in Atallus' palm, Thanos had marched off with his soldiers to try to capture her.

He chuckled to himself. Ludicrous indeed, but in all of his thirty-five *annos* Thanos had always trusted his instincts. And as he'd set off to find the 'spawn of

Hades', as Atallus and his men had named her, he knew he was being guided by the gods to seek this spirited woman out.

"You're not dead, because I have no reason to kill you," he answered truthfully.

"But I killed all those men."

"They were not my men, so you are not my enemy. Those soldiers meant nothing to Atallus. In the end, all he cared about was making a hefty profit out of you—"

"So it is *you* who has purchased me." Her eyes darkened. "It is you I now *belong* to."

"I did," he acknowledged, his belly twisting with her last words. The way she said them, the melodic lilt of her voice caressing him even as it brimmed with anger, did something to him. What would it be like to have this woman belong to him? Though not in the way she spoke of. She thought she was still a slave, but he needed no slaves—nor did he want one. What he wanted—what he truly needed—was something *more*.

"I will not deny that I acquired you from Atallus, but you do not belong to me. I have no desire to make you my slave, or my servant."

"Then why did you purchase me from Atallus?" She frowned. "What is it that you desire of me?"

She nibbled on her bottom lip, slowly inching away from him until her back once again touched the wall behind her. He understood her fear, but she had nothing to fear from him. He was not Atallus. He would *never* take a woman who was not willing. And when it came to this woman, her willingness was the only thing he desired.

How did he even begin to explain to her? That he was a practical, almost cynical soldier who didn't believe in chance or coincidences. The gods orchestrated the lives of mortals, bringing them together for a single instance, a single purpose, or for a lifetime. And when it came to the gods and this woman, they'd certainly sent him a very clear sign.

As he'd sat in Atallus' office listening to the men refer to her with a mixture of fear and awe, and had glimpsed the look of trepidation on the governor's face while his soldiers spoke of her, Thanos had been overcome with curiosity to lay eyes upon the woman who could conjure such fear in the hearts of men. His thoughts had been noble at the time, and they'd remained so when he came upon her in the *agora*. He'd told himself he would purchase this woman then set her free so that she could have a life away from Atallus, where her spirit would not be broken.

Noble thoughts, indeed—he stifled a wry snort—until he'd stared into flashing topaz eyes and found himself captivated.

There was something about this woman—her steady, unflinching gaze, the fiery challenge blazing in her eyes, how she refused to be cowed even though her future was uncertain. Everything about her called to him, taunted him, daring him to breach her walls and *master* her. Such a challenge to a man of his nature was impossible to ignore, even harder to refuse.

She wanted to know why he'd purchased her. The response, even to his own ears, sounded absurd—because it was—but Thanos prided himself on honesty, so, instead of sparing her with a lie, he met her steady gaze and gave her the only answer that he could—the truth.

Chapter Two

Lamia's mouth fell open. "Your pardon?"

"I said I have no need for a slave or a servant. What I have need of, however, *is*..."

A wife.

Yes, she'd heard him the first time, and she wanted to tell him her ears were just fine — it was his words that gave her pause.

His eyes softened then, obviously glimpsing her inner turmoil across her face. He seemed so earnest, so genuine, which puzzled Lamia. Thanos Aristaeus did not appear cruel, and it was apparent to all he was a handsome man — the chiselled muscles of his arms, which strained against his tunic, impossible to ignore by any woman, including her. She experienced a soft, warm stirring in her belly as her gaze unwittingly strayed to the sprinkling of dark hair along his broad torso, taut and defined. A man such as Thanos should have been wed by now. She had no doubt there were many women who clamoured for his attention, his *affection*.

"I know my words were quite unexpected, and I am sure you must think I am mad."

That was exactly what she thought. He'd purchased her…to *wed* her? To purchase a woman as a concubine was quite common, as was a wife, but such arrangements were typically not made between a man of his station and a woman such as herself—a foreign slave.

Many would have seen it as an honour for him to even offer her a place in his bed as his concubine, a position far more elevated than most would think she truly deserved.

But Lamia was not honoured by propositions from a stranger, no matter that he wished for a wife instead of a whore.

"I assure you I have no intention of pressing you on this," he said gently. "I know you need time to consider my offer, mull over the notion. And I shall give you that time—"

"Time?" Her eyes widened. "You purchased me to wed me. The way I see it, I have no choice in the matter. After all, you *own* me." By law, he could command her to do *anything*, including wed him.

He shook his head, a frown marring his handsome face. "You are wrong—you do have a choice, as I do not own you and I will not force you. I simply ask that you consider my offer." He gestured around the small space, and her eyes lit on his fine garments and expensively made weapons. "In Sparta, I am well respected. I could offer you a good life, a secure one. The way I see it, there is nothing for you here in Athens."

She was incredulous. So, because she had nothing left, she should just cast her lot with him—a stranger? She bit back a snort. This was lunacy, and yet she acknowledged he was correct in many ways. There was nothing for her there—or anywhere else for that matter—but she had no desire to wed him, or any other man.

But what of him? She wondered of his desires. She knew he desired a wife, but she had a feeling there was more to his reasoning than he'd revealed.

"Tell me truly. Why is it that you seek a wife...and why have you decided that woman should be me?"

"Truthfully?" When she nodded, he let out an uneven breath. "I need an heir. I am a soldier—a general. With war coming to Greece there is the very real possibility that I could die, and I have no child, no son to carry on my father's name."

There it was, but Lamia knew that was only half of the story. The rest was right there in the crystalline depths of his eyes and a fist closed around her heart at the glimmer of sadness that crossed his face. He was lonely, and for just a moment she wanted to reach out and comfort him with the slightest touch of her hand against his. She wondered if he was a widower, if he'd lost his wife in the passing *annos*. But then she realised what she was doing and with a quick shake of her head she immediately set those thoughts aside. She could not feel compassion for this man. He was not part of her plan.

He'd spoken the truth. She had nothing left and no one to return to—all because of one man. *Atallus.* She intended to make Atallus suffer for all he'd done to her and Darius. She would snuff out his life, the way he'd so callously snuffed out the life of the only family she'd had left.

She was indebted to Thanos for what he'd done for her, and she truly hoped he found a woman to ease his lonely nights—to give him the heir he so desired—but that woman was not her.

"I am sorry, Thanos." She pleaded with her eyes for him to understand. "I will be forever in your debt for freeing me, and I will find a way to repay you, but I have no desire to wed you or any other man. I fear my destiny lies elsewhere."

Thick lashes obscured knowing eyes as he studied her, and she fought the urge to fidget beneath the weight of his stare.

"I know not of what happened before I came upon you, though I have heard of Atallus' cruelties," he said finally, his expression gentle. "I can see you plan to go after him. The desire for revenge burns in your eyes, but I would not suggest it."

"You have no idea what he did. I cannot just let him get away with it."

Thanos' gaze did not waver and Lamia knew what his next question would be.

She steeled herself to recount the horrible memories of Darius' death and Atallus' brutality, so he would understand why her desire for vengeance was so great, but Thanos never got the chance to question her.

A young soldier burst into the tent, his expression intense.

"General. We have spotted a band of soldiers advancing towards us. They move with great stealth as if they intend to come upon us by surprise given the late hour."

Thanos snapped to his feet. "Do you recognise their crest?"

"Athenians, sir, about half a kilometre out."

Thanos frowned and then his gaze slammed into her.

"Atallus. I would think he has not given up on you as easily as he would have us believe." He turned to the soldier. "Break down camp and prepare to move out. We need them as allies against Rome. We do not want to fight them over her. Tell the men we will not engage unless they attack."

"Yes, sir," the soldier said with a crisp nod and marched out of the tent.

"Come," Thanos said. "We need to leave now, and, once we're safely away, I think you need to tell me the entire tale of how you ended up with Atallus because it is now apparent you are no ordinary slave girl."

* * * *

Lamia soon discovered one of the reasons why the Spartans were heralded as the most formidable military in the world. In minutes they broke down camp and were on the move, their battle horses taking them away from the advancing Athenians under the cover of eve.

Lamia rode with Thanos, her hands clasped around his waist, clutching him tightly as they galloped over the rough terrain. She had no idea for how long or how far they rode, but it felt like dawns, though it probably was just an hour before they came to a stop and set up camp.

Thanos put up his tent first and once she was settled inside he went back to attend to his horse and give his men instructions.

She sat huddled on the makeshift bedding, listening to the sounds of the men moving about camp, as she warmed herself beside the small fire. That was where Thanos found her when he pushed his way inside the tent.

The harsh planes of his handsome face were severe and riotous anger simmered in his eyes as he stared down at her.

"Who are you? I want the truth."

The accusation in his voice ignited her temper. She had not brought this upon them. He had taken her—not the other way around.

"Do not look at me like that, as if I am some spy or thief. You brought me here, remember? You brought this on—not me."

"I thought you were a simple Berber slave, but the governor of Athens does not send his personal guard to retrieve just a common slave." His eyes narrowed. "Who are you?"

She glared at him, bristling at the offensive word he'd hurled at her. She was a free woman, not a *slave*. "My name is Lamia, and I am a simple Berber *woman* from Carthage—"

"I do not believe you—"

"Well, that is your dilemma because I speak the truth," she snapped. "In Carthage, I worked as the swordsmith apprentice to an old soldier from the Persian army. One sun rising, Atallus came into the shop to purchase weapons from Darius. His beady eyes followed me the entire time." She shuddered as she remembered that dawn—Atallus' cloying eyes and the wretched, sinister air that clung to him.

"Later Darius told me Atallus had tried to purchase me from him, but Darius had refused. I was Darius' apprentice, not his servant or his slave. Darius rescued me from the streets when I was just a little girl and raised me as his own after my parents died in the war. He was like a father to me, the only family I had. Darius could not sell me because he did not own me."

She swiped at the hot tears that had fallen against her will.

In the span of dawns she'd lost everything. She'd been ripped from her home, her entire world destroyed as if it had never existed, and now this man heaped his anger upon her—a man who might have saved her life, but had altered it yet again.

"Two sun risings later, Atallus returned with his soldiers. He burned down our home and kidnapped me. He left Darius to die in that fire," she choked out, forcing back a sob.

She dipped her head, hating that she cried before him, but she found she couldn't force herself to look away or blot her tears when he lifted her chin, his eyes now gentle.

"I am sorry." He spoke softly. "I had no right to cast my anger upon you. You are the only victim in this, and I fear my actions have only added to your turmoil."

He sighed as he released her chin, and she studied him when he dropped down beside her, his expression pensive. She sensed he had more to tell.

"What is it?" she asked finally.

He shoved a hand through his dark mane, his gaze locking with hers.

"I had every intention of letting you go. Yes, I want a wife, and for a moment I was convinced that woman was you—"

Lamia gaped. "But why? Why would you ever think such a thing? We have never even met—"

"I saw you...in a dream."

"What do you mean you saw me in a dream?" She breathed out slowly.

"Well, not *you*, exactly. There was a woman who wielded a sword—I never saw her face." His lips crooked into a small smile. "When I visited the Oracle, she told me my destiny was tied to this woman — a foreign woman whom I would meet on the other end of a sword." His gaze never once wavered. "She told me I would wed this woman. I thought you were her."

The Oracles were renowned for their prophecies...their *accuracy*. Her heart thudded faster in her chest. If the Oracle spoke the truth...

She shook her head. *No.* The Oracle must have spoken of someone else. For her destiny was not tied to this man, but to Atallus. Returning to Athens to seek Atallus' death — *that* was her only destiny.

"You said you had every intention of letting me go," she interjected, deliberately changing the subject. "I sense that something has now changed."

He nodded, but he appeared guarded as he spoke. "Atallus sent his men after you under the darkness of eve to kill you *and* us if it came to that. I sense that his humiliation at being bested by you ate at him." Thanos sighed, frustration heavy in his voice. "But we have no time for these petty squabbles right now. War is coming to the city-states of Greece and we need to be united. I cannot jeopardise our tenuous peace with Athens for anything...or *anyone*."

She had an idea as to the deeper meaning of his words, and somehow knew his altered plans did not bode well for her and her plans. "What are you truly saying?"

"That if I let you go, Atallus *will* find you and he *will* kill you."

"So let him try —"

"I cannot. I am honour bound to protect you."

She shook her head. She was not his property — his responsibility. What did he care if she died trying to kill Atallus?

"But you do not own me. Of your very lips you said you purchased me and that I was free —"

He placed a single finger against her mouth, halting her words. That's when she glimpsed the weariness in his eyes. This ordeal weighed upon him, and she had no doubt he now regretted freeing her.

"You are free, but since by all accounts I am your last owner, and you are a woman —" He cleared his throat. "I must see to your welfare until you are under the protection of your husband."

"*What?*"

"If you were my freed *helot* in Sparta I would have arranged for you to be married, but I see no reason to adhere to the laws of my homeland since we are not in Sparta, and you are not truly my slave..."

"But?" she snapped, when he didn't rush to finish.

"*But* I cannot release you *knowing* that soldiers are after you. I know you wish to return to Athens to seek revenge, but I cannot in good conscience allow you to go, nor can I seek revenge on your behalf so that you shall be safe — at least not now. I simply cannot jeopardise Sparta's truce with Athens."

"So you want me to journey to Sparta with you?" she asked, knowing already that he did. He was basically holding her prisoner, because his *honour* demanded it.

"I am bound by the laws of Sparta, and my honour. You will be safe with me, and under my protection. Once the threat from Rome has passed, you will be free to go to seek your revenge." He shrugged then, a small glimmer lighting up his tired eyes. "Of course, if you were the *wife* of a Greek citizen, charges could then be brought against Atallus for his crimes against you —"

She glared at him. "I see that you find my situation amusing, but, to me, I find none of this humorous—"

"And I did not mean to make light of your situation." He sobered, or at least his voice grew serious, but Lamia did not mistake the twinkle of amusement still brimming in his eyes. "I was simply explaining your options—all of them."

He thought this was funny. Her only options were to either go with him to Sparta as his charge or go with him to Sparta as his *wife*.

Her nostrils flared in anger. "I will not wed you. And you cannot force me to stay and journey with you to Sparta if I do not wish it so—"

His actions were so quick and quiet that he had her by the arm before she could even gasp. In an instant the man before her was Thanos—the soldier. He trained his steely gaze on her.

"Let me be clear, Lamia. If you try to leave, I will find you. I will not let you endanger this truce—nor will I let you dishonour me. In Sparta a man's honour is everything. I will not send you to your death, and that is final."

He released her and stood. Moments later he stormed out of the tent.

She'd angered him—well then, that made two of them.

She glared at the flap of the tent. Thanos may have been the general of the world's finest army, but she was certain he'd never met an adversary such as her. If he thought she would simply bend to his will and do his bidding because he said so, then he was sorely mistaken. He'd spoken of his honour, but what of hers?

There was no honour in allowing the man who'd killed Darius and kidnapped her to continue to breathe, as if the lives he'd shattered were meaningless. Her destiny was to return to Athens — and she was bound by *her* honour to deliver death to Atallus' door.

Chapter Three

Lamia felt a gentle nudge against her shoulder. With a sleepy moan, she stretched out her arms and legs, easing the knots in her still sore muscles.

The rasp of the soft wool across her skin jolted her fully awake, and for several moments she was startled to find she was not on the cold, hard earth of Atallus' floor. She looked about the unfamiliar room, while at the same time the events of yestereve flooded her mind. A sigh trembled out of her. She was no longer Atallus' prisoner, his slave.

She was safe.

Stifling a yawn, she blinked her eyes as she struggled to adjust to the faint light in the small space. That was when she saw him, and her breath thinned in her chest as her blurred gaze clashed with his.

On this day, his crystalline blue eyes were translucent as the sky as he peered down at her, his raven hair curling around his shoulders. His locks were wet—from a bath, perhaps—and the heavy tendrils clung tightly to his skin. Her attention left his face to travel the length of his body, and she stilled, her breath catching in her throat as she stared at him.

He was nude.

His chest rippled with muscles, meeting the hard planes of his chiselled stomach, while powerful arms, corded with sinew, rested along his sides, perfectly defined. She dipped her gaze lower, swallowing the hard lump in her throat when his manhood stiffened before her eyes, as if awakening from its slumber. His root stood thick and long, jutting out proudly from its nest of coal black hair that coiled around it.

She snapped her wandering gaze back to his face, her cheeks boiling hot with embarrassment.

His lips furled into a wicked grin, his eyes dancing with laughter. "I came to wake you. We depart shortly." He nodded before turning to leave.

And as he stalked away, she ogled his massive legs and taut ass, admiring how the muscles in his back flexed with each powerful step he took.

She remained transfixed by his muscular back, but her appreciation soon gave way to alarm as sickening horror settled in the pit of her rolling belly. What seemed like hundreds of tiny lines crisscrossed his entire back.

He'd been whipped — repeatedly — and she gulped in dismay, wondering whatever he had done to receive such a horrible punishment.

* * * *

The scorching waves of the desert heat crashed down upon her, choking her, and Lamia wiped at the sweat trickling along her brow as the blistering sun battered them mercilessly. They would travel south towards Sparta—the journey taking at least half a fortnight, if they were lucky.

Already her muscles ached and she released a soft groan as she shifted in the saddle, tensing when her buttocks brushed against Thanos.

"Relax," he murmured close to her ear, the sound of his deep voice washing over her like a gentle breeze. She shivered as his warm breath feathered across the sensitive skin along the side of her neck, coaxing tiny goosebumps from her heated flesh.

"I am fine," she gritted out, but she was far from it. Her backside was sore, her back hurt, and her muscles throbbed with pain from holding herself so rigidly.

He chuckled, the husky rumble resonating through her entire body as it seemingly crossed the narrow space between them to enfold her in its intimate warmth.

"I do not bite," he said with laughter in his voice.

Lamia whipped her head around to glare at him. "I said I was fine."

By the gods, he was handsome when he smiled. The harsh planes of his face softened and his piercing eyes danced with merriment as he stared down at her. Afraid that her eyes would betray her, she twisted her head back around.

He tightened his hold on his reins, enclosing her in his embrace. And when he leant forward, his chest brushed against her back.

She stifled a moan and her eyelids drifted shut the moment she felt her body hum to life, her nipples budding so tightly that the sensation was almost painful. Yestereve, she'd noticed him as a man—his handsomeness, his virility. Yet at the same time she'd been so consumed by her fate that she'd purposely ignored her awareness of him.

But ever since earlier that dawn in her tent...having seen his wet physique, the droplets of water that clung to his hair-roughened skin... She swallowed at the memory. Thanos was just so blatantly masculine that it was hard not to be affected by him—it was hard to be around him and still pretend that she did not notice, especially when his body was pressed to hers.

"Move back and relax against me," he said firmly, his warm breath fanning the tiny hairs behind her ear.

She shook her head. The last thing she wanted was to have his strong arms wrap any tighter around her, so that, with each step of his horse, his solid chest would rub her back and the insistent press of his cock would nudge the swells of her ass, just as it was doing now—

"Do it, Lamia."

"No."

He dropped the reins, and she gasped when his hand snaked out to splay across her belly, to gently but firmly scoot her back so that she rested against the hard wall of his body.

"Stop that, Spartan," she snapped, struggling to lean forward, but it was useless. He had trapped her with his large frame.

"You are the most stubborn woman I know," he shot back, his voice strained with exasperation. "Your back will be sore by dusk if you remain so rigid. Relax against me. We have a long journey ahead and you will ache all over before it is done. It is foolish to start off in pain," he argued.

She silently fumed but said nothing. She hated that he was right. But, more than that, she hated how the tender folds of her womanhood were now warm and swollen, the slick, wet juices of her blossoming body now pooling between her thighs. She let out a ragged breath, trying to fight back a moan while her gaze desperately roamed over the expanse of land that lay ahead of them. There was no way she would survive a fortnight with her body pressed against Thanos the entire time. She needed to concentrate on plans to escape…and the sooner the better, because her body threatened to ignite into flames with the slightest touch.

It was shameful, it was shocking and it terrified her, the power this Spartan now wielded over her without any effort.

Yes, it was imperative she escape him—and fast—for she could only imagine what would come of her if he were to do more than just touch…

* * * *

Thanos stifled the bubble of laughter that threatened to slip past his lips as Lamia's face darkened with irritation.

"Then where shall I sleep?"

"Right there." He nodded at the bed mat.

She pinched her lips into a frown. "But then where will you sleep?"

"I just told you, Lamia." His voice was patient.

"Absolutely not. Why can you not sleep wherever you slept last eve?"

He smiled slowly, surprised by how much he was enjoying her discomfiture. "Last eve, I slept outside my tent, while you slept *inside*." He didn't bother to add that she'd slept inside *alone*, which apparently was what she wished for again this eve.

"Very well, then. I shall put up the tent and *outside* the tent is where you may sleep again," she argued.

He drew in a deep calming breath, pinching the bridge of his nose.

"I know you have another bed mat," she hedged.

"I do, but it is folded up in the tent and I just told you we are not putting it up this eve. It takes too long to break down camp when we do that. If Atallus' men are still after you then we need to be able to move quickly. Now...if it rains, then we shall build the tents." He didn't add that only one would be put up...*for her*. Spartan soldiers were conditioned to endure any climate—rain, hail, snow. "Otherwise, we will sleep under the sky."

Her lips pressed tightly together while her eyes threatened to scald him alive. He ignored her. Thanos was tired and he would not waste his last bit of energy arguing with her.

"I set up our sleeping mat over here to give you some privacy from my men. I suggest you relieve yourself and prepare for bed. We have another gruelling dawn ahead of us," he said as he began to remove his heavy leather *curiass*.

He rolled his neck on his shoulders, glad to be rid of the smothering armour, as he stretched and flexed the muscles in his torso.

He started at the soft brush of fingertips along his back that was so unexpected his entire body jerked. The gentle touch of her hand ignited a simmering heat deep in his belly and he fought back a low groan as his body slowly awakened to her warm caress. It had been so long since a woman had touched him like this—had touched him at all—that he had to drag in a deep breath to gain control of himself.

Wiping all traces of the effect she was having on him from his face, he twisted around to glance over his shoulder.

"Who did this to you?" she asked, as she continued to run her fingers over the raised scars.

There was something in her voice that caused him to still. It was concern, but it was more than that. There was something else lingering there, just beneath the surface, which stirred him. He sensed her compassion for his pain, and it warmed him inside. A small spark of hope flared within him. He knew she sought not to wed him — that she was only with him because he'd forced her. But he gathered she was beginning to soften towards him, even if it was just a tiny measure.

"Have you ever heard of the *agoge*?"

She furrowed her brow. "Isn't that a Spartan school?"

A small smile pulled at the corners of his mouth. "Somewhat. Spartan boys enter the *agoge* at seven *annos*. It is where boys become soldiers. We are trained and educated in the *agoge* until we reach twenty." He turned to face her, grasping her fingers in his hand. "Flogging is one such method of training."

Her eyes widened. "But there must be hundreds of scars there."

"Thirteen *annos* is a long time."

"But that is just barbaric."

He tightened his grip around her fingers when she tried to jerk them from his grasp. "No, Lamia — war is barbaric. Spartans simply train their men for the horrors of war."

"I disagree. They whipped you as a boy. You were just a child."

He let out a long sigh, knowing most could never hope to understand the ways of his people. He hoped Lamia would not be one of them. He hoped she would keep an open mind but he knew her grasp of Spartan culture would not take place in a single eve. "As we journey to Sparta, I will tell you more of my people, my home, and with time maybe you will come to understand our ways."

"If they whipped you as a child then I seriously doubt that, Spartan."

His lips twitched. "Well, if you ever have a change of heart and decide to wed me, and we have a son, then at the least you will have to accept Spartan ways, even if you do not agree."

He teased her, his words meant in jest, but Lamia did not share his sense of humour in that moment.

"You truly think our situation is amusing, but as I've said before, I find none of this funny." Her topaz gaze flashed with anger. "We will have nothing together, Spartan. I have already refused to wed you, so I certainly will not be bearing you any little Spartan soldiers."

His lips quirked higher and he released her fingers only to grip her arm with the same hand and drag her against his body, reaching out with his other hand to caress her face.

His movements were so quick that she had no time to react and she stared up at him, her eyes wide with surprise and her mouth agape.

"I wish you would reconsider. Any son we have together would turn out to be a magnificent soldier. With your spirit and my skills, I have no doubt he would grow to be one of the finest warriors the Spartan army has ever seen."

"I cannot believe you even speak of children when we shall never wed." She snorted. "You are mad. Release me," she demanded and raised her hands, flattening her palms across his chest to push against the solid muscle.

He ignored her words and did the exact opposite. He tightened his hand around her arm, pulling her closer. "You enjoy fighting me at every turn. You think it sours me to you, but I find your fire..." He searched for the right word. "Enchanting," he whispered, leaning into her.

Thanos knew she glimpsed his intent in his eyes. She knew he was going to kiss her, and she could have resisted when his head descended, but she didn't. She didn't offer up a single protest, not even when his lips gently met hers and he clasped her body tighter.

He groaned against her mouth as he moulded her lush curves to his larger frame, the heat of her body scorching his flesh. He released her just long enough to wrap his arms around her waist, dipping his hands to cup the firm globes of her backside. Squeezing gently, he massaged her ass softly, slowly, and he felt her shudder against him as a moan escaped her soft lips. Slipping his tongue inside her mouth, he stroked in and out of the moist cavern, letting his mouth mimic the rhythm of his hips as they pumped back and forth to grind his burgeoning arousal along her mound.

"Touch me," he rasped.

Her eyes grew wide, and her fingers were hesitant as she traced an agonising path along his shoulder blades, down his arms and across his back, before skimming back up his arms to twine her hands behind his neck. His skin heated wherever her teasing fingers stroked his flesh. He wanted to lay her down right there on his mat, spread her thighs and, beneath the dark sky, sink his rigid cock into her moist heat until his seed erupted inside her.

He deepened the kiss and devoured her mouth, squeezing her ass tightly, rocking her firmly against his engorged length. His body demanded that he release himself from the confines of his leather *pteryges* and plunge inside her, but he resisted. She wanted him. For all her protests—her body was her betrayer. But he could not push her on this, not yet. She was not yet ready for him to take her, to brand her, to make her his—for that was exactly what he would do if he made love to her. So instead of doing what his body demanded, he lifted his head, slowly ending the kiss.

Her eyes were still closed and he smiled down at her upturned face. He'd been surprised that she'd succumbed so eagerly. He'd fully expected her to strike him before she yielded to him so wantonly—

Whack.

His head snapped sideways, and he would have visibly winced had he not been a better trained soldier. *Gods*, he'd forgotten just how strong she was. Rubbing his burning jaw, he hid his smile. Apparently, he'd been too hasty in his thoughts.

"Do not ever touch me again, Spartan."

He lifted a single brow at her words. After such a passionate kiss, he had definite plans to touch her—*many* more times. "Do not strike me again, Lamia, or I will be forced to punish you."

"I will cut your hands off with your own sword if you flog me."

He grimaced at the vision of her doing just that. He would have to watch her…*and* his sword.

"I would never flog you, Lamia. The punishment I have for you would serve only to teach you a lesson, not to cause you undue pain. It would be pleasurable for you—and for me."

She emitted a rude curse. "I doubt any pleasure could be found in your type of punishment," she retorted, her arms folding across her chest, but the flash of interest brimming in her eyes betrayed her. She was curious about his brand of punishment that also promised pleasure.

Desire heated his body and blood simmered in his veins at the challenge she'd unknowingly just issued. "Any pain I give will also bring pleasure. I am not a cruel man, Lamia. I would never hurt or humiliate you. As you learn to surrender to me, you will learn the joy of my punishments," he murmured softly.

He held her gaze for just a moment longer, making certain she understood the promise of his words, because, with the long journey ahead of them, her wanton behaviour and their desire for one another, there would surely come a dawn when she would find herself on the receiving end of one of his punishments, of that he was certain.

He spun away from her then, turning towards the dense forest area where they were camped in order to relieve himself. Alone, hidden by the thick foliage, he drew in a deep breath as he counted silently, a technique he'd developed as a young boy to calm himself.

He could have forced her to wed him, but he hadn't—his honour and his pride would not allow him to take an unwilling woman to wife. But she was not as *unwilling* as she pretended to be. The explosive heat of their kiss, its intensity, had revealed her desires—that she wanted him just as much as he wanted her.

He could not explain why he yearned for her so fiercely, why he longed for her so intensely, even though she was a stranger to him. He could only guess it was her inner fire that captivated him, drew him to her and enthralled him so completely that he would not be satisfied until he claimed her as his.

Despite his longings, however, Lamia was not yet ready to confront the intensity of his desire for her. For now it was more important for Lamia to have the opportunity to awaken to her own passion for him, which would take...

Time.

He was certain that with time he could make her see that tying her life to his was destined by the gods and that it would not be a bad life if she were to wed him. But he would not succeed in convincing her if he pressed her as he'd just done moments ago. He had not intended to reveal to Lamia his true nature. He wanted her to come to know him better, because the last thing he wished was to scare her away—not when, in all his *annos*, he'd never imagined he would come to find a woman such as her.

While most Spartan men wed at twenty and had sired all of their children by thirty, at thirty-five *annos* he had yet to do either. It was not because he didn't want a family, quite the opposite. The difficulty had always arisen when it came time to find a wife.

Spartan women were dominant outside of the bedchamber—and equally dominant inside— sometimes indulging in several lovers or taking more than one husband. He had no desire to share what he considered to be his with any other man, which was why he'd given up hope of ever finding a Spartan wife. And yet women not Spartan born were submissive both in and out of the bedchamber, which was something he could not endure either. He had no desire to tie himself to a woman who could not think for herself. He wanted a wife, not a servant.

The gods had driven him to Lamia—a woman who would challenge him in all areas of his life, except in the bedchamber. Her response to him that eve had hinted at her true nature—a nature he was certain she had no idea she even possessed.

His manhood began to swell and lengthen as he recalled how easily she had submitted to his kiss, her body opening and yielding to his desires. Her actions told him that, while at dawn she would fight him at every turn, by dusk she would willingly submit to his complete dominance over her body.

Chapter Four

Lamia sipped from her cup of wine, watching Thanos from above the rim. He shuffled back and forth across the camp, barking out orders to his soldiers, his lithe muscles flexing with every stride he took. Just like the dawn they'd met, when they'd fought in the *agora* at Athens, his very presence commanded attention and she found it impossible to tear her gaze from him.

A droplet of wine spilled from her lips, and she ran her tongue across her mouth, catching the tiny bead. Thanos chose that moment to turn his attention to her and she froze beneath his hooded gaze, stifling a small shiver when his eyes settled on her lips.

His eyes darkened, a dark feral glint swirling in their depths, before he abruptly spun around.

She touched her fingers to her lips, his fleeting gaze so intense she could still feel the heat of it upon her skin. Or maybe her lips were simply still swollen from the heat of his erotic kiss. She'd lain awake beside him for most of the eve thinking of him, that kiss, and what he'd meant by pleasure being found in punishment. More than anything, that notion intrigued her. The punishments she knew of only brought pain, so she was curious what it was that Thanos did—and if he actually could bring pleasure to punishment.

She set her cup aside and drew her legs up to her chest, the soreness creeping into her body firmly brushing aside all thoughts of Thanos. Their pace had been harder and faster than the dawn before, and every muscle now ached. Closing her eyes, she rotated her neck, trying to ease the tightness that knotted the tendons.

The unexpected brush of fingertips across her back startled her, and she twisted around, her gaze clashing with that of Thanos.

"What are you doing?" she demanded, slightly bewildered that he'd been able to get so close to her without her realising it.

"I'm trying to help you ease the aches in your back." He emphasised his words by pressing his callused fingers against her flesh.

She forced back a moan. The rhythmic motion of his hands brought such a welcome relief to her body that she almost forgot she'd told him never to touch her again after what had happened last eve.

When her breasts grew heavy and her nipples drew tight from his skilful touch, she jerked away, as if his fingers had been dipped in a pit of fire.

"Have you already forgotten my words to you? *Do not touch me again, Spartan* should have been quite clear."

His lips twitched with amusement, which only infuriated her more. She scurried away from him to sit on the other side of the fire, far out of his reach.

Nadia Aidan

"You persist in being stubborn, even at great cost to yourself." He sighed as he settled against the log she'd just vacated. "Suit yourself, but we will not stop next dawn when you complain that you are too sore to go on."

"I shall not complain."

He must have heard the belligerence in her tone, or maybe by now he was starting to realise that her wilfulness was not a ruse, because he smiled.

"Of course you will not complain." She noticed that he inched towards her as he spoke, but she didn't move. She simply watched him with wary eyes. "You would rather faint and expire from exhaustion than allow a man to take care of you."

He now sat at her feet, his laughing gaze meeting hers. He was taunting her, daring her to back down and move away. She refused to let him see that his nearness affected her. Even as the heat of his body seemed to surround her, engulf her. She sat up straighter, battling against the embers of desire that tiptoed across her skin and flickered inside her belly.

"I do not need a man to take care of me when I can take care of myself."

He arched a single brow as he studied her with such forceful scrutiny she had to tell herself not to fidget.

"But do you ever wish there was someone who would?"

She didn't know which affected her more—his softly spoken words, or the piercing intensity of his turquoise yes. She wrenched her gaze from his, unable to allow him a closer glimpse inside her soul. She hated herself for doing it, for silently revealing that he'd got to her, but she could not allow him to see that she *did* long for someone to care for her, although she

44

knew that, with Darius gone, there was now no one who ever would.

She inhaled deeply. "My wishes are unimportant. I am more curious as to yours, Spartan."

His grin was smug as he leant back, his every gesture hinting that he knew she was purposely evading his question. Lamia ignored the self-satisfied gleam in Thanos' eyes, refusing to be baited into a discussion she did not wish to have.

"I already told you what I wish for."

"A wife."

She gave a derisive snort, but he didn't seem to notice or care, when he shrugged and said with a half smile, "But not just any wife."

She frowned. "What do you mean, not just *any* wife?"

His eyes closed as he settled his back against the log. "You're not ready for such honesty, Lamia."

She glared at him. How did he know what she was ready for? Besides, it did not take a scholar to figure out what *type* of wife he wished for.

"You want a woman who enjoys pain."

He opened one eye, his lips furling.

"Is that what you think?"

"I'm only repeating what you said last eve."

"And what was it that I said, Lamia?"

She stared at him, his eyes now closed once again. This was a game to him. He wanted to force her to say the provocative words that he knew would embarrass her. He enjoyed baiting her, just to see how much she would squirm. Well, she was tired of playing.

She shot up from her perch atop the felled tree. "This is ridiculous."

It was amazing just how quickly and quietly he could move. She'd barely taken a step, before he seized her by the arms and dragged her to him.

She struggled against his hold. "Is this what they teach men in Sparta? How to maul women?"

"It is so apparent you are curious as to how I can make punishment pleasurable for you, but you are too much of a coward to simply come out and ask the question."

His voice was as soft as a lover's caress, but his words stung and she drew back as if he'd slapped her. She was many things, but a coward was not one of them.

"Release me, Spartan."

"Or what? Will you strike me again?" Mischief flashed in his gaze. "That is going to be a bit more difficult this time, since I have your arms."

She glowered at him, fury bubbling over inside her. "This is a game to you, but I do not wish to play. Release me right now."

He ignored her and pulled her closer, trapping her to him. He leant down, his face settling within the crook of her neck, and despite the protests ringing in her mind she could not stop the tiny tremor from rocking her body. When he chuckled, she knew he'd felt it. In that moment, she hated him—him and the power he seemed to so easily wield over her.

"Just so we are clear. I never said I liked pain. I only said that pleasure could be found in punishment."

His warm breath teased her sensitive skin, and she found it nearly impossible to find her voice, but somehow she managed it.

"Pain, punishment…what is the difference?"

He groaned, and she had to bite back her own when his body hardened against her belly.

"There is a vast difference." His words were choppy, and he lifted his face to rest his forehead to hers, his eyes clenched shut. "I ache to show you the difference, but you are not ready, *agapetos*. Far from it."

She traced the taut lines of his face, somewhat awed by the effect she was obviously having on him. It was a heady feeling to realise that Thanos — the Spartan general who possessed such strength of will — was having trouble controlling himself around her. From somewhere deep within, she revelled in her feminine power over him, though she would never admit it.

Maybe it was the startling realisation that a man as desirable as Thanos actually seemed to want *her*. Or perhaps it was that he was so close to her that she could almost taste him on her lips, every part of him seemingly seeping into her pores. She truly didn't know what it was that possessed her, but in that moment she yearned to once again feel his lips melded to hers, coaxing her to surrender to his kiss.

"Thanos," she whispered, the soft plea barely audible.

He dragged in a deep breath as his eyes fluttered open, and, before she could change her mind, she closed her lids and tilted her head back just as he crushed his mouth to hers.

His kiss was hard and demanding, his tongue insistently probing inside her mouth to claim her. He deepened the pressure of his mouth and she moaned when their tongues scraped together. He was branding her, his kiss igniting a bone-melting fire that singed through her blood. Her entire body was set ablaze as heat gnawed at her belly before settling between her thighs, causing the plump lips of her core to grow slick and heavy with her desire.

She was a bit dazed when he pulled away from her, his chest heaving, although he didn't release her.

"I am afraid if I let you go you will strike me again," he said with a smile.

"I have no plans to strike you, but this has to stop, Thanos." She sucked in a shaky breath.

She would never know what had come over her, what made her desire his touch so wantonly, but she knew it was madness to continue this flirtation, for their actions were those of lovers, of a couple set to be wed, when she knew that would never come to be.

He unclasped his hands from around her arms to settle a single finger against her lips.

"Do not ruin this, *agapetos*, with talk of how you do not wish to be my wife—how you do not wish to journey to Sparta—"

She opened her mouth to tell him just that, for it was the truth, but he shook his head.

"Please." His gentle request struck a chord deep inside her, and she nodded. They both knew how she felt. There was no need to hurl it in his face at that very moment.

He let his hand drop from her mouth. "I must speak with my men, so you will have plenty of privacy to prepare for bed."

She nodded again and neither of them said another word when he turned and disappeared into the centre of the camp.

Settling down on the bed mat, she stretched out beside the fire, mesmerised by the wild blaze that echoed her inner discord. What she'd done moments before—seeking out his kiss—had been madness. This burgeoning desire between them was dangerous and she'd be wise to steer clear of him—a man who was but a stranger to her, a man she would soon flee from, never to set eyes upon ever again.

The twinge of regret that nicked at her with the thought of never seeing Thanos' laughing gaze again, Lamia refused to acknowledge. It was impossible to harbour feelings for a man she'd known for only three dawns, and yet there was no denying the carnal desires he'd awakened within her. She sat up straighter with the sudden thought that sprang forth. The effect he had on her, it was the same for him.

Yestereve, her almost desperate response to him had frightened her, making Lamia that much more determined to flee him, but this eve had brought with it a new understanding of the man who still held her fate within his hands.

She'd witnessed Thanos struggle to control himself earlier, and it had come as a shock to her to discover that she possessed the same power over him. A plan began to form in her head. Now, if she could just keep her wits about her and her own attraction to Thanos at bay long enough to see her plan through…

* * * *

Thanos stalked Lamia with his eyes, digging his fingers into the cool sand. The sun was setting in the horizon and she reminded him of an ethereal water nymph as she playfully frolicked in the Gulf of Argolis.

They'd had another gruelling dawn of travel, and he'd promised her she would be allowed to bathe when they stopped, but now he was regretting his words.

She knew he was watching her, his eyes slowly appraising her. She was purposefully taunting him, laughing softly when she lifted herself in the water just high enough so that he could catch a brief glimpse of the swells of her breasts, before dipping beneath the surface.

He swallowed the lump in his throat, digging his hands deeper into the mushy sand, so that he would not reach inside his *pyterges* and stroke his cock.

He narrowed his eyes when she waded closer to shore to settle against one of the sand bars. With her back facing him, she gracefully parted her legs. The shadows of the approaching eve made it difficult to see, but he swore she was touching herself.

With a muttered curse, Thanos shot to his feet and marched on stiff legs towards her. As he drew closer, he became convinced that she was pleasuring herself. Her unbound hair dripped with water as it clung to her arched back, while uneven breaths caressed his ears.

"What are you doing?"

She moaned softly, her entire body tensing. Twisting her head around, she looked squarely at him, and despite the encroaching darkness he easily glimpsed the laughter in her eyes.

"What does it look like I'm doing?"

He frowned at the teasing lilt of her soft voice. This was out of character for Lamia. She had to know how she affected him, but nothing about her actions before had spoken of wanting to encourage his desire. Actually, quite the opposite.

"What are you doing, Lamia?"

"You already asked me that. And I would think it should be obvious."

Frustration seized him. She knew what he was truly asking.

"Not *what* you're doing, but *why* are you doing it? Why are you touching yourself?"

"Again, that much should be obvious, but, if you must know, it's because I need to find release." She quirked her lips into an alluring, seductive pout. "That is, unless you would like to give it to me."

His heart battered the wall of his chest until it threatened to burst, a furious rush of blood surging into his pulsing cock. He was almost tempted to wade through the water and do just that, but he came to his senses before he could make a fool of himself. Just like the sirens who'd ensnared Odysseus, Lamia sat there spinning her web, trying to trap him, but he wouldn't be so easily fooled. He knew she was up to something.

"Get out of the water."

He realised his mistake too late when she shrugged and stood. His next breath lodged somewhere between his lungs and inside his throat when she spun around and sauntered towards him, her movements sensual, erotic. His gaze followed every single droplet of water that clung to her nude figure, tracing the trail that a lone dewdrop made as it slithered between her breasts and across her middle, before disappearing into the thatch of dark curls that hid her womanhood.

Buried deep within his foggy brain, somehow he managed to recall that his men stood on the ridge behind him. Snatching up her garment, he stalked over to her and wrapped it around her wet body.

"What in *Hades* are you doing?"

"You keep asking me that and —"

"I do not know what game you are playing, but it shall not work."

She shrugged away from him, slowly donning her *peplos*, and he struggled not to follow her every move with his eyes, but it was just that—a struggle.

"You are overly suspicious, Thanos," she said when she was finally fully clothed. "Come, drink some wine with me, and let me help you relax."

He knew her docility was a trick. Even as he followed behind her, his gaze fixed on the gentle sway of her hips, he knew. And when he sat beside the fire and relaxed against her, drinking from his cup of wine, while she soothed the aches in his shoulders with her delicate hands, he knew. In his arrogance he determined that, because he recognised her ploy, he would not be fooled by it—but later he would realise his mistake in underestimating her.

Chapter Five

Lamia snapped her eyelids open, and she tried to stretch, but a solid wall of muscle hampered her movements.

Thanos' nude body lay pressed against her back, while his arm was draped around her waist. She glanced down the length of her body—his leg was entwined with hers and his hand gently cupped her breast. Thanos always slept nude, and until last eve he had politely stayed on his side of the mat, but, likely owing to all the wine, he'd drifted beside her until their bodies lay intertwined.

She swallowed down a needy moan, her nipples tightening as molten heat furled in her belly at the coarse hair of his rough legs brushing across the smooth skin of her thighs. Everything about Thanos screamed of untamed, masculine virility, and, while she was loath to admit it, his large, powerful body— with its rough planes and hard edges—called to her as a woman, making her feel delicate and feminine, something she'd never felt with any other man before.

He shifted again and his thumb brushed her now stiff nipple. She bit back the sigh that hovered on her lips as lightning shocks of pleasure sizzled down her spine. Everywhere he touched her skin tingled, causing dewy warmth to pool at the juncture between her thighs. She wrestled with the feverish heat that now claimed her body, hating the desperate need this stranger had awakened inside her from the moment their lips had touched and they'd shared their first kiss.

She shook herself — to gather her wits. And then she shook him.

"Thanos," she whispered.

She rolled her eyes when he mumbled a series of muffled words but did not budge.

She nudged her back harder into his chest. "Thanos," she hissed. "I need to relieve myself. Wake up."

Somewhere in the back of his sleepy mind he must have understood her because he loosened his embrace and rolled away from her.

Thank the gods. Her ploy had worked. He'd been suspicious at first, but, between the wine and her gentle hands, he'd eventually relaxed before succumbing to the arms of sleep. Her only hope was that the wine would keep him asleep long enough for her to escape.

She wasted no time in scrambling off the mat. With measured steps she tiptoed into the sparse forest that surrounded the camp. After relieving herself, she waited. Several moments passed without a sound.

Thanos was still asleep.

She carefully made her way towards where the horses were tied up for the eve. With stealthy movements, she untied Thanos' white stallion and slowly guided him away from where the Spartan soldiers were camped. She walked beside Zeus until she was sure the sound of her galloping away would not be heard by the sleeping soldiers.

* * * *

Lamia's hair whipped violently about her face as she urged Zeus to go faster.

"Come on. Come on," she yelled, trying to coax the stallion to pick up the pace.

Leaning forward, she grasped his mane tightly and dug her heels into his flanks.

"Faster, Zeus. Please," she begged, her lungs burning with every frantic gulp of air she struggled to take in.

She didn't need to turn around to know who was chasing her. She could feel his angry gaze burning the skin off her back. Still, she desperately wanted to turn her head, if only to gauge his distance. But she couldn't afford to take her focus away from pressing the horse to go faster.

As the blistering sun blazed down upon her, she knew that it would only be a matter of time before he caught up to her. She'd been confident in the success of her escape...too confident.

In one moment she was sitting astride the galloping stallion and in the next she was wrenched off Zeus, only to remain suspended in the air, her body dangling above the ground. A startled scream rushed out of her and she winced in pain when her body collided with what felt like a crushing boulder, although she knew it was just the flank of Thanos' horse. She barely had time to brace herself against Thanos' mount before he abruptly released his hold on her, sending her flailing wildly to the ground with a loud thud.

"Ouch," she cried as she crashed down, before rolling over to sit up. She had broken her fall with her hands and knees, scraping them in the process. Rubbing her palms across her chafed skin, she dusted away the dirt, trying to soothe the dull throb of pain from her scratches.

At the sound of footsteps, she lifted her head, her gaze colliding with stormy blue eyes swirling with fury.

"You promised. You gave me your word that you would not try to run."

She thought of Darius, her need to avenge his death, and the fact that this Spartan still stood in her way. "I lied," she spat out. "I lied, Spartan. I have no intention of going to Sparta with you."

His entire expression hardened as he closed the distance between them, while she tried to widen it again, scooting backwards.

She had barely put a yard between them when his hand shot out to grasp her ankle, and he dropped down to his knees, jerking her roughly across the rocky and uneven ground, tugging her closer.

"Ouch, Spartan. Stop," she protested as her barely covered backside scraped against the hard, arid earth beneath her.

Struggling wildly, she kicked her arms and legs out, slashing at anything in their path as she desperately fought to get away. She knew Thanos had taken several hard blows when her knuckles began to throb from what she could only guess were punches to his jaw.

But instead of relaxing his hold, his grip only tightened until he managed to drag her beneath him and cover her body with his own. He clasped her wrists in his hands, pinning her to the ground as he clamped her legs between his bulging thighs.

She struggled beneath him, twisting in every direction, but her resistance was futile, and eventually she yielded, relaxing into the solid earth, limp with exhaustion.

Frustrated tears burned the backs of her eyes, but he was not swayed as his expression darkened. "You will have much to cry about soon, *agapetos*," he said harshly.

In one fluid motion he rolled off her, to rest on the ground in a seated position. Before she had gathered his purpose, he'd pulled her across his lap, her backside facing the sky.

He wouldn't.

The steely glint in his eyes said otherwise

"No, Thanos. Please, do not do this," she pleaded, using his given name this time, hoping it would endear her to him, but, just in case it didn't, she resumed her desperate struggling.

He remained silent.

Grasping the fabric of her *peplos* in one hand, he wrenched it upwards, balling it at her waist, her ass now completely exposed.

She continued to kick and protest, but her efforts were wasted. Fury boiled inside her until her veins pumped with churning, hot lava. In all her twenty-eight *annos*, no one had *ever* spanked her. No one had ever dared. Not even Darius.

She swore worse than a *tavernas* whore when his first strike came, his hand slamming down against her buttocks. Her back arched instinctively, the sting of the blow jolting her entire body.

She cried out when another stinging blow came. But, as tears slipped from her eyes, she gave up yelling and simply tried to ignore the jagged needles of pain.

Thanos said nothing, although he continued to spank her...*hard*.

The sound of flesh meeting flesh echoed across the barren plain as sharp arrows shot from her lower back to the rest of her body with each slap.

She expelled a shaky breath when he finally stopped, grateful that it was now over.

With a tenderness he'd not displayed moments ago, he cupped her buttocks, gently squeezing the soft, full globes, and she shivered when a new throbbing ache settled in the lower regions of her body.

His hand continued to stroke her rounded flesh, back and forth — massaging first, then lightly squeezing before gently stroking again.

A soft hiss forced its way past her lips when his finger dipped below her cheeks to slide through the now moist folds of her core.

It came away coated with her juices, glistening beneath the sunlight. "You're wet, Lamia," Thanos said softly and the deep gravel of emotion in his voice was unmistakable.

She tried to turn over to look at him, but he placed a palm against her back, gently nudging her down.

"Did you enjoy being spanked?" he asked, his finger lazily encircling the tiny nub at the mouth of her sheath.

A sharp breath pulsed in her chest, while a steady, unrelenting throb began to build between her legs.

"Did you, Lamia?" he demanded, emphasising his words with the press of his finger inside her.

She shook her head, balling her hands into tight fists. She refused to answer him, refused to reveal to him the truth because she was shamed by it. But his skilful hands were driving her mad, making her want to do things she'd never dreamed of. Of its own volition, her ass lifted to meet the shallow thrust of his finger, and she let out a deep moan.

"No," she protested, needing to say something to make him stop or else he would continue his assault upon her senses, her body making a liar out of her.

"I think you're lying, Lamia. I think you enjoyed being spanked." She could tell he was smiling by the amused tone of his voice. The bastard. She would not admit the truth and give him the satisfaction of knowing that she *had* enjoyed it.

"N-no," she managed to croak out, her traitorous hips now rocking in a steady rhythm, eagerly meeting each probing thrust of his finger.

"Then why are you so wet?" he groaned as he roughly shoved two fingers inside her.

Her answer was a deep, soul-stirring moan and she gasped when his hand suddenly slapped her ass.

She began to squirm against his lap. She was so close to coming she could feel herself on the edge of release and she strained towards it, another moan escaping her lips.

His hand came down hard again as he shoved his fingers deep inside her. A primal sound rose up out of her, and her hips now bucked furiously against him. She was so close, so close to release as the tremors quaked harder within her...

Lamia's mouth fell open then, as her eyelids clenched shut and violent shudders thundered through her body. The wave inside her began to crest, but, before it could break apart and carry her away to blissful fulfilment, his hands stilled.

A strangled sob escaped her. "No. Don't stop," she pleaded, her hips lifting instinctively, desperately seeking out his hands — his fingers.

He chuckled softly, his palm stroking her soft, reddened cheeks, but not that place where she ached for him to touch more than anything else.

"You do not get to come, Lamia. You disobeyed me. So that is your punishment."

She stiffened, his words slowly piercing the fog that had settled in her lust-filled mind, her fury chasing away the last remnants of her arousal.

Whipping her head around, she speared him with her gaze. "Now I see why you are not yet wed, you twisted deviant. Who would ever wish to wed a man such as you?"

Out of frustration, she'd lashed out at him, but the tiny ember of pain she glimpsed in his eyes instantly had her regretting her harsh, rash words.

"Thanos, I did not mea —"

The rest of her apology caught in her throat as she was unceremoniously rolled from his lap and dumped on the hard ground.

Wariness settled in her gut when she glimpsed the tiny muscle in his jaw twitching uncontrollably. He shot to his feet and began to march towards the horses.

He's going to leave me. Panic gripped her and her stomach tightened into knots at the thought that he would leave her out here alone with nothing. Without food or water or a horse, she would surely die — that was if the thieves that trolled the coast didn't get to her first.

But, when he headed back over to her with a twine of rope in his hand, she decided she would rather he'd deserted her.

He is going to hang me.

She jumped to her feet and turned to run, but only managed two steps before his hand shot out, grabbing her around the waist. She struggled against him but he easily overpowered her, just as he'd done before. He spun her around to face him and, with his free hand, he clenched her wrists in his grasp.

She could try to run again, but she quickly abandoned that thought. As tight as his hold was on her, she would only manage one step this time, at the most. Lamia resigned herself to her fate. She'd survived Atallus only to die out here by the hands of the man she'd thought had saved her —

Thanos ripped her *peplos* down the middle to throw the tattered remnants to the ground — her first clue that maybe he was not going to kill her as she'd assumed. By the time he'd secured her wrists and ankles with the rope, Lamia was too shocked to do anything but stare at him, mouth agape. She'd been expecting to die, but he didn't seem intent upon using the rope to hang her at all. When he was satisfied her restraints were secure, he gently lowered her to the ground onto her knees, her hands behind her back.

Her face flushed with embarrassment as his gaze leisurely roamed over her nude body, now openly displayed before him. With her hands tied as they were, her breasts jutted forth, the large, brown nipples standing to attention.

His eyes fixated on her breasts and he began to stroke his cock through his leather *pteryges*. Had it been any other man, the entire display would have been perverse and lewd. That it wasn't — that she experienced the hot press of desire and not revulsion — caused her cheeks to burn with heat. She lowered her gaze to the ground, mortified that, when it came to Thanos, she knew no shame.

"Look at me," he commanded, his voice ragged.

Her gaze snapped to his face.

Hunger. Hunger and longing scorched in his hooded gaze, and her heart stuttered in her chest at the intensity she glimpsed in those blue depths, along with the same desperate need clawing inside her own body.

"Do you want to know why I am not yet wed, Lamia?"

She shook her head. Truly, she did not want to know at all. She had a feeling that his revelation did not bode well for her. And yet she was curious...

He moved closer, his eyes never leaving her as he undid the laces of his *pteryges,* his fingers unhurried.

"I like a woman with spirit, a fire in her. A woman who is my equal in every way...*except* in our bedchamber." His last words came out as little more than a hoarse whisper, but she'd heard them quite clearly, and her eyes grew wide when the meaning of them began to sink in.

"Do you understand what I am saying, Lamia?"

She nodded stiffly, wary of what he would say next, what other intimate details he would reveal.

Slowly he removed his long, thick cock from the confines of his *pteryges,* the mushroom head already glistening with a tiny pearl of liquid arousal.

"And do you know why I wish to wed you, Lamia?" he asked thickly as he began to stroke his hand up and down, pumping his ruddy flesh.

She fixated on his engorged length, the purplish head, the blue veins running along his swelling shaft. Her cunt began to throb with her need to seize his hard length within her channel and wring him of every last drop of seed he possessed.

He stepped closer to slip one finger beneath her chin, forcing her hungry gaze from his cock to his face. He smiled knowingly, and her face grew hotter at the look in his eyes. That was when she remembered he'd asked her a question, and she'd failed to answer. He knew. He knew she wanted him, desired him, longed for him as she'd longed for no other. No matter how much she tried to deny him with her lips, he knew her body ached for him.

A denial hovered on her lips but she was powerless to speak it, just as she was powerless to answer the question that still lingered between them as lust and desire hammered inside her, making every breath an arduous one. Yet, even if she physically could form a response, Lamia decided only Thanos was the one who could truly furnish such an answer. For only *he* knew why he wished to wed *her*.

"I desire to wed you, Lamia, because I believe you to be that woman," Thanos said gently.

That woman? *A woman who is my equal in every way...except in our bedchamber.* Submit to a man in bed when she'd never submitted to a man in anything before? She shook her head. Thanos was wrong about her.

"Thanos, I... I do not think—"

"Shhh, *agapetos*. Words are not necessary, for your body shall soon reveal the truth."

With his finger still beneath her chin, he shifted his hips, bringing his cock closer until the very tip of him was poised at the entrance of her mouth.

"Suck it," he commanded softly.

Her gaze climbed his body until their eyes met.

She battled against Thanos' command, wanting a taste of him but afraid to give in to him, knowing he would think she enjoyed his dominance over her when she did not.

He repeated his command and this time she opened her mouth at the same instant Thanos slid his hard shaft between her lips. She told herself that just because she'd obeyed him did not mean she was of a submissive nature — she was simply driven by her desires, nothing more.

He groaned, the harsh, ragged sound vibrating through her as his hand gripped the back of her head, tangling in the coiled locks of her hair.

She wrapped her lips securely around him and sucked hard, taking him deep into her mouth, letting the tip graze against the back of her throat. Her gaze never left his face. Back and forth, she bobbed her head, working her mouth furiously at sucking him.

White hot lashes of pleasure whipped across her skin at the feel of his iron-hard length beneath silken flesh powering between her lips. She wanted to feel ashamed. She was naked and bound on her knees before a man she barely knew, allowing him to do things to her she'd never allowed a man to do before. Thanos' words haunted her in that moment and she worried he'd spoken the truth. Was she a woman who enjoyed a man's dominance? She'd never considered it before. But then she'd never met a man such as Thanos, who had the ability to bring her to the brink of arousal with just one look, a single caress, a softly spoken word against her heated skin.

She moaned around his thrusting length at the thought of Thanos coaxing carnal responses from her body, introducing her to the ways of lovemaking, then branding her, claiming her as his own.

Thanos. His…
Belonging to him and only him.

Her heart contracted, the very thought slicing her open and leaving her raw and vulnerable, but in its wake came a desperate longing to belong to someone, to have him belong to *her*. The ache, the need—it settled in her breast, and lent a passionate fervour to her wet strokes up and down his cock that had not been there before.

"Fuck, Lamia," Thanos groaned as he cupped her head with both hands, his fingers digging into her scalp, to tunnel his cock deeper.

She swirled her tongue around the thick base of his length before she shifted back to run it across the slit in the centre of the head, lapping eagerly at the droplets of seed gathered there. The metallic taste of him exploded on her tongue—salt and desire—and she closed her eyes, wanting to savour his unique flavour. She wanted to experience all of him—his taste, his touch, his smell. Lamia inhaled deeply, trapping the scent of leather and sweat—the scent of Thanos—within her lungs.

Opening her eyes, she let his cock slip from her stretched mouth to flick her tongue around the crown before dipping under the sensitive fold of skin.

"Lamia," he grunted her name, the feral sound slipping past clenched teeth, and she knew his release was imminent as he began to tremble. With his hands still desperately clutching her head, his eyelids drifted shut and his head rolled back on his shoulders, the pulsing blue veins in his neck bulging beneath sun-bronzed skin.

She hummed against his pounding, hot shaft, letting the vibrations slide over him, forcing a violent shudder to rock his entire body. Already treading thin, his control disappeared with a blinding rush as he pumped his hips and held her head firmly, feeding her more and more of his cock. She strained to take him deeper, struggling with the girth and length of him.

"Wider, *agapetos*. Open your mouth wider and take it deeper," he begged. "Take me down your throat."

The hoarse plea trembling out of him spurred her. Flicking her tongue back and forth over the head of his cock, she descended upon his shaft on a single swallow and sucked furiously, taking him further and further until her throat quivered along the tip of his shaft.

Thanos' hips thrust back and forth, his cock surging inside her mouth and Lamia relaxed her jaw as his fingers stiffened in her hair and every muscle in his body tensed. A loud roar erupted from his lips at the same time that hot spurts of his seed shot into her mouth.

She swallowed his warm essence down her throat until Thanos wrenched his cock from her mouth and, with his hand curled tightly around his still spewing shaft, pumped hard and fast, spraying the last of his release across her breasts.

She gasped when hot droplets trickled down her chest to drip from the pebbled peaks of her nipples.

Thanos pumped his cock until it grew soft. Finally spent, he slipped to his knees, his breath coming in short pants. With shaky hands, he untied her restraints.

His hands trembled as he redid his clothing and, when he had finally regained himself fully, he stumbled to his feet and walked to his horse, returning with a small bundle. When he unrolled it she saw that it was a strip of cloth and a clean *chlamys*. With surprisingly gentle hands, he cleansed his seed from her body with the fresh cloth, and, when he was done, he draped her in the thin woollen *chlamys*, before securing it at her waist with the same twine of rope that had bound her only moments ago.

Tugging her to her feet, he helped her on to Zeus, but this time he did not ride with her.

A tense silence hung between them as he mounted the other horse. Lamia emitted a soft, short sigh as she settled against Zeus, staring out over the large expanse of land she now had to cover *again*.

Her gaze slipped to Thanos, who sat astride his mount with his jaw tight, his mouth set in a firm line. In that moment, he was Thanos, the disciplined Spartan soldier, and not Thanos, the man who'd just lost control and found pleasure within her mouth and across her breasts. A tiny smile tugged at the corners of her lips. She decided then that she liked Thanos the man better.

As they rode, she cast furtive glances in his direction, wondering what thoughts brewed in his head. But when she realised what she was doing, she shook her head sharply. It was foolish to care what he was thinking, because it would only lead her to care for him. And she didn't want to care for Thanos. She only cared about plotting to escape him when the next opportunity presented itself. Despite her failed attempt, her plans had not changed—she would return to Athens to make Atallus pay for what he'd done.

Revenge—that was the only thing she seemed to care about these dawns and she could not—she *would* not—let anyone or anything distract her from her larger purpose, not even Thanos...*especially* not Thanos.

Chapter Six

Thanos clenched the reins in his hands so tightly that his knuckles turned white. Loosening his grip, he dragged in a long breath, struggling to ease the tension that invaded his body. He hadn't intended to lose control. He'd set out to punish Lamia, but that had been his only intent. Yet, when he had stroked the full mounds of her rounded backside, lust had seized control of his mind and body, and he'd been powerless to stop what came after.

He felt her eyes burning holes into his back, and he longed to turn around and reassure her—to say *anything*—but he could not look at Lamia just yet. He definitely could not talk to her, for he was certain that, if he did, the last vestiges of his control would finally dissolve and in an instant he would be wrenching her from his horse, settling between her legs and burying himself deep in her hot wet channel until they both could not walk for many sun risings.

A groan yawned out of him and he closed his eyes, as if he could banish the image of his seed coating Lamia's lovely breasts. Forcing out a long breath, he ran a hand through his wild mane in frustration. How was he going to make the long journey alone with her without fucking her at every turn? He'd sent his men ahead of them, not wanting to slow their progress. They needed to return to Sparta to deliver the news that the Roman army was once again gathering in the territory of Carthage, which was not good news for the city-states of Greece.

It would only be a matter of time before the Romans turned their greedy eyes towards Greece. The thought made him weary. He had more than enough to worry about, if war was in fact coming, but now he had a recalcitrant woman on his hands, who stubbornly fought against journeying to Sparta with him, who claimed she would never wed him even though her body craved him — and he had brought that problem upon himself.

He lifted his hand and shielded his eyes to scan the horizon. Her foolish plan of escape had cost them one full sun rising and he was fairly certain they were now almost two sun risings behind his men. It would be a miracle if he caught up to them before they reached Sparta. And, again, he only had himself to blame since he was the one who had offered to purchase her from Atallus in the first place.

Buried so deep in thought, he almost missed the familiar tingling along his skin when his instincts told him something was amiss. Immediately, Thanos brought his mount to a halt and listened. All thoughts of the war and Lamia instantly vanished as a sharp pang of unease settled in the pit of his stomach. The soft staccato of riders approaching on horseback was unmistakable. He glanced over his shoulder to meet Lamia's concerned gaze, before he shoved his hand into his satchel and grasped his spare sword.

"Take this," he shouted and flung it towards her.

She caught it easily with one hand, testing its weight in her palm.

The ground began to quake as several riders sped towards them, their horses galloping at a frenzied pace. Thanos squinted, straining to see into the distance. Clouds of dust gathered around the riders as they closed in on him and Lamia.

He stiffened as they drew nearer, and despite the distance, he could see the riders' faces were filthy, covered in grime, and their tattered garments hung off them like grungy rags. They were thieves. The one road from Athens to Sparta that ran along the coast of the Gulf of Argolis was rife with bands of thieves. He cursed under his breath. He was certain that the men had targeted them as soon as he had sent his soldiers ahead, probably gathering that two lone riders would be easy to pick off.

He met Lamia's gaze again, determination flashing across her stern face. When they saw her, they would think her a helpless woman. They certainly would not be expecting a fight.

"Can you ride and wield my sword?"

She nodded.

"Then we ride to meet them." Pressing his heels into the sides of his mount, Thanos set off. Moments later came the steady sound of Lamia's horse trailing close behind.

With his sharp eyes focused on the fast approaching thieves, he transformed into the ruthless, battle hardened *hoplite* he'd been born and bred to be. Lifting his sword, Thanos barrelled into the centre of their formation, surprising the riders who'd expected him to battle them from outside their ranks. With precise movements, he slashed at the inept thieves and cries of pain erupted from the wounded men as their crimson blood splattered across his arms.

A sharp cry dragged his attention to his right and he saw Lamia wrench her sword from her attacker's chest. Seconds later the man fell like a dead weight from his horse. His breath caught in his throat when one of the thieves reached up from the ground to grasp her leg. He turned his horse in her direction but another rider blocked him. Without a moment's hesitation, he cut the man down with a deft swipe of his blade. A wretched scream burst from the man and he tumbled from his horse, clutching desperately at his chest in a futile to attempt to staunch the blood that flowed like a river from the deep gash. Thanos rushed towards Lamia, his heart pumping wildly in his chest. The knots in his stomach loosened when she disentangled her ankle from the thief's grasp and delivered a deafening blow to the back of the man's skull with the butt of her sword. The man instantly crumbled to the ground, his body limp.

She sat on the back of her horse, her chest heaving. Their gazes clashed and he glimpsed a familiar churning in the depths of her eyes. He knew that look. It was the same one she'd given him on the day they'd fought in Athens. And he was reminded of the thought he'd had then as he'd faced her, standing at the edge of her sword. She had a warrior's heart, a fighter's strength of will, a fearlessness that was etched deep within her soul.

He glanced down at the bloodied and wounded men piled on the ground groaning in pain. Two were eerily still and silent.

They were done here.

"Let's go," he called.

Nudging his mount in the direction of the setting sun, he took off with Lamia riding by his side.

* * * *

Lamia ran her hands across Thanos' now clean and freshly polished sword. She smiled at her reflection that flashed in the blade. It looked better than new. Sheathing the sword, she set it down on the ground beside her.

She caught a flash of movement and she glanced up. A small grin tugged at her lips and she shot Thanos a tentative smile when he sat down beside her, bare from the waist up. Her stomach knotted as she let her gaze wander over him. His sculpted body glowed beneath the soft flickering of the firelight, ripples of corded muscle bulging and flexing with his every movement.

Her nipples tightened and she sucked in a sharp breath, quickly averting her gaze. What was wrong with her? She had known him less than half a fortnight, yet her body responded to him as if it had known him for many *annos*. If she was willing to be honest with herself then she could admit that she had never been attracted to any man as strongly as she was now attracted to Thanos. But she wasn't quite ready for such honesty.

"You fought bravely today."

She met his gaze, glad for the distraction.

"Thank you. You as well."

He smiled at her compliment. "Was Darius the one who taught you how to wield a sword?"

A knife of pain twisted in her gut at the thought of Darius. "That, and the art of fighting," she said brokenly, the bittersweet memories of Darius threatening to overwhelm her. It was only her vow to avenge his death that kept her sane most dawns, that kept her from succumbing to the soul-wrenching grief that was never far away.

Her vow of revenge *and* Thanos, she acknowledged. The handsome Spartan was an unwelcome distraction, but a distraction nonetheless.

"I am sorry. I did not mean to upset you."

Her smile was faint. "Do not be sorry. It is not your fault that my memories sometimes cause me pain."

He shifted next to her as he sheathed his sword. "Very few women could do what you did earlier, or what you did when we first met," he said, deftly switching the subject, for which she was grateful. "I worried earlier that you would be hurt."

"You are a man... Of course you worried. Men are the only ones who believe they can fight," she joked.

"I am serious, Lamia. You are a superb fighter, but still a woman. I fear there may come a time when the battle will be beyond your skills."

"And so what if it is?" She shrugged. "I will either be wounded or killed —"

"'So what'?" He scowled down at her. "Your life deserves far more than your flippant response, and I would feel responsible if you were ever hurt —"

"You are not responsible for me, Thanos. Besides, you were outnumbered. What was I supposed to do? Just sit there and twiddle my useless thumbs?" She knew if he'd had his way she would have been mending garments instead of galloping into the middle of a battle, but she wasn't that kind of woman.

"I am a soldier, Lamia. I am trained to fight uneven odds."

Defiance fuelled her words. "And I am a fighter as well, who does not run from any fight, no matter what."

"A fighter you may be, but you are not a soldier," he argued. "You are but one woman."

"And so now I'm helpless?" she scoffed. "I have been defending myself since I was a child, and I am one woman who does not need you or anybody else to protect me."

"You may not need my protection, but that will be my duty as your husband. When we are wed—"

She halted him with the roll of her eyes, but for only a moment.

"You can sit there and mock me, Lamia, but you must now see that there was some truth to the Oracle. You are foreign born. We met in a sword fight. And now it would seem your fate is tied to mine."

She'd thought he would abandon any notion of wedding after she'd run away. Didn't he see how ill-suited she was for marriage? For him?

She shook her head. "Thanos, cease with this nonsense. Can you not see that we are not well suited?" She sprang to her feet in an effort to put distance between them. She had no desire to be any man's wife—least of all Thanos' with his domineering ways—and especially now that she feared she was growing to care for him. If she wasn't careful she could lose her heart to the handsome Spartan and find herself tied to him after all. And she knew she would hate it, for Thanos was far too rigid a man, far too unyielding. Darius had always allowed her freedom— probably too much. With Thanos, his dominant manner would simply not allow her the freedom she was used to—and she would come to hate him...and he her.

"You cannot accept my independence," she continued. "And I do not take well to your arrogant commands. I've already tried to escape you once. Even if I lost all my senses, and we were somehow wedded, I would not stop trying to escape you. I answer to no other, and your dominant ways would only stifle me."

She'd barely got the last of her words out, before she was abruptly yanked by her *chlamys* down to the hard ground.

She met Thanos' simmering gaze. Before she could protest, he flipped her over, pressing her back deep into the cold, jagged earth.

She struggled to sit up but his solid frame was unyielding. And when she pushed against his chest, he gripped her wrists with his large hand, lifting her arms above her head, effectively restraining her.

She gritted her teeth, anger boiling through her, but she eased beneath him, leashing her fury for the moment because she realised it was useless to struggle, if her still sore behind was any evidence.

"You will not leave me again," he growled out, the muscle in his jaw thumping beneath golden skin.

"This is what I'm referring to, Thanos. You are a bully," she snapped.

A smile lifted the corners of his lips, but it did not reach his eyes, and she knew her insult had struck a chord.

His free hand shot out and he dragged her *chlamys* from her body, leaving her completely nude.

"You truly are a bully if you think you can force my hand. But I still will not wed you, Thanos. Not ever, not even if you rape me," she warned with a steely glare.

The anger in his eyes dimmed, giving way to surprise, before she glimpsed the wounded expression on his face. For the second time that dawn, she'd lashed out and injured him with her brash words. She knew instinctively that Thanos would never take her if she was unwilling but it was too late now to take back what she'd said. Still, she opened her mouth to apologise, but shut it at the chilly expression etched across his face.

"I would never rape you, Lamia, and you know it. I have never taken a woman by force and I never shall." Cupping one breast in his large hand, Thanos flicked his thumb across her hardening nipple, earning a traitorous gasp of pleasure from her lips.

Leaning down, he traced the shell of her ear with the tip of his hot, wet tongue and she shivered against him, eliciting a soft chuckle.

"You say you hate my dominance, but I think you realise the difference between a husband who seeks full control over his wife, and a man who seeks her submission in their bed. You know I do not seek to control you, Lamia. I only wish to master you in our bed, but I think that frightens you. I think your mind is frightened of what I do to you. But when it comes to your body, it tells an entirely different story than the protests tumbling from your sweet lips."

His mouth furled into a grin full of arrogance and she shuddered at the triumph blazing in the cobalt depths of his eyes. "Even now your cunt is wet for me. I've barely touched you and I can already smell the scent of your arousal wafting in the air.

"But you're so afraid of your own desires for me, that you must convince yourself the only way I could ever have you is if I force you." The chuckle rising out of him held a note of censure that was mocking to her ears. "That is fine, Lamia. Tell yourself whatever lies you must so that you may escape your shame. Because know this—when I finally do take you, your pleading cries will echo so loudly on the wind that you shall never be able to deny that you begged for my cock. And you will beg, *agapetos*. You will beg for me to fuck you any way that *I* desire."

Chapter Seven

Lamia squirmed beneath Thanos when his free hand lingered over her breast. He took its softness in his palm and massaged gently, plucking her nipple until it was fully erect.

Her channel clenched and she clamped her thighs together as moisture seeped out, hating that he spoke the truth. She couldn't deny what he already knew, what they both knew, that before the eve was done she would shamelessly beg for his touch.

Her body ached to surrender, to give in to the need that he had created within her, but her mind resisted.

"Thanos," she protested on a low moan while his hand traced the plane of her belly, teasing her navel before dipping lower to rake the soft nest of curls between her legs.

"Open for me," he whispered within the hollow of her neck.

Lamia's mind screamed in protest, warning her of what her surrender would mean, but she was powerless against the insistent desire clawing through her, and her body rebelled, obeying his command as her thighs drifted apart. Parting her folds with his fingers, he encircled the tiny nub at the apex of her womanhood, rubbing it back and forth, pinching it lightly. Her back stiffened as the pressure built inside her and her legs fell open wider, her hips rocking slowly, pushing her mound harder against his hand.

"Thanos," she moaned when his fingers dipped inside. Her wet heat embraced him and she glanced down to see her juices glistening on his fingers beneath the silver moonlight. She let her eyes drift shut, savouring the feel of his fingers gently ploughing in and out of her wet cunt, pushing past the tight muscles of her sheath.

A needy gasp passed her lips as he eased out of her shuddering body, and, when her eyes finally opened to meet his, she melted at the crooked smile he greeted her with. Her heart galloped to an abrupt stop as his handsome face softened and a single dimple creased his cheek. She curled her lips into a slight smile and in that moment something passed between them, a fleeting emotion that warmed that small space where her heart rested.

As quickly as it had come, the moment passed and he leant forward, raining tiny kisses across her forehead, against her lips, down her neck and along her breasts. He gently kissed a trail down the length of her body until he reached her belly, where he swept his tongue along the sensitive skin before dipping inside her navel. She moaned louder, her skin tingling where the cool eve air stroked her wet flesh.

With both hands, Thanos hooked her legs over his shoulders and he glanced up from kissing her belly to hold her gaze, his lips poised at the mouth of her dripping opening. His eyes never left her face even as he pressed forward, the tip of his tongue shooting out to flick the hardened bud before sliding through her slick folds. Her vision blurred as she watched him watch her while his mouth hungrily feasted upon her cunt. His long, thick tongue shot out again, stabbing at her tight hole, plunging inside, and she cried out at the sensual invasion, her head falling back.

"Look at me," he commanded in a harsh rasp.

She struggled to lift her head to train her gaze on him. But she did, then held his penetrating stare even as her legs began to tremble, forcing him to grasp her thighs tighter in order to steady her, driving her hard against his tongue. Back and forth he plunged in and out of her clenching hole, his searing gaze imprisoning her.

The rough, wet press of his tongue across her most intimate flesh awakened a feral response in Lamia. Her skin flushed with heat. A broken sob tore from her mouth and tiny tremors gathered at the centre of her womb until every part of her shuddered with pleasure. Throwing her hips at him, she rocked her cunt against his mouth as she grasped his head in her hands, digging her fingers into his scalp. His lids drifted shut and he moaned as he devoured her in earnest, a look of bliss crossing his face. That was her undoing. Her body trembled and quaked as she exploded against his lips.

She cried out his name, clenching her eyes shut as violent shudders racked her and she came, her sticky warm juices gushing forth.

He moaned again, licking up her liquid pleasure, his tongue flicking out rapidly to lap up every last drop of her essence.

"You taste like the sweetest ambrosia from the gods," he groaned as he moved up the length of her body.

Bending down, Thanos pressed his lips to hers and she opened her mouth to accept his kiss, savouring the erotic flavour of her juices on his tongue. He kissed her deeply, drawing her bottom lip between his teeth to nip gently before plunging inside her mouth. She grasped the back of his head to crush her lips against his, delighting in the heady taste of his tongue sliding deeper inside the moist cave of her mouth as it had just slid into her hot tunnel only moments before.

He slowly dragged his lips from hers to place soft kisses against the column of her neck and she sighed, roaming her hands across the uneven flesh of his back before tangling in his soft, dark spill of hair.

With him nestled in her embrace, Lamia felt the brush of his rough knuckles against the inside of her thigh as he undid his *pteryges* before shrugging them down his powerful legs to toss them aside. Grasping her thighs with callused palms, he once again lifted her legs over his shoulders, opening her wide.

She was wide and spread before him, her knees resting against her shoulders and he hovered above her, the weight of his solid body pinning her to the ground. Thanos coiled his hand into her hair, twisting it in her mass of curls, while he used the other to grasp his pulsing shaft and guide it to her now dripping core.

With his hand still in her hair, he gently nudged her head to the side and buried his face against her neck. His breathing was stilted, warm puffs of air along her throat as his tongue licked the sweat-slicked skin while he pushed the thick, mushroom head of his cock against the entrance of her cunt, powering forward. She released a low hiss at the sweet invasion as he fed her his length slowly until just the crown of his cock rested inside her walls.

"Fuck, Lamia," he gritted out in a hoarse whisper. His jaw was clenched tight, the muscles in his arms straining, and he drew back just enough to thrust deeper. "You're tight, *agapetos*."

Slowly he sank into her until the pressure welled up inside her. The feeling of fullness, of being stretched, overwhelmed her and she dug her nails into his back.

"Thanos!" she cried out, her body tightening around him.

"By the gods, you are so wet, so warm," he groaned, already plunging hard into her. He ripped through the thin barrier within her passage, sinking his engorged length so deep that the heavy sac beneath his cock slapped her tender flesh.

Pain sliced through Lamia and she stiffened, a sharp cry erupting from her lips as she curled her nails into his back.

Thanos tensed above her, the air around them suddenly thick with an ominous chill.

"Why did you not tell me?" he demanded in a broken whisper, his voice shaking, the muscles in his neck and arms bulging into tight knots as he strained to remain still inside her.

She did not speak as she lowered her gaze.

Thanos' eyes dipped shut, the jagged breath he drew in vibrating through her. "You should have told me you were a virgin," he whispered. "I would have stop—"

Pressing her fingers to his mouth, she halted him. She'd protested and denied the insistent pull of attraction between them, but never had she resisted.

"I did not wish for you to stop," she replied truthfully. "And I do not wish for you to stop now," she insisted when he began to withdraw from her.

His body trembled above hers, his expression uncertain until she slowly rocked her hips against him, taking him deeper. A lewd curse whispered out of him as his gaze became hooded, and he began to move within her, setting a lazy, languid rhythm. He eased his shaft into her, gently stretching her until Lamia relaxed, the pain eventually giving way to the burgeoning flames of pleasure that now licked within her belly. Desire's warm embrace curled around her, stoking the fire that now raged within. Her hips jerked and her nails pierced his weathered skin while the tender muscles of her sheath pulsed and tightened around him.

Desperation flashed in Thanos' eyes. "Stop it, Lamia. I c–can barely –" He sucked in a sharp breath. "Fuck," he groaned helplessly as if powerless against the need surging through him. His eyes clenched shut and he fell forward to nestle his face into the crook of her neck.

His thrusts quickened, his hips furiously pistoning back and forth, tunnelling the ruddy length of his cock in and out of her tender flesh at a frenzied pace.

"I am sorry," he croaked out. "I cannot stop." He drove his hardened shaft deep inside her, his ass clenching tight beneath her hands as he rode her hard. The pungent scent of sweat and desire tickled her nose as his naked flesh pounded hers, the erotic din of skin slapping skin echoing on the wind.

She dug her fingers into his back as he rammed his stiff flesh inside her, his cock brushing hard across her engorged nub with each brutal stroke. The pain mingled with pleasure as he held her open wide, making her a vessel for his seed.

Heat furled in her belly as he mounted her roughly, hurling her body to the brink of pleasure until spasms fluttered within her tight tunnel.

Her mouth fell open. Thanos thrust harder. A strangled cry escaped her lips as the muscles in her thighs tensed and the walls of her channel collapsed. She erupted—a raging, tumultuous inferno—her release coming so swift and hard that Thanos had to struggle to plough his cock through the tight vice of her spasming cunt. With her release thundering through her, her body convulsed uncontrollably as her hole gushed with sticky fluid to coat his thrusting length.

Thanos stroked his stiff erection faster and harder inside her, the heavy weight of his sac slapping against her skin as her slippery cunt made faint suctioning noises with each thrust. She released a tortured moan, her raw voice calling out his name as the last tremors of her climax ripped through her.

Clinging to her, his blunt nails dug into the flesh of her thighs as he pounded wildly into her—every trace of the disciplined Spartan soldier having vanished the moment he'd entered her cunt. Sweat dripped from him, and Lamia arched just high enough to swipe her tongue across his chest. The spicy taste of him exploded on her tongue. A moan of pleasure filtered through her lips mingling with his strangled moan. His shuddering release soon followed and he stiffened above her, releasing a harsh roar, as he drove into her one final time.

Burying his cock deep, her name rushed out of him on a stilted sigh as a pool of warmth settled against the back of her tunnel. She clenched and tightened around him, squeezing hard, milking him of several more hot spurts of his seed until he shuddered violently, collapsing atop her.

With a harsh grunt, Thanos settled atop her, nestling deeper into her embrace, and she held him tightly. Her limbs wrapped around his slick body, his back expanding with each laboured breath. When his breathing grew even, he rolled off her and dragged her against him so that her body rested at his side.

They lay there for a long while before he pulled away from her and stood. She stared up at him, her eyes feasting on his battle-honed physique, glowing beneath the moonlight like that of the war god Ares, who stood enshrined in marble within the stone columns of the Parthenon.

Dragging a cloth through the basin of warm water beside the fire, he twisted it in his hand, until it did not drip with excess liquid. Returning to her side, he stooped down before her to part her thighs. Heat gathered in her cheeks when he dipped the cloth between her legs to wipe away all traces of their lovemaking, the warmth of the rag soothing her tender flesh.

When he was done, he placed the cloth aside and drew a woollen blanket over her naked body to once again settle beside her, pulling her into the circle of his arms. Lamia did not resist the intimate gesture, not after what had already passed between them. Instead, she rested her head against his solid chest and closed her eyes, desperately trying to ignore the soft flutters of pleasure that danced inside her belly at the thought of Thanos' tenderness towards her.

She hated that she was softening towards him, but it was hard not to. Despite his gruff manner, Thanos was a man of great gentleness and kindness. Of its own volition, her body snuggled deeper into his embrace, even as her mind fought against what it already knew. Thanos was steadily chipping away at the wall she'd erected between them, and, most importantly, the one that had long guarded her heart.

* * * *

Conditioned to function on little sleep, Thanos lay awake long after the sound of Lamia's gentle snores echoed in the silent eve. He glanced down into her sleeping face, stroking a single finger across her cheek and along her chin. He lifted his lips into a contented smile when a heavy weight settled in his gut. Lamia had yet to realise it, but according to Spartan custom he'd just wed her. Marriage ceremonies were very simple to his people and by the act of simply taking her he'd made her his wife.

She would not be happy when she learned of this particular tradition, but that was not what kept him awake this eve. His growing need to protect and cherish this woman unsettled him greatly. Marriage in Sparta was not typically based upon love, at least not initially. It was seen as a contract a couple made with the state to produce children and future *hoplites*.

When he'd decided he wanted to take her to wife, his first thought had been that she would suit him well and bear him strong sons. Thanos had not considered that she would raise his most basic need as a man, his most primitive instinct—the one to protect. Nor had he imagined that he would grow to feel something for her that went beyond his duty to Sparta.

Lamia was revealing herself to be a woman of many surprises. He'd never have guessed she was a virgin by the way she'd pleasured him with her mouth. But that was Lamia—seemingly experienced in some ways, yet innocent in others. She was proving to be a far more complex woman than he'd first suspected. With each layer she revealed, he found himself fascinated by her and drawn to her even more, which made him wonder if maybe he'd found a woman who could be his wife in the truest sense. His heart stuttered at the thought. What if Lamia proved herself to be more than the woman in his dreams? What if she could not only ease the loneliness in his bed, but also the ache inside his heart?

Chapter Eight

Carthage, 176 BC

"What are you thinking?"

Lamia twisted in the arms of her young lover, Mythos, to stare down into his handsome face.

Darius would be gone for most of the dawn, out purchasing more materials to fulfil all of the orders they now had from the Roman army. Business was thriving, and Lamia was grateful, since it kept her and Darius from starving. Yet, she hated that they sold weapons to the marauding Roman army, weapons they would now use on some unsuspecting, vulnerable village, just as they'd done with her, killing everything in its path, leaving nothing in their bloodthirsty wake.

"What am I thinking?" she asked Mythos, struggling to chase away the dark thoughts that still haunted her.

"Yes, well, what were you thinking? For a moment you were wistful, but now you have that faraway look on your face that you get whenever you're lost in the past."

At nineteen annos, two annos older than herself, she thought Mythos was considerably astute, especially considering their courtship had only begun three moons *ago. He had a way of reading her moods that spoke of the sort of familiarity between them she knew didn't always happen until much later. She appreciated that about him, among many other things. Unfortunately she could not seem to muster up deeper feelings, beyond that of admiration and a fleeting attraction. But Mythos was a good man, one of the few who'd dared to court her.*

"I was thinking of how I wish we could spend more time together, without having to sneak around."

His handsome face twisted into a scowl as he slowly traced the lines of her jaw with his fingers.

"If you would tell Darius, we would not have —"

She shook her head sternly, not letting him finish. She thought of her adopted father, Darius — the great general of the once unstoppable Persian army. He guarded her virtue quite closely, believing very few men were worthy of her, and most times she had to admit he was right. She knew the interests of the men who'd turned their attention to her as she'd grown into a woman were not genuine. Their thoughts were of how best she could warm their bed mats. They had no desire to court her, to make her their wife.

She knew Mythos was different. He was kind and attentive, generous with his affection, and not once had he pressed her to go beyond stolen kisses and gentle caresses. Even if she did not love him, she was at ease with him, but she had yet to tell Darius of Mythos, afraid he would forbid her from seeing him, as he'd done so many times before with other suitors, which was why their time together was always fleeting, relegated to the shadows so they would not be caught.

"I am sorry, Mythos, but Darius does not yet understand. He still sees me as a child —"

"But you are not a child, Lamia. You are a woman of marriageable age. Do you not think it is time for you to leave his home for that of your husband?"

Nadia Aidan

She frowned at his words. She didn't want to leave Darius. He was the only family she had, and, without her, there would be no one to watch over him, no one to take care of him as he grew older with the passing of time. She parted her lips to tell Mythos that, but never got the chance when he spoke again.

"Lamia, I want to wed you," he said softly. "I want to ask Darius for permission to take you as my wife."

Her eyes rounded, her next words forgotten. She liked Mythos, enjoyed his company, but she wasn't sure she could ever be his wife. Maybe in time, as she grew to know him better, she could...but then there was the chance that she would never change her mind. She didn't want to hurt his feelings, especially since no other men were particularly eager to offer for her hand, but she could not lie to him.

"Mythos – "

"The sooner we wed, the sooner I can begin to make a proper woman out of you," he said, as if she hadn't spoken, but his words struck a chord deep inside her, making her abandon what she'd been prepared to say.

"A proper woman? How am I not a proper woman already?"

She knew, before he even spoke, what he was referring to, but she wanted to hear him say it. She wanted to hear the disgust in his voice, see it revealed on his face when he reviled the masculine garments she wore, her prowess with weapons, and how she preferred to work rather than seek a husband.

"Lamia, I am certain I do not need to tell you where you are lacking."

Lacking? No, she did not need to be told what she already knew. She'd been taunted as a child because of her preference for things unbecoming of a woman. She knew all too well that she wasn't a traditional woman, but that didn't mean she was lacking. So she couldn't mend *garments very well, but how many women knew how to wield a sword and forge weapons with their bare hands?*

She pulled out of Mythos' arms and got to her feet, her heart weighing heavy in her chest. She'd thought he was different, more open-minded, but he was no different from the others. Finding her completely unbecoming and unattractive, men usually just steered clear of her, but what Mythos was doing was far worse in her opinion. He didn't like who she was, what she was, so he thought he would change her, mould her into someone more acceptable in his eyes. She would have preferred him to have done as other men did, just left her alone, instead of pretending to want her when, truly, he did not.

"I need to get back before Darius returns."

He released a long sigh as he ambled to his feet, brushing the blades of grass from his body.

"You know there are very few men who would want you as their wife."

She stilled at his words. The mild resentment she'd felt only moments ago was now long gone, replaced by indignation and open fury.

"So why do you want me then?" she snapped as she folded her arms across her chest.

He shrugged, and his entire expression transformed into one she'd never seen before. His eyes were cruel, and she knew then that she'd been very wrong about him.

"To be honest, I do not want you, at least not as you are now, but I see potential beneath all of your masculine ways."

"So, if I were to wed you, you would expect me to wear a chiton, and then pretend I didn't know how to use weapons. I certainly would not be allowed to make them – "

"Lamia – " he tried to cut her off, realising the fire he'd set off inside her, but it was already too late. Mythos had revealed his true self, his true intentions, and she wasn't impressed.

"You know what, Mythos? I am not so desperate to wed that I would change my entire self for a man." She thought of the girls she'd known as a child, and how they'd grown apart as they'd reached womanhood because she did not recognise them anymore. They'd disappeared into their husbands, serving only their needs, until they were little more than mindless slaves. She'd vowed long ago never to become that type of woman, even if it meant she would remain alone for the rest of her dawns.

"I believe a husband should respect his wife, and wed her for who she is, not who he wishes her to be. I am flattered by the honour you do me, and I know you will make some woman a fine husband, but that woman is not me." That was mostly a lie, but she was trying to be gracious. Yet Mythos was far too intelligent not to know when he was being patronised.

His laughter was harsh to her ears, full of bitterness and the promise of cruelty, and she hated the sound. "You live in the realm of the gods, full of dreams and enchantment, if you think you'll find a man who wants you for you." He emphasised his words by slowly raking his gaze over her dishevelled chlamys and wild hair.

"Good dawn, Mythos," she said tightly, her sandalled heels digging a shallow hole into the soft earth as she spun away from him. The sound of his mocking laughter trailed after her, and she fought not to run, to flee from him, for she had far too much pride to let him see that he'd succeeded in his desire to wound her. But the words he shouted at her back she would never forget — not one dawn would pass that she did not recount them, until she came to believe them.

"No man will ever want you, Lamia. No man who wants a real woman."

She didn't stop as she walked away from him, her back rigid and her head held high, even as she blinked back tears that she would shed into her bed mat later. She'd been a fool to let Mythos into her life – giving him the power to wound her – but never again.

No man would ever have such power to wound her as Mythos had done, for she was determined to forever guard her heart, her body, her very soul.

* * * *

"How are you faring this sun rising?"

Lamia glanced over at Thanos, trying her best to meet his concerned gaze even as embarrassment stole over her, warming her cheeks. He'd taken her two more times before they'd risen that dawn and she knew what he was truly asking. She finished securing the goat-hide sack, which held a few figs and one pomegranate, to her horse before she spoke. "I'm faring well."

He scrutinised her for several long moments before he seemed to accept her answer, which she knew to be somewhat of a lie. She was pleasantly sore, but sore nonetheless. More heat crawled along her skin all the way to her face when an image of Thanos ploughing inside her with gentle strokes flashed into her head. He'd bestowed upon her unimaginable, indescribable pleasure that even now left her tingling all over, and afterwards he'd been gentle and tender as he'd bathed her, trying to ease the ache between her thighs.

"We will ride until we reach the town of Sellasie. I sent most of our food with my men so we will need to stop and replenish our supply before we continue on."

She nodded as he mounted Zeus and she moved to follow suit, but stopped when her body protested and she winced in pain.

"What is it?" he demanded, his face darkening with alarm as he jumped down from his horse to stand by her side.

She braced herself against her mount with her hands, curling her lips into a weak smile. "I am still a bit sore, after all."

She grimaced at the sharp curse he expelled. "I asked you if you were sore and you said that you were fine." He reached down to hoist her into his arms.

"No. You asked how I fared and— What are you doing?" she demanded when Thanos hoisted her up on to Zeus with her body sideways so that her knees touched.

"You will not make it a single metre in your condition if you sit astride." Lifting himself on to Zeus, Thanos grasped the reins so that his body trapped her in the small crook at the back of the horse's neck.

She opened her mouth to object but just as quickly she snapped it shut because he was right. She would be in pain within moments if she tried to ride.

"Wrap your arms around me and rest your head against my chest. It will make it easier for me to ride with you," he added, apparently glimpsing the question in her eyes.

She nodded as she curled her arms around him and laid her head against his broad chest, listening to the even rhythm of his heart beating beneath her ear.

He flicked the reins once and eased into a slow trot, the echo of steady hoof beats in the distance revealing that the other horse followed behind Zeus.

She closed her eyes and inhaled the rich, masculine scent that was unique to Thanos as the muscles in his torso flexed within the rough *curiass* beneath her cheek. Her mind easily drifted to the eve before and she found herself balling her fists at his back just to keep from running her fingertips along the hard planes of his chest. She wished he hadn't donned his battle armour because she ached to feel the rough skin of his torso beneath her palms —

"What are you thinking?"

The deep rumble of his voice vibrated beneath her cheek, jolting her back to the present. She lifted her head to meet his open gaze.

"Why do you ask?" She danced around the question with a coy retort, refusing to admit the truth — that she'd been thinking of *him*.

"You sighed a moment ago. It was a pleasant sound and you seemed happy. Made me wonder what you were thinking."

Had she sighed? Lamia blinked furiously, now at a loss for words. "I-I —" she stammered.

"You do not have to share your thoughts if revealing them to me makes you uncomfortable. It was the first time you've seemed happy since I met you, so I just wondered what thoughts could have the power to bring you such joy."

She swallowed the lump that gathered in her throat at his softly spoken words.

"Why do you care what brings me joy?" she asked wearily, the rough edge to her voice sharper than necessary but she hated the warmth flooding her belly because it was thoughts of him that had brought her joy. She felt as if she was being pulled in two different directions as a battle raged within her, where one Lamia wanted to open herself fully to him, while the other wanted to maintain the distance that separated them.

Thanos brought Zeus to an abrupt stop and dropped the reins. He then lifted one hand to cup the back of her head. Tangling his hand in her hair, he nudged her head, forcing her eyes to meet his.

"I care because I would simply like to know what it is that makes you happy. Is it so wrong for a man to know what pleases his lover?"

She struggled to ignore the wild thumping of her heart beneath her breasts, but it was no use. "Why, Thanos? Most men care not for the happiness of the women who warm their beds."

"You should know by now that I am not most men." He untangled his hand from her hair to trail a finger along her cheek as he spoke softly. "I care about your happiness, Lamia, just as I hope that you will come to care about mine."

* * * *

They rode into the small town of Sellasie at high noon, but Lamia barely saw the cluttered shops that lined the streets as the *agora* bustled with merchants peddling their goods. Her mind was at a distance as she once again repeated Thanos' words in her head. He cared about her happiness. With the exception of Darius, no man had ever cared about her happiness, nor she theirs. She'd grown up in Carthage, surrounded by men who feared her and her mannish ways. No man was impressed by a woman who could wield a sword as well as him or possibly best him in a fight. Her suitors had been non-existent, so she'd accepted many *annos* ago that she would never wed. But here was Thanos, offering not only to wed her but also the promise that she could become his wife in the truest sense—not simply a body to bear children, but one with whom he could share true affection.

What if she agreed to his foolish plan and actually wed him? Could she truly make him happy? *Her?* The woman who everyone said no man would ever want. Could she learn to give him what he needed just as he promised to give her what she needed in return? Or would she only disappoint him?

She frowned at the thought. With any other man she would not have cared what he thought of her, wanted of her, but here she was again thinking of a future with a man who up until a few dawns ago she hadn't even known. What was it about Thanos that made her forget herself…made her forget her promise to Darius' ghost?

The absence of Thanos' warmth beneath her cheek tugged her out of her trance and she glanced over her shoulder to see him slide down from his horse and tether the reins of both mounts to a post beside a watering hole.

"I will purchase food and return shortly. Remain here until I return."

She glowered down at him, irritated by his arrogant command, but she didn't argue. She was too tired. Besides, with her stiff legs and aching muscles she had no intention of going anywhere at all.

Yet he hesitated as he peered up at her, and she realised he was waiting for her to respond.

"I will not run," she said dryly. "I would not get very far even if I did."

He arched a single brow and studied her more intently as if trying to ascertain from her expression the truth of her response. Seemingly satisfied with what he read upon her face, he visibly relaxed.

"I shall return shortly," he said again before he strode purposefully towards the *agora*.

Her eyes never left him as she followed every move of his powerful body, his muscles rippling beneath the harsh rays of the sun. He walked with the confidence of a man who was always in charge, so he easily drew the attention of curious onlookers. She scowled when she noticed she wasn't alone in her admiration. Several women turned their heads, ogling him as he passed by.

He strolled through the *agora* until he stopped at a pretty young woman's cart who looked to be no more than eighteen *annos*.

"*Barely* a woman." She snorted when the young merchant flipped her dark, glossy hair over her shoulder and fluttered her eyelashes. She was flirting with him. Lamia narrowed her eyes when Thanos smiled down at the girl as he gathered several figs, loaves of bread and a large chunk of goat cheese and placed them into his sack. When he was done he handed her several coins. The woman beamed as she closed her hand around them and said something that caused him to chuckle. Lamia frowned as his eyes sparkled with laughter before he waved farewell to the little temptress and strolled back to where he'd left her with the horses.

As he drew near, she forced herself to school her features into a blank mask, hoping that her irritation didn't show on her face. But she needn't have bothered because he busied himself with packing the food and checking on the condition of both horses, barely sparing her a glance.

Once he was done, he once again lifted himself atop his mount, but this time she did not wrap her arms around his waist. Instead she crossed her arms beneath her breasts and rested the side of her body against his chest. She knew she was being childish, but she could not help it.

He'd flirted with that girl although he'd known she was watching. Despite all of his flowery words and his displays of tenderness, he was still a man no different from any other. For just a moment, she'd allowed herself to believe his words, that she could be the woman he desired, that she *wanted* to be the woman he desired. But Thanos was a virile man, and far too handsome to ever be satisfied with just one woman. And, if his flirting was any evidence, she certainly wasn't the woman who could satisfy him if she couldn't even hold his attention for more than a single sun rising.

* * * *

After leaving Sellasie, Thanos followed the main trail that ran along the northern edge of the Laconian plain until it was almost dusk. He knew he was pushing the pace a little hard, but he was trying to make up for the time he'd lost by going after Lamia and then stopping for food.

By the time he found a suitable area to make camp, they were both exhausted. Tossing several more small branches of wood onto the fire so that it would burn through the eve, he looked up when Lamia returned from relieving herself. She didn't meet his gaze as she sulked all the way to their bed mat and lay down with her back to him.

He frowned at her rigid back. She had been sullen and distant from the moment they'd ridden out of Sellasie. At the time he hadn't questioned her, thinking that she was simply weary from their journey, but now he knew it to be more than that.

He stood to remove his *curiass* and crossed the short distance to where she lay pretending to be asleep. He slipped beneath the heavy woollen blanket and snaked his arm out to wrap around her waist, pulling her soft body flush against his. At the first touch of his hand she stiffened and she remained tense as he held her to him.

Thanos released a long, weary sigh. He was exhausted and had no desire to fight with her, but he could no longer ignore her surly disposition.

"Would you care to tell me what is wrong?"

Her breathing was measured, but not even, so he knew she was not asleep even though she remained silent. He sighed again, the gesture more exaggerated this time.

"I know you are awake."

Several moments passed until he became certain she would continue to ignore him when finally she said in a small voice, "What makes you think something is wrong?"

"You've been silent from the moment we left Sellasie. Did something happen while we were there?"

There was a pregnant pause, and Thanos held his breath, waiting.

"Actually, something did happen while we were there and I am surprised you do not remember."

He wrinkled his forehead as he searched his memories, recounting the brief trip to the city. He hadn't spoken to anyone except the Thespian girl at the market. He drew up short when he recalled his hurried exchange with the merchant. *She could not possibly be upset over that?*

A small smile tugged at the edges of his mouth at the notion that Lamia was angry because he'd shared a joke with a girl who was young enough to be his daughter.

Lamia? Jealous? His smile hitched higher.

"If you're referring to the time when I bought food from the girl in the market, then yes, I remember." He pressed his open palm firmly against her abdomen and drew her deeper into his embrace when she stiffened and tried to pull away. "I remember because she was the only person I spoke to while there, so I am assuming she must be the source of your anger."

"*She* is not the source of my anger. And I am not angry. Just—just—"

She stumbled over her words and he knew she was either having trouble voicing her feelings or she didn't yet realise what it was she was feeling, so he finished for her.

"Jealous?"

She shook her head, launching into a litany of protests.

"I am *not* jealous. That is ridiculous. You flirted with the girl right before me and it was simply rude—"

She stopped in mid-tirade when, without warning, he rolled her over onto her back and covered her with his frame. Holding himself still above her, he settled his weight on one side of his body and used his free hand to cup her cheek, dragging her gaze to his face.

"I did not flirt with that girl. I admit that I joked with her but I was simply being polite. If you saw it as flirting then I apologise. It was not my intention to upset you."

She nibbled on her bottom lip, her expression full of scepticism.

"I did not flirt with that girl," he repeated, his voice firmer. He *hadn't* flirted with the girl. The young merchant had been pretty enough, but he was a man of single-minded focus. He'd focused all of his attention on one woman and that woman was Lamia, and *only* her.

"I believe you," she whispered after a long silence.

He quirked his lips into a grin. "I'm flattered to discover that you are jealous—"

"I am *not* jealous."

"Yes, you are," he remarked quietly before dipping his head to capture her sputtering mouth with his lips. He slowly ran the tip of his tongue along the seam of her lips, gently teasing her, before plunging inside.

The kiss was unexpected so she gasped softly when he slipped his tongue between her lips to taste her. He knew the moment her surprise gave way to her own desires, because she arched into him and lifted one hand to tangle in his hair, causing her breasts to jut out and press against his bare chest.

He groaned at the feel of her hardened nipples stabbing into his torso. Grasping the back of his head, she held him locked to her and he deepened the kiss as he intertwined his tongue with hers.

Thanos rocked his hips in a gentle rhythm, the evidence of his arousal pressing into her belly. Skimming his hands down the length of her body, he teased her honey-smooth skin with his fingertips as he pushed her *chamlys* upward until he'd released her breasts from the loose confines of the garment. Cupping the soft weight of her fullness in his hand, Thanos gently rolled her stiffened peaks between his fingers only to pluck at them when they were fully erect, eliciting a sharp gasp from her lips.

She writhed beneath him, her hands roaming over his back as she twisted her legs apart and he easily settled beneath her spread thighs.

"Thanos." She rasped out his name on a hoarse sob when he rocked against her again, grinding the bulge in his *pyterges* into the moist heat of her feminine mound.

Wrenching his lips from hers, he trailed his tongue down the column of her throat until he reached the soft spot where her neck and shoulder met then nipped and sucked at the sensitive flesh, dragging another moan from her pretty lips.

She clung to him, her nails digging deep into his back as she locked her ankles at his waist, desperately meeting the thrusting of his hips with wild, jerky movements.

"Make love to me, Thanos. Please," she begged.

He stilled, lifting his head to meet her lust-drunk gaze. "Are you still sore?"

Sable lashes brushed her cheeks, shielding her eyes, and he had his answer. He ached to sink into her body, knowing that her dewy sheath would grip him as tightly as a wet fist. But to take her again would only cause her pain. He berated himself for making love to her as often as he had the eve before. Even though he'd been gentle the second and third times, he knew it would be a few dawns before her body became accustomed to the act. He should have stopped after they'd first made love, but she was an erotic temptation, and when she'd begged him to take her again, and then again in that soft, sensual voice of her hers, he was powerless to resist her siren's call.

His gaze roamed her lovely face, drinking her in. Her lips were puffy from his kisses, while her cheeks were tinged scarlet with the rush of pleasure stealing through her body, but it was her eyes that felled him. Her glittering eyes were glazed with wanton desire and a burning need that scorched him to the core of his soul. She was exquisite. Even now, despite her soreness, she begged for him, but this time his restraint and good sense kept him from giving in to her husky pleas.

Placing a gentle peck against her lips, he murmured, "To make love to you now would only bring you pain and not pleasure. Your body needs time to recover—"

She groaned in protest and he smiled down at her. His little wanton was insatiable. He lowered his head again to kiss a pathway along the length of her body, determined to give Lamia the release she craved, knowing he would probably wind up in a painful state of arousal for the rest of the eve. He stifled a wry smile. Watching her face as she climaxed would be worth the slight discomfort.

He showered her breasts with kisses, moving lower to sweep his tongue across her bare belly. He dipped the tip into her navel and she nearly shot up off the bed mat, her fingers clenching the back of his head tighter. He didn't linger at her belly. Instead he continued on his languorous journey down her body until he reached the mound of her womanhood.

He darted out his tongue to slide between the slick folds, tasting her arousal.

"Thanos…" she hissed, clamping her knees against his head. He chuckled at the catch in her voice, letting his warm breath glide across her feverish skin.

He teased her again with the slow slide of his tongue through her tender, pink flesh before he devoured her completely. Parting her outer lips with one hand, Thanos stroked his tongue inside her at the same time that he seized her tiny nubbin with his other hand, rotating it gently between his fingers.

She thrashed wildly beneath him, his name tearing past her lips on a sharp cry. Her body pulsed and vibrated around him as he fucked her with his tongue. Increasing the pressure along her tiny nub, he dragged hoarse sobs of pleasure from her lips until she was panting wildly, her body trembling as she neared her release.

He made love to her with his mouth, his hands, until he joined her in the spiralling cyclone that threatened to obliterate his control. He'd never found release from pleasuring a woman in this manner but the urge to spurt was so strong that he found himself undoing the laces of his *pyterges* to pull out his aching shaft.

Returning his hand to her cunt, Thanos shoved two long fingers inside her, coating them with her juices. She responded instantly to the probing of his fingers by arching against his hand, but he was eager to taste her juices on his lips, so reluctantly he withdrew his fingers from the hot, tight centre of her body only to replace them with his questing tongue.

Her sticky liquid glistened on his fingers and he snaked his hand down his body to rub her essence over his cock until it was coated with her arousal. With his hard length slick and wet, Thanos pumped his hand along his shaft, keeping rhythm with the thrusting of his tongue inside her clenching hole.

He rotated his thumb against her stiff bud harder and faster while he shoved his tongue into her core with deep, stabbing strokes.

Her thighs clenched tighter around his head and more of her essence trickled from inside her, warning him of her impending release. Thanos pinched her nub hard and curled his tongue against the roof of her sheath.

She exploded around him as she screamed out his name on a long, hoarse cry, her juices flooding his mouth. At the same time he felt his heavy sacs draw tight against his body. He fisted his cock with one last hard stroke and then he, too, exploded. A harsh roar slipped from his mouth as he poured his warm seed onto the bed mat in long, thick spurts.

Lapping up her essence, he savoured her sweet taste, her musky scent, as the last tremors of both their climaxes meshed together and rocked their bodies. When finally she relaxed her thighs from around his head, he eased away from her.

With deft movements he quickly tucked himself back inside his *pyterges* and redid the laces. He then rolled over to grab a cloth from his sack and wiped his seed from the bed mat. When he was done, he set the rag aside to lie down beside Lamia.

Rolling her to her side, he hooked his arm around her waist and settled her into the crook of his body, with her back pressed to his chest. She sighed, burrowing deeper into his embrace, causing a curious ache to settle in his chest. Refusing to examine the unfamiliar feeling, he closed his eyes and relaxed against her.

Exhausted from the long dawn and satiated from their lovemaking, they soon drifted off to sleep.

Chapter Nine

Lamia stifled a groan when her body jerked against the horse. Her muscles ached and several beads of sweat gathered along her brow. She was beyond weary from the many long dawns of travel.

She glanced over her shoulder at the crystalline blue water of the Gulf of Argolis, the choppy white waves hurling towards the sand. She couldn't stop the sigh from escaping her lips as she stared longingly out over the water, wishing she could ease her stiff and sore body into the churning water as she'd done once before — though she doubted Thanos would let her do it again, after her antics the last time she'd been allowed to bathe alone.

"We shall stop here."

She started at the husky timbre of Thanos' voice and whipped her head around to face him. "Why? We're only a dawn away, and you told me you wanted to arrive as soon as possible."

"I do," he said, jumping off his horse to tether the reins to a nearby tree. "But you are tired, so we shall camp here for the eve and rest, and then ride in early on the morrow's dawn."

"You do not need to make exceptions for me," she insisted as she slid from her mount. "I am well enough to ride into Sparta this dawn."

He grinned at her as he removed his armour, and for just a moment he appeared boyishly handsome…flirtatious even.

"You do not need to prove yourself to me, Lamia. I know you can ride all the way to Alexandria if need be, but there is no need to push you to the point of exhaustion."

She narrowed her eyes, her lips pursed into a tight line as she battled against the embers of warmth that his tenderness towards her always sparked inside her. It touched her that he always sought to please her, and yet, as much as she appreciated his protectiveness towards her, she wrestled with it. She didn't need him to coddle and shield her.

"What is it that I've done to upset you now?"

She frowned at him in exasperation. How was it that he could seemingly read her thoughts just by gazing upon her face?

"It is just what I said." She sighed. "I do not need you to make exceptions for me."

He drew nearer, and she had to force herself not to let her eyes stray to the bronzed muscles rippling across his bare chest.

"It is your nature to hate that I try to protect you, and yet it is my nature to always see to your needs."

He was so close she could feel his breath against her cheek, and she couldn't stop the shiver that raced through her body. It was more than just his physical presence. His words also stirred something deep within her. It was beyond frustrating that he kept trying to take care of her, and yet, deep down inside, it warmed her that Thanos was the first man who didn't look at her and see her as other men did—as a woman far too strong to be cherished and protected.

She didn't know what it was—maybe it was the way he regarded her, with such intense passion smouldering in his eyes. Or maybe it was the sincerity of his words that made her feel so cherished. But, for the first time since they'd met in Athens, she felt emboldened with him, and she found herself initiating the intimacy between them—not because she was trying to escape, but because she truly wanted him.

She slid her palm across the bare flesh of his chest, tunnelling her fingers through the sprinkling of dark hair. "And what of your needs, Thanos? Who shall see to them? Who shall protect *you*?"

He grinned, the tiny dimple creasing his cheek. "I imagine you would fulfil that role."

She arched her brow. "A woman?" she queried with a chiding smile. "You would entrust your welfare to but *one* woman?"

He chuckled, and the sound was rich and warm as it curled around her. It was a sound she'd grown accustomed to. Over the passing dawns, there had only been one another to talk to, and she'd been surprised by just how easy it was to talk to Thanos, how natural it was to banter with him.

"I guess I deserve to have my words thrown back in my face. But if ever there is a woman to protect me, I know it is you, Lamia."

She wondered how much of his pride he'd had to swallow to admit that maybe he'd been wrong before when he'd referred to her as 'but one woman' after she'd helped him battle those thieves. She smiled inwardly. Maybe there was hope for him after all.

And, with that thought, she realised that maybe there was hope for her as well. After all, she was keeping her word and travelling to Sparta. She didn't know how long she would stay, and, despite what Thanos believed, she still had no plans to wed him. But he was a kind man and he'd saved her life. At the least, she owed him her word—she would not jeopardise Sparta's truce with Athens. She wouldn't have to as long as she just bided her time.

With war coming, Athenian and Spartan soldiers would soon be marching into battle with Rome. And with Greece at war, Thanos would have to leave at some point to defend his state. When he did, she would leave Sparta and Thanos far behind and return to Athens to deal with Atallus.

It was the perfect plan. She would keep her word, Sparta would have its truce, and she would have her revenge. She just needed to be patient.

She gasped in surprise when, without warning, he scooped her into his arms.

"What are you doing?" she questioned when she realised he wasn't walking towards the bed mat he'd rolled out, but away from it.

"I want you to bathe with me."

She shook her head vehemently. "Thanos, this is the last *chamlys*," she complained as she wriggled around in his arms, but he held fast.

He ignored the warning in her voice, his clear, blue eyes twinkling with laughter.

"We'll leave it out to dry beside the fire this eve."

"Thanos, no—" Her next words died on her lips when she was hurled into the air, her body suspended for a scant heartbeat, before she plummeted into the chilly water.

When her head finally broke the surface, she glared at him as he waded into the water with a smile on his face.

"That wasn't funny," she sputtered. "What if this doesn't dry by dawn?"

"Then we shall both ride into Sparta nude, since I still have on my *pyterges* and it may not dry by dawn either."

She started to tell him that wasn't exactly the answer she'd been searching for, but found it hard to form words when he clasped his hands around her arms and drew her flush against his body.

"I thought we were bathing."

"I find the idea of bathing less exciting right now." His eyes twinkled. "I would have never thought it possible, but you are even more beautiful wet."

His voice was deep and husky, and his eyes darkened to twin pools of sapphire. She knew she should stop him before they went too far. She was much too sore from riding and their vigorous lovemaking of the eves past to take him inside her body this eve.

"Thanos, I—"

"Shhh, *agapetos*," he whispered, silencing her with a single finger against her lips. "I know we cannot make love. I just wish to kiss you."

He'd barely said the words before he pressed his lips to hers, his tongue eagerly searching inside her mouth. His hands settled along her hips, and he held her close, rocking gently against her. She twined her arms behind his neck, a low moan tumbling from her lips as the evidence of his need dug deep into her belly.

She ached to feel him inside her, pressing her back into the bed mat as he rode her body, but knew she just couldn't. So she poured every single measure of her desire into their heated kiss. She hungrily devoured him, until every centimetre of her skin grew flushed with heat despite the chill of the water.

When their kiss grew more insistent and urgent, Lamia forced herself to pull away, although her movements were slow and unhurried.

"We had better stop," she breathed, her words choppy.

He rested his forehead against hers, his eyes sealed shut as his chest heaved and he panted. He struggled for several heartbeats to gather his control before his eyelids fluttered open.

"I will leave you to bathe, and when you are done I shall take my turn."

She nodded when he released her and trod through the water towards the shore. She missed him immediately but batted aside the unwanted neediness as she set about cleansing herself. How was it that whenever he touched her she somehow forgot that at one time, not so long ago, she'd vowed he never would?

"You're becoming soft and weak," she muttered under her breath as she finished bathing and waded towards the bank. She settled her gaze on Thanos, who was watching her with steady eyes.

It was unacceptable to her that she was growing soft towards him...and yet, if ever there was a man whom she could be vulnerable with, Thanos was that man. She didn't know why all of these thoughts bombarded her now. Maybe she'd been alone with him for too long on this journey.

That had to be it.

Lamia never would have imagined she'd come to accept being dragged to Sparta, but right now she actually welcomed the distractions that would come with their arrival. Being alone with Thanos for so long was wreaking havoc upon her senses, but as soon as they arrived in Sparta, she and Thanos would thankfully part ways, and she could once again focus on her original purpose, and not one temptingly handsome Spartan general who now occupied almost every single one of her thoughts.

* * * *

"What is Sparta like?"

Thanos had just returned from his bath and was wringing the excess water from his hair when she spoke. He studied her from the other side of the fire, the burnished flames casting a golden shadow across her lovely face.

He bit back a smile. He'd known her for less than a fortnight, and yet he could glimpse the truth of her intentions so effortlessly. She'd never been eager to talk of Sparta before, and that she was now had little to do with their impending arrival. They were growing closer, developing a deeper intimacy. If he could feel it, then he knew she could, too. And while it unsettled him to know she'd turned his world upside down and so soon, he accepted it, for he believed the words of the Oracle. But he knew the feelings growing between them frightened her — that she did not welcome them.

And now she thought she could somehow escape this unyielding attraction between them once they were in Sparta. She naively believed he would throw himself so fully into whatever she imagined he did there, while she went about plotting her return to Athens, and eventually they would just drift apart until the dawn came when she would simply slip out of Sparta without him noticing or caring. His lips twitched. If Lamia believed that, then she was woefully mistaken. They would only grow closer once they were in Sparta — of that, he was determined.

"Sparta is a very simple place," he answered finally. "We live comfortably, but not extravagantly. It's not like Athens or Thebes where there is a great emphasis placed upon the arts and politics." He settled down on the bed mat beside her, tucking his knees to his chest. "In Sparta, we have one purpose and that is to protect Sparta. So the men train to defend the city, while the women run it."

Her nose wrinkled. "You mean the women run the government?"

He smiled. He certainly found the notion of women running the government, as opposed to the current cadre of stuffy old men, far more appealing. "Not quite. I meant that they own most of the businesses, they run the households. The men are soldiers, so the rest of the duties in the city are seen to by the women."

"Interesting."

"I think so. It is certainly very different from the rest of Greece, and I think that is why you will like it."

She smiled at him, a teasing gleam in her eyes. "You seem so certain of that, Spartan. But what if you are wrong? What if I hate it? What will you do then?" She balled her fist against her mouth as she yawned, then lay down to stretch out across the bed mat.

He didn't flinch at the challenge in her eyes as he spoke truthfully. "I've already told you that if you hate it then you will be free to leave once the threat from Rome has passed." *But you won't,* he said to himself, purposely not voicing his thoughts when her eyelids drifted shut, because that would only provoke her to disagree with him, and right now he didn't want to argue with her. He wanted her to do as she was doing — sleep.

He couldn't stop the warm grin from spreading across his face as he watched her rest. Despite her endless protests, he knew she would come to find a place for herself in Sparta, and he was determined to make certain that was the case.

He listened to the sound of her even breathing until the moon was high in the sky. Stretching out beside her, he pulled her into his arms, a smile tugging at the corners of his mouth when she instinctively curled up against him. He couldn't ignore the invisible knot that tightened inside his gut. It wasn't just how she unconsciously sought him out in her sleep, but also the words she'd spoken earlier that made him hope she could come to accept Sparta, just as he knew she was coming to accept him. She still struggled against it, but, when she'd asked who would see to his needs and protect him, he'd glimpsed a tiny flicker of longing in her eyes.

He'd done well in masking his own reaction to her words, but he could not deny that until she'd spoken them he'd never once thought he'd want or need someone to actually see to *him*. He was so used to being in charge and in control. All of Sparta relied upon him and turned to him for guidance and leadership. It wasn't until he'd met Lamia and had her voice the question that he'd realised what he'd been missing in his life. He'd had no one to see to his needs, to help shoulder the heavy burden that he carried around. He'd been trained not to need anyone, to be completely self-reliant, and yet, it was a lonely existence.

He glanced down at the woman nestled in his arms, the heat of her body warming his as the cold eve air swirled around him. Until she'd barrelled into his life, he'd never thought he would need anyone else, but he was quickly starting to realise that maybe he'd been wrong.

Chapter Ten

Nestled between two mountain chains—the Taygetus to the west, and the Parnon to the east—Sparta was a large city-state that sat on a fertile plain just north of the Eurotas River. Unlike all other Greek city-states, Sparta was the only one without protective walls. Legend had it that Lycurgus, the founder of modern Sparta, had had them torn down, proclaiming that the men should be the walls of Sparta. And so the *agoge* and the legendary Spartan *phalanx* had been born.

Early the next dawn, Thanos and Lamia rode into Sparta, their arrival a bit earlier than he'd expected. He was glad the journey had been swift because he knew the Spartan government was eager to hear his report from Athens.

As they neared the city from the east, he tugged on the reins until Zeus came to a stop.

Lamia brought her own mount to a halt beside him, a frown spreading across her face when she glimpsed the disquiet in his eyes.

"What is it, Thanos?"

He'd dreaded this conversation from the moment he'd spotted the city buildings in the distance, but he knew he had to tell her the truth.

He turned towards her, meeting her searching gaze as he released a long sigh, gathering up the courage to finally speak. "Before we enter Sparta, I must tell you something."

"All right," she said, waiting for him to finish.

He dragged in another long breath, hesitating for just a moment longer.

"There are actually two things you should know. In Sparta, the ceremony of marriage is quite simple." He paused to glance at her, choosing his next words carefully. "The simple act of bedding one's intended is enough to constitute a marriage."

She narrowed her gaze but remained silent, although, from the awakening fury he glimpsed in her eyes, he surmised that she was already connecting the pieces.

"I know you have no desire to wed me, but when we enter Sparta I will have no choice but to declare you as my wife, because according to Spartan law that is exactly what you are."

Her nostrils flared and anger darkened her swirling eyes, but he praised her for not railing at him. It actually troubled him somewhat. Her outbursts he could handle, but her quiet, seething fury he found unsettling.

"You said *two* things," she bit out tightly. "You said there were two things you needed to tell me. What other piece of information have you neglected to share?"

He gulped deeply at the murderous look that flashed in her deep, topaz eyes. Oh yes, her quiet fury was definitely unsettling.

"In Sparta there are two generals, just as there are two kings—one from the House of Eurypontids and the other from the House of Agiad. I am from the House of Agiad, the oldest family in Sparta."

He stopped, not certain of the best manner in which to deliver the news.

"I do not understand your point, Thanos," she snapped impatiently.

He lifted his lips into a wry smile. She wouldn't. Especially since he'd done his best to speak in circles. He cleared his throat, and tried again.

"Before we ride into Sparta, I thought it best you should know that I am both general and co-regent of Sparta. Here they are one and the same."

When she shook her head, her expression still puzzled, he just blurted it out.

"I am one of two kings, Lamia." A sheepish grin tugged at the edges of his mouth as he shrugged. "Welcome to your new home, my *queen*."

* * * *

"My queen, my *ass*," she muttered under her breath. She forced herself to maintain her counterfeit smile as she accepted congratulations and gifts from the citizens of Sparta she passed by on her journey towards Thanos' home. She was going to strangle him—with her bare hands if she could manage it. He had a thick neck so she figured it would be quite difficult, but she was certainly going to give it her best effort.

Lamia's mind conjured a host of deviant punishments for Thanos while they trotted on horseback along the narrow streets paved with lava stone. It wasn't until a little girl stepped away from the throng of onlookers, blocking their path, that Lamia's thoughts grew pleasant. She and Thanos brought their mounts to a halt, and the child stuck out her hand, her little fingers curled around the stem of a flower. Reaching down to accept the lotus blossom from the girl, who could not have been more than five *annos*, Lamia smiled warmly.

"Thank you."

"You are welcome, my queen," the girl replied shyly as she bowed her head and scurried away, disappearing once again into the crowd of people who'd left their homes and shops to catch a glimpse of the 'exotic' new queen of Sparta.

She struggled to stifle a frown. She had no desire to be a wife, let alone a *queen*. At the thought, her anger returned in waves. Oh, she could not wait until she reached Thanos' home. He would be lucky if he survived the eve.

She glanced over at the object of her nefarious thoughts.

As if sensing her eyes upon him, he turned to meet her gaze, his expression contrite. The look on his face tugged at her heart, but she refused to allow it to sway her. She was furious with him. He had deliberately deceived her — not once, but twice.

He'd tried to apologise outside the city, but she'd refused to listen. He'd known what he was doing by waiting until the last possible moment to reveal the truth to her and she had not been of a forgiving heart at the time. She wasn't of a forgiving heart now, either, and she doubted she would be any time soon.

She pursed her lips into a tight line and tore her gaze away from him to get her first glimpse of Sparta. The actual city of Sparta was quite simple in its design, as sturdy mud-brick homes and stores blended effortlessly into one another. Unlike Athens, there were no elaborate statues of marble or impressive archways and columns. It was pleasant enough, but she had to admit that there was nothing remarkable about the city.

Soon the crowds began to thin and, as they drew closer to the edge of the city, away from the centre of town, the streets widened.

They trotted along in silence until they reached a small colonnaded courtyard with elegant marble statues of the patron god and goddess of war. The lavish gardens burst with a rainbow of colour. Green grass and flowers of every kind greeted them as a fountain gushed with sparkling water in the centre. A glimmer of sunlight shimmering against pure marble snared her gaze, and she glanced just beyond the courtyard. Shadowed by the thick foliage, an opulent home peeked out from behind the garden, one that could easily dwarf many of the estates she'd caught glimpses of in Athens.

Thanos guided Zeus through the gardens until they reached an impressive arched entrance that opened into a cylindrical courtyard. Supported by six large Doric columns, there were two wings that fanned out from the open space and stretched for several metres.

The magnificence of Thanos' home did not escape her and she struggled to close her gaping mouth as they drew closer to the archway where more than a dozen servants waited to greet their king.

Thanos stopped just before them and dismounted from Zeus. She, too, slid from her horse to stand beside him.

She stood there while he greeted his servants and introduced them to her, but her astonishment at the opulence of Thanos' home left her mum, so the introductions passed by her in a blur. Given the simplicity of Sparta, and Spartan life, she'd expected Thanos to bring her to a modest home, not a veritable *palace*.

She only vaguely recalled Thanos gently taking her hand in his to lead her towards their bedchamber.

As soon as he ushered her into the inner room of their chambers and closed the door, he pulled her into his arms.

"I am sorry," he whispered against her ear. With their bodies pressed together, his heartbeat joining with hers, she found it difficult to hold on to her anger as warmth suffused her skin. And yet she did not completely absolve him of his trickery and deception.

"I do not like being deceived. I do not like being forced—"

"I know and I am—"

She stopped him with the swift shake of her head. "I was under the impression that when I arrived I would find work, that I would seek out a room at the boarding house, but with your revelation I know that shall not be the case. I will be expected to remain here as your wife—to attend to duties as your queen." She sighed. "*This*, I was not prepared for."

His eyes were gentle as he peered down at her. "I know, but every time I thought to bring up the subject it never seemed an appropriate time. I never meant to deceive you. I never meant to force your hand."

His expression was earnest, apologetic, and she believed he truly had not set out to deceive her. She imagined he'd wanted to tell her, but had feared her explosive response. She blew out a long, weary breath. She wanted to find the nearest horse and ride out of here, but she'd given her word that she would stay.

Yet the thought of being Thanos' wife was overwhelming enough...and now she was his *queen?*

"You've won, Thanos. You have me as your wife." She shrugged. "So what now?"

Frown lines creased his brow. "This was not a competition. I did not seek to win. You must know your unhappiness does not please me." He rubbed his thumb against her lips, drawing an involuntary quiver from her body. "I want a willing wife...a *happy* wife," he said softly. "I want a woman who desires to share my bed, my home, my life" — he leant down to kiss her neck — "my children."

She had to suppress the shudder that racked her body at the image of him filling her womb with his seed, her belly swelling with his child — *their* child. The curious stirring in her heart alarmed her. What was it about this man that made her forget all reason? That made her want to draw him inside her body until they were fused so tightly, she would not know where he ended and she began.

She wrapped her arms around him and joined their lips in a kiss, their tongues duelling, meshing, and she melted into him, absorbing his warmth.

Just like that, her anger was long forgotten, for she could not be angry with him when she knew the truth. She was just as culpable as he, and if she was upset with him then she needed to turn that anger upon herself as well.

Deep down, she'd known the consequences from the moment she'd given her body to him and allowed him to claim her. Truly, she hadn't expected that to mean he'd claimed her as his wife, but she'd known that Thanos had marked her as his when they'd first made love...and she'd allowed it. She could have resisted, but she hadn't. She'd let him take her, brand her as his. That she'd allowed him to bind her to him as his wife was her own damned fault.

The wet glide of his tongue against hers sent a raging wave of heat rushing through her until her nipples were achingly stiff, and the space between her thighs grew damp with her desires. When the bulge of his arousal dug into her belly, she gasped, and he swallowed the desperate sound. The way she responded to him, awakening beneath his touch, was evidence enough for her — she may not have wished to be his wife, but she'd belonged to Thanos from the very moment she'd surrendered her body. The notion was terrifying, but she had no time to dwell upon it as his warmth engulfed her, his kiss bombarding her senses, her entire body. When he pulled away she had to force herself not to whimper.

"I ache to be inside you, making love to you until dusk chases away the dawn." He rested his forehead against hers. "But I must go."

"Go? But we only just arrived."

He cupped her cheek with his hand, gently stroking his thumb along her jaw. "I must meet with the leadership of Sparta to discuss what I learned while in Athens. But when I return we shall talk. I will do everything I can to ease your settling in here."

The tenderness in his eyes stirred her heart and she cupped his hand, gently kissing his palm.

"And after we talk? What shall we do then?" Her smile was teasing and his brows lifted. "Well, since you now have a wife, I would think you should return swiftly and *attend* to her."

He chuckled. "Only wed a few dawns and already you nag me, woman." He kissed the tip of her nose and, with a reluctant sigh, released her.

"I will do my best to speed matters along, but while I am gone, Armine, one of my *helots*, shall see to you."

As if he couldn't get enough of her, he lowered his head to kiss her gently again, and she returned his kiss with a heated urgency until he lifted his head and their lips parted.

He nodded farewell and she gave him a small smile as he turned to leave their chambers.

She released a long breath at the sound of the soft thud of the door closing shut.

So what now?

She'd barely formed the thought when the door burst open again and a little bundle of a girl barrelled inside.

Lamia did her best not to laugh at the small child who nearly tripped inside the room. The girl looked to be no more than ten *annos* and she knew instantly from the look in her wide copper eyes that she was a fiery girl with a precocious spirit.

"Master Thanos told me that I was to attend to you, but he told me not to bother you until after you rested, but I had to meet you. I was told you were from Carthage and I had to see for myself. I am from Carthage as well, you know. I was found there as a baby during the second war and brought here as a *helot*. You're pretty, I see. Everyone said you were very pretty."

She chuckled as the child panted, trying to even her breathing after rushing through her words.

Lamia crossed the room and stooped down before the girl to meet her at eye level. *This had to be Armine.*

She flashed the child a warm smile. "Well, hello. My name is Lamia. And you are?"

The girl bowed her head. "My name is Armine, Mistress Lamia, and I am ten *annos*."

Lamia struggled not to laugh again. "Well, I am honoured to meet you Armine, who is all of ten *annos*." She did laugh when Armine's eyes widened as if she couldn't believe Lamia would be honoured to meet *her*.

She leaned closer to Armine and whispered to her as if she had a secret to tell. "Will you do me a favour, Armine?"

"Of course, Mistress," the girl said, nodding her head vigorously, flashing her a toothy smile.

She got to her feet and took Armine's small hand in her palm. "Will you lead me on a tour of Thanos' home?"

The child's smile grew wider and, before she could catch her breath, the little girl, who was surprisingly strong, tugged her by the hand and led her off on the grandest, most animated tour she had ever experienced.

* * * *

Thanos walked along the open colonnades of the *bouleterion*, down the long hallway to where Sparta's city council convened regularly to deliberate the political affairs of the state.

He hated politics. He found the tedious dialogues and petty arguments tiresome, but as a king of Sparta he could not escape his duties.

His sandalled feet echoed against the hard stone floor as he climbed the three small steps to enter the large arena-like structure where the council was now assembled. Low chattering vibrated off the walls around him as he stalked towards his seat on the throne beside the other king of Sparta, Cleomenes the fourth.

He nodded in greeting to Cleomenes and took his seat. The other king returned his greeting with the slight dip of his greying head. Cleomenes was twenty *annos* older than him, but there was nothing about the king that was frail or weak. The older king was a virile man who was every bit as fit as he'd been thirty *annos* ago. Thanos had always admired Cleomenes, who was a sharp and astute man, and many times had looked to him for guidance and wisdom.

He glanced around the cylindrical chambers as Cleomenes called the council to order. On each side of him sat fourteen elders, from the wealthiest and most prestigious families of Sparta, to make up the twenty-eight member *gerousia*.

Seated in front of him were the *ephors*, the five men directly elected by popular assembly to represent each of the five villages that made up the city-state of Sparta and provide oversight to the ruling kings.

For the most part, when it came to political matters, he did not come into conflict with the other bodies of government, Cleomenes included, mainly because Sparta had enjoyed a measure of peace and stability since he'd assumed power. But now he feared that was about to change.

At the sound of his name, he glanced over at Cleomenes to meet the older man's sharp emerald gaze.

"It is time for your report," he said.

Thanos nodded and rose to his feet to offer greetings to the entire council and deliver the news they had all waited to hear upon his return.

"As you well know from the reports I sent by my men, I met with Governor Atallus, who informed me that the Roman army has once again settled in Carthage."

A cacophony of murmurs broke out in the chambers, forcing him to raise his voice in order to be heard.

"What I wanted to share with you in person is that, from what I could gather, the settlement in Carthage is far from benign. I suspect the Roman army is planning to invade Athens and they will use their strategic location in Carthage to launch their attack."

The room erupted then, as he'd suspected it would. Several questions were thrown at him.

"How do you know the Athenians are telling the truth?"

"Why do we care if the Romans attack the Athenians?"

"What does this all mean for Sparta?"

Cleomenes raised his hand to bring order once again to the room and Thanos spoke as soon as the men had quieted.

"Those are all important questions, to which I shall say this — if the Romans plan to attack, they will enter Greece from the Aegean then, starting with Athens, one by one they will pick off the weaker city-states until they reach Sparta, where they will trap us within our own territory. Even if they are unable to defeat Sparta, the rest of Greece will become Roman territory, and we will be forever surrounded by our enemy, always waiting for them to attack. We as the council must decide if we intend to aid the Athenians. And it is my opinion that we should if we want to stop the Romans from invading Greece."

Again, the chambers erupted into chaos, but he could tell from the expressions on their faces that, even if they did not fully support his plan, they saw the wisdom in it. He sat back down, knowing they would not come to a decision on this sun rising. The council would need to mull over all their options and belabour every point before they would even call for a vote.

He settled into his seat, already weary at the thought of what lay ahead. A war was coming to Greece, and, while stubborn politicians talked, Roman soldiers were preparing to march.

* * * *

Dusk was on the horizon when Thanos finally arrived home, the orange embers of the sun fanning out like fingertips to caress the mountains that surrounded Sparta.

As he trotted up to his estate, he stopped his mount to greet Panos, the young *helot* who'd come to him as a boy and who was now in charge of his stables. Dismounting from Zeus, he handed the reins to Panos and let him lead the hulking warhorse away.

He dragged his weary body along the cobbled pathway towards his chambers, thoroughly exhausted. He'd been forced to sit before the council for several long hours, only to watch them arrive at the conclusion that they would have to reconvene in half a fortnight to call for a vote.

While he'd known to expect such a decision, he'd still been furious as he always was with the sluggish political process in Sparta. He would have preferred to be on the battlefield, training *hoplites*. Or better still, in his bedchamber, twisted in the bed sheets, making love to his new wife. The latter thought had consumed his mind the entire time he'd been away from her, and he found he needed to see her, if only to catch a glimpse of one of her rare, teasing smiles.

With purposeful strides, he hurried towards his chambers, fully expecting to find her curled up in his bed, fast asleep after their long journey. So he was certainly surprised when he entered the courtyard that separated the gardens from the main residence to find Armine with one of his steel blade short swords in her firm grip, and Lamia behind the young girl calling out instructions.

"That is good, Armine, but next time you pivot, be sure to keep your sword higher. Whenever you give your back to an opponent, you have to be prepared for him to take advantage of your folly and go right for the attack, so you want to be ready. All right?"

Armine nodded. "Yes, Mistress."

"Again."

He nearly choked on his laughter when Armine's eyes widened at the command Lamia had issued. The girl was drenched in sweat, her woollen *chamlys* clinging to her skinny body, and he was sure she hadn't been prepared for the intense session Lamia was putting her through. He had no doubt that Armine was tired, but if she was, she didn't show it. Her wide mahogany eyes darkened with purpose and he watched in shock when the girl executed a perfect parry of a forward advance, her right foot shooting out as she ducked below the would-be opponent's sword, then twisted around to meet the blade that would be crashing down if this were a real fight.

Now it was his turn to stand there wide-eyed. There were probably dozens of Spartan boys in the *agoge* who would kill for such grace and poise in executing the difficult move. How old was she again? He was stunned as he looked at the girl through fresh eyes. The child demonstrated an aptitude for battle instruction — a talent that was held in high esteem in Sparta.

He glanced over at Lamia when she barked out another order. Armine had been in his residence since she was four *annos* and he'd never realised she was possessed of such a quick wit. Yet Lamia had discovered this in a matter of hours. His wife had been in Sparta for less than one sun rising and already she'd found herself a devoted admirer and pupil, if the awestruck gaze that Armine studied her with was any evidence.

"I would say we have the makings of a fine soldier on our hands," he said with a grin as he stepped from behind one of the columns where he'd hidden from their view.

Two sets of nearly identical brown eyes swung in his direction as he strolled into the courtyard.

Armine's cheeks darkened with colour and she averted her gaze to the ground. "I am sorry, Master Thanos, for neglecting my duties—"

"You are fine, Armine. Your only duty was to attend to Lamia." He stopped to rake his gaze over the dishevelled child. "But from the looks of it, I see she was the one who attended to you. We will retire shortly so you are free for the remainder of the eve."

She smiled up at him, her eyes bright. "Thank you, Master Thanos." She glanced over at Lamia then. "May I continue to practice?"

Lamia nodded with a smile. "As long as you promise not to practice what you've learned on anyone else. However, I suggest you rest this eve. You will have more lessons on the morrow."

"Thank you, Mistress. I promise." She nodded as she beamed all over, before she scurried off in the direction of the servant quarters, dragging *his* sword behind her.

He arched an eyebrow. "On the morrow?"

131

"Of course, on the morrow. Thanos, that child is brilliant. She is a quick study who picks up things after one simple demonstration. Did you know she can read and write?"

No, he didn't.

"When I asked her about it, she told me she'd taught herself. *Herself*, Thanos."

Now, that *was* impressive.

"That girl belongs in school, not attending to me or anyone else for that matter."

If what she said was true, he could only agree with her. Armine's talents were being wasted as a *helot*.

"You make a fine point. So you plan to instruct her—"

"Until you help me get her into school? Yes."

He lifted his arched brow higher at the determined look on her face. Not even one dawn Lamia had been here, and already she'd found a devoted admirer, who she was planning to instruct until the child could enter the *agoge* for Spartan girls. For all her protests of not taking to Sparta, Lamia seemed to be settling in quite well, which pleased him greatly.

Crossing the short distance that separated them, he pulled her into his arms. "You will hear no argument from me. For once I agree with you. Had I known the girl was so skilled, I would have seen to her education myself." He smirked at her then. "Although, maybe I should have put up more of a fight. It would have been amusing to watch you *convince* me," he whispered, dipping his head to press his lips firmly to hers.

A small sigh escaped her mouth as she opened it to allow his searching tongue to explore the heady taste of her. He groaned against her lips, pulling her tighter to him to grind his growing bulge into her soft belly. It had been three sun risings since he'd lain with her, and he ached to feel the clenching vice of her snug, wet heat surrounding him, sucking him in.

Reluctantly, he lifted his head, dragging his lips from hers. "We should take this to our chambers."

She flashed him a wicked grin as she turned with him and headed for their bedchamber, but drew up short when two figures advanced towards them, their faces shadowed.

Chapter Eleven

"I hope you do not mind us arriving without announcing ourselves, but Panos allowed us in," a deep masculine voice boomed. "He said you'd just returned from meeting with the council and I'd hoped to catch you before you retired for the evening."

Lamia grinned at Thanos when he groaned low in his throat, clearly not happy that their journey to their bedchamber had been thwarted.

As the figures moved closer, she smiled to greet their guests, and it took her less than a heartbeat to realise that the man standing before them was kin to Thanos. She stared up at the hulking man who possessed the same coal black mane and familiar turquoise eyes.

"Ulysseus, brother. Welcome." Thanos greeted the handsome man with the firm handshake between soldiers as he gripped his forearm tightly. When the two men released one another, Thanos moved once again to her side, wrapping his arm around her waist and pulling her close.

"May I introduce you to my lovely wife, Lamia." He turned to her. "Lamia, this is my younger brother, Ulysseus, and this stunning woman by his side is his wife, Basha."

She'd shivered at the word...wife. To know she was his, and only his, did strange things to her insides. For when he called her his *wife*, it was a declaration—a clear statement to the world that she belonged to him.

Struggling to ignore the fluttering in her belly, she turned her gaze towards Ulysseus' wife and realised then that Thanos had not lied about the woman's beauty. Stunning almost did not do her justice. She had never seen a more beautiful woman in her entire life.

Framed by the setting sun, Basha's bronze skin glowed under the tawny rays while her inky black hair, as straight and soft as the finest silk, hung to her waist. She raked her gaze over the lithe woman, taking in her charcoal-lined silver eyes, specked with amber, and her supple, womanly figure encased in a straight-fitting ivory linen *chiton* that hung from one shoulder. She wore heavy golden bracelets on her slender wrists and matching sandals of spun gold. In a word, she was exquisite.

Lamia nodded in their direction. "It is a pleasure to meet you both."

Ulysseus immediately embraced her with his thickly muscled arms, welcoming her into the family with kind words, but Basha held back, her dark silver eyes not cold, but not welcoming, either.

The look in her eyes told Lamia that she was being assessed very closely, and Basha's next words only further confirmed her suspicions.

"Why don't you two give Lamia and I a moment to acquaint ourselves?" She glanced over at Ulysseus. "I am sure you are eager to hear of what Thanos learned in Athens, given the rumours of war."

Thanos hesitated, but she nodded for him to go with his brother, her expression telling him she would be fine. Lamia knew what Basha was doing, and she also knew she could handle her.

With a slight nod Thanos left her and joined Ulysseus in the *oikos*, the private dining room in Thanos' home, where they could recline on couches and enjoy food and wine while they talked.

"Come," Basha said as she linked her arm under Lamia's elbow. "We shall join them shortly."

They walked in silence into another open courtyard that held several weapons chests and targets. She'd learned from Armine that this was where Thanos sometimes trained when he was at home.

Basha stopped almost in the centre of the courtyard, and released Lamia's arm to face her.

"Ulysseus and I were quite surprised when we learned of you. We worried that Thanos would never wed."

Lamia studied Basha with probing eyes, almost as intently as the woman had studied her earlier. She was trying to read the hidden meaning in her new sister within the law's words. If Thanos never wed, then he could never produce an heir...and that would mean Thanos' title would pass to Ulysseus and his children. She regarded Basha warily, wondering if she was one of those ambitious wives.

"I know what you are thinking, but you are wrong. Ulysseus and I have been wed for almost four *annos* but the gods have not seen fit to give us a child. Ulysseus also lacks the patience and diplomacy of Thanos. He is a soldier at heart. We have no designs on Thanos' throne, for either ourselves or our unborn children."

Lamia was careful to keep her expression blank, mainly because she didn't want her face to betray her sympathy for this woman. She hadn't missed the slight catch to Basha's voice when she spoke of being unable to have a child. While she didn't know Basha and the woman hadn't been particularly warm towards her, she still felt compassion for her. She was fairly certain that Basha wasn't the sort of woman who wanted anyone's pity or compassion, so she let the comment pass without acknowledgement. Instead she got straight to the matter and voiced what she knew Basha was implying.

"You don't think Thanos made a good choice in picking me as his wife."

Basha cocked her head to the side, her silken strands falling over the shoulder that was bare, and scrutinised Lamia with eyes of a hawk stalking its prey.

"I do not know you well enough to make such a statement," she said bluntly before she spun away from her and walked towards the edge of the courtyard to where several archery bows hung from iron nails jammed into a wooden shelf. Pulling one down, she tested its weight then gathered several arrows in her fist. "But I do know Thanos well enough to say this." She placed all but one arrow aside. With the single arrow in her hand, she centred it in the middle of her bowstring, lifted the bow and drew the string back until her fingers brushed her jaw. "Thanos is a steady man, but with war coming to Sparta he has a great deal of responsibility now resting upon his shoulders," she said and released the arrow.

Lamia followed the soaring arrow across the courtyard until it hit its mark at the centre of the target painted in red.

"He needs a woman who can handle all of this. Someone who can keep her head if there is war and will not become hysterical should Thanos need to leave Sparta for several moons to lead the army."

She bit her lip to stop herself from saying something rude. What had given Basha the impression she was prone to hysterics? She wrestled with that notion for several silent moments, but never being one to mince words she simply decided to speak directly.

"You do not know me well enough to know whether Thanos and I are well suited, and yet you have already managed to diagnose me with hysteria. Interesting."

"Foreign-born wives tend to have a very difficult time adjusting to the ways and customs of Sparta." Basha shrugged, her expression indicating that she was not offended by Lamia's caustic statement, but neither was she apologetic regarding her own.

Lamia swept her gaze over Basha, noting the tattoo of a tiny *ankh* that was visible on her bare shoulder. "Are you speaking from experience?" she asked pointedly, still trying to decide if she was going to dislike this woman.

Basha arched one elegant eyebrow, following Lamia's gaze to the tattoo she knew to be the Egyptian symbol for eternal life.

A wry grin tugged at the corners of Basha's mouth. "I am the daughter of an Egyptian priestess and a Spartan soldier. I have not forgotten the ways of my mother's homeland, but I was raised here in Sparta. I grew up alongside Ulysseus and Thanos, so I know them both quite well and—"

"You only want the *best* for Thanos," Lamia interrupted, fighting to temper her voice. In her opinion, this conversation was at an end. Lamia may not have wanted to be Thanos' wife, but that did not change the fact that she now was. If Thanos thought they were well suited, then no matter Basha had grown up with him or knew Thanos well, what right did this woman have to question otherwise?

She crossed the courtyard towards Basha and held out her hand for the bow. "May I?" Surprise briefly flashed in Basha's gaze before she nodded and handed it over.

"I realise you know Thanos probably far better than I do." She stooped down to gather a single arrow from the pile at Basha's feet. "And I can tell you care for him a great deal and only want him to be happy. It is certainly clear to me that you do not want Thanos tied to a woman who is a hindrance to him and his duties." Lamia lifted the bow and, just like Basha had, she centred the arrow, pulled the string back until the arrow was in line with her jaw, then released it.

Again, she followed the motion of the arrow sailing across the courtyard and watched it hit its mark, splitting Basha's down the middle and breaking it into two pieces, which limply clattered to the ground.

She turned to face Basha, who, much to her amusement, stood there completely still, staring wide-eyed at the target. "But I can assure you, Basha, Thanos is a wise man and he certainly did not take this long to find a wife just to pick one that is unable to handle the pressures of being both his wife and his queen."

They locked gazes then, openly assessing one another until Basha apparently came to the same conclusion as she—that the woman standing before her was her equal in every way.

Basha's entire countenance changed then. Her face softened and, for the first time since they'd met, she smiled—a genuine one, full of warmth. Lamia returned her smile, grateful she'd passed her test. She would have hated to have this formidable woman as her foe.

"I have to agree with you, Lamia. Thanos is a wise man who has indeed made a very wise choice in you. Welcome to the family, *sister*."

* * * *

"So was it that blasted Oracle or did you finally realise Cleomenes was right?" Ulysseus chuckled. "I bet it was probably both."

Thanos' brow knitted into a frown. He tightened his fingers around his goblet of wine as he struggled to tamp down his irritation with Ulysseus and his pointed words.

"Right about what?" he asked, pretending he had no idea what Ulysseus was referring to. The struggle he'd faced with Cleomenes, his brother and Basha—even the *gerousia*—had been a constant one. He needed an heir, but he'd refused to take a wife for that purpose alone. Thus far, Cleomenes and the *gerousia* had been tolerant of his position, but with war on the horizon, their patience had been starting to wane. Sparta's two kings needed heirs, and he was long overdue in producing one.

He'd resisted their pressure because he was looking for more than just a woman who would simply bear him sons. The mother of his children, his wife, had to be a woman strong enough to lead in his absence, strong enough to mould his sons into Spartan men if he was not there to do it. Yet her strength could not come at the expense of her tenderness, her compassion for others, the very essence of her femininity. He'd almost given up his ideal—that such a woman even existed—until he'd met Lamia.

To say that everyone else had already given up on him ever finding a wife was an understatement. So when he'd shared with Cleomenes and Ulysseus the prophecy of the Oracle, and the news had spread, all of Sparta had rejoiced. They'd seen it as a sign that he'd finally take a wife, but Thanos had not been so certain. He trusted the wisdom of the Oracle, the truth of his own dreams, but he'd still wondered if maybe this woman was a figment of his imagination. Not until he'd met a fiery-eyed beauty on the other end of his sword had he realised she was indeed real.

"Do not act as if you have no idea what I speak of. You finally realised everyone was right about you taking a wife, having an heir." Ulysseus took a sip from his cup, wiping the corners of his mouth with the back of his hand. "It is good you've heeded their advice, but could you not have found a *Spartan* woman?"

Thanos clenched his jaw tight at the censure dripping from his brother's voice, although Ulysseus' reaction was not wholly unexpected. Most Spartans were not particularly welcoming when it came to foreigners, although, with Lamia as their queen, those who were likely to have a problem with that would be wise to hide their displeasure—but not Ulysseus apparently. "You know what the Oracle said."

Ulysseus shrugged. "I know, but I still think Sparta's queen should be...well, *Spartan*."

"I disagree. I believe Lamia is Spartan at heart. And besides, I believe Lamia and I are well suited. That is more important to me than where she was born."

Ulysseus eyebrows arched. "You *believe*?" his brother questioned.

"I *know*," Thanos said firmly, struggling to bite back a groan at the image that flashed in his head of Lamia writhing beneath him, lost in the throes of pleasure, as he thrust into her supple body. Physically, there was no doubt that they were well suited, but it was more than that. It was her passion, her fire, her strength of character—all of which had drawn him to her, convincing him she was strong enough to stand by his side and face the perils that lay ahead of them.

"You know." Ulysseus snorted. "You don't *know* this woman at all and yet you bring her here as your wife. Sparta has waited for you to give her an heir by a suitable woman, and this is your choice?"

Thanos tensed, Ulysseus' words igniting a hot spark of fury inside his belly until his vision blurred into a crimson haze. Separated from him in age by just two years, his brother was one of the few individuals who was not afraid to challenge him, who did not fear his wrath. For most things, he relied upon Ulysseus' sound judgement, but in this instance he needed no such help. He'd already made his decision, and his brother would simply have to accept it.

"Do you have a problem with my choice, brother?"

Ulysseus stared at him, apparently noting the sharp, icy edge to Thanos' voice. He narrowed his gaze.

"What is it about this woman that has you so enamoured? You have only just met her and yet you are ready to strike me for some perceived insult. Do not try to deny it." He smirked. "Your hands are balled into fists. You only do that when you're fighting to rein in your temper." Ulysseus leant back against the couch, studying him from above the rim of his wine cup. "I just hope the faith you've placed in her is justified. Sparta faces many challenges on the horizon and she will need a strong queen to support her when you are off fighting to defend her."

Thanos thought of Lamia the dawn he'd met her, her eyes full of determination, and then the dawn they'd been attacked by thieves. She was courageous, fearless even, and he had no doubt that she was strong enough to lead Sparta in his absence.

He had no doubt that she could lead... His only worry was that she would not follow.

Lamia enjoyed making love with him, but she was not tied to him. There was nothing but her promise to him that she would stay with him in Sparta until the threat from Rome had passed. She may be his wife, but by all accounts, she was not truly bound to him...to Sparta, to his people.

He could plant his seed in her womb, and with any other woman that would keep her by his side, but Lamia was unlike any other woman he'd ever known. That was what drew him to her, and yet it was what made him doubt her, made him unsure of himself before Ulysseus.

She was strong enough to lead Sparta as her queen, but was she strong enough to be his wife, when she truly had never desired to be?

* * * *

Lamia rode Thanos, her body tensing above his as she took him inside her one last time before heat whipped through her and she splintered into pieces.

143

She cried out at the same time that his hands clutched her hips, a hoarse moan spilling from his lips as he shuddered. His warm seed stirred in her womb and she collapsed against him, curling herself into a ball, like a sleeping kitten, as she lay in Thanos' arms basking in the warm, contented haze of their lovemaking.

Basha and Ulysseus had departed a short while ago and she and Thanos had wasted no time in intimately reacquainting themselves with one another within their bedchamber.

She sighed as she snuggled deeper into Thanos' embrace, loving how his coarse hands traced the delicate curve of her thighs.

"You must admit, being my wife does have its advantages."

She lifted her head from his chest to stare into teasing eyes. "I cannot believe you dare to boast of your prowess in bed."

He answered with a shrug, a smirk fixed upon his face.

"You are unashamedly arrogant, you know that?"

He chuckled and she shook her head. He may have spoken the truth—their lovemaking was one of the definite advantages to being wed—but he was incorrigible, she thought as she ran her fingers through the sprinkling of hair along his chest. Laying her palm flat over his heart, she bit back a sigh at the feel of it thumping beneath her palm in perfect rhythm to the pulsing beat of her own heart.

This...this *thing* between her and Thanos was becoming more complicated by the moment. At first she'd brushed his talk of dreams and the Oracle to the back of her mind, but as she'd stood in the courtyard earlier, defending her place in Thanos' life before

Basha, she'd been forced to admit they were seemingly a perfect fit.

What if the Oracle was right? What if their destinies were intertwined? She looked up at him and her heartbeat quickened at the desire that burned in his gaze. But it was more than that. In his eyes shone something deeper and it made every butterfly in her belly flap their wings.

She glanced away, unable to hold his gaze when she knew she would one day betray him. She so desired a real home, a real family, but the guilt that beat inside her was so overwhelming it threatened any happiness she sought to find. She did not deserve to be happy as long as the man who'd killed Darius still walked the lands. Her sense of honour, her need for justice, would not allow her to simply let her hatred go and seek bliss with Thanos. She just couldn't.

As if reading her thoughts, Thanos tightened his arms around her and sighed. "I fear for you and these storms that sometimes rage in your eyes."

She glanced at him, plastering a small smile across her face. "There is nothing to fear, Thanos. All is well," she lied.

He knew she lied, his penetrating stare told her as much. She'd forgotten how attuned he was to her. Yet he didn't press her. Instead he nudged her head to his chest, placing a gentle kiss to her temple.

"You are not alone, Lamia. If you would but trust me with your demons, I would slay them all for you."

She closed her eyes as he stroked his hand through her hair—his words nearly made her weep. Thanos was so good—so just. She was not worthy of him. She had no doubt he would fight all of her battles, without question. And yet, even now, she still plotted to leave him.

She hated that this battle she had to fight would cost her the happiness she knew she could find with Thanos—would cost her Thanos himself—but she would never be truly happy if she did not do this.

She didn't answer, for she could not speak. The words stuck in her throat as unshed tears choked her voice. Thanos just did not understand—he never would.

There were just some battles one had to fight alone—even if this one cost her everything she was starting to hold dear.

Chapter Twelve

Lamia glared at the offensive garment in Thanos' outstretched hand. When he'd told her she would wear the traditional attire for her formal presentation to the nobility of Sparta, she'd been expecting something far more…substantial.

The crowning of Sparta's queen was steeped in a myriad ancient customs, and while she'd barely accepted that she was now his wife, and still inwardly rejected the notion that she was officially Sparta's new queen, she would not embarrass Thanos by electing not to participate in the ceremony. However, she refused to attend the ceremony without proper garments, no matter what tradition dictated.

"No. Absolutely not," Lamia protested, shaking her head vehemently.

"Lamia, we talked about this."

She searched her brain, mulling over the conversation they'd had last eve just before they'd fallen asleep. Not once did she recall him telling her she was to dress herself as an Egyptian harem girl.

She'd barely arrived in this new land, only to be thrust into an awkward and humiliating public ceremony. At the least, she should be allowed to wear attire that would affect a sense of courage, not garments that would leave her feeling completing exposed in every possible way.

"No, you told me there would be a coronation ceremony in my honour. You never said I would be expected to prance around naked, too."

She once again stared crossly at the garment he held—if she could even call it that. Besides the bejewelled necklace that encircled the neckline, the rest of the *peplos* was sheer white silk that fell to her ankles.

"You will not be naked. You will be clothed in the traditional attire of the newly crowned queen."

She was incredulous as she stared at him. That was easy for him to say because he was fully clothed. He was clad in a white *tunica* that was draped by a scarlet robe. She would be expected to walk in there nearly nude, while he wore two layers of garments. Now that was not fair, and she said as much.

"Lamia, my mother wore this, just as my grandmother did, and the queen before her and the queen before her... It is tradition."

She balled her hands into fists as she bit back a snappish retort. He was trying to charm her. His eyes were soft, along with his voice. He was trying to coax her out of her garments—*literally*.

"What if we broke with tradition just this once? After all, I am not Spartan—"

"Lamia." She could tell he was reaching the end of his patience with her. Already they were late, and her continued resistance was only delaying them further, and she knew Spartans *hated* to be tardy.

"Given how liberated you are, I did not expect you to put up such a fight about a simple *peplos.*"

She narrowed her eyes at him. "You are not clever, Thanos. I can see what you are trying to do, but insulting my character will not yield a favourable response from me."

His brows lifted and he sauntered towards her. "I am merely pointing out that you fought me so bravely, and then battled a band of thieves, but now you are somehow cowed by a simple little garment. I thought you were stronger than that. After all, you are not afraid of anything."

Lamia glowered at him as she gnashed her teeth together. His antics were transparent—just like this *peplos*, she decided—but, accomplished general that he was, he knew the right tactics to ensure a victory.

"You will pay for this, Thanos. I promise you," she snapped, snatching the flimsy garment that was a poor impersonation of a *peplos* out of his hand, all the while ignoring the smug grin on his face.

* * * *

Lamia blew out a long breath as she walked down the corridor with Thanos.

As they neared the *kapelia*, she could feel the energy radiating from the room, raucous voices mixing with the festive music of the performers. She tightened her hand around Thanos' palm, trying to ignore the nervous jitters that settled in the pit of her stomach. Up until that moment, she'd been mostly anxious about walking into the dining hall wearing the translucent *peplos*, but now, as she neared the *kapelia*, other nagging doubts began to creep in.

Thanos had explained to her the brief ceremony. He'd made it seem so simple — all she really had to do was stand there and recite a few words swearing her loyalty to Sparta, its people, and her king. Still, she couldn't help but feel apprehensive. Thanos was used to this — he felt comfortable in a room full of the wealthy nobility. She, on the other hand, was out of sorts.

It seemed only yesterdawn she'd sat astride Thanos' horse, looking down upon the city-state of Sparta. She'd been Lamia — the simple orphan from Carthage. And in less than a full dawn she'd become Thanos' wife — the new Queen of Sparta. It was all a bit overwhelming, to say the least.

"If you squeeze any harder, I will not be able to use my hand for several dawns."

She started at the sound of Thanos' teasing voice against her ear and relaxed her grip, flashing him a sheepish smile.

"I am nervous."

He grinned. "I never would have guessed."

They stood just outside the *kapelia*, their bodies obscured from view by the archway. Thanos tugged her into his arms, holding her firmly to his chest.

"You will be fine, *agapetos*. And if you need reassurance, just look to me."

He kissed her gently, the intimacy of the moment doing more to assuage her nerves than anything else had.

"Just remember, I am right here," Thanos whispered when he lifted his head, softly stroking her cheek with his hand.

She nodded. Taking his hand once again, she allowed him to lead her into the *kapelia*.

As soon as they stepped into the dining hall, silence descended upon the room, the attention of every guest arrowing in their direction.

Beneath the dancing firelight, glimmers of appreciation flickered in the gazes of the men as they regarded the silhouette of her figure revealed beneath the translucent *peplos*. Gripping Thanos' hand tighter, Lamia struggled against the urge to run.

Just as he'd told her to do, she looked to him for reassurance, but what she saw on his face did not reassure her at all.

Crimson splotches stained his cheeks, and his blue eyes were sharp as granite. When the circulation in her hand began to wane, she leaned into Thanos.

"You have to relax, Thanos. Now I cannot feel *my* hand."

He didn't look at her. Instead he glared at every man in the room, but the pressure in her hand eased.

The brief ceremony was mostly a blur, mainly because she could not get past the notion that Thanos was *jealous*. She would later recall that Cleomenes called her name, and she released Thanos' hand to step forward and kneel before the older king. A golden, bejewelled crown was then placed atop her head as she recited her oath of loyalty, and when she stood, everyone in the *kapelia* were on their feet, clapping. In the distance, she heard Cleomenes proclaim her the new queen of Sparta, and Thanos grasped her hand once again.

But as she was led towards the dais by her husband, who was as rigid and stiff as a statue, her thoughts kept returning to the notion that Thanos was jealous because several men in attendance were treating her with appreciative stares.

It was surreal.

Men never gazed upon her with desire in their eyes—with fear or trepidation, maybe. Or even disgust. But never desire.

She glanced at Thanos as he settled her onto the couch, none too gently, she decided, given his preoccupation with glowering at a number of the male attendees. She snuffed a small grin, longing to tell Thanos his jealousy was unwarranted.

In all of her *annos*, he was the only man to touch that place inside her she'd thought long dead—the one capable of tender, intimate emotions, the place deep within that allowed her to care for another when everyone she'd ever cared for she'd lost. If Thanos knew just how deeply he affected her, he would have realised he had no reason to be jealous. Still, his possessiveness was endearing, and she certainly would not deny that she secretly revelled in the male attention, not after being told for so many *annos* that no man would ever want her.

Recalling all the cruelties whispered behind her back, Lamia wished those same people could see her now, for she would tell them they'd been wrong—the men of Sparta thought otherwise.

Lamia nearly jumped out of her seat with the sudden touch of Thanos' hand against the small of her back.

"I am sorry." Her smile was sheepish. "I guess I am still trying to get used to the attention."

"It is because you are so radiant and beautiful," Thanos whispered, biting back the mixture of lust and jealousy that seized him.

She was doing more than trying to get used to it—she was revelling in it—although, he could not fault her. Even if it was driving him mad, the attention was certainly warranted. There was no denying her obvious beauty as her shimmering copper skin glowed against the gauzy *peplos* that barely covered her ripe figure.

Several men in attendance could not tear their riveted gaze from the exotic queen, and Thanos did not know whether to beat his chest with pride or unsheathe his sword and strike them all down. Never before had he experienced such an overpowering sense of possessiveness towards a woman and he was astonished at how much of a struggle it was to rein in his primitive need to shield her. Now he wished he'd given in to Lamia's demands and allowed her to wear something more substantial after all.

Hundreds of guests filled the dining hall, the din of low chatter filtering through the room. The official announcement had been made, and Lamia had been crowned the new queen of Sparta. Now everyone celebrated in her honour as they indulged themselves with goblets of wine and an assortment of only the finest dishes that Sparta had to offer.

His gaze darted about the room, and he nodded at Basha and his brother before turning his attention to Cleomenes, who he raised his goblet to. He gestured politely towards several members of the *gerousia*, although, he noted with a tight frown, they could barely meet his gaze because their attention kept wandering back to his wife.

His wife. The words shuddered through him, warming him. In the past, the thought of taking a wife had always filled him with dread, but now…

He glanced over at Lamia. She was still a bit nervous, but the twinkle in her dusky eyes told him she was enjoying herself. He could not stem the smile inching across his face. Whenever he gazed upon her, touched her, made love to her, a contented peace settled over him. Dread was the last thing he felt when Lamia was near, when he held her tight within his arms.

Still gently caressing her back, Thanos leaned his head into the curve of her neck. He knew the moment she felt his kiss because she drew in a sharp breath. He licked her flesh, kissing in the same spot. She tasted of the sweetest honey, and he teased her, nibbling her skin from neck to her shoulder.

"Thanos," Lamia whispered brokenly. Closing her eyes, she arched into him.

He groaned within the curve of her neck and shifted closer, snaking one hand down the length of her body to stroke the moist curls that covered her womanhood. A moan brushed against his ears, and dimly he wondered if the guests could hear her over the noise.

He did not care.

Lovemaking in plain view was not uncommon in Sparta. No one would be shocked or revolted by their display.

Trailing his fingers through the soft curls of her mound, he gently stroked the lips of her womanhood, but he did not push inside her.

"Thanos," she begged, and he knew she ached for him to slide his finger into her heat and bring her to climax, but he held back, wanting to continue their intimacy in private.

It took every single measure of his will to pull away from her. Resting his brow against hers, it was several moments before either of them opened their eyes. And when they did they discovered that silence had descended upon the *kapelia* and that every guest had stopped to watch them.

"I think it is time for us to retire."

He grinned, pleased by the envious gazes of Lamia's admirers. After such a display, there would certainly be no doubt as to whom Lamia belonged to—not that there ever was before. Any who knew Thanos knew he guarded what was his very closely…and when it came to his wife, that statement was never truer.

Others might look, but that was all, because Thanos would never share.

* * * *

How they made it to their home with their garments still intact would always remain a mystery to Lamia. As soon as they stumbled into the courtyard, they carefully removed the ceremonial attire and set it aside, before once again falling into each other's arms.

Their movements were frenzied as Thanos backed her against the archway leading into the inner courtyard.

She wrapped her legs around his hips, dragging him deeper into her embrace. She kissed him hungrily, devouring him, her tongue duelling with his as she explored the hot, wet cave of his mouth.

She gasped when his fingers dug into the soft flesh of her hips, pinning her against the hard stone. Her back scraped the rock, but she ignored the slight twinge of pain. Thanos must have caught her brief wince because he pulled her away from the wall, and with her body still coiled around his, he marched into the courtyard and straddled the marble bench, so their legs were draped across the sides.

"I want you to ride me."

Lamia did not hesitate as she shifted up his body to settle on the tip of his shaft. A carnal storm erupted in her belly, her swollen folds moistening with need at the first brush of his hardened flesh against her.

Thanos clenched her hips and, before she could inhale her next breath, he jerked her down at the same time that he surged up into her clenching body.

The waiting breath exploded from her chest as he invaded her body, stretching her. She clung to him, clawing at his hair as she rode his cock wildly, taking his length inside her. Her arousal had been ignited at the coronation ceremony by Thanos and his searching fingers, so she was already close...so close. She clenched her eyes shut, parting her lips when warmth gathered at the centre of her core. Her entire body began to shudder, but just as the wave inside her was about to crest, Thanos lifted her off him.

"Thanos!" Her scream was so primal, so needy, she flushed hot with embarrassment that such a sound had erupted from her. "Thanos. Don't stop. I need to find release," she rasped.

His cobalt eyes darkened and beneath his fan of lashes she glimpsed a look within them, one she'd been treated to before.

"Beg me. Beg me, Lamia, to give you the release that only *I* can."

His words were husky, hoarse and they were a command, full of the arrogance she'd come to recognise was as natural to him as taking a breath. He trembled against her, his own control threading thin, and yet he held back, watching, waiting for her to *beg*.

Dominance clung to him, dripping from his every word, and she shivered, understanding dawning upon her.

When he'd spanked her...

When he'd told her pleasure could be found in punishment...

I desire a woman who is my equal in every way...except in our bedchamber.

The words he'd spoken as she'd knelt before him, primed for his lust.

"Beg me," he whispered again.

She understood now, as she'd never understood before.

Her surrender was not enough—Thanos demanded her complete and absolute submission.

"Please, Thanos." She lowered her gaze, and her body shook. "Please, Thanos, *fuck me.*"

A deep growl rumbled from his chest, her lewd words, her complete submission, shattering the last of his control. He seized her hips and, yanking her down, he pushed into her clasping channel.

She cried out, the raw sound mingling with his harsh groan as her sheath pulsed with seemingly endless nerve endings. Cupping his shoulders, she clung to him while he drove into her, his pounding thrusts unrelenting as he took her, as he claimed her.

"Thanos..." she pleaded, because she was close, and she knew what would bring her the culminating bliss of release, just as she knew Thanos wanted to be the one in control—the only one responsible for her pleasure.

Whether driven by instinct or understanding, Thanos slid a hand between her thighs, teasing the hardened nub with his fingers until the storm tossing violently within her broke free, hurling Lamia over the edge into ecstasy.

She dug her nails into his flesh and stiffened, her head thrown back as she arched into him. She couldn't move, she couldn't breathe, but in the deep haze of her release she felt him spurt inside her as he belted out a harsh grunt of completion.

Coming on soft whooshes, her breath clawed through her chest, interrupted only by stilted moans until she slumped against him. Closing her eyes, Lamia settled into the warmth of Thanos' arms, satiated and content.

She would never know how long they remained in the courtyard locked together, or how she ended up in their chambers nestled in Thanos' embrace.

The next time she awoke, the sun was streaming through the window, bathing them in its shimmering, amber glow.

Chapter Thirteen

Lamia had been in Sparta for over a fortnight now, and when she awoke that dawn, bright-eyed and restless, she decided she'd had enough of lazing about in Thanos' bed all dawn. But it was no wonder she'd been doing nothing since she'd come to Sparta. Thanos had encouraged it. Even he'd brushed off his duties to indulge in the pleasures of their bed, until he could no longer avoid the demands of his station.

Thanos would be gone for several hours, his duties taking him to the barracks to train the newest *hoplites*. So, with Thanos away for most of the morn, Lamia had decided to visit Sparta's *agora*. While there, she was hoping to look for meaningful work, too.

Thanos had protested, of course, saying Sparta's queen did not need to find work, but she'd insisted — if he wanted her to be happy while she was there then running his household was not enough. She was used to long dawns and gruelling labour — the thought of idling about at his estate made her want to yawn. Outside of instructing Armine and running a household that could run itself, she had little to do.

Making her way into the outer courtyard of Thanos' home, she greeted Panos as he turned over the reins to her mount. The sun beamed brightly this morn, encouraging her high spirits as she lifted herself on to the chestnut mare and headed off towards Pylos, the main square in Sparta.

Her coronation ceremony had been attended by only the nobility of Sparta, so the common citizens were still curious about their new queen, having caught only a few glimpses of her. Lamia was not surprised that when she rode through the streets many of the city-state's dwellers stopped to stare. Their expressions were open and friendly and she greeted them all as she passed by.

She rode along, stopping occasionally to assess her surroundings. She'd only been in Sparta for less than a single moon, and, while she was becoming familiar with the city with each passing dawn, she still ended up getting turned around every now and then. Most of it was owing to the architectural design and layout of the city-state. Many Spartan homes and shops were built in the same nondescript fashion, so they easily blended into one another if one wasn't paying attention.

Well, she *had* been paying attention, but somehow she'd managed to get turned around again. With a small sigh, Lamia slid from her horse and tethered the reins to a nearby post. It would be easier if she walked the rest of the journey, affording her a closer look at each of the buildings so she would not get lost this time.

Deciding to continue north towards the main square, she spun away from the post, her steps faltering as she barely avoided colliding into a small woman.

"Sorry," the woman said with a sheepish smile. "I should have warned you I was here. You appeared lost, so I thought maybe you needed directions."

"My apologies. I should have heard you coming, but I was too preoccupied with finding my way," Lamia reassured her, surprised that the woman had crept so close without her hearing. Only Thanos had ever been able to catch her unawares. "But as you've now guessed, I am certainly lost and would welcome any assistance." Giving the young woman a grateful smile, she thought to introduce herself. "My name is Lamia—"

"Yes, the new queen." The woman grinned good-naturedly. "Welcome to Sparta. My name is Callisto."

Lamia stifled a grimace at Callisto's words. It was strange to have everyone know her.

"Where are you off to?" Callisto asked, her golden curls bobbing in the wind as her almond-shaped eyes sparkled a rare aquamarine.

Callisto was a pretty woman—not classically so, but there was something very interesting, very intriguing about the fullness of her lips, her pert nose and high cheekbones, not to mention those almost bewitching eyes of hers.

She was short in height, barely making it to Lamia's chin, but what she lacked in height she made up for with her generous curves. Some might have described Callisto as plump, but Lamia decided her figure was beautifully feminine, perfectly rounded in those places that would easily tempt a man.

"I am actually off to Pylos. I plan to visit with Diomedes."

Callisto's eyes brightened. "Ahh, the swordsmith. We are not far from there." She scrunched her lovely face into a frown. "He's an ornery old man, though. Are you sure you wish to seek out his company?"

She laughed at Callisto's expression. When she'd asked Thanos about him, he'd also said as much. "I have already heard, but I shall take my chances. Will you lead me to him?"

"Of course. It would be an honour. This way," she offered, and tipped her head in the direction of the main square.

They strolled the short distance, making small talk, and she soon discovered that Callisto was a very bubbly and chatty woman, so she found herself listening most of the way. Callisto was a young seamstress of twenty-three *annos* and—much to her father's displeasure—was not yet wed. She, on the other hand, did not seem the least bit upset by her status.

"Unlike the other city-states, it is not uncommon for a Spartan woman to marry at an older age, own property or even live alone. Nor it is unusual for her to work outside the home. Father knows this. I think he just wants grandchildren. My brothers still have some time left in the *agoge* and father keeps complaining that he is an old man and needs grandchildren." Callisto giggled. "He is just being dramatic. Father is far from old."

Lamia smiled down at Callisto, whose laughter was infectious. She had taken to her almost immediately. The Spartan woman had a natural way about her that made Lamia feel as if she was speaking with an old friend.

"Well, we are here, my queen—"

"Lamia. Please call me Lamia."

"Well, Lamia, then." She smiled. "We are here. It was a pleasure speaking with you."

"As it was a pleasure to have your company, and your guidance. I don't know many people yet so it was refreshing to have someone to talk to. I hope to visit with you again soon."

"I would like that. Farewell, Lamia, and good luck with old Diomedes."

She chuckled as she watched Callisto walk off, her curls flapping behind her in the wind. Lamia was certain she was going to need all the luck she could get if Diomedes' reputation was at all true.

Giving the weathered, wooden door of his shop a fleeting look, Lamia sucked in a deep, fortifying breath. She then pushed opened the door and stepped inside.

* * * *

Carthage, 183 BC

"Again, Lamia."

She scowled at Darius' back as he walked in the direction of the target that was several yards across the courtyard.

Sweat trickled down her brow, and her garments clung to her small body, soaked from her perspiration. When she was seven annos, he'd rescued her from the streets, given her food and shelter, taught her to read and write the languages of the Greeks, the Egyptians, the Persians. Three annos later, she was on Latin, the language of the Romans.

His first instructions in the art of battle had been to wield a dagger, and she'd mastered that quickly. She was eager to learn how to wield a sword, but, before he would teach her that, she would first need to learn how to master her lessons in archery, which was proving far more challenging than she'd expected.

"I don't see why I have to learn archery. No one even uses the bow and arrow anymore. It's so ancient," she muttered under her breath, blowing a tendril of hair from her face.

"I heard that," Darius boomed from across the room.

She gulped, quickly wiping the scowl from her face. How he could hear her whispering from several yards away she would never know, but her hushed comments had landed her in more trouble than she wanted to remember.

And with every muscle in her body sore, and considering she was already dripping in a pool of sweat, she had no desire to find herself in an even worse state, so she kept her mouth shut.

"You're not focusing, Lamia."

She wanted to protest that she was – she was focused so intently on the target before her that all she saw were big red dots – but somehow she knew that wasn't what he meant.

"Your mind is scattered, and your thoughts are all over the place, but, to be a skilled archer, you must see nothing but your target. You must envision what it is you want to hit and then focus only on that."

"But if I focus only on that, won't I leave myself open to attack since I won't see anything else coming?"

"That is why you must learn to use your other senses as I've taught you. You must learn to hear someone approaching, to sense the presence of someone who means to do you harm. Even when you cannot see, your other senses are alive, and you must focus them, even as you focus your sense of sight on your target."

She raised her bow again, but hesitated when Darius came to a stop just to the right of the target.

"Father, you are too close. I may hit you." She glanced at the pile of arrows littering the ground by his feet. For some reason she kept wanting to shoot to the right of her, no matter how hard she focused on centring her shot.

"I am right where I wish to be. Now arm your bow, aim and shoot."

Her eyes widened and sweat gathered on her top lip, but this time it wasn't from the sweltering heat.

She opened her mouth but snapped it shut at the stern look on Darius' face. This was another one of his unorthodox lessons. He had many of them, each seemingly more dangerous than the last. She wondered how many times he would need to put himself in peril before she actually ended up hurting him. He claimed that she thrived under pressure, that she rose to the occasion when the risk was great, but, at that moment, she wasn't quite so certain.

Darius was as close to the target as he could be without standing directly in front of it. If she kept missing to the right – as she seemed bent on doing – he would be struck by her arrow.

Her fingers shook as she loaded her bow, and her heartbeat quickened. She lifted it and aimed it at the target before letting it fall back to her side with a heavy sigh.

"I – I cannot do it."

His eyes darkened with anger. "Yes, you can. Now lift your bow, and release your arrow."

"But – "

"Lamia, if every time you face a challenge you believe you cannot overcome it then you won't. Self-doubt is normal, but you must not let it weaken you. You must learn to use it, just as you should learn to use rejection, failure, and any other obstacle you face. Use them to drive you and you will become greater. Now release your bow."

She lifted her bow and arrow. At the same time she drew in a long, deep breath. She focused her sight and her mind on hitting the target before her, and after several moments she saw nothing else, not the blue ring on the canvas that circled the red eye, not the other arrows in the target, not even Darius.

When all she could see was a glaring red orb, she uncurled her fingers and let her arrow fly from her bow, following it with her gaze as it sailed through the sky to pierce the centre of the target.

She smiled when she finally came out of her trance and realised she'd actually done it.

"You must see a challenge as something to test your will, not as something that can break you," Darius said once he stood by her side.

She'd never forgotten those words. From that dawn forward, every challenge that had fallen across her path, she'd met head on.

* * * *

Slam!

Thanos smiled as he turned towards the door. Lamia was home, and from the looks of it she was furious. He'd told her that Diomedes would be difficult, but had known she would have to discover that for herself.

"I take it your sun rising has not fared so well."

Lamia's eyes darkened with fury, her hands balling into tight fists.

"Do you know that arrogant swine had the nerve to tell me that only a *Spartan* could make Spartan weapons?"

He lifted his eyebrows but said nothing. He'd learned when Lamia was angry it was best to just remain silent while she ranted then speak once she was spent.

"He said not even Spartan women should be making weapons and that since I was not *born* Spartan I had no business trying to work as a swordsmith. Thanos, that's just ridiculous. Can you believe he told me

Spartan weapons were the best and they should only be made by the best?"

She angrily kicked off her sandals, only to pace before him, barefoot. With great effort, he schooled his face into a stoic mask, trying to hide his smile. "I take it you had a talk with Diomedes—"

Her eyes widened. "*Hardly.* The blustering fool talked while I barely restrained myself from smashing my fist into his jaw. The *pig.* I will show him. You just mark my words, Thanos."

That was what he was afraid of. His voice was gentle when he finally spoke. "Lamia, please do not do anything—"

She rounded on him, her hand waving wildly in the air. "Oh please, Thanos. I am not going to hurt him, although I should." She scowled. "No, I am going to show him that a *foreign* woman can be a swordsmith too—and a damned good one at that." Catching the amused look on his face, she stopped suddenly, balling her hands against her hips.

"What?"

He smiled as he stood, tugging her rigid body into his arms. Maybe a heartbeat passed before she relaxed into him, her tense muscles softening.

"Most women, most *people,* would abandon the idea at the first sign of defeat, but not you. Rejection fuels your determination and I admire that about you." He held her in his arms, placing a gentle kiss against her forehead, but he knew that was all they could have for the moment. He was expecting company.

"I know you are still upset, but I must warn you that very shortly we shall have a visitor," he said, as he grasped her hand in his, ushering her from their *oikos* towards the courtyard.

One brow peaked. "So what you're saying is that you want me to behave and not take my foul mood out on our company."

That was precisely what he was saying.

"I will be good, Thanos," she said sweetly. "But may I ask whom we are expecting?"

He opened his mouth to tell her but never got the chance.

"None other than the great Adonis, son of Cleomenes the fourth, and future king of Sparta."

Thanos turned to greet Cleomenes' eldest son, a frown creasing his brow when the young man sauntered into Thanos' courtyard, full of arrogance.

At twenty *annos,* Adonis was a skilled fighter with impressive instincts, but he was also brash and conceited and thought himself to be as handsome as the god whose name he carried. The boy was like a son to him, and he knew Adonis would become a great leader in time—that was, if he ever learned to rein in his rampant and wandering lusts.

Adonis' eyes twinkled as he came to a halt before them, bowing low before Lamia. "It is certainly an honour to meet such a vision of loveliness," he murmured, lifting her hand to gently kiss the inside of her palm.

He scowled and deliberately tugged Lamia's hand from Adonis' grip, clasping it within his.

Lamia stared into the piercing blue eyes of the wickedly handsome Adonis, coming to the conclusion that he was every bit as attractive as his namesake proclaimed. His glorious blond hair curled at his shoulders and when he smiled a single dimple creased each cheek. She could tell from the look in his eyes that this was a man who knew his effect on women and he revelled in it.

She glanced over at Thanos, who wore a ferocious expression. Squeezing his hand lightly, she grasped for his attention, recognising the moment she had it because his body relaxed and his hard expression eased. Adonis may have been handsome, but he was a boy…and, from the looks of it, one who was free with his charms. She had no interest in boys who liked to play when she had a man in Thanos.

Lamia's every gesture conveyed this, and she knew Thanos understood when he winked at her before turning to greet Adonis.

"Welcome, Adonis. I would like to introduce you to my wife, Lamia." Thanos nodded to her. "Lamia, this is Adonis, the son of Cleomenes, and the future king of Sparta — as he so *eloquently* proclaimed," he added dryly.

"A pleasure," she greeted.

"I agree, *my* queen" he said huskily, and she did not mistake the double meaning of his words.

With the shake of her head, she rolled her eyes.

"You are bold to flirt with me so openly before my husband," she chided, but instead of being put off by her reprimand, which had been her intent, Adonis appeared confused as he cast Thanos a quizzical look.

"Did you not tell her?"

Did not tell her?

Lamia stilled, a sense of foreboding washing over her. *Not again.* What had Thanos neglected to tell her *this* time?

"Tell me what?"

Thanos seemed uncomfortable and a dark flush crept along his neck all the way to his hairline.

When it seemed that Thanos would not answer, Adonis did not hesitate to speak up.

"Flirting is quite natural and common in Sparta. It's not seen as rude or offensive to flirt with one's husband or wife because here boundaries of marriage are not so *rigid*."

She narrowed her eyes. "And that means what, exactly?"

"It means that the state is the central unit here, not the family."

She shook her head, still confused. "I do not understa—"

Thanos sighed. "What Adonis is trying to say is that the main goal of the Spartan state is to produce strong soldiers." Thanos paused as if searching for the right words and he appeared almost embarrassed. "The *preferred* method is from a wedded union, but however children are produced is unimportant."

She gasped when she realised what he was implying. "So what you are saying is that we have an...*open* marriage?"

"In a manner of speaking, yes. If you wish to take other lovers, then, by law and custom, I cannot stop you any more than you can stop me... *But* we can agree not to," he added, apparently glimpsing her stunned expression.

She could not believe he had neglected to tell her this...*too*. She was now wedded to him—a decision she had not willingly made at the time. Did he not think it was also important to share with her that they had an open marriage, since after all she *was* his *wife*. She could not look at Thanos, she was so furious.

Turning to Adonis, she pinned him with a hard glare. "Open marriages? Are they common here?"

"Relatively." He shrugged. "As long as babies are born, no one really cares who the fathers are."

That was where he was wrong—*she* cared.

All of a sudden she felt ill, unable to stomach the realisation that Thanos had not told her the truth of their marriage.

"Excuse me. I am not feeling well." Ripping her hand from Thanos' grasp, she turned away from the two men.

"Lamia," Thanos called after her. "Lamia!"

She felt Thanos reach for her, but she shrank away from him as she raced from the courtyard.

A single moon ago, after he'd neglected to tell her of Sparta's marriage ceremony—after he'd neglected to tell her he'd made her his queen—she'd made him promise not to keep such things from her ever again. *He'd promised.* He'd given his word. Did that mean nothing to him? Again, he'd deliberately kept the truth from her, and her heart stuttered at why that was and what it meant. Did he desire an open marriage? Did he fear that, if he'd told her, she would seek out another man?

She shoved a hand through her unbound locks. She did not want any man but Thanos…and she would rip him to tiny little pieces if he took another woman to their bed. She sensed that Thanos did not desire an open marriage—any more than she did—so that he had failed to reveal the truth of this custom was telling.

After all his gallant words, she still could not quite trust him…and, apparently, he did not quite trust her, either. Her heart skipped a beat at the thought, a mocking laugh catching in her throat. Of course he couldn't trust her. Did she not plan to leave him the moment he marched out to battle?

It was not fair to hold him to standards she herself could not be held to. And yet it still hurt—that he had such little faith in her, in her desire for him, her affections for him. His trust she may not have won, but she'd more than earned his faith in her by keeping her word. She'd travelled to Sparta with him, entrusted her protection to him.

Even *she'd* put her faith in him—a woman who put her faith in no one. She now wondered if that had been a mistake. If Thanos had kept not one, not even two, but now three secrets from her—how many more did he still guard?

* * * *

Basha raked her gaze over her husband, drinking in the sight of his sweat-slicked back, glistening beneath the heavy rays of the waning sun.

She loved him like this, lost in his training, his mind far away as he focused on executing every single move with thorough precision. Besides Thanos, there was no finer Spartan soldier than Ulysseus…and even on that point, she was still somewhat partial.

She crept towards him, her lips curling into a smile, her sandalled feet as quick and quiet as a spirit moving through their courtyard. As she drew closer to him, she knew the moment he sensed her presence, because his body tensed, before he abruptly spun around to face her, his sword pointed at her chest.

His expression darkened. "How many times do I have to tell you not to sneak up on me like that, Basha?" he growled, his clear blue eyes flashing with anger, but she knew it had less to do with any fury towards her, and more to do with his fear that he could have mistakenly hurt her.

She slid a single finger along the blunt edge of the blade, holding his gaze until she stood within a hair's breadth of his panting chest.

"I am sorry. I did not mean to disturb you." Curling one arm behind his neck, she brushed her fingers against the damp locks of his dark mane. "But I could not take my eyes off you. You know how I love watching you train."

He grinned down at her, all traces of his anger gone as his body hardened against hers, adding kindling to the flame that already burned inside her.

They'd been wed for almost four *annos*, and every dawn her feelings for Ulysseus grew deeper, stronger. If only she could give him a son, everything would be perfect—their union complete—but as long as the gods continued to curse her, that blight would always remain, and with it the knowledge that there would come a dawn when she awoke and Ulysseus would not be by her side.

A heavy weight settled in her belly, the same weight that always threatened to drag her down and bury her.

"What is it that troubles you?" His palm gently stroked her cheek, and his eyes bored into her, seemingly probing the layers of her soul.

"Nothing troubles me," she lied, slipping her other arm behind his neck. She knew he loathed these discussions about having a child, which was why they never talked about it anymore. Basha knew, however, that they could not ignore the obvious forever, no matter how much they wished to.

A sigh escaped his lips, but he didn't press her for the truth, even though his shrewd expression revealed he knew she was lying. She was grateful because she did not wish to fight with him.

He let his sword fall from his hand, and it clanked loudly against the hard ground at their feet. Desire clouded his stormy gaze, and he cupped her other cheek with his hand, tilting her head back. "You know you can tell me anything," he whispered.

She didn't cry—always so in control of her emotions, she *never* cried—but his softly spoken words caused a sob to well up inside her, even as she swallowed it. He was a far better man than most, far better than she truly deserved. Few would have stayed with her, remaining true to their single union, and although it was his right to seek out a lover, especially with no heir, he hadn't.

She wished she could say the same.

Basha closed her eyes, the guilt and shame assaulting her all at once, weighing heavily upon her heart, threatening to strangle her. She didn't deserve Ulysseus, and if he ever found out what she'd done, he would never forgive her. He would refuse to stay, and there would be nothing she could do to stop him from leaving.

No, she couldn't tell him any and everything, and she hated herself because it hadn't had to be that way.

"Basha—"

Her eyes flew open, locking with the shimmering blue of his concerned stare. She halted his next words with a single finger against his lips. She didn't want to talk, she just wanted to feel. She wanted to lose herself in her husband's touch, where everything that was wrong between them somehow was made right.

"Kiss me," she whispered, tipping her head back, offering her lips to him. He didn't hesitate as he crushed his mouth against hers, his tongue seeking entrance, and she eagerly gave it, openly surrendering to his heated kiss.

He moaned into her mouth, the rigid length of his iron-hard cock pressing deep into her belly. She curled one leg around his, rubbing her mound against his large bulge, teasing them both with the friction of their bodies.

"Basha," he rasped, his words warning her to stop, to cease the rhythmic gyrations of her hips, but she couldn't. Her body was on fire for him, a raging inferno that burned hot and completely out of control. It had been so long since she'd felt the urgency of his need coupled with hers. In recent moons they'd drifted apart, more her fault than his, the obsession of having a child having made their lovemaking more duty than pleasure. But this dawn was different.

She'd sought him out because she missed him—the thrusting of his cock inside her, his heavy body pressing her into the furs of their bed. In that moment she simply wanted him as a man, as her husband…because she desired him, because she craved him, because only he could give her body the release it ached for.

He slid the single clasp of her *chiton* down her shoulder, revealing her pert breasts as they spilled forth. Dipping his head to capture one pebbled nipple between his teeth, she sucked in a sharp breath when he nipped her flesh. The small bite of pain brought a needy gasp to her lips. Her gasp soon dulled into a moan as he soothed the aching bud by drawing it deep within the moist, hot cavern of his mouth, where he suckled her hungrily. She shuddered against him, tangling her hands in his soft locks, her eyelids slipping shut.

Her head lolled back, and she arched into him, her breasts thrusting forward as if offering themselves to him. He seized the weight of her other breast, massaging the ripe mound, drawing a series of ragged moans from her lips as tingles of pleasure tiptoed down her spine.

She whispered his name when he moved to her other nipple, sucking the berry-ripe peak into his mouth, rolling it around with his tongue, laving it with his cool saliva. She hissed through clenched teeth, the pleasure of his mouth and hands almost too much to bear.

"Ulysseus, please. I need you inside me," she begged, her voice sounding needier, more urgent than she could ever remember.

He chuckled, his warm breath feathering out to singe her skin, her nipple still between his sensual lips.

Releasing the perky globe of her soft flesh, he slid his hands down the length of her body, leaving fire in the wake of his touch. Dipping beneath her *chiton*, he inched his fingers up along the bare skin of her thigh, tracing a path straight to her swollen heat.

"How is this?" he teased, shoving a single finger deep inside her.

She shattered around him, small vibrations ricocheting though her neglected body. Her greedy tunnel clenched and unclenched around him, seemingly grateful for whatever attention it received as it rewarded him with the gift of her essence. He pumped his finger inside her, gently at first, building her until she was feverish, dragging her towards the edge, but never letting her fall, never letting her go.

"Ulysseus," she cried out sharply when his thumb grazed against the tiny nub at the mouth of her entrance, but he ignored her urgency as he continued to explore her body, taking his time as he rediscovered the deepness of her cunt, the way her body tightened around his. He moved inside her faster, harder, her sheath dripping with her juices as he fucked her with his finger. She nearly exploded when he slid another finger inside her, and then another.

She was nearing the pinnacle, the place where she would find release, complete and utter bliss.

"Let go, Basha, do not hold back. Just let go, and drench my fingers with your sweet honey."

His heated words struck a chord inside her and she sobbed. Her entire body pulsed around him as she gave herself over to the euphoria of her climax, the sweet contentment that only Ulysseus could give her with just the sound of his whispered words in that deep, husky voice of his.

He held her to him, his arm clasped around her waist as she shook with the after-effects of her release. With his free hand, he undid the laces of his *pyterges*, releasing a ragged moan that was a mixture of relief and desire as his cock sprang forth, bobbing in the air.

"Wrap your legs around me," he rasped.

She didn't hesitate to obey his command and he shoved her *chiton* out of the way, his callused hands stroking the bare skin of her thighs, goosebumps dotting her skin everywhere he touched.

She quivered in his arms, the strength of him easily holding her suspended against him, almost as if her weight was that of nothing but a feather.

Clasping her arms tighter behind his neck, she clung to him, while his hands beneath her *chiton* clutched her hips, as he slowly guided her down the length of his engorged shaft.

"Ulysseus," she gasped, clenching her eyes shut as she lost herself in the wondrous sensation of him stretching her, filling her with his hard, unyielding flesh until he was buried to the hilt.

He growled out her name, his face tucked against her neck, his warm breath tickling her skin. "I have missed this," he whispered, and this time the sob she'd held back did break free. She had too, and she imagined that, when he finally did leave her, the loss of him would be unbearable. But in that moment she didn't want to think about that, didn't want to ruin the time they still had left together.

"Fuck me, Ulysseus, please," she begged, and, not waiting for him, she moved her body up and down on him, impaling herself on his cock, taking him deep within her gushing wet sheath until she thought she would die from the pleasure.

She rode him, her movements frenzied, and he let her—he simply held her hips while she set the pace.

"Basha," he groaned against her neck, that single word a tortured plea to her ears. She clenched her channel around him, dragging another ragged moan from his lips. She was on fire, felt as if she would burst into flames at any moment. Her body was needy for him—it ached for him, every single vessel inside her straining to absorb his essence.

Her entire body trembled in his arms as she rode him, taking his thick cock deep within her welcoming body. She closed her eyes, letting her other senses take hold of her as she filled her lungs with the scent of him, revelled in his skin sliding against hers, driving into her. Even now, she could taste him on her lips and she wanted more.

She moved faster, taking him harder, burying his ruddy shaft inside her with deep, stabbing strokes. He was close—she could feel it, his loosening restraint vibrating through him. She worked herself harder and faster on his cock, until he was panting, his breaths shallow.

"Come for me, Ulysseus. Fill me with your seed."

It was as if her words sparked a flame inside him, and he went up like a wild blaze, his body jerking as he came on a violent shudder. His climax triggered hers and she found herself bucking wildly against him, her cunt dripping with liquid heat as she coated his thrusting length.

She screamed out her pleasure at the same time that he grunted her name, and his hands tightened around her hips, holding her against him as he continued to erupt inside her, filling her with his essence. He pumped his warm seed deep within her until the walls of her cunt were drenched, and their combined juices spilled forth from her channel.

Breathless, they clung together, their sweat-soaked garments sticking to them like a second skin. She slowly uncurled her boneless body from around him, her legs wobbly. He held her against him, steadying her until she could stand on her own.

Lifting her head, she smiled up at him, but it quickly died on her lips when she glimpsed the expression on his face.

"Ulysseus, wha—"

"Is this what our marriage has been reduced to?" he demanded harshly. "Your obsession with having a child?"

The blood in her veins ran cold, and for just a moment she feared he'd discovered the truth, but she knew that was not possible. She'd been so careful.

"I do not know what you speak of," she said tentatively, wondering what it was she'd done to reveal that she hadn't let go of her desire to have his son, even though she'd assured him otherwise.

"Of course you don't. With you, it is so unconscious you do not even realise you do it."

"Do what? I have no idea what you speak of, Ulysseus—"

"*Come for me, Ulysseus. Fill me with your seed.* You said that right before I came," he mocked, and she hated it, the sound grating her ears.

Had she said that? She couldn't remember—she'd been lost so deep in her own climax—but if she'd said such a thing then she could understand why he was upset.

Those were the same words she used to call out before, while in the throes of her release, back when she'd been on the edge of desperation to conceive. It had not always been that way. In the beginning she'd screamed them out of passion, but her obsession had twisted their erotic meaning. Ulysseus hated when she said them now. *You make me feel as if I am some breeding animal and not your husband.* She'd been careful never to utter them again, something that had not been difficult, since they hardly made love these dawns.

"I do not remember uttering those words, but I am sorry if I did. I promise you I did not mean it in that way."

His eyes flashed. "But of course you did, Basha." He tunnelled his hand through his dark hair, something he only did when he was furious. "I thought we agreed to concentrate more on *us* and less on having a child."

Before she could stop herself, she snapped, "No. *You* agreed." She quickly realised her mistake when he froze, but still she did not regret her hasty words.

His idea of agreement had been to tell her to stop thinking so much of having a child, and that had been it. There'd been no discussion, no communication—he'd simply stormed out, and she'd been supposed to accept his words as final.

He sighed, his expression sad, and it hurt her heart to see the look upon his face. "Our marriage is falling apart, but you do not seem to care. All you care about is one thing —"

"That is simply not true."

"Yes, it is, and we both know it." His eyes darkened, and anger swirled in their murky depths. "You still think we should take lovers. I can tell," he added, cutting her off when she tried to protest. "You know how much I am opposed to the idea and yet you still will not put it to rest."

"But it is the only way, Ulysseus," she said quietly, her gaze dipping when his expression twisted into a harsh frown.

"Damnation, Basha. Can you not even hear yourself?" Anger poured off him in waves, the heat of his fury blistering her skin.

"Where are you going?" she asked when he spun away from her with a sharp curse.

"I need some time away from you. To think —"

"But —"

He slashed his hand through the air, cutting her off. "I do not wish to hear you, Basha. You think if you take a lover and you get with child that I would accept it as my own — and I would, because you are my wife — but what you suggest is not the solution to what ails our union, for our problems are greater than just having a baby. I wish you could see that. I wish you could understand that the reason why I will not take a lover has nothing to do with my pride, and everything to do with how I feel about you."

"Ulys —" His retreating back silenced her momentarily. She called after him again, but he was already gone, his large frame disappearing from the courtyard.

* * * *

Ulysseus was so full of anger by the time he made it to his brother's home that, when he stormed into his courtyard, he didn't even take notice that Thanos already had a guest.

"Basha still wants to take a lover."

"Basha wants a lover? Then what am I still doing here?"

The seemingly disembodied voice startled him and he whipped around to confront whoever was foolish enough to even dare go near his wife.

"Adonis." He glared at Sparta's future king, not surprised at all. Adonis had graced the bedchambers of many Spartan wives, widows and *tavernas* whores. But Basha would not be one among them.

"You will not go anywhere near my wife."

"Why not?" Adonis' lips twitched. "If she needs a lover then I am happy to see to her needs, since it is obvious you have neglected them."

He advanced on the smirking boy, but stopped when Thanos' hand grasped his shoulder.

"Adonis, don't you need to return to the barracks shortly?" Thanos boomed from behind Ulysseus.

"Actually, no, I—"

"Well, then I am *ordering* you to return to your barracks."

Adonis wanted to protest, the displeasure was there on his face, but he didn't even part his lips. As foolhardy as Adonis could be, he was still wise enough to realise how unwise it would be to challenge a direct order from his general.

"Yes, Sir," he said crisply, as he snapped to attention, and, in the blink of an eye, he transformed from a playful youth to the battle-ready *hoplite*.

Seconds later he filed out of Thanos' home, heading back to the barracks where the rest of the young men in Sparta's army lived.

"I apologise. He's—"

"Adonis," Ulysseus finished for Thanos, since they both knew how the young soldier could be. One dawn, Adonis would grow and mature to become a great king and general, but there was a daring about him that sometimes worried Ulysseus. He'd trained the boy into a man, had watched him grow under his and Thanos' tutelage, so he knew Adonis' skills were impressive, but Adonis was a risk-taker, sometimes forsaking his training and acting on instincts alone. Thus far, his gambles had paid off, but Ulysseus knew the dawn would come when Adonis would act on impulse, without thinking first, and he worried about the price the young man would have to pay for his hasty actions.

"I know you did not come here to talk about Sparta's resident charm-wielder."

Despite his sour mood, he could not help but grin at Thanos' very accurate description of Adonis, and he twisted around to face his brother.

"No. I think I've had enough of Adonis for one dawn."

An almost helpless breath rose out of him as Ulysseus raked a hand through his hair. He didn't even know where to begin. It was hard to admit the failures of his relationship with his wife to anyone, even Thanos. Most men in Sparta wouldn't have even bothered, but he didn't always think and act like most Spartan men, and that was what made him different, what set him apart, which was something Basha didn't seem to realise...or she just didn't care. He hoped it was the former, but of late he couldn't be so

183

sure. Basha had done everything in her power to push him away, and, had he been like most Spartan men, he would have taken a lover and ignored the deep-seated problems in his marriage, but he couldn't do that. He loved her too much.

"Basha wants to take a lover—that much I caught when you stormed in here."

Ulysseus gave his brother a weak smile, grateful that Thanos had broached the subject, since he couldn't seem to, now that his anger had waned some.

"She thinks it will solve everything. Actually, she wants us both to take lovers, but she does not realise doing so will solve nothing."

Thanos nodded. "I could imagine how that would make you feel. Most men would prefer not to know if the child their wife bears isn't actually theirs."

Most men wouldn't, but that was not what troubled him. "You and Lamia have recently adopted your *helot* Armine, no?"

"Yes," Thanos answered with a puzzled frown.

Ulysseus nodded, gesturing for him to hear him out. "I know it takes time to develop a bond with a child you've adopted, but, even in this short time, I see how you dote on her, how focused you are on her instruction. You care about that child."

"Yes. She's lived in my home for many *annos*, but, until Lamia came, I rarely saw her. Now that Lamia and I must prepare her for the *agoge*, I am with her quite often, and our bond has grown in a short time...but I do not see your point."

"Let me ask you this," Ulysseus continued. "Do you somehow feel less responsible for Armine because she is not the child of your loins? Do you think Lamia cares that she did not carry Armine inside her body and give birth to her?"

Ulysseus watched a myriad emotions cross Thanos' face, and he knew his brother was sifting through his words.

"No. I care for Armine as if she were my flesh and blood, just as Lamia does."

"How you feel about Armine is how I would feel about *any* child of Basha's. She is my wife. I care not about whom the father is, because it would be the child of my wife, and that is all that matters."

"But?"

He smiled at his brother, who, besides Basha, knew him better than anyone else. Of course he realised there was more. "I know Basha does not feel the same as I do. She hasn't said it, and she won't, but I know her far too well. She *hopes* she would conceive with a lover, but if she didn't, and in turn I planted my seed inside another woman, it would destroy her. She doesn't say it, because she doesn't even want to think it, but if I were to have a child with another woman she would never forgive me."

That was the truth of it...mostly. He'd never thought the dawn would come when he would believe his wife could ever be dishonest with him, but it had. He'd offered her many opportunities to tell him the truth, but she hadn't, and that was also why he'd refused to entertain the notion of going outside of their union to conceive a child.

If he took a lover and they had a child, he would tell Basha, no matter how painful it was, no matter how much he knew it would hurt her. He would tell her the truth because he wouldn't be able to live with himself if he didn't, but he knew Basha did not share his sense of honour, at least not when it came to this. She would carry another man's child and pass it off as his for as long as she could hide the truth, and that was unacceptable to him.

She was his wife, the other half of his very soul. They should have been able to share anything with each other, but they couldn't, and that was why he refused to bring an innocent child into their union.

Their marriage was broken — splintering apart at the very seams. And Basha's 'solution' would only add more tribulations to a union that already had far too many to contend with.

* * * *

Lamia knew as soon as she glimpsed the strained expression on Basha's face that her sister within the law and Ulysseus had quarrelled. Yet, even if she hadn't seen Basha's face, Ulysseus barrelling out of the courtyard, nearly knocking her over with just a muffled apology, would have been her first clue.

She walked with hesitant steps towards the woman, who stood as still and frozen as a mountain of ice.

"I came here seeking advice about my own marriage, but I am wondering just how sound this advice will be, since I believe you might be a bit partial at the moment."

A faint grin tugged at Basha's lips as she shook her head. "I do not even want to laugh, much less smile, but thank you."

"For what?" Lamia moved closer, only realising then that Basha had been crying, if her swollen eyes and red nose could serve as testament.

"For making me laugh." Basha smiled. "I needed that."

"Do you wish to talk about it?" she asked quietly, still reeling from her surprise that this woman, who seemed as impenetrable as the Spartan *phalanx,* could actually *cry* – that Basha wasn't without her own weaknesses, her Achilles heel. She was human just like the rest of them, just as flawed and vulnerable as everyone else.

"Of course not. When does one ever want to admit they are not perfect?"

"None of us is perfect, Basha."

Basha curled her lips into a bitter smile as she stared off at something behind Lamia's head, and it was clear to Lamia that, wherever Basha's thoughts were taking her, the journey was far, far away.

"I know that. I hear your words, but believing them is something else entirely."

Basha's gaze snapped to her face, as if she was coming out of a trance, and when she finally spoke, Lamia had to strain to hear, her words were so faint.

"I was the only child of the union between my parents, but like most Spartan men my father wanted a boy, had to have a boy. So I had to be better than everyone in everything in order to prove that my Egyptian half did not make me weak, just as being a girl did not make me less valuable as his child."

Lamia moved towards Basha, not sure what she would do, but sensing that the woman needed comfort. She grasped Basha's hand in hers, holding her gaze. "I am sure your father loved you."

"In his own way." Basha smiled, but it was hard and brittle, making Lamia wonder if she should even call it a smile.

"And in his own way he loved my mother, but he hurt her, most of it unknowingly. When they did not have a son, he looked for someone else who could. She'd left her homeland, everything she knew, and it killed her to watch him take lovers. He never managed to have another child, but it did not matter. My mother never forgave him, and deep down, I knew she hated him for what he did."

Basha's words crawled over her skin like an icy serpent, chilling Lamia where she stood. Her heart ached for Basha and a woman she would never know, but whose story could one day be hers. How could she hate Thanos for being who he was, for living according to how he was reared? But, like Basha's mother, she knew she would.

Thanos' actions suggested that he did not desire an open marriage, but what if they didn't have children…or what if they had girls, but not a son? She had no doubt that his position would change, because in Sparta one *had* to have children and they *had* to be boys.

"I thought we were listening to your problems, but this sounds like a cautionary tale for me," Lamia joked, although it was forced, as was her smile.

"I did not mean it to be—a cautionary tale for you, that is. Thanos is a good man, a far better man than my father," Basha whispered, her beautiful eyes darkening with sadness.

"Same could be said for Ulysseus," Lamia offered quietly, wondering if Basha had considered how lucky she was. Four *annos* was a long time to go without having a child. That Ulysseus hadn't strayed rang true of his depth of character.

When Basha didn't respond she realised that the woman was withdrawing from her. Lamia didn't want to push her, knowing how hard it must have been for her to even reveal that she and Ulysseus had a problem.

"I realise this must be difficult for you," she acknowledged gently.

Basha shook her head. "Talking is not what is difficult. Admitting that I am not perfect, well, that is a bit harder. But what is truly difficult is having to accept that I cannot be the woman my husband needs."

Basha's last words came out as little more than a tortured whisper, and Lamia's heart broke for her and the pain she'd undoubtedly carried around inside for so long.

"That is not true. You are the woman Ulysseus both needs and wants. Ulysseus love—"

Basha's eyes flashed. "Do not say he *loves* me," she snapped, abruptly snatching her hand from her grasp, and just like that Basha's walls fell into place. "You will soon learn, Lamia, that love has no place in Sparta. Ulysseus *cares* for me, but eventually he will leave once he realises I cannot give him the child he so desperately wants."

Crossing her arms over her breasts, Lamia shook her head, because it was sad that Basha could not see the obvious—that her stubbornness, her need for perfection, her inability to heal from the wounds of her past had left her blind to the true needs of her husband. For, it was apparent to Lamia, Ulysseus wasn't the one desperate to have a child—it was *her*.

She regarded Basha thoughtfully, carefully choosing her next words. "I saw Ulysseus walk out of here and he looked like a man who was hurting, a man who was in pain. The look in his eyes wasn't one of a man who only cared for his wife, it was one of love. You cannot judge Ulysseus by the actions of your father—"

Basha parted her lips to speak, but Lamia shook her head. She was not yet done.

"You must take him for whom he is, and open your eyes to the feelings he carries inside his heart for you. I have no doubt you could lose Ulysseus, but it will not be because you cannot have his child—it will be because you refuse to love him back."

She didn't realise she was shaking until she was done. Basha was a lucky woman to have a man, a Spartan man no less, who wore his love for her across his face. She thought fleetingly what it would feel like to have Thanos love her so deeply, but she refused to dwell on such a thought because it was one born of futility, one that would only lead to disappointment.

Basha claimed that Ulysseus only cared for her, but the woman was wrong. She needed to take a lesson from Thanos on the depth of caring, because he did it well. He was tender and considerate, kind and attentive...but he did not love her. Not that she needed his love, she told herself, because she didn't, just as she was determined to ignore the feelings she'd begun to nurture for him. Thanos' lack of trust and disregard for the promise he'd made to her was the reminder she'd needed, because over the passing dawns she'd lost her way, becoming distracted from her purpose.

For a moment, she'd allowed herself to forget that her destiny had been sealed the dawn Atallus had burned down her home and ripped her from Carthage. A few fortnights spent in Thanos' arms, experiencing bliss, and she'd allowed herself to dream—allowed herself to hope that maybe she could lay her demons at his feet. That maybe she could find happiness with him in Sparta.

Yet such dreams were foolishness.

She could not allow herself to forget, not even for one moment, that Atallus was her destiny, and, when she'd dealt with him, she would return to Carthage and rebuild the ruins of her life...alone.

Chapter Fourteen

Thanos walked briskly towards his bedchamber, knowing that Lamia would be inside and hopefully in a better disposition than when they'd parted. It had been a long dawn for the both of them and he'd given her the space she'd needed after she'd returned from Basha's.

Thoughts of Basha reminded him of his conversation with Ulysseus earlier. His brother and Basha had many problems to work through, but he knew they would sort their union out in due time. They cared far too much for one another not to, and he was starting to understand that feeling.

Lamia was too important to him to leave things as they were. She deserved an apology for his high-handed actions, and he would humble himself before her because she was worth the small slight to his pride.

His father, Icolos, had taught him that. And when it had come to his mother, Illythia, his father had never hesitated to set aside his pride—at times, even his own needs—to see to her happiness, for in turn she would always do the same for him. His parents had maintained a joyous single union for thirty-five *annos* until Icolos' death, and Thanos reasoned that that was why he and his brother were somewhat different from most Spartan men when it came to how they demonstrated their affection for their wives.

He pushed open the heavy oak door to his bedchamber, pleasantly surprised to discover that it wasn't locked. As soon as he entered, his gaze fell upon Lamia, who sat with Armine in her lap, holding a book in front of her.

She glanced up and he was relieved to see that the fury that had burned in her gaze earlier had cooled...somewhat. He'd been furious with Adonis for telling his wife the truth of their marriage, but he was mostly furious with himself for not thinking to share it. Truthfully, he'd never thought to share the information because he'd assumed...no, *hoped* that Lamia would not want anyone else. He certainly didn't.

"Armine, just this sun rising I am going to ask that you finish your lesson in your chambers so that I may speak with Thanos," Lamia said, placing a gentle kiss against the girl's flowing russet curls, which were starting to look a lot less unruly since Lamia had begun taming them.

"Yes, Mistress." Armine hopped down from her lap, but before she left she turned to give Lamia a hug and kissed her cheek, and gave the same to him as he bent down to the child's height to scoop her into his arms. She then bounded out of the room with her book tucked beneath her arm.

He'd been successful in securing Armine an audience before the council who would decide if she was suited to attend Sparta's *agoge*. For now that meant Armine was going to have to demonstrate that she was at the same level as the rest of the Spartan girls her age, so Lamia had doubled her efforts and added instructions in archery and Latin to Armine's curriculum. He in turn had taken over her blade instruction. Knowing she would be expected to demonstrate her abilities against a seasoned *hoplite,* he wanted to adequately prepare her. By the time she tested, they both hoped Armine would more than impress the council, leaving none with any doubt that she belonged in the *agoge.*

"I am sorry," he said as soon as the door clicked shut behind Armine.

Lamia stood, meeting his gaze, but her expression was inscrutable and it worried him that, for once, he could not read her. "Thanos, we need to talk—"

He crossed the space separating them to pull her into his arms. He heard the distance in her voice and it tore at him like a knife.

"Lamia, I did not tell you about the issue of an open marriage because truly I never thought we would ever take lovers. I know I do not want to—"

"Thanos, I—"

"Lamia, please, I do not want to argue with you. *Please,*" he said again at the hesitance in her eyes. He knew she had more to discuss, but he feared her words from the resigned look upon her face. He didn't want to hear what he knew she would say, what he deserved to hear her say—that she didn't trust him—and he could not blame her, but she had no reason to doubt him. He cared for her, needed her in his life. He would never do anything to cause her pain, but it was difficult for her to see the truth of his words when he was always away.

With Armine's lessons and his meetings with the *gerousia*, they had both been so drained. Nearly a week had passed since they'd last made love. They needed time alone, where he could show her just how important she was to him, how much she meant to him. He'd been hoping this eve they would make up the time they'd lost and he didn't want an argument to ruin his plans. Especially when there were far more enjoyable ways for them to spend their time.

The look in her eyes told him she was still eager to talk, but she must have sensed his need for her. And when she tugged his head down to touch her lips to his, he reasoned her need for him was just as great. He kissed her deeply, his hunger for her evident in the urgency of their kiss. He teased her with his lips, his tongue, until he dragged a soft moan from her mouth. He kissed her passionately until he was forced to lift his head to draw a breath.

Blood rushed to his face as his heated gaze roamed over her figure in her revealing *peplos*, yet it still covered far too much.

"Remove your *peplos*, Lamia."

She instantly obeyed his command without protest.

Lust burned in his eyes as he watched her reach for the bronze clasp that held the flimsy material together on one shoulder. He had to remind himself to breathe when the soft fabric slipped from her beautiful figure, pooling at her feet. Lamia's full breasts jiggled slightly as her chest rose and fell with rapid breaths, her large brown nipples hardening to stiff peaks.

He drank in her rich sienna skin, loving how it glowed beneath the moonlight that streamed through the window behind her. He ached to touch her, knowing her skin would be soft and silken, but he resisted. She was not yet ready for what he planned for her this eve.

"Bend over the bed."

Again, there was not a moment's hesitation. Resting her hands flat, Lamia pressed her chest into the bed, her backside high in the air.

Thanos' steps were deliberate as he stalked behind her, enjoying the sight of her trembling before him. She was ignorant of what he would do next and that excited him — that she was wholly at his mercy.

Grasping the ends of his *chlamys*, he pulled the garment over his head, tossing it aside. His *pteryges* followed soon after as he released his aching cock. Gripping his staff in one hand, Thanos pumped his flesh with measured strokes, while he palmed the silky flesh of Lamia's backside with the other.

"Spread your legs. Wider," he demanded when she failed to part them to his satisfaction.

He feasted on her round ass raised before him with her legs spread and her folds glistening wet. The vision hardened his shaft even more as lust scorched through him, burning an agonising trail from the sac beneath his cock all the way to his temple.

With her shivering before him, poised and waiting, the possessive urges within him beat harder, more insistently, until he shook with his baser need to possess her. She was *his*. His to do with whatever he pleased. His to pleasure. His to fuck any time, any way, anywhere he wanted. Why would he want another woman, another lover, when he had her?

He groaned at the thought, unable to stop the sound from pouring from his lips. There was no need for them to have an open marriage when she satisfied him in every way.

"Lamia, I'm going to spank you for running off earlier. Do you want me to spank you?"

Her affirmative reply was a soft, seductive purr, and he smiled at how easily she'd yielded to him, submitting to the dominance humming low in his voice.

He smacked her backside, the sharp crack reverberating against the walls, and she released a low hiss but did not cry out. Again he struck her cheeks, her supple mounds bouncing from the force of his strikes. He delivered several stinging blows, desire stirring in his gut as he fixated on the jiggling flesh of her backside.

The breath stuttered in his chest when, giving her reddened cheeks one last swat, he stepped back and glimpsed the steady trickle of her juices trailing down her thighs. The possessive streak that had raked through him before raged out of control as he fixated on her trembling form. Taking lovers, having an open marriage — the very thought shadowed his gaze with crimson. He could never — *would* never — share Lamia with another, and neither would he ever desire another as he desired her — not when her carnal longings so perfectly echoed his. It was as if she'd been created solely for him.

"Whom do you belong to, Lamia?"

"Y-you, Thanos." She shivered when he palmed her ass, caressing softly.

"You were made for me, *agapetos*. Strong, fierce, intelligent. And your body was made for me — supple, curvaceous, *yielding*. Your body responds to my touch as no other." His voice hitched with desire, gripping her soft mounds. "I love the way your cunt grips me whenever I am inside you. I love how it milks my cock so sweetly when I fuck you."

He leaned over her, whispering into her ear while he pressed his hardened length against the small pucker of her anus, teasing her. "You are mine, *agapetos*. I have no desire to take another lover just as I have no intention of sharing you with another man."

She moaned and he knew his possessive words had aroused her. He placed a soft kiss against her neck as he shifted down her body. Clutching her hips in his hands, he held her firmly against the bed.

Rearing back, Thanos waited for several pounding heartbeats until they were both panting with longing. Only then did he thrust forward, plunging hard into her juicy cunt, a loud groan erupting from his throat.

She screamed his name, the wild sound blending with his own hoarse shout.

"Fuck, you are tight." He began to stroke inside her, his length ramming deep. "I could fuck you forever and still never get enough of your cunt." He groaned, bucking his hips wildly as he pounded her with furious thrusts.

He rode her, the rhythmic echo of sweat-drenched skin coming together barely muffling Lamia's cries of ecstasy.

"You feel so good," he growled out, moving his hands to grip her shoulders.

With one hand, she reached behind her body to grasp his ass, encouraging him to deepen his strokes as he pummelled her harder.

Every muscle in his body clamoured for release as he rode her ass harder, faster—tunnelling deeper, impaling her roughly against his cock.

Wrapped around his thrusting shaft, her cunt sucked him in, tiny flutters trembling along his length. A shudder of pleasure raced through him, and he barely leashed his waning control, wanting her to surrender first before he would join her. As if she could hear his thoughts, she began to buck beneath him. Throwing her hips back, Lamia eagerly met each thrust until there was no space left in her snug sheath for him to go any deeper.

"I'm coming," she gasped, the words rushing out. Her body pulsed and vibrated around him as she gripped the woollen cover atop the bed, her knuckles reddening beneath the firelight.

He took her harder, his guttural moans joining her soft cries as he pounded wildly into her sopping wet cunt.

"Yes, Thanos. *Yes!*" Her screams rent the air, her back arching, and she held herself perfectly still while he drilled her with mindless thrusts.

Plunging into her over and over, Thanos lost all control as he rode Lamia's body through her release, ploughing roughly inside her dripping sheath as it clenched tightly around his cock. She climaxed so intensely that her juices flowed down her legs, coating the nest of hair surrounding his shaft. He inhaled the musky scent of her release, dragging it deep within his lungs, trapping it there where he savoured her unique perfume.

Tiny, waning tremors rocked her until she collapsed against the bed, breathing heavily, her body seemingly spent.

His body demanded release, that he take his pleasure and join her, but he tamped down his desperate needs. With his teeth clenched tight, he withdrew from her, his cock still hard as a rock.

She glanced over her shoulder at him, a quizzical expression upon her face.

He lovingly stroked her back as he smiled. "Your pleasure is mine, *agapetos*," he whispered. "I restrained myself only so that I may take you where I have wanted to take you since the very first time I punished you."

Her eyebrows arched over her still questioning eyes, so he reached down to part the cheeks of her backside, his smile hitching higher when she realised his intent. Her lips formed a tiny circle and her eyes blazed with renewed passion.

"Trust me, *agapetos*. I shall be gentle," he assured upon glimpsing the tiny flicker of uncertainty she tried to hide.

Trailing his palms across her skin, he slowly eased his shaft back into her. She gifted him with a delicate moan, all traces of unease disappearing from her hooded gaze as he worked his cock in and out of her sheath, coating himself with her juices.

After several lazy thrusts, he pulled out of her only to replace his hard staff with three fingers. A soft whimper rose out of her when he removed them, now dripping with her slick wetness, to press a single digit against the tight pucker of her anus.

"Relax, Lamia. Relax," he urged when she stiffened. He gently probed into her forbidden tunnel. Even as her tight rectum bore down upon him, he pushed inside until her ring of muscle surrounded his knuckle. He shivered in anticipation of feeling her anus clenching his cock as tightly as her snug hole now gripped his finger.

He pressed deeper, until his finger disappeared inside her and her body eased. When her breaths settled into a steady rhythm, he added a second finger, stretching her wider. Thanos probed and prepared her hole, not ceasing until she easily welcomed the three fingers he'd coated with her wet essence.

Satisfied that she was ready to accept him, he withdrew his digits from her tight pucker to curl his other hand around the iron length of his pulsing cock. Dipping his shaft into her cunt one last time, he pulled out slowly to position the tip of his staff against her opening. He leaned into her, pressing forward, his cock burrowing against her hole. Letting the head of his member slowly slip inside her, he didn't stop pushing forward until he was past the first ring of muscle.

She gasped but he gripped her hips tighter when she moved to pull away. "You will not move," he ground out, struggling not to impale her on his shaft, even as she clenched and shuddered all around his sensitive flesh.

She whimpered softly but did not protest as she stilled.

He gave her more of his length until the head of his cock was fully lodged inside her.

A groan rumbled out of him, hoarse with his need. "You are so tight, *agapetos*. So very tight," he gritted out, holding himself perfectly still until she relaxed around him, every passing moment testing the last vestiges of his restraints.

The muscles in his arms bulged and he dug his fingers into her hips, willing himself not to plunge into her. Slowly, so achingly slow, he fed her his cock.

He closed his eyes on a deep, shuddering growl when he finally buried his length to the hilt, his heavy sac pressed against her ass. He didn't move for several seconds, her rectum stretching to accommodate his cock. Only when he was certain that he could move within her without causing her pain did he begin to push inside her with shallow thrusts. She gasped with each thrust, gentle tremors shaking her as Thanos stroked in and out of her body, his pace unhurried.

He rocked into her, tunnelling deeper and harder into her virgin anus, and what was left of his restraint began to vanish on the wind.

A growl escaped his lips when she moved to pull away again.

"You are not to move," he rasped, pumping his hips faster, pounding harder.

"But it hurts, Thanos."

Instantly, he reached around her waist to give her the pleasure that would soothe her pain. Cupping her mound, he found her tiny nub. With vigorous strokes, he rubbed it between his fingers until she cried out in pleasure.

He gritted his teeth, straining against her.

With one hand still furiously stroking her bud, he grasped her shoulder with the other and began to ream her anus, his strokes quickening. He ached for her to find release, but his impending climax threatened to sweep him away. He battled against the desperate demands of his flesh, wanting her to experience the pleasure of coming with him inside her virgin tunnel.

But when her tight hole seized around him, he lost his battle.

"I'm about to spurt." He did not even recognise his voice as every word came out on a strangled cry and blood rushed to his ears.

Powering inside her with a flurry of strokes, he could barely breathe when she erupted beneath him, her anus nearly strangling his cock as she climaxed.

She threw her head back, her long hair whipping across his face. No sound came from her mouth when she stiffened, her body convulsing with pleasure.

He exploded with her, his entire body trembling.

"*Lamia!*" he shouted hoarsely, a wave of sensual heat washing over him, as his cock erupted, his warm seed coating the walls of her rectum.

Dragging in a breath was akin to swallowing fire, and with harsh pants he lowered his head to her back, falling limply against her, his body draped over hers as they both struggled to catch their breath.

When finally their panting ceased, he eased out of her, his gut balling with knots when she winced. He could not stomach the thought of having caused her undue pain, and he gently settled her against him, his brow furrowed with concern.

"I am sorry. I... I lost control —"

"But I love when you lose control," she whispered, her eyes warm.

Easing from his embrace, she stood up, lazily lifting her arms above her as she stretched.

When creases remained in his brow, she reached out to caress the tiny lines.

"Do not fret, Thanos. I am fine. And I spoke the truth. I love when you lose control in my arms. I love many things about you." The last of her words whispered out of Lamia on a hushed sigh, but, as attuned as he was to her, he was certain that he had not mistaken the note of regret in her soft declaration, which gave him pause.

Leaving the bed, he grabbed a warm towel from a nearby bowl and cleaned the evidence of their lovemaking from their bodies before tossing it aside.

With her legs crossed, she sat atop the bed, his *chamlys* casually draped around her.

Thanos watched her warily, only to realise then that the conversation he'd tried to put off, the one he'd hoped he could make her forget with his lovemaking, was coming — and he dreaded it.

Although desire still swam in her gaze, and her cheeks were still flushed with pleasure, her eyes were sharp. She may have been basking in the afterglow of their lovemaking, but that did not mean she'd been rendered mindless.

He let out a long sigh, finally accepting that she was determined to have this discussion this eve. In that moment, she was closed off from him, her emotions harder to read, but he knew...deep down in his soul, he knew. He was losing her. She was pulling away from him, and, if he was not careful, he would lose her for good. A woman such as Lamia did not give her trust easily, and when it was taken for granted, as he'd so callously done by withholding truths from her, she took it back, and it was never to be given again.

"I can sense there is much on your mind." He sat down beside her on the bed. "You wanted to talk earlier, but I stopped you. I am listening now."

Lamia nodded slowly, uncertain whether she was quite prepared to reveal what was haunting her now that she had his attention. She dragged in an uneven breath.

Just part your lips. The words will sort themselves out.

"You know already I am still upset that you did not tell me of the marriage customs in Sparta." She hesitated. "But it is more than that — it is the *deeper* meaning of it all."

He furrowed his brow when she did not rush to continue. "What are you saying?" he asked quietly, the deep rumble of his voice so earnest that out of cowardice she averted her gaze, not wanting to have to stare into his eyes when she said her next words.

But Thanos would not let her retreat so easily. Reaching out a hand to stroke her face, he lifted her chin so that she had no choice but to meet his gaze. She almost faltered at the tender look in his eyes, but she forced herself not to be swayed by it. She resolved to tell him what she truly felt in her heart.

"Thanos, I meant what I said. I truly do love many things about you and my life here, *but* there is also much about you and your life that I know nothing about. Things you should have told me before you thrust me into this position. It's my ignorance that makes me question what else you have neglected to tell me. You have intentionally kept matters from me, thinking to protect me, but all you've done is make me doubt my ability to trust you—"

The frown he wore tugged at her heart. "I was only trying to shield you. It truly was never my intention to deceive you and I never meant to hurt you. You must know this. I do not blame you for not yet being able to trust me, but you must know that I would never deliberately do anything to hurt you—"

"I don't know that, Thanos," she said gently. "Because I do not know *you*. And I think I just need some time—"

She faltered at the darkness forming in his eyes. The lines along his mouth stood out when he frowned. "Time for what?"

She sighed. There was no turning back now. She had to say it. "Time to make some decisions," she finished quietly.

"Decisions?" He nodded as if he'd resigned himself. "All right. I can give you time. You shall have plenty of time to make whatever decision you need to mak—"

She placed a single finger against his lips to halt his next words. Thanos was a good man. Most women would kill to be in her sandals, but she wasn't most women. She hated having decisions made for her and choices taken out of her hands. She hated feeling like she would make a mistake and embarrass herself and Thanos at any moment because of her ignorance. She hated not knowing if one dawn she would return home to an empty bed because he was now sleeping with his lover. Had she known him better, or known the ways of his people, she probably would not have felt this way, but that was beside the point. The truth was that they did not belong together — their destinies were leading them in opposite directions. Thanos wanted a wife, a wife to give him children who would bear his name for many generations, while all she wanted was revenge — an act that would most certainly lead to her swift death.

"You are not hearing me, Thanos. When we spoke in Athens we both agreed that it was safer for me to return with you to Sparta. I kept my word. I came with you to protect your truce, in exchange for your saving my life. You then told me of the Oracle, and, though I was not prepared to wed, you took me to wife. Even after that deception, I accepted my lot and you — "

"Your *lot*?" His expression hardened. "I did not realise wedding me was such a burden — "

"Thanos — "

"I thought you were happy here. I thought you'd accepted your destiny."

"I *am* happy, but do not twist my words and turn this back on me. You have kept truths from me that make me doubt — "

"But I only di — "

"No, Thanos. There is no apology to explain this away. We may be wedded, but we do not trust one another, because we do not *know* one another."

The lines in his forehead deepened. "You may not trust me, Lamia, but I do trust you. Yes, I have made many mistakes, but I never expected you would come to distrust me. I know my trust in you has never once wavered, not even after you ran from me."

The sincerity of his words burned in his gaze, and a hard, painful lump welled up in her throat, but she swallowed it down.

You have to do this. You must tell him.

She had to do this now before she could not, before she lost her heart to Thanos, before she forgot her purpose and never left Sparta. Thanos *said* he trusted her, but his actions belied his words. She could not let his earnest gazes and sincere words sway her, not anymore.

Gathering up her courage, Lamia released a long, strained breath knowing her next words would shatter the bliss they'd shared this past moon, but it was necessary. He had to know that she did not plan to stay.

"Thanos," she said carefully. "I cannot stay here — you know this."

Anger brewed in his gaze. "I actually know no such thing."

"Please, Thanos, be honest with yourself — you know I cannot stay here as your wife. We agreed that I would come to Sparta so as not to threaten your truce with Athens, but when the threat from Rome has passed...I shall leave," she said quietly.

"I see."

She could tell he didn't — that he did not truly understand — and she ached to ease the lines upon his face, she ached to kiss him soundly until the storm raging in his gaze quieted. She cared for him, truly she did, but...

I am afraid to love him.

That was the heart of it. She was afraid to love Thanos, only to lose herself to him...and then lose him.

"And what should I tell the people of Sparta?" he asked tightly. "How should I explain to them that my wife and their queen has simply decided to leave."

She reached for him, but he jerked away.

"Thanos, please be reasonable. Please understand my position."

He shot to his feet and grabbed a blanket from the bed to wrap around his waist.

"Trust me, Lamia, I *understand*."

She shook her head. "No, y— Where are you going?"

He was already at the door when he spun around, and the look in his eyes was so ferocious she had to suppress a gasp.

"I want a wife, Lamia. A woman who will stand by my side. Who will be my partner. Who will lo—" He cleared his throat. "Who will trust me, and forgive me when I have wronged her."

"Thanos—"

"I do not want a scared girl, too afraid of being vulnerable with her husband, too afraid to trust, nor do I want a woman to warm my bed as her pastime until she decides to move on with her life."

He raked her with his gaze, and her heart seized when he dismissed her with the blink of his eyelids. "I thought I'd found something special in you, in our union. I thought you were my destiny, that you were happy as my wife." He turned from her. "But I was very wrong."

He slipped from their bedchamber, the door closing behind him with a sombre finality.

Long after Thanos had left, Lamia fought back the tears until she just could not stem them any longer and every emotion she'd bottled up inside her spilled forth and she cried into her pillow.

That was why parting now was for the best. She cared too much—she needed him too much. Thanos was furious now, but he would thank her later. In time he would realise just how wrong she was for him and he would find someone else—a woman who could be all the things he wanted...needed. A woman who was *nothing* like her.

Chapter Fifteen

Lamia hammered at the sword before her, moulding it to perfection, her strikes brutal as the metal yielded beneath the weight of her anger.

A fortnight had passed since their bitter argument, and she missed Thanos, missed his laughter, his smiles, the intimacy they'd shared, his hand caressing her flesh as he pushed inside her.

She shuddered, nearly striking her hand with the hammer as her thoughts wandered.

This was for the best, she chanted to herself. *For the best*. But she worried…that maybe she'd been wrong. With Thanos absent from her life, she should have been focused on returning to Athens — her preparations filling her days — but she wasn't. Actually, quite the opposite. She spent more time thinking of Thanos than anything else, more time missing him, longing for him —

"*Damnation*," she cursed into the wind when her strike missed the metal blade, the hammer jamming her thumb instead. She shoved her throbbing finger into her mouth, trying to soothe the pain. She rarely hurt herself when she worked, but lately she was a walking accident, and it was all Thanos' fault. He consumed her waking thoughts and haunted her dreams with his teasing smile, his husky voice.

She shivered when the image of him seemingly materialised before her eyes, and she nearly groaned aloud when she saw them as they'd once been, entwined in each other's arms, his body covering hers as he thrust between her thighs, deep into her womanhood, her legs curling behind his back, her entire body trembling from the pleasure of his passionate lovemaking.

She struck the metal viciously with her hammer. This had not been the plan she'd mapped out on her walk home from Basha's nearly a fortnight ago. Her plan had been to put distance between herself and Thanos before her feelings grew any deeper for him, and then leave as soon as he marched out for battle.

Yet, with each dawn, she found herself becoming more entrenched into the fabric of Sparta, her own life weaving seamlessly into the lives of every Spartan she met. The more time she spent here, the more she realised that it wasn't just Thanos she cared for, but now there was Armine and Callisto, Basha and Ulysseus, even Adonis. They were her friends, the family she now belonged to. There was nothing but ashes and bitter memories back in Carthage — there was nothing and no one to return to. She had a thriving, vibrant life here in Sparta —

But what of Darius?

Had he not been her family too? Had she not loved him as her own father? She'd promised to avenge his death and she would not abandon her vow to him — but moons had passed since she'd made that promise.

A ragged, weary sigh tore through her, slicing open her conflicted heart.

Her vengeful vow – it now choked her, weighed her down. Like an obsession, it would eventually destroy everything she loved – including herself.

And yet she could not abandon the promise she'd made. She would not abandon her vow to Darius for a life of happiness that would always be haunted by his ghost as long as Atallus still lived.

The wind whipped through her hair, the gentle breeze carrying with it the scent of sweat and leather, reminding her of Thanos.

How she wished he was there to talk to. She could have confided in him, shared with him those demons he'd once declared he would slay for her, but he wanted nothing to do with her, and she couldn't blame him. Thanos had offered her everything – his entire world – and she'd turned her back on him, rejected him.

Even after their bitter argument, he'd still kept his promise. He'd loaned her the coins for her to begin plying her trade as a swordsmith. When Basha had handed her a purse full of silver *drachma*, she should have been overjoyed, but she'd been filled only with regretful sadness. He'd kept his word, despite everything, but she'd wished it had come directly from him, and not through Basha. As heartwarming as his gesture had been, it had been impersonal, leaving her feeling cold inside, reminding her that Thanos had no desire to even lay eyes upon her. And now she feared that whatever affection he'd once harboured for her she'd all but destroyed.

Thanos was never around anymore – his instructions with Armine the only times she saw him at their home, and even then he did not speak to her.

He'd taken up separate chambers, rising before dawn and creeping in late into the eve.

But last eve…

Her heart squeezed so tight in her chest she could hardly breathe. She inhaled sharply, even as the very thought of Thanos' betrayal clogged her throat with a heart-wrenching sob.

Last eve Thanos had *not* been in his chambers, for she'd gone to him, ready to humble herself, hoping to at least find a way to bridge the distance that separated them…but he hadn't been there. And she'd spent a lonely, heart-breaking eve in their bed, wondering whose bed he *was* in.

Her hammer crashed down upon the forming blade, striking the metal with the full force of her anger. That was probably why it slipped again and slammed against her finger.

"*Fuck!*" Two of her fingers were well on their way to being broken while her hand now throbbed with pain

"If you keep that up you will have no fingers left to finish my dagger," a teasing voice chimed from behind her.

A familiar voice. Lamia scowled at her approaching visitor.

"Oh, do not give me that look. Of late you have become quite inept. I wonder why?" Callisto smiled prettily, mischief sparkling in her aquamarine eyes.

"I am in no mood, Callisto," she muttered under her breath and turned back to her work, but her friend was far from offended, let alone deterred.

"Yes, and if you say that to Thanos as prettily as you just said it to me it is no wonder you are so…frustrated."

Lamia spun to face Callisto, her cheeks heating with embarrassment. She was still trying to get used to the

Spartan humour or the *laconic* wit as they called it. Crass and abrasive was more accurate a description in her opinion.

She flung the sword aside, dimming the smelting fires. With Callisto, there was no telling when she would get back to work.

"It is not *me* you should ask about their moods," she said irritably.

Callisto's brows knitted above startled eyes.

Immediately, Lamia surmised the direction of her friend's thoughts. "You mistake my meaning. Thanos has no physical trouble—he just chooses not to," she said softly, her eyes drifting to the ground, embarrassed to say even that much.

"But it was not like this before," Callisto remarked. "You two were always tearing at each other's garments. I repaired at least *four* of his—"

"We had a fight," she interrupted before her friend could continue. She did not need Callisto to recount the tales of the arduous lovemaking she and Thanos used to enjoy.

"Over what?" Callisto questioned as she plopped her curvy backside down on one of the marble benches in the courtyard.

Lamia sighed. It would be a long while before she got back to work now that Callisto had got comfortable.

Although her time with Callisto would undoubtedly set her back another dawn, she didn't mind—she welcomed it, actually. She had not left many friends behind in Carthage and it was nice to have friends like Callisto and Basha to confide in.

Lamia recounted the gist of her fight with Thanos, and when she was done she expected Callisto to be outraged by Thanos' stubborn behaviour, his unreasonableness, his complete inability to see her point, so she was surprised when, instead of agreeing with *her*, Callisto took *his* side.

"I am not taking Thanos' side, Lamia," Callisto argued, brushing aside Lamia's heated accusation. "Of course I am your friend. That is why I am pointing out that you are a fool to think you could tell Thanos you wanted to *leave* him and that he would not grow cold towards you. To Thanos' way of thinking, you were rejecting him. And for a man as proud as Thanos, rejection is a hard blow to his pride, especially coming from the woman he loves."

Loves? Whatever made her friend believe Thanos loved *her*? She shook her head sadly. "You are wrong, Callisto. Thanos does not love me."

"Of course he does. He wed you. Made you his queen. Everything he does, he does to please you."

"Again, you are mistaken. Thanos *cares* for me, and before our fight we shared a deep affection, but that is not love. Not once has he even said the words."

"Is that what you think?" Callisto's brow wrinkled with tiny lines. "That Thanos does not love you because he does not tell you? If that is what you believe, then you still have much to learn about the men of Sparta." She chuckled. "Our men do not so openly declare their love, wearing their affections upon their brows, but that does not mean, once a man of Sparta has claimed a woman as his, he does not love her, for he will show it in his actions, in how he treats her. Thanos loves you, Lamia, but it will be some time before he says it, if at all. That is just how our men are made. You have to listen to their actions, not their words."

Lamia snorted. *Well then, that was easy now, wasn't it?* She had her answer, since Thanos' actions were nothing but cold and distant—clearly not a symbol of love.

"Thanos does not love me, Callisto, and I cannot blame him. I told him I planned to leave him. That I was going to walk away, and so he did it first."

"Ahh, Lamia, Lamia," Callisto chided. "Thanos' pride was wounded, so he is sulking right now. In time he will get over it, especially if you admit what you've just admitted to me. That you miss him, that you were wrong. But, even if you do not, that will not stop Thanos from trying to win you again. He has not walked away, Lamia, of that you can be certain. And if you even doubt my words, just see what happens if another man comes near you. You belong to Thanos, and I can assure you, no matter what has transpired between the two of you, that is exactly how he still feels."

"But that is not love," Lamia argued. "Thanos is just possessive. What man isn't?"

A tiny smile spread across Callisto's face and she shook her head, as if to say *Lamia, you have much to learn.*

She could not argue that. She had much to learn about Sparta, its customs, and the man she still called her husband.

"There are no boundaries here, Lamia. If a couple decides to go outside their union, that is acceptable, so if Thanos is possessive that does mean something, because most Spartan men are not. There simply is no need to possess what belongs to everyone. It is like coveting the air of your neighbour, and yet Thanos covets you because he considers you his and *only* his.

"Thanos loves you," Callisto pressed. "And, if you ever desire evidence of this, simply turn your attentions to another man or let another man turn his attention to you, and Thanos will reveal himself as he never has before."

* * * *

"Don't you think it is time for you to return home and talk to your wife?"

Thanos glowered at his brother. He didn't need this. He'd come here to escape his problems, not confront them directly. Besides, Ulysseus had enough of his own, certainly far too many to take on his.

"Have you talked to Basha since your argument?"

"I know what you are trying to do, but it shall not work. To answer your question, no we have not talked and we have not done much else for that matter, but, thus far, neither one of us has moved into separate chambers or taken up residence at our brother's home."

Thanos glared at Ulysseus, itching to wipe that smirk from his face with his fist.

"Basha does not have a brother —"

"You need to go home, Thanos," Ulysseus said firmly.

But Thanos was too sullen to heed warnings. His brother talked to him as if he didn't have problems with his own wife. "Just as you need to talk to Basha about why it is you two haven't conceived a chi —"

Ulysseus lunged for him, and he let him ball his fist into his *chlamys*. Thanos wanted a good fight — it would help ease the ache inside him that cried out for release.

"You can strike me all you like," Thanos growled. "Just know that I shall hit back, but no matter how many times you strike me it won't silence the guilt inside you. Try fucking your wife for once, and maybe she could actually have a bab—"

"You need to stop right there because you know nothing of what keeps me from Basha's bed." Fury raged in Ulysseus' gaze, but Thanos also glimpsed a soul-stirring pain, and it instantly quieted his own anger.

It was as if all the air inside him had been let out, and he felt completely empty and deflated. He wasn't angry with Ulysseus—he was only lashing out at him because his brother was convenient and he could not lash out at the one person whom he truly was furious with—himself.

"I am sorry, brother. My anger is directed towards the wrong pers—"

"Ulysseus, release him," Basha snapped from the doorway. "I grow weary of all the things that disappear from my home because you two are constantly tussling like children."

Ulysseus released his hold on him as Basha sauntered into the *oikos*, her hips swaying gently. For just a moment, a look passed between Basha and his brother that was so intimate he felt as if he should cover his eyes. It was a look of longing—their eyes, their bodies saying what their lips would not—but it passed just as quickly as it had come, and he almost thought he'd imagined it when Basha turned towards him with a smirk on her face.

"There is a messenger here with a note for you, Thanos. He says it is from your wife."

* * * *

Thanos walked towards his home, dragging his feet slowly. He'd wondered how long he could go before

Lamia's patience ran out. He was surprised she'd lasted as long as she had. He'd avoided her for a full moon, by rising early and returning long after she'd gone to bed. But he'd known she wouldn't stand for it forever so it had been no surprise when he'd received the *summons* for him to return home.

Ulysseus had roared with laughter when the *helot* had arrived with the terse message, trembling as he delivered it—'*Come home now or I shall drag you home myself!*'

"For all your searching I do believe you wed a Spartan woman after all," Ulysseus had taunted, falling over himself with laughter.

With his foul mood, he would have actually punched his brother that time had Basha not kicked him out, saying, "I can see where this is headed and I have no intention of letting the two of you destroy my pottery again. Go home to your wife, Thanos. You are very lucky she did not actually come and drag you home, as she threatened. I know I would have if you stayed gone until dusk for as long as you have."

He'd scowled at her words. Basha had always been his champion. They'd rarely disagreed on anything and she had always been quick to defend him, so he was more than surprised that she'd taken his wife's side.

Women.

No matter he'd known Basha all his life, after just a few moons her and Lamia had now banded together against him. And Thanos knew it had been from her co-conspirator that Lamia had even discovered his whereabouts in the first place.

For the last full moon he'd spent his eves hiding out at his brother's until he was certain she was asleep and only then would he return home. Last eve he'd overindulged in too much wine, and had passed out on one of the couches in his brother's *oikos*. He'd finally stumbled home well past dawn. He knew it was cowardly to hide from his wife, but he saw no other way. It was hard for him to be at home with her, in separate chambers, pretending to be her husband when he was not.

Leaving his brother's home behind, Thanos walked the short distance towards the spot where he'd left Zeus tethered. It was well into the eve, and the moon winked out from behind weaving clouds, piercing the charcoal night. The streets were empty, eerily silent, and for a fleeting moment a chill of unease crept down his spine, leaving the hairs on the back of his neck tingling. He tightened his hand around the reins.

Thanos glanced up, his gaze searching into the darkness, but he saw nothing but barren, mud-brick pathways.

For some time now, he'd felt as if someone was watching him, but nothing had ever come of it so he'd just brushed it aside. Yet again, he felt someone's eyes upon him, but as he raked his gaze in every direction, he didn't see anything that was amiss. He shook himself with a mocking curse. He had far more tangible problems than the imaginary ones he'd created in his head.

The most important one being the very real troubles with his wife. He acknowledged that he'd made a mess of things by pushing Lamia away, but he didn't yet know what else to do with her. She planned to leave him. What was he supposed to do?

He was not a man who existed in grey spaces. Either she wanted to be there with him, or she did not, and he could not pretend to be her husband in the truest sense when so many uncertainties lingered between them—when he knew she would one dawn pack her belongings and disappear from his life.

With a pained sigh, he lifted his hand to untie the knot that held Zeus to the post. These were all questions he could not answer alone. He needed to return home. It was finally time for him to face Lam—

Raucous laughter echoed on the wind, snaring his attention. Two young men stumbled onto the street, bloated with wine and staggering on wobbly legs.

They were drunk and Thanos curled his lips into a small grin as he watched them tumble along. *Ahh, the stupidity of youth.* He knew they would curse themselves at dawn when they awoke with pounding heads.

He let his hand fall to his side and followed the same pathway the boys had just taken. It had been several moons since his last visit to the *tavernas* but he could use a nice full cup of wine. As soon as he was done, he would then go home and face his wife.

* * * *

"Thank you for coming with me."

Basha sent her a sidelong glance as if to say she owed her many coins for this. "I couldn't let you go alone. I hope he's here because if Ulysseus awakens before I return then I will never hear the end of this."

"He has to be here—"

Basha sighed deeply and Lamia knew what was coming, but she did not wish to hear it.

"Lamia, I have tried to prepare you for the possibility that he may have taken—"

She halted immediately, rounding on her sister within the law. "Don't say it. Do. Not. Say. It." She punctuated each word softly, coldly.

Basha sighed. "Fine."

Lamia nodded and resumed her hurried pace towards the *tavernas*. When Thanos had failed to return home an hour past the time he should have, she'd gone in search of Basha. Luckily for her, Basha had still been awake, although Lamia had not been pleased to hear Basha's news. Thanos had departed from Basha's home over two hours ago. He should have been fast asleep in his bedchamber by now. But he wasn't. And she refused to believe he was in another woman's. But this was two eves now and—

Stop it.

She shook her head firmly as if she could banish the notion from her mind. *Do not torture yourself this way.*

Just the thought of him warming another woman's bed made her heart wrench so she refused to even think about it, which left only one other place where Thanos could be—the *tavernas*. She prayed to the gods he was there, because, if he wasn't, she didn't know what she would do. After their fight, she'd known that Thanos wouldn't simply idle about, twiddling his thumbs for her to make up her mind about them— after all, she'd told him she was leaving with such a finality that it would not have been erroneous for him to believe her. She'd still never considered he would seek out another woman, however. Foolish it may have been to think such a thing, but she never would have imagined Thanos could betray her so cruelly while he still called her *wife*.

She caught sight of the torches blazing in the distance and quickened her pace. When she reached the rickety old building with its crumbling façade and nauseous stench, she hesitated. She had no idea why people would wish to spend their time in such a dreary place, but that wasn't her concern. Her only concern was Thanos, and with thoughts of him firmly fixed in her mind she stepped inside.

Her heart sank when she swept her gaze over the room. About two dozen men crowded the dingy space, along with a few women, whom she assumed to be prostitutes, but Thanos was nowhere in sight.

She choked back a sob and spun around to leave.

"Where are you going?" Basha questioned, blocking her path.

"He's not here," she whispered brokenly, hating how her voice now quivered. It was humiliating. How could Thanos do this to her?

Basha stared at her as if she was mad. "What do you mean he's not here?" She pointed over Lamia's shoulder. "Look there, in that corner, behind the prostitute."

She followed the direction of Basha's hand until it landed on Thanos, who sat at a table off in a corner. She'd missed him before because three men sat across from him at the table as well, obstructing her view, along with the prostitute who kept dipping in and out of her line of sight. She frowned then when the woman completely blocked her view of Thanos by sitting in his lap.

She was going to kill him, Lamia decided, as she marched towards him with Basha on her heels.

She stopped before Thanos to glare down at him. His pupils were dilated from all the wine he'd consumed, but he was sober enough to realise he was in a wealth of trouble as he stared up at her, alarm spreading across his face.

She swung her gaze towards the woman, who looked to be barely older than Adonis. She felt nothing but sadness for her. This was no way for a woman as young as she to make a living. However, her pity was short-lived when the woman ran her palm along Thanos' thigh.

She glowered at her. "I suggest you remove yourself from his lap if you do not desire trouble."

Anger flashed in the girl's eyes, and Lamia stepped closer when the woman did not so much as move.

"It would be wise for you to remove yourself as she asked," Basha called from over Lamia's shoulder.

The prostitute's gaze darted between the two women, realising immediately she was outmatched. With a nod, the girl quickly scrambled off Thanos' lap and disappeared.

With the young woman gone, Lamia turned her attention to the three men sitting at the table, their rapt gazes riveted on her and Thanos.

"Could you spare us a moment?" She did not wish for an audience to hear what she had to say.

The men were slow to shuffle off, but eventually they disappeared from sight as well.

When Basha backed away to give them privacy, Lamia finally turned her full attention to Thanos. Mindful of the curious eyes and alert ears, she kept her voice low.

"We can do this two ways, Thanos. You can walk out of here with me and we can go home and have this conversation in private. Or you can stubbornly refuse to leave and we can stay here and give all of Sparta something to talk about for the next fortnight."

Thanos may have been drunk, but he wasn't stupid. Moments later they departed from the *tavernas* and headed home.

Chapter Sixteen

Lamia jabbed her sword into her imaginary opponent's chest.

No, she corrected, he was not imaginary at all. Thanos would fit perfectly on the other end of her sword.

As soon as they'd arrived home last eve, Thanos had passed out in his bed, fast asleep. And when she awoke at dawn, he was still there, *still* fast asleep. She'd left him there. He was lucky he hadn't been awake because she was furious. As if carting home a drunk husband wasn't enough, before they could leave the prostitute had demanded payment from them, which had been promised to her by *Thanos*.

She had a pretty good idea what he'd promised the woman payment for and, if she and Basha hadn't arrived when they had, the woman probably would have earned her coins. Pain knotted her belly at the realisation that Thanos no longer wanted her. That he'd sought out a prostitute to ease his lusts was hurtful and humiliating.

A fresh wave of fury hit her and the boiling emotions fuelled her precise movements as sweat poured from her body, soaking her *chlamys*. When needing to expend her anger, Lamia had always turned to her training, so she'd risen that dawn and headed to the open *gymnasium* near the *agora*. It would be good for her, she'd decided—to practice her swordsmanship, but also to work through her frustrations away from Thanos and the home they shared before she would have to confront him. Maybe, when she was calmer, they could have a fruitful discussion and not the simmering argument that was sure to come if she was upset.

She snorted. *Not upset?*

Not likely.

Already, she'd been there for three hours and every time she thought of Thanos her anger redoubled. What also appeared to be steadily increasing was the number of curious spectators hovering around the open field. She noticed then that several *hoplites* had joined the crowd, their raucous cheers echoing loudly across the open space whenever she executed a particularly difficult move. She rolled her eyes when they cheered again. Did they not have better things to do than watch Thanos' 'exotic Berber wife'? Certainly there were lands to conquer, she thought dryly.

"Your husband should know better than to leave you unattended. You could kill someone."

She turned at the sound of the deep, familiar voice, letting the heavy sword rest against her hip. Instantly groans of protest erupted from the growing crowd.

"Oh, calm down my friends," Adonis shouted to them. "I have not come to spoil the fun. Quite the opposite. I wonder if the lady would care to try her skills on me." He crooked his lips into a smile.

With a grin of her own, Lamia shook her head at the handsome *hoplite*, who she'd discovered lived up to his namesake as she'd first suspected. Adonis was breathtakingly handsome and he knew it. He was also a notorious flirt and quite free with the ladies. Still, his shameless flirting aside, a genuine friendship had blossomed between the two in the passing moons.

Unsheathing his sword, he dipped his head with a curt nod, his dimples creasing his cheeks. "Care to join me in a friendly round?" His eyes sparkled. "If you dare."

"You are incorrigible. You know that? If Thanos finds out about this, he will flog us both."

"Then we shall not tell him," he said in a conspiratorial whisper. "Come now, Lamia, show me what you can do with one of your little girl swords," he taunted as he gestured towards her ruby-jewelled sword of pure steel, its hilt an intricate design forged out of silver. It was one of her more elaborate designs. It was also one of her more expensive pieces. She really shouldn't have even been training with it—

"Do not tell me you are fearful of one as lowly as I," Adonis teased, glimpsing her hesitation. "Not when you have battled thieves and governors, even our great general himself."

She sighed, knowing she was going to regret giving in to Adonis' dare. Her mind screamed at her to tell him *no* but she had never been particularly adept at resisting a challenge—even one as foolhardy as this.

Cheers erupted from the crowd when she lifted her sword.

"All right, *Spartan*. Show me if you're as *good* as you boast," she taunted, smiling when his eyes widened at her double meaning. He wasn't the only one who could flirt. She may be out of practice, but she still knew how to play the sport.

Besides, if her husband could canvas prostitutes, the least she could do was enjoy the attention of a handsome young man.

* * * *

Thanos wearily dragged himself towards the post where he'd left Zeus, eager to make the short ride home. He was going to be sick and he wanted to be in his chambers when he vomited.

He'd awakened late and had to rush to his meeting with the council. He'd then sat through another two hours of deliberation before they'd taken a vote on what to do about the Romans. His bad mood had taken a dive for the worse when the results had come back.

The fools had voted against sending soldiers to Athens—a grave mistake on their part. Fortunately, he and Cleomenes had suspected that would be the outcome and so they'd devised a plan. A plan that, if it was to work, would mean that he would have to leave soon. His only regret was that he would have to leave Lamia at such a tumultuous time in their relationship.

After last eve, he'd awoken with new hope for them. A wife who did not care would not demand he come home then threaten to fight prostitutes over her husband.

He dreaded leaving Lamia with so much of their future still uncertain, but it was necessary, if they were to even have a future, for the very existence of Sparta was at stake. He only hoped that, when he returned, he could convince her that she hadn't made a mistake by coming to Sparta and becoming his wife, and that, if she left, she would regret leaving him behind — that was, if she was still there when he returned, he thought glumly. With Lamia, he had no way of knowing if she would vanish from Sparta the very moment he marched out.

Boisterous shouts and cheers rose up from Pylos, drawing his attention and bringing with it a fresh wave of nausea as the loud noises ricocheted in his head. Thanos promised himself then that he would never imbibe wine *ever* again as he dragged his feet towards the large crowd, curious as to what could have drawn so many spectators. While the *gymnasium* normally enjoyed a steady trickle of people, this dawn it was overflowing with visitors as they crowded on the grass around the open area. That was an unusual occurrence, especially this early in the morn.

With unhurried steps, he pushed himself through the throng of people trying to get a closer look.

His forward progress was momentarily halted when cheers rose up from the crowd, the crush of people boxing him in tightly as they jumped and clapped.

"That's it, Lamia. Get him!" someone shouted out.

He froze, his body rooted to the spot.

The craggily old Spartan beside him squinted hard as he stared up at him, a smile slowly spreading across his wrinkled face.

"Your wife is holding her own in there with Adonis. You two will have fine sons," he exclaimed excitedly.

Holding her own?

With Adonis!

Numbly, Thanos pushed his way through the throng of people until he made it to the edge of the field. He saw her immediately and his belly lurched at the vision before him. Her mass of flowing chestnut locks were wild, her topaz eyes even wilder as she wielded her exotic sword effortlessly. She looked as unbridled and untamed as he knew her to be. And a frown crossed his face when he saw, much to his displeasure, that her *chlamys* was bunched up mid-thigh so that she could easily dodge Adonis' attacks, leaving her shapely, toned legs on display for all to see. In a word, she was stunning…and as soon as he got his hands on her he was going to spank her stunning ass, right after he killed Adonis, he concluded as he stomped angrily onto the field.

Lamia stopped in mid-thrust, her sword high above her head.

"Thanos!" she exclaimed breathlessly.

He glanced in her direction but did not address her. As furious as he was, he was afraid of what he would say. Besides, he would see to her shortly, right after he dealt with the larger matter…

Turning towards Adonis, he raised his fist high, crashing it into Adonis' jaw before the boy had the chance to react. The young man stumbled back, but, much to his annoyance, did not fall.

Adonis' blue eyes darkened with anger as he readied himself to charge Thanos.

"Adonis. No," shouted Lamia and she grasped Thanos' arm, her eyes pleading. "Thanos, please do not do this."

Shrugging her off, he gently nudged her aside.

Unsheathing his sword, he pointed it at the younger man. "How dare you raise your sword to my wife? She could have been hurt."

"Hurt?" Adonis laughed dryly. "The only way I could have hurt her was if she'd been blindfolded and tied up. Lamia and I were simply enjoying a friendly sparring match—"

Friendly? There was nothing *friendly* about the way the boy looked at his wife whenever he was around, which seemed to be quite often of late. His eyes turned cold. "Stay away from my wife—"

"Oh, so Lamia is your wife now? How convenient for you all of a sudden. One dawn she is your wife, the next dawn you don't even acknowledge her presence. Maybe on the morrow she shall be your wife again, but who knows? You may decide to ignore her agai—"

"Enough, Adonis," Lamia warned, but her warning came too late.

"How dare you!" Thanos thundered, rage scorching hot and violent through his veins. He advanced towards Adonis but was forced to halt his steps when Lamia blocked his path. Throwing herself between Thanos and the young *hoplite*, she braced her hands against Thanos' chest.

"Thanos, he is just a boy. He is brash and hot-headed. Do not do something you will later regret. It is not worth it," she said quietly.

"Move, Lamia," he gritted out, his eyes never leaving Adonis.

"No, Thanos."

"Move, Lamia. *Now!*" he shouted.

When she still refused to budge, he grasped her by the waist, picked her up and set her aside.

Before either Lamia or Adonis could react, he rounded on Adonis and smashed his fist into the boy's face again, much harder than before. This time Adonis crumpled to the ground in a heap.

"*Thanos!*" Lamia cried and she tried to run towards the fallen Adonis but Thanos wrapped his arm around her waist, halting her mid-stride. Lifting her up, he slung her over his shoulder and held her firmly against him with his hand splayed across her backside.

He turned to face the nearby *hoplites* and nodded towards Adonis' unconscious body.

"Get your soldier," he said before he stalked off, still holding a wildly struggling, fuming Lamia.

As Thanos stalked away from the *gymnasium*, the crowd erupted with a flurry—clapping and cheering wildly. They had enjoyed the show.

Thanos barely heard any of it as blood pounded in his ears, his entire body coiled tight with barely leashed fury.

Lamia beat wildly against Thanos' back as she was carried unceremoniously into their home. He'd even held her over his shoulder as he rode atop Zeus, which had been the ultimate humiliation. Curious and sympathetic eyes followed her while she'd flopped like a limp doll against him. *Help me,* she'd wanted to say. She had never been so mortified in her entire life.

Once they were safely ensconced in their bedchamber, Thanos finally lowered her feet to the floor and released her.

Face to face, their angry gazes clashed.

"How could you!" they shouted simultaneously.

Lamia's eyes rounded. "How could I? Adonis and I were simply sparring, nothing more. But you have to charge in there, beat him up and then drag me off like I am a disobedient child. You are nothing but a bully, Thanos."

"You should be grateful all I did was knock your boy lover out. I should have killed him. How could you take that philanderer to your bed? He has fucked everyone in this cit—"

She drew back sharply. "Adonis is not my lover. He is my *friend*, Thanos. Nothing more."

"Then why did he feel at liberty to say such things about what goes on between us in the privacy of our home? How does he even know we have had our differences if you did not tell him?"

"Everyone knows that you have cast me aside, Thanos. That you have rejected me for a prostitute," she said bitterly, hating the slight catch in her voice as she fought against the painful ache now engulfing her heart.

"What are you talking about? I have not cast you aside for any woman and certainly not a prostitute."

She was incredulous at the blatant lie he now told as she folded her arms across her chest. "Just last eve Basha had to pay a prostitute the coins you *promised* her before we could drag your drunken self home. Do you not remember that?"

"I do not remember much from last eve," Thanos admitted with a frown. "But I am certain I did not even have my purse upon me, and I never would have promised coins to another without it. I believe this prostitute you speak of has cheated you out of your *drachma*."

She considered his words as she studied him closely. Thanos was not a liar—withholding truths regarding important matters he was certainly guilty of, but not once had he ever lied to her—and something told her he never would.

That prostitute had better hope they never crossed paths again because Lamia was going to give her some coins all right—a fist full of them.

"So, you are telling me you did not seek out a prostitute last eve?"

"I just told you *no* —"

"So you have not bedded any other women since I have come here."

Thanos exploded. "Are you even listening to me? No, I have not bedded any other women. Certainly not since you've been here, not since I've met you, even, and not for almost an entire *annum* before." He stalked towards her, seizing her arms. "And you had better reply the same. If you have bedded another man, *especially* Adonis, I shall march back out there and kill him."

"Another man? There has been no other man but you, Thanos. And as for Adonis, he is simply my *friend,* which I keep trying to tell you—"

"He does not think so. He desires more than friendship from you. I have seen it in his eyes. He covets you. He covets what is *mine.*"

His? Thanos' words stilled her, sparking fury in her heart. He had some audacity. He'd ignored her for over a full moon, but now all of a sudden she was *his.* She struggled to break free of his grasp. "Yours? I am no longer *yours,* Thanos. Not anymore."

Anger scorched through his gaze, so intense that she almost trembled. She had never seen him so angry and, had he not still held her, she probably would have taken a step back.

"You just told me that you had bedded no other man but me," he whispered coldly.

"And I haven't—"

"Then whom do you belong to if not me?"

Her lashes shuttered her eyes, for she could not gaze upon him as emotion welled up in her throat. She *was* his, she had been from the very beginning, but it was obvious he no longer desired her.

"I *want* to belong to you, Thanos," she choked out softly, amazed she'd found the strength to admit even that, despite how vulnerable it left her to him. And yet she could not stem the words of her heart now that she had begun. "But you do not want me anymore. You never look at me, you never touch me or even speak to me, and we have not made love in over a full moon."

With a gentle hand, he cupped her cheek, forcing her gaze to his face. Disbelief softened his eyes, chasing away the last of his anger.

"You told me you wished to leave me, Lamia. How could I treat you as my proper wife, knowing you planned to walk away from me? I wanted you to *want* to stay with me — but you do not. I will not lie and say it does not pain me to know you wish to leave, because it does. I hate that you could so easily walk away from what we have built here, and yes, every time I think of this, I find myself angry with you, but that does not mean I stopped wanting you, Lamia. I have never stopped desiring you," he said softly, his thumb stroking her bottom lip.

The ache that had torn apart her heart since their bitter fight began to ease. His gentle touch, the longing in his eyes, his earnest words... Thanos had not cast her aside, he still wanted her, and that knowledge freed the tender emotions she'd guarded so carefully and for so long, hoping to spare herself from knowing pain. In the end, those walls she'd erected had not spared her any measure of pain, for Lamia had still experienced it in the deepest regions of her soul when she'd believed she'd lost Thanos forever.

It was because she loved him.

She loved Thanos — with her whole heart, her entire soul.

She'd been trying to fight it, then she'd tried denying it, but her efforts — they'd been futile. Almost from the moment she'd met him and had discovered how different Thanos was from the other men she'd known, she'd let him inside her heart. His compassion for others stirred her, along with his tenderness, his strength. When she was with him she always felt safe, cherished, and even if he did not actually feel the emotion for her, he made her *feel* loved.

Her feelings overwhelmed her as her heart burst with love for Thanos, an emotion she never thought she would ever feel for a man. She ached to reveal herself to Thanos, but it was still so new, so foreign to her that she found she did not yet have the courage to speak her heart. Instead she said softly, "I never stopped wanting you either, Thanos."

He threaded his hand through her hair, and she read both tenderness and longing in his gaze as he tilted her head back and slowly lowered his head to kiss her lips.

She closed her eyes as she welcomed his kiss. It had been so long. So long since she'd felt the brush of his lips, the heavy weight of his body against hers, the tight feel of his cock inside her.

She trembled at the first taste of his lips. Twining her arms around his neck, she held him close, caressing his tongue with hers, savouring the essence of him. She moaned, grasping for his garments, tearing at them.

Thanos smiled down at her and in a single fluid motion he wrenched off his *chlamys*, casting it aside. She lifted her arms to shrug out of her own sweat-drenched *chlamys,* hurriedly tossing it to the floor.

Their movements were frenzied as they touched each other, their hands stroking everywhere their lips could not reach. A groan escaped his mouth when she nipped his lips with her teeth. She could feel his control waning. They had been without each other for far too long.

Thanos grasped her hips and lifted her. "Wrap your legs around my waist," he commanded.

Instantly, she clamped her thighs around him, gasping when her back slammed into the wall, the cool marble sending chills across her flesh. She stroked his shoulders as he pressed her deeper against the stones, his body trembling, his breath coming in stilted pants.

Sensing the urgent need in him she tilted her head to the side and whispered in his ear, "It is fine, Thanos. I am ready."

She felt him shudder with relief moments before he plunged into her waiting warmth.

"Lamia," he groaned, his face twisted in agony.

She cried out in response, her eyes slipping shut as his thrusts came fast and hard, pounding her into the wall.

She was so wet for him as liquid fire filled her clenching tunnel. "Fuck me, Thanos," she begged as she threw her hips at him, her ass bucking furiously, her heavy breasts bouncing against his chest.

A guttural roar escaped his lips and he surged harder, deeper into her sopping wet heat.

She dug her fingers into the skin along his shoulders and her mouth fell open. Just one more. Just one more thrust *and...*

"Thanos," she cried, arching as her body convulsed violently. Her channel fisted tight around his cock as her release roared through her, her warm juices drenching his thrusting length.

"Lamia," he moaned, riding her harder, the sounds of their sweaty flesh sticking together echoing off the walls of their chambers.

His cock slammed furiously into her, once, twice, three more times before he stiffened against her.

"*Fuck*," he rasped lewdly, his eyes clenching shut. The veins in his neck strained as his muscles bulged into tight knots. His cock jerked then twitched inside her, jets of his warm seed pouring into her waiting cavern.

Lamia held Thanos through the tumultuous throes of his release, his entire body shaking with tremors. When he was no longer able to stand, he collapsed to the floor, taking her with him. They lay there, a tangled mass of arms and legs, their breathing laboured as they stared into each other's eyes.

She smiled warmly, stroking the stubble along his jaw, her eyes saying what her lips could not. Lamia knew the very moment he glimpsed the depth of her emotions in her open gaze because his eyes widened. He blinked, and, when she looked into his face again, his gaze was dark and hooded. He pulled away from her both physically and emotionally, his every emotion now closed off from her.

He was afraid.

She understood his fear, because she'd struggled with her own until just moments ago. Before, she would have erected her wall out of defence, locking herself behind it to protect herself from the pain of Thanos' rejection. This time, she did not.

Thanos may not love her, he might never love her, but that did not diminish her feelings for him, feelings she could not deny.

Lamia understood the fear of baring one's soul to another and daring to love. Ironically, it was her love for him that gave her the strength to remain vulnerable before him despite the uncertainty of his feelings for her.

Her gaze did not waver.

She wanted him to realise that, if he would only dare to open his heart to her, she would treasure it for the gift that it was.

She wanted Thanos to know he had nothing to fear.

Thanos held Lamia's gaze, her beautiful eyes blazing with an emotion that startled him, that terrified him.

He could feel the heat creeping into his cheeks but he furiously tamped it down. He had not blushed since he was a boy. But here he was beside this enigma of a woman who made him do things that he had never done before, things he'd never dared to do with anyone but her.

He turned from her to stand, shrugging on his *chlamys* with jerky movements, his hands trembling.

There was no room inside him to feel what he was feeling for this woman, but, damnation, he —

He *loved* her.

He'd practically blurted it out the eve of their bitter fight. He'd never expected to feel for his wife what he felt for her and was not prepared for the intensity of his emotions — the feelings she aroused deep inside him. He was a Spartan. It was weakness to crave the presence of this woman so deeply. And yet he constantly ached for her whenever she was away from him. Even when she was beside him, a second could not pass before he had to touch her.

She was his obsession, and he loved her.

He glanced at Lamia.

And she loved him. It was there in her eyes, but he did not trust it.

How long would she love him? Until he admitted the intensity of his own feelings, and she decided his love was simply too much to bear? Too overwhelming? Too much of a burden?

Just one moon ago she'd told him she'd planned to leave, that she was determined to turn her back on him and the life he'd made with her, and for what? Revenge? He had the power to bring Atallus to justice, but he knew she would accept nothing less than that man's blood on her hands. He understood her need for revenge, but didn't she see that, if she pursued this to the end, it would destroy her? It would destroy *them*? It had already consumed her—already cast a shadow over them. And now he had her love, but he wondered how deep it ran? Did she love him enough to abandon this obsessive need for vengeance? He doubted so.

He struggled to clothe himself, now desperate to escape from her presence.

"Thanos?"

He jerked away from her when her fingertips brushed against his back.

"I must go," he murmured, tilting his head over his shoulder, yet avoiding her gaze. "I have to meet with Cleomenes and I am already late."

With angry strides he left their bedchamber without another word or a look back, closing the door behind him harder than he'd intended.

He stood outside his chambers for several long moments, drawing in a long, ragged breath as he argued with himself.

I should return to her.

I should simply reveal myself to Lamia and talk to her.

A storm of conflicting emotions jostled within him, fighting for dominance, and every time he thought he would go back inside he found he couldn't.

What would he say to her? He had no answer, for the emotions brewing internally were far too intense, much too raw. He'd never expected to fall so deeply in love with his wife, nor had he been prepared for the doubts and uncertainties that came with this love.

No, he could not go back inside and talk with her because he knew not what he would say. At once, he felt both foolish and helpless, emotions he had not felt in many *annos*.

With a curse, he shoved a hand through his hair and stalked off, hating that he now doubted himself. Not until Lamia had he ever known the weakness of such feelings since becoming a man.

But not until Lamia had he ever known the deep completion of an intimate love.

Chapter Seventeen

Carthage, 185 BC

Lamia was seven annos when she lost her parents, her tribe, everyone she knew in the war. Those who survived the attack, and weren't captured and sold into slavery, retreated deep into the shadows of the city, where few would notice a beggar child.

For one anno, she lived on the streets with other orphans of the war, moving constantly, trying to avoid Roman soldiers who would pick them from the streets and send them into the far reaches of the empire as slaves. Food was scarce and their existence was hard, living in abandoned homes destroyed in the war, but which had not yet been torn down.

Lamia was one of the youngest, but she was particularly skilled at pilfering from city dwellers walking about empty roads and busy markets. The dawn the Romans raided her home, taking all of her friends where she would never see them again, she'd been out roaming the market looking for someone to steal from.

Darius had not been her first choice. She usually liked to stay away from big, scary men, but he wasn't Roman and he appeared to be wealthy, so he was more ideal than some of the other targets she'd selected.

She was young and unassuming, a dirty little street child whom no one noticed, her hands so small and her touch so light that she could easily make off with their purse of coins and be safely home long before they discovered it was gone.

That dawn in the agora, she should have had no problem. His purse was tucked lightly in his ballooning sherwal, the full pants worn by the men of Arabia and Persia. He should have never felt her between the heavy material of his garments and the bustling market as people were jostled about.

She hovered near him for several moments, eyeing the gold-embroidered sack of coins. He stopped to talk to a merchant and that was when she reached for it. She closed her hand around the bundle and she tugged lightly, pulling it from its owner. She twisted around, but never even took one step when her head snapped back as something, or rather someone, jerked on her long braid.

"Owwww. You are hurting me," she cried out, tears gathering in the corners of her eyes from the pain shooting through her skull.

"Good. You deserve it, you little thief." He easily snatched his purse from her hands then wrapped her braid around his other hand, pulling her from the market.

She had no idea where they were going as he shuffled her down the street until he said, "Where do you live? I am taking you home to your parents."

"Don't have any parents. Died in the war," she gulped out past trembling lips. If he turned her in to the Romans, she would be sent somewhere far away – to Briton perhaps, where she'd heard it was cold the entire anno and freezing white grains fell from the sky.

"Well, where is your home?"

"Don't have one," she said quickly, maybe a little too quickly when he glared down at her.

"Look, you can either tell me where you live so that I can take you there, or I can leave you with the Praetorian Guard. I am sure they would know what to do with a thief like you – "

"I am not going to tell on my friends so you can bring the Romans back there and send us to strange lands as slaves."

He drew up short, and she winced in pain when he jerked her head violently, although she quickly realised he hadn't meant to when he apologised. "I am sorry. I forgot I still had you by the hair." He released her braid. "Are you all right?"

She nodded. "I am fine." Not really. She had a pounding headache now.

He grasped her frail arms and stooped down on his haunches to meet her gaze. "I promise I will not tell the Romans where you live. I only wish to take you back to your home and caution whoever watches over you that it is not safe for you to be on the streets stealing from strange people."

She studied him with narrowed eyes, searching for any small granule of deceit. His grey eyes seemed earnest and she sensed he was telling the truth, but she'd learned never to trust anyone.

"Look, the next time you try to steal from someone, he may not be as lenient as me. If you allow me to escort you to your home, I will give you the coins you sought to steal."

Her eyebrows snapped up. She wasn't sure she should trust him, but they really needed those coins. They hadn't eaten in three dawns — they could use them to buy several loaves of bread. If he was lying and he came back with soldiers…well, they would just do as they had always done – slip out through the tunnels beneath the city and roam until they found another place to settle.

She nodded slowly and turned in the direction of the old abandoned house where she lived. They walked in silence side by side through the winding streets. She glanced up at him, thinking he was awfully tall and still really mean-looking, although, with the exception of pulling out her hair, he seemed like a nice man. She was so engrossed in her task of studying him that she did not realise she'd been about to walk into a trap.

She let out a tiny yelp when the man's strong hand clamped around her arm and he pulled her back against him.

"Where are you going?" he reprimanded. "You were just about to walk into that raid."

A raid? She glanced at the hollowed-out building she called home, her eyes widening as she watched her friends, one by one, being dragged kicking and screaming into the streets by Roman soldiers.

Instinct propelled her forward, but the man's hands around her arms held her back.

"There is nothing you can do. Come, before they see you, too."

She knew he was right, even as tears stung her eyes and she fought against his words, feeling so helpless, wanting to do something for the friends who'd been her family for the past anno.

"Come, let us go – "

"You! Over there! Come here!"

The man beside her stiffened, and she froze as they turned towards the voice that called out to them.

A young soldier jogged towards them, his gaze roaming over her, before snapping to the man at her side.

"Where are you going with her?"

"Excuse me?"

"The girl," the soldier said, pointing to her, before jerking his head in the direction over his shoulder. "She's one of those street kids."

"I am sorry. You must be mistaken."

The young man's brows knitted together as he stared between the two of them, and she knew he was taking notice of the impeccably dressed man, and her filthy garments.

"Ahhh, I do not think so. We were told there were twelve kids. We only have eleven and the one child we're missing happens to be a girl about what looks to be her age."

"Well, I am sorry, but you have the wrong girl." His arms tightened around her shoulders, as he inserted his body between hers and the soldier's, shielding her from the boy's view.

"But she fits the descript — "

"I am sorry that you are missing a child, but she isn't one of them. This girl is my daughter."

Before the soldier could say another word, the man grasped her hand and tugged her back down the street, holding her by his side. From that dawn forward, she became the daughter he'd spoken of, just as he became her father.

* * * *

Lamia felt a shadow fall over her as she sat with Armine on a marble bench in the outer courtyard of her home. She looked up with expectant eyes, hoping it was Thanos, knowing it was foolishness to so openly pine over a man who'd rejected her, but she could not seem to stop.

It was not Thanos, but she smiled anyway, recognising her visitor.

Well, she smiled, that was, *until* she saw his right eye. She opened her mouth to say something, but Armine beat her to it.

"What happened to your face?"

Adonis scowled at Armine before he turned his eyes — or *eye* rather, since one was swollen shut — on her.

"Your husband decided to tamper with the perfection of the gods."

She swallowed a smile at Adonis' arrogance. His eye may have been bruised but obviously not his ego. "I am so sorry, Adonis. I tried to stop him—"

He held up his hand to halt her words. "Do not apologise. It is not your fault." He grinned. "Besides, I know you tried to stop him. I heard you yell for him to halt just before he knocked me out, but we both know your husband is an ill-tempered bull. Not even the gods could have stopped him once he decided to charge."

She chuckled at the vision Adonis described. That was one of the things she liked about him—his good humour. "You know, if Thanos returns and finds you here, you are a dead *hoplite*."

He winked, taking a seat on the ground at their feet. "I shall take my chances. Besides, he is at my father's home for the moment and I expect he shall be there for some time. They are plotting a campaign to Athens using some error in the constitution to supersede the directive of the council."

She frowned. Thanos had mentioned needing to meet with Cleomenes, but he hadn't mentioned anything about a campaign to Athens. "When are you expected to march out?"

He shrugged. "I honestly do not know, but I imagine soon. There is word that Roman ships have already been spotted in the Aegean."

Lamia did well in masking the alarm now roiling in her belly. She knew Thanos was a soldier and this was his way of life, but it still did not make it any easier to hear that he could soon be leaving for war.

"What are you doing?" Adonis asked and she was grateful for the interruption. She did not need to succumb to the hysteria Basha had warned her about, she thought wryly.

"Armine was recently accepted into the *agoge* under Thanos' sponsorship." She glanced down at the sketch tablet in her hands. "So we are now working on a special design for the sword she shall use for her blade instruction."

His eyebrows lifted. "Congratulations. It is not easy for a foreigner to be accepted into the *agoge*. I am impressed. You must be very special."

"Thank you." Armine nodded as she blushed very prettily for Adonis, and Lamia thought it amusing that no matter the age, no woman, girl or newborn babe seemed to be unaffected by Adonis' charms.

She stroked her daughter's hair and smiled down at her, remembering the first eve she'd spent in Darius' home after the raid and how he'd lovingly stroked her hair while she'd cried in his arms. The bittersweet memory brought tears to her eyes, but she smiled through the sharp pain as she glanced down at Armine, vowing she would be to this child what Darius had been to her.

"Armine is *very* special indeed and she deserves a special sword. Is that not right?"

Armine returned her smile and nodded again. "I need a *great* sword because when I grow up I shall become a great soldier just like father and—"

Armine stopped at the sound of Adonis' laughter, and Lamia cringed, knowing already what Adonis was sure to say. For his sake she prayed he would temper his words, for she feared, if he angered the child, that Lamia would not be able to stop Armine before she took out his *other* eye.

"That is quite ambitious of you, but in Sparta girls cannot be soldiers."

His tone was placating and Lamia inwardly sighed when Armine balled her fists against her lap. The girl was too astute not to know when she was being patronised.

"Yes, I can."

He shook his head. "No, you canno— *Ouch*!"

"Armine!"

Adonis stared up at the scowling child. "Did you just kick me—?"

"Yes, because you are mean-spirited and you lie."

Adonis shot Lamia a helpless look as if to say *How should I respond to that?* but she rescued him before he could dig himself into a deeper hole. Besides, Armine could not go around striking people just because they disagreed with her.

"Armine, apologise to Adonis this instant," Lamia admonished, her voice firm.

"I am sorry," she murmured, her arms folding across her chest as she bowed her head, duly chastised.

Adonis graciously accepted her apology, although Lamia noted with a measure of amusement that he deftly scooted away from them so he was out of the girl's kicking range.

"While I disapprove of Armine striking you, I must admit, however, that I do not agree with you." She put her sketch tablet aside, giving him the full weight of her attention. Spartan men could be arrogant and presumptuous and she did not care for anyone telling Armine that she could not be anything that she desired simply because she was a girl.

"I believe Armine can become whatever it is she desires when she reaches womanhood. And if she was still in our homeland, she *could* be a soldier."

Adonis leant back on his hands and watched them both warily. "Everyone in your family seems to be prone to hitting people so I am afraid to speak."

She chuckled softly. "I shall not strike you, Adonis, for having your beliefs, especially since I understand where they come from. Sparta is very progressive in many ways, except when it comes to warfare. Spartans seem to believe men are the only ones capable of being soldiers."

"And I take it you disagree."

She grinned good-naturedly. "Of course I do. I come from a place with a long and distinguished history of female soldiers, so I see no difference between the genders when it comes to battle." She arched a single brow at his sceptical expression. "You do not believe me?"

"That you come from a long line of female soldiers? Yes, I believe that, having sparred with you myself. But that there is no difference between men and women on the battlefield?" He snorted in response.

A smug smile spread across her face and she folded her arms beneath her breasts. "I am certain you have heard of Alexander of Macedon."

He shrugged. "Of course. Who hasn't?"

"So you would agree he is one of the greatest military leaders in the history of Greece?"

"With the exception of Leonidas and Lysander, certainly."

Lamia cast him a dour look. Of course he would think two legendary Spartan generals greater than Alexander.

"Well, can we at least agree that he was a formidable military leader?"

"One of the finest." He nodded.

"Yes, he was, but apparently he doubted his abilities when he encountered the Queen of Meroe."

Adonis' brow creased with frown lines, but he remained silent, allowing her to continue.

"It is not widely known, but Alexander had no desire to invade Egypt. He actually coveted the far richer kingdom of Meroe but was forced to conquer Egypt instead of the lands to the south because he feared that, with her well-known acumen for battle and her impressive armies, the Queen of Meroe would easily defeat him and ruin his legendary reputation for being unbeatable. It is even said that, when he tried to march on Meroe, she met him with her army of both men and *women*, sitting astride a war elephant.

"It is amusing, don't you think? One of the greatest generals in the history of Greece and he left Meroe untouched because he feared losing to a *woman*."

* * * *

Adonis shook his head as he departed from Thanos and Lamia's home.

He had stayed for longer than he'd intended and, if he did not hurry and return to the barracks before curfew, he would be cited and fined a hefty tax. Despite his father's position, Adonis himself was nothing more than a lowly *hoplite* in the greater hierarchy and would be without coins for a full moon if he had to pay the tax. Still, the threat of having no *drachma* for two fortnights was a small price to pay for the eventful eve he'd just had.

He'd spent over an hour listening to Lamia recount stories of her homeland, stories of warrior women just like her and that feisty daughter of hers. He chuckled to himself, recalling how stunned he'd been when she'd kicked him in the shoulder. For the rest of the eve, he'd tried to charm his way back into her good graces, but it hadn't worked. He'd insulted her with his 'mean-spirited lies' and she was not going to be so quick to forget that. He smiled at the thought. There were few members of the fairer gender, young or old, who weren't susceptible to his effortless charm, but apparently she was one of those few.

He shook his head again as he thought of the child. He should pity Thanos and Lamia. She was a pretty girl and from the looks of it she promised to blossom into quite a beauty when she grew older. He had no doubt that men would one dawn flock to her, but with her fiery spirit, she would prove quite a handful for the man who took her to wife. The more he thought on it, the more he doubted that any man possessed of a sane mind would be up for the challenge, no matter how beautiful she turned out to be, for it wasn't just her fiery nature to contend with, but in her eyes he'd glimpsed a wildness that refused to be tamed. Not even in Sparta—where men lived to conquer and many would appreciate her spirit—did he imagine there was a man who would be quite up to the challenge of taming *that* one.

"What are you doing at my home?"

Adonis halted, drawing up short before he could collide into Thanos. With careful steps, he backed away from the fearsome general, just far enough so that if the older man threw a punch he would have time to counter, unlike last time. He needed to be able to see out of at least *one* eye if he hoped to make it back to the barracks in time.

"I stopped by to apologise." That was only a half truth. He'd wanted to apologise to Thanos for his disrespect but hadn't come by that eve to do it. He'd actually stopped by to see Lamia, but he didn't think it wise to tell Thanos that he had a crush on his wife, especially since Adonis wanted to live.

"But you weren't home, so I visited with Lamia and your adopted daughter for a while. Your daughter — quite a charmer," he said with a wry grin. "Seems you taught her a couple of moves." When Thanos' brows peaked above curious eyes, Adonis added, "She kicked me."

"I shall have to buy her a gift then." Thanos grinned. "Besides, you probably deserved it."

He didn't bother responding to that. "Well, it is almost time for curfew. Again, I apologise for my words earlier." When Thanos nodded, a silent gesture that he accepted his apology, Adonis moved to walk around him and leave, but stopped after taking only one step.

Spinning around, he met Thanos' questioning gaze, knowing that it was none of his business and that the older man would probably pummel him for overstepping his boundaries *again*, but he felt he had to say something. Lamia was his friend, and he had not missed the sadness lingering in her eyes every time one of the servants entered the courtyard and she realised it wasn't Thanos returning home. Adonis wasn't a frequent guest in their home, but the times he'd visited he'd noticed that Thanos was never there.

"I know it is not my place to say this, but I hope you realise there are many men here who would kill to be in your place and they would treat her far better than you if they were."

He didn't stick around to see if his words had taken root. He was in a hurry and had no wish to die that eve.

* * * *

Basha stared out of the window in her bedchamber, her heart thundering in her chest.

The door creaked open, followed by the dull thud of it closing shut.

"You must have heard," said Ulysseus and she didn't miss the weariness in his voice as she spun around, tearing her gaze from the silver moon that hovered in the dark eve sky.

"Everyone has heard." She crossed the room to stand before him, and before she thought of what she was doing, she fell into his arms. They had not made love since that dawn in the courtyard, both far too stubborn and angry to cast aside their pride, but there was no place for pride before war.

He held her close, and she let her eyes drift shut as she listened to the steady sound of his heartbeat beneath her ear. They had much they needed to discuss, but neither seemed to wish to ruin their tenuous truce.

"You know eventually we will need to talk," he said with a sigh, giving voice to her thoughts.

She lifted her head to meet his gaze. It was obvious that the problems between them weighed heavily upon him, just as they weighed on her. She was usually the one who wanted to talk, not Ulysseus, so she thought it a bit ironic that he would even broach the subject. She knew he deserved to know the truth, just as they both needed to come to an agreement about the future of their marriage, but now was not the time for such a discussion.

"When you return we can—"

"Basha—"

"Please, Ulysseus." She cut him off, not wanting to hear him say the dreaded words.

He seemed to want to pour out his heart so that his soul would find peace in the afterlife should he not come back to her alive, but she didn't want to hear any declarations, any last words, not when they could be said upon his return. Just giving voice to his thoughts gave them power, injecting seeds of doubt within her heart. She didn't believe in last words, or lofty declarations — had promised herself she wouldn't make them — but, in that moment, Lamia's words suddenly came back to haunt her.

The reality of the life she shared with Ulysseus was that she'd been his wife for four *annos*, and yet she'd never once told him she loved him, had never let him even speak the words to her, even when he'd tried. She'd convinced herself that his love was fickle, false, just as fleeting as her father's love, but Lamia had been right that dawn. Ulysseus was not her father, and every time he went off to battle there was the very real possibility that he would not come back.

How had she lived this long without telling him how she felt? How could she ever imagine living with herself and the guilt she would carry inside her if Ulysseus were to die without knowing what lay buried inside her heart?

"Ulysseus, I — I..." She forced out a breath when the words stuck in her throat. Trying again, she blurted out in a rush before she lost her nerve, "I love you."

He stilled, his eyes rounding. "What did you say?"

Her gaze dipped to the floor. She was unable to meet the intensity of his stare now that she'd opened herself up to him, now that she'd made herself vulnerable.

"Say it, Basha," he demanded with a slight shake. "I want to hear you say it again. I want to know that I did not imagine it," he whispered and a sharp knife of pain sliced through her heart at the look in his eyes.

So much time had passed without her telling him she loved him that he'd come to believe she never would — that the reason why she didn't say it was because she simply *didn't* love him.

She read it right there on his face, and it almost broke her heart, realising that for so long she'd been so afraid of being hurt that she'd ended up hurting not only him, but herself as well.

"I love you, Ulysseus." The words came out on a faint whisper, but she knew he'd heard every one of them as his hands cupped her face, lifting it so that he could crush his lips to hers, branding her with the heat of his kiss.

She melted into him, weaving her arms around his neck to clasp him within her embrace as he deepened the kiss, drawing her into his web of unyielding warmth.

His shaft hardened against her, his hard flesh digging into her belly, and she moaned as her body responded in kind, trembling with the need of him, the folds of her intimate space growing heavy and slick with desire.

"Basha…" Her name was a hoarse cry on his lips, and she wound herself tighter around him, holding him closer. She didn't want to let him go, not physically, and certainly not off to war, not with so much still left unsaid between them, so she tried her best to tell him with the words of her body.

Their hands tore at their garments until their clothing lay in a tattered mess, strewn about the floor.

She tugged her lips from his to meet his gaze, sliding her hands across his chiselled torso. His muscles flexed beneath her fingers, his breathing harsh as his entire body vibrated against hers.

She loved touching him, the feel of him beneath her palms confirming that he was real, that he was alive. She lifted on her toes to beg for his kiss, and he eagerly gifted her with his lips, plunging them headfirst into the tempestuous storm of desire.

He hoisted her into his arms to lay her across the bed, covering her body with his. He captured her lips again, his tongue probing deep inside her mouth, as it swept between her parted lips, dragging hoarse sighs from her throat, only to be muffled by the press of his insistent mouth.

He raised his head, and for a moment their eyes met. The love they felt inside their hearts shimmered between them, just as clear and radiant as a sunny dawn in the middle of spring.

He dipped his head to trace a path of tiny kisses along the column of her throat, against her chest, between the valley of her breasts. He teased her with his kisses, coming close to the aching nipples of her breasts but never taking them inside his mouth, instead taunting them to tighter peaks as his hot breath sent shivers of searing pleasure fanning out across her entire body. He continued his sweet torture as he gently kissed her belly, sweeping his tongue inside her navel.

She gasped, his wet tongue sending another series of tingles washing over her. She curled her toes into the bunched and twisted blankets, wondering if she would explode into tiny pieces, the pleasure was so intense. She thought she couldn't take any more—couldn't endure the teasing touch of his hands as they gently caressed her thighs, the warm kisses of his lips, or his sinfully skilled tongue—but found she was wrong when he moved just a few inches lower to slide his tongue through the dripping folds of her heated womanhood.

"Ulysseus!" she screamed, clutching the back of his head, holding him to her.

He chuckled, the deep rumble of his voice sending tiny vibrations across her sensitive flesh. He loved taunting her, knowing that when they were together like this she was powerless to the needs of her body and his masterful touch. She let her legs drift farther apart, and he braced himself against her parted thighs as he devoured her cunt, drinking in her essence as his tongue probed deep inside her glistening channel.

She was a mindless, writhing bundle of nerves beneath him, lost in the sensation of just feeling. She trembled against the bed, her climax slowly building inside her. Tears gathered in the corners of her eyes at the thought that, when Ulysseus left for war, she would be bereft of his touch, his kiss, the hard press of his cock inside her, stretching her, making her his.

His lips fastened around her engorged nub and everything seemed to stand still, as time froze and her entire body tensed. Her breath came out as gentle whooshes and the tremors that shook her were almost violent as they roiled through her. She moaned low in her throat, her climax just on the horizon, and Ulysseus must have sensed it.

"Ulysseus…" she cried out on a tortured rasp when abruptly he tore his lips from her wet folds and moved up the length of her body.

With his muscled frame draped over her, she clasped her legs behind his back, locking him to her. He pressed the tip of his hardened shaft to the opening of her cunt, and she spread her thighs wider, her body pounding with need, her channel flooding with wet warmth, every wanton gesture silently begging for the stroke of his cock deep inside her.

There was no more love play, no languorous frolicking—not this time. Their bodies were urgent, hungry for one another.

He nudged the head of his cock against her wet slit before thrusting inside her on one smooth stroke. They cried out in unison, and she clung to him, squeezing her eyes shut at the intensity of the pleasure roaring inside her. He filled her completely, stretching her, claiming her as his, and she shattered around him, a tiny climax gently rocking her.

He pumped his hips back and forth, riding her body through her subtle release, setting a steady rhythm, driving them both closer to the edge of fulfilment, building her back up for what she could feel would be a stronger, more violent climax than the one before.

"Fuck me, Basha," he whispered against the hollow of her neck, his fingers digging deeper into the flesh of her hips as he pounded into her body. She lifted her hips in answer to his plea, sending him tunnelling deeper, so with every stroke he brushed the back of her sheath.

The balmy air from the open window streamed inside, heating their dripping flesh, as they writhed against each other in a tangled mass of limbs. The musk of lovemaking permeated the room, staining the blankets that draped the bed, reminding Basha that, when Ulysseus left, their room would carry his scent, and, no matter how hard she tried, she would never be able to escape the visions of that eve, their wild lovemaking as their bodies came together as one.

His strokes grew faster, more frenzied, and she clenched her legs tighter, causing him to rub harder against the tiny nub at the apex of her cunt.

She could feel he was close, as she was too, and Basha simply closed her eyes, losing herself completely to the moment, when there were only the two of them in that special place where nothing else mattered but them.

She tightened her legs around him, drawing him deeper inside as his body slid against hers, dripping with sweat. He drove into her harder, faster, his brutal thrusts now urgent…desperate, even.

"You're mine, Basha. You belong to no other man but me."

Tiny butterflies fluttered in her belly as his possessive words slid over her, warming her from the inside out.

"I am yours — only yours," she whispered in his ear, because it was true. No matter how much distance separated them, she was still his. She would always be his.

She belonged to him, and only him.

There was no other man who could ever rival Ulysseus in her eyes. And Basha knew, as long as she lived, that she would never love any other man but him. No matter what happened in this battle or the next, her heart would always belong to him, and only him.

How had she thought she could ever take another man between her thighs, allow him to spill his seed within her, bear his child, tarnish and ruin what she'd built with her husband? Even if she could never give Ulysseus the child she'd once so desperately wanted to give him, she would never — *could* never — give herself to another man, just as she would die before she allowed another woman to feel the weight of her husband pressing her deep into the bed they shared together. No other woman would feel her husband's seed stir inside her belly when he found release, no other woman would ever know that type of pleasure but her.

That single thought caused something deep inside her to shatter and she splintered apart, finally giving herself completely to Ulysseus and the joys and pains of their mutual love.

She dug her nails into his back as her hips jerked uncontrollably, rocking in time to the pounding of his wild strokes. And, when her climax exploded, his release soon followed as he burst deep within her spasming sheath, filling her with his hot liquid.

A roar of completion tore past his lips, mingling with her ragged cry, just as the juices of their climaxes joined together.

He collapsed against her, and Basha held Ulysseus tight, caressing the hard, muscled planes of his sweat-drenched back, absorbing the essence of him as his heart hammered out the same beat as hers.

"I love you," he said softly, his voice faint, but she heard every word.

She curled her lips into a tired smile as she drifted in and out of consciousness, lethargy creeping inside her, gently enticing her into the arms of sleep.

"As I love you," she said, letting her eyelids flutter shut, her last thoughts of Ulysseus, and only Ulysseus.

* * * *

Thanos was in a foul mood by the time he entered his bedchamber. Adonis was lucky that he'd taken off as soon as he had because if he'd stayed just half a second longer, Thanos would have grabbed him by his *chamlys* and beaten him to a pulp.

He didn't need to be reminded that other men coveted his wife and it shamed him to admit that he was certain other men could treat her far better than him. She had openly revealed her feelings for him earlier, shining bright in her gaze, and he'd run like a coward because he didn't know how else to respond. He knew he didn't deserve her, and he hated that every man, including Adonis, knew this as well.

He pushed open the door to his chambers, squinting against the brightness of the burning oil lamps as he stepped inside. Darkness crowded the space and shadows flickered off the walls as the glow from the flames danced about. Yet, despite the muted light, the sensual awareness coiling at the base of his spine revealed her presence immediately.

His breath caught in his throat when he saw her, his gaze instantly snared by her wondrous beauty on display in a delicate *peplos* that clung seductively to her generous curves, its amber hue shimmering against her skin. She was absolutely breathtaking and she was in *his* bedchamber. He remembered then that they hadn't shared the same chambers since the eve of their fight.

"Adonis visited earlier. He told me you are planning to march to Athens soon. I thought, if you have such little time left here in Sparta, that it would be best if we were not separated by chambers," she explained.

He dragged a hand down his face. He was going to flog Adonis. The boy had interfered once again. He'd had no business telling his wife news that should have rightfully come from him. Adonis was quickly becoming a thorn in his side with his meddling.

Obviously misreading the anger in his eyes, however, Lamia moved to step around him.

"But I see that you would prefer to keep separate chambers so I will go — "

Thanos shot his arm out, snaking it around her waist.

"My anger was not directed towards you, but Adonis. It was not his place to tell you of our march to Athens, but mine. Please, do not go," he said quietly.

She nodded and, when he was certain she would not leave, he relaxed his arm.

"When do you depart?" she asked softly.

He and Cleomenes had invoked the Rite of Gorgo, an emergency directive implemented by Leonidas' widow after the disaster at Thermopylae. It allowed the two kings to veto a vote of the *gerousia*, but only if it concerned the Spartan military. He and Cleomenes would meet with the council at dawn to deliver the news, and then he would prepare his soldiers for their campaign to Athens.

"Within half a fortnight."

"So soon?"

He nodded stiffly, the look of dismay he glimpsed in her eyes like a dull blade sawing in his gut. He ached to pull her into his arms and reassure her, but he held back. If she was to be a queen of Sparta then she needed to harden herself to the reality that he could go off to war at any time...and that he might never come back.

"How long do you plan to remain in Athens?"

"I truly do not know. But we must remain there until we are certain the Roman army will not wage an attack."

"And what of Sparta? What if this is a trap to draw her soldiers away from the city?"

He smiled to himself, pride swelling in his chest. His wife's mind was ever sharp, ever assessing as one trained in the art of battle. "We are leaving a sizeable contingent here. If this is a trap, the city will be well protected and, with Cleomenes in command, he will be able to lead our men should there be a need."

"And what do you need of me, Thanos?"

He reached out a hand and dragged her flush against him. He'd just promised himself he would not do this, but he could not stand it any longer. He had to touch her. Right now he just needed to hold her in his arms and succumb to the warmth of her tender embrace.

"Truthfully, I need you to write to me and keep me abreast of what is going on here. I also need you to make sure the council does not try to go behind our backs on this. Cleomenes will be alert to this, but I want you to be present if they call a meeting."

She nodded against his chest. "I can do that," she whispered.

He let out a ragged breath when he felt her arms wrap around his waist. "Thank you," he said quietly, dipping his head to capture her lips.

She returned his kiss as she clung to him, drawing him within the circle of her warmth. Not since their quarrel had they been like this — together without anger driving their passions.

He'd missed this. He'd missed her.

He stripped out of his garments then easily removed her *peplos*. She gasped as he took the weight of her breasts into his hands, cupping them gently, drawing her nipples inside his mouth.

She trembled in his arms, her hands in his hair. He backed her to the bed, covering her body as she spread out across it. Her skin was like spun silk against his, heating his body, inflaming his senses.

By the gods, he loved her, couldn't imagine what his life would have been like had he not met her. He could feel the words on the tip of his tongue, but held back, the doubts that hovered in the shadowed corners of his mind paralysing him.

But he could show her. With everything inside himself, his body could utter the declaration that his lips could not. He cupped her face between his hands, claiming her lips in a deep, bone-melting kiss until she opened beneath him, the juices from her cunt wetting his thighs.

With their lips still locked together, he turned her onto her side to face him. Draping her leg over his hip, he held her to him so that her body was perfectly open, perfectly poised to accept his searching cock. With one hand on her hip he cradled her against him, while he tangled the other in her wild rush of hair. Tearing his lips from hers, he stared into her eyes, drowning in their dark depths as he pushed his way inside her dripping wet heat.

"By the gods," he groaned, his body straining to drive deeper, to fill her completely.

Her cunt wrapped around him so tightly, her juices coating him, making the journey of his cock in her passage slick and slippery.

She clutched him, her arm twisting around his neck while her other hand was braced against his chest. In this position he couldn't surge as deep as he wished to go, but he liked that he could see all of her. The light blush upon her cheeks, the tiny circle of her lips, her eyes dancing with pleasure.

"Thanos," she gasped, her body moving sensually against his, her rocking hips sending him tunnelling deeper.

He couldn't withhold his desires any longer. He needed to fuck her, mount her, spill his seed inside her until she overflowed with it.

He rolled her beneath him and drilled her into the bed with his driving thrusts. Grunts spilled from his lips as he took her hard and deep until she shattered beneath him, her tight channel clamping down hard upon his surging length.

She screamed his name, her head falling back, her eyes clenching shut as her nails dug into the flesh of his shoulders. Her release triggered his own and with one last powerful stroke he buried his shaft inside her and erupted, coating her walls with his essence until he had nothing left to give her. He shook and shuddered, his hoarse groans filling up the room. Completely spent, he collapsed atop Lamia then rolled to her side to cradle her in his arms.

They lay there entwined, their breathing erratic, their hearts pounding. The tenderness of the moment reminded him of their first time together, and he sighed, remembering how she'd shattered so sweetly in his arms, crying out his name beneath the stars before curling up in his embrace.

He didn't want to leave her, not after he'd just found her, not after they'd just repaired the fragile bonds of their union. The Oracle had revealed he would wed this woman, that their fates were intertwined...but she'd never said for how long.

He closed his eyes and breathed in the scent of Lamia. If their dawns were numbered then he would cherish them, just as he planned to cherish *her*.

Chapter Eighteen

Lamia's sandalled feet brushed against the cobblestoned street, barely making a sound as she walked with purposeful strides towards Basha and Ulysseus' home. Time was drawing near for Sparta's men to march to Athens and the entire city was abuzz with anxious energy as everyone prepared for their departure. She was eager to speak with Basha, who'd been through this before, who understood the politics of Sparta and what would be required of her in Thanos' absence.

She couldn't believe her turnabout—that she actually planned to stay. She didn't dwell on what it meant, or for how long she would remain in Sparta. All she knew was that she loved Thanos and he needed her right now. She could not betray her love for him and steal out into the night like a thief while he risked his life on the battlefield. For now, she'd put her thoughts of revenge aside. Thanos' need of her was more important. She would sort out her business with Atallus once this crisis with Rome had passed.

She nodded at the young *helot* who stood outside Ulysseus and Basha's home as she passed by. Following the stoned pathway through their gardens, she headed into the vestibule.

The din of muffled voices caused her to slow her steps. The hushed sounds were that of a man and woman, clearly engaged in an argument. She started to turn around, not wanting to intrude upon the intimate moment between Ulysseus and Basha, knowing that if they discovered she'd overheard them they would be embarrassed. Yet, before she could leave, she caught a brief glimpse through the thick foliage to see that Basha was indeed the woman involved in the argument, but it was not Ulysseus whom she was now quarrelling with.

Basha's face was flaming red, her eyes flashing with anger as she glared at the handsome man who stood before her. He was younger, *much* younger, as if he'd just graduated from the *agoge*. His golden hair floated against his broad shoulders, his sapphire gaze swimming with fury. She recognised him immediately as Zenos, a prince of Sparta and Adonis' younger brother.

She wondered what he was doing there, arguing with Basha, until he moved towards her sister within the law, his expression intense. Basha shook her head and held out her hand, pressing it against his broad chest. Lamia stood there transfixed by the sight of them, watching the interplay of emotions that crossed their faces. They were lovers. She knew so immediately by the intimacy of their actions. Even the way Basha touched him was familiar.

A battle raged inside her as she spied upon them, struggling with what she would do next. She felt betrayed, betrayed by Basha and her deceit. Ulysseus was a man of honour. He did not deserve a wife so cruel that she would bring her young lover into the home they shared.

Lamia wanted to intrude upon them, but realised it was not her place...and, more importantly, that, even if she disagreed, there was nothing amiss about Basha's actions — at least not according to the customs of Sparta. She backed away, trying to slip out before the couple took notice of her presence, but the slight movement caught their attention, and two pairs of eyes slammed into her, halting her where she stood.

She ignored Zenos, her gaze settling on Basha, her eyes conveying every emotion she felt inside, none stronger than disappointment.

Now that she'd been discovered, Lamia didn't move to apologise or turn to leave. Quite the opposite. She stepped through the low arch into the vestibule, forcing Zenos to mumble a quick goodbye as he made a hasty departure.

"It is not what you are thinking," Basha said as soon as the young *hoplite* disappeared behind Lamia.

"I am listening." Lamia moved closer to Basha, forcing herself to wipe her face of any expression that would betray her. Before she accused her of any wrongdoing, Lamia would hear Basha out.

Shoving a hand through the silky locks of her dark hair, Basha inhaled a sharp, deep breath as she settled down on a nearby stone bench.

"It is no secret that Ulysseus and I have been unable to bear a child, just as it is no secret that it has mostly been me who has been desperate to have one." She stared at her clasped hands as if they held the answers to all her questions, all her problems. "Several moons ago I became so desperate that I convinced myself it would be good for us to take lovers, but Ulysseus was against it—"

"And yet you went ahead anyway, despite his wishes."

Basha's gaze snapped to her face, at the same time that she shot up from the bench. "Do not judge me. You have no idea what it is like for people to whisper behind your back that you are inadequate, that you are less than a woman because you are only *half* Spartan—"

"You are right, I have no idea what that feels like." Lamia stalked towards her, feeding off Basha's anger as her own fury whipped through her.

No, she had no idea what Basha was going through exactly, but that didn't mean she didn't carry around her own set of troubles, her own set of insecurities. No one was without them. Basha was not unique—nor was her situation. As much as Basha didn't want her to judge, it was hard not to, especially when it was clear that her sister within the law had done something that was beneath her dignity, had resorted to actions she knew she would later regret.

"I have no idea what you are going through, but what I do know is that your husband is leaving for war soon and it is unthinkable to me you would invite another man into your bed while he is away just so you can have a baby."

Basha's eyes widened. "I have not invited anyone into my bed—"

"But you've thought of it." She knew she was right when Basha seemed to shrink right before her eyes. "Did you take Zenos as your lover so that you might bear a child?"

"No," Basha sighed. "But I considered it. I did more than that. I came very close, but I could not go through with it." Her words came out on a tortured whisper, her expression one of agony.

Lamia recognised then that Basha was telling the truth. The anguish in Basha's eyes was one of self-loathing, not guilt.

"You have to tell Ulysseus," Lamia said finally.

Basha's eyes rounded. "*No!* It would crush him."

Lamia wanted to say that she should have thought of that before she'd acted, but she bit her tongue, at least on that point. "Don't you think he deserves the truth? Don't you want him to hear it from you, instead of an angry Zenos? Whatever you did to encourage Zenos has nurtured the boy's feelings. I would not be surprised if he reveals the truth out of spiteful jealousy."

Basha flattened her lips into a tight line, the expression on her face acknowledging that Lamia was right, even if she refused to say it.

Lamia let out a loud sigh, brushing aside a single lock of hair that tickled her brow. "I know how stubborn you are, so I know you will refuse me on this, but think about what I have said. If Ulysseus finds out from someone else besides you, it will be that much worse for you both."

* * * *

That eve, as Lamia lay in Thanos' arms, she recalled her words to Basha. She'd judged Basha for not being truthful with Ulysseus, and yet here she was keeping her own secrets from Thanos, secrets that were not as blatant as Basha's but still just as powerfully destructive. As long as she kept them to herself, there was no risk that Thanos would find out. There was no risk that he could be hurt by the truth, but *she* knew the truth, and the guilt of carrying that knowledge around was like a heavy weight upon her heart.

"What is it, *agapetos*? Your entire body is stiff."

She lifted her head from Thanos' chest, a small smile curling her lips as she met his searching gaze. There were many obstacles that stood between them, which left her wondering what their future together held, but there were moments like this, when Thanos guessed her inner turmoil without her ever having to say a word, which made her believe with time that they would come to bridge the distance still separating them.

She dragged in a long, deep breath. Trailing her hand across his jaw, she grazed the pads of her fingertips along the stubble just starting to grow out.

"There was a time when I considered leaving you as soon as the opportunity arose. Planned to go as soon as you rode out of Sparta to war." He tensed beneath her and she stopped tracing the hair along his cheek to meet his blue gaze, which was now clouded, revealing little of his true emotions. He'd wiped his face clean, afraid to show any emotion that would betray him, afraid to reveal that her words had hurt him, even though she knew they had.

"And do you still feel that way? Do you still plan to whisk out of Sparta like a thief and disappear as soon as I am gone?"

"No," she whispered softly.

"Then why are you telling me this?" he asked, his eyes still wary. Some of the tension had begun to ease from him, though not all of it.

"Because I needed to be honest," she confessed. "I had to be truthful with you so that you would understand."

The arms wrapped around her held her almost too tightly as his muscles knotted. "And what am I supposed to understand, *agapetos*?"

"That at one point I wanted to leave and had no intention of looking back, but I cannot do that now, not when you need me."

"But...?"

She smiled weakly, because he knew there was more—he'd heard it in her voice. "But I will never be happy here as long as Atallus lives. I promised myself I would avenge Darius' death and I plan to do that no matter what."

He was quiet, too quiet as he studied her face. "It is dangerous for you to go after Atallus on your own, but I understand your need for revenge and I know if I tell you 'no' that will not stop you—which is why I won't—*but...*" he added, heading her off just when she'd been on the verge of thanking him for understanding how much this meant to her. "I ask you to put your trust in me and let me see to this matter."

She shook her head. This was her fight, her battle for revenge. She couldn't let Thanos risk himself for something that had nothing to do with him, and she said as much.

His eyes darkened as he drew her deeper into his embrace. "And how do you think I feel about you? I cannot allow you to do this alone, no matter how much you wish to. You are my wife now, Lamia, an extension of me, a *part* of me. You shall have your revenge, but you have to trust me. Did I not promise you, if you would but trust me, I would slay every demon for you?" He tightened his arms around her. "Well, I meant it."

She wanted to argue with him, tell him to let her do this on her own, but the expression on his face left no room for any protests.

"I trust you," she finally said quietly, because she did. "So, I will let you see to this in your own way." *For now*, she added silently. She'd given him her love. If she could trust Thanos with her heart, Lamia *knew* she could trust him in this matter. But she was still determined that this was a battle he would not fight for her, which was why she did not argue further. They would never come to an agreement on this.

Besides, with him headed off to war, she wanted Thanos to be secure in the knowledge that she would be there when he returned, that she would not do anything foolish to jeopardise her well-being. He had enough to worry about as it was. She did not wish for him to worry for her as well...so she *would* be there for Thanos when he returned from war, but after...

Despite her words, Lamia knew she would not turn this battle over to him. She'd vowed that Atallus would die by her hands, and she would see to it that he did.

Chapter Nineteen

"I must go."

Those softly spoken words had come five sun risings from the eve when Adonis had revealed to her that Sparta was going to war.

Thanos had whispered them against her ear, just before dawn, and they had pierced her heart like a sharp dagger as she lay there wrapped in the strength of his arms, battling her fear for him.

She'd twisted around in his embrace, reaching for him. They'd moved towards each other in unison, their bodies straining together as they made love, not knowing if they would ever lie in each other's arms again. Lamia had poured all of the love she felt for Thanos into every single touch, every gentle caress, every passionate kiss. When he was away, she wanted him to think of their time together, remember these moments and know that she'd given him pieces of her soul. Because when he was gone and she rested her head against the bed, inhaling the scent of him, imagining the touch of him, she would remember these stolen moments and cherish every single memory of their time together before they'd had to say goodbye.

While she had desperately longed to tell Thanos that she loved him, every time she'd tried, she had choked up. Still, she had not wanted him to depart without a symbol of her love for him.

"What is this?" he'd asked after he'd slipped from their bed to begin donning his armour.

She had stood before him. "I made it for you." Lamia had held out her hand for him to take the gift from her. "I know you have plenty of blades, but I have never seen you with a dagger."

He'd unsheathed the small weapon and stared down at it, his expression full of awe. It was one of her finest designs and she'd made it thinking only of him.

The arrow-tipped blade was forged of bronze and iron, the hilt cast from gold and silver. Two snakes twisted around the length of the hilt, their bodies framing a rare sapphire that was the same unique colour of Thanos' eyes.

He'd been surprised by the gift, but from his pleased expression, she could tell it had touched him. Somewhere deep inside, Lamia knew she was not alone in her feelings. Everything about Thanos hinted at deeper feelings for her. Just remembering the eve he'd told her he would soon leave for war, she recalled how he'd made love to her with such tenderness, such reverence, that she'd felt cherished...*loved.*

Thanos was a man of few words, not one to show his feelings so openly. She now understood Callisto's advice. He would not be quick to such declarations, but she could accept that, because his actions said it all.

"Now I know it is not Spartan or masculine, but a dagger—"

"It is beautiful. Thank you," he'd whispered as he'd pulled her into his arms and kissed her soundly. They'd made love one last time then she'd watched helplessly as he'd dressed for battle.

Later that dawn, thousands of Spartan soldiers marched towards Athens, their metal armour reflecting the blazing sun with blinding flashes of silver. At the head of the army, Thanos had long since passed by her. He'd held her gaze for as long as he could—his eyes strong, confident, reassuring. She hoped her own face had reflected those same emotions, but she could not be sure. She was worried for him.

She sighed as the last of the soldiers filed out of the city.

To let her tell the story, Thanos had practically dragged her kicking and screaming to Sparta...but then he'd given her a new life, full of friendships she'd never had, and a love she'd never thought she'd ever know. Now he was gone—and gods only knew for how long...if not for good. She bit back a strangled sob as she shook her head, forcing the thought from her mind. She could not think such thoughts. She refused to lose another person she loved. She refused to even consider the notion. Thanos was a brilliant soldier. He had to come back to her.

He has to.

"Spartan men are born to be warriors. I know it is difficult, but you must endure this with dignity and strength."

She smiled at the familiar voice from behind her. "Basha," she acknowledged simply.

"It gets easier."

She shook her head. She did not want it to get *easier*. She wanted him to never leave her. "I am sure it does but I find that hard to accept right now."

Basha's face softened. "Spartan soldiers are the best in the world. You must have faith in Thanos and his training."

And she did, but Basha's words would be empty to her until Thanos returned home alive.

When she remained sullen, Basha sighed, linking their arms together.

"Come. Let us return to my home and drink all of Ulysseus' good wine. We will be well and truly drunk by dusk."

Her smile was slight as she let Basha lead her away. She didn't really want to get drunk, but at least it would dull the ache in her heart—even if only for a moment.

* * * *

The Outskirts of Carthage – Meshwesh Lands, 186 BC

The last memory Lamia had of her parents was of her mother singing her to sleep – an ancient Berber lullaby – as she tucked her into bed, while her father smoked a shisha by the fire.

Her younger brother, Umar, had fallen asleep as soon as he'd lain down on the bed mat, but she'd fought against sleep, straining to keep her eyes open as her mother's lovely voice drifted around her.

"Lamia," her mother chided softly. "Close your eyes and go to sleep."

A tiny yawn escaped her lips as she shook her head. "But I am not sleepy. Can you sing to me again?"

Her mother laughed harder, her warm, brown eyes flowing with love as she gently stroked her cheek before once again her beautiful, melodious voice began spinning the tale Lamia loved to listen to just before she floated off to sleep.

She didn't know why she loved the song so much, because it was a sad one. Her mother had once told her it was about the evils of the world, the evils of men who visited their horrors upon the land only when the eve was dark and the moon was high, which was why the moon was always sad, why she refused to sleep.

But at seven annos, Lamia didn't quite understand sadness and horrors – her dawns were filled with the love of her parents, the herding of sheep with her tribe, and playing with Umar, who'd just turned three annos. She didn't grasp what could make the moon sad enough to cry. Lamia would not understand the cruelties of men...not until she awoke later that eve.

That was when the warning sound of the horn came, when the bone-chilling screams of children being slaughtered and women raped singed her ears, the charred stench of burning animal flesh turning her stomach and acrid smoke choking her lungs.

Lamia shot up from her bed mat at the same time that her mother herded her and Umar together.

Terror flashed across her mother's face as her father raced from their small hut. There was panic and chaos all around them, but her mother held them close, her voice soothing when she and her brother began to cry.

From inside their home, she caught a glimpse of the shadow of angry red flames rising from the clearing where her people kept their livestock. She tried to block out the panicked sound of horses neighing as they struggled to escape what was now a fiery pit. The squeal of animals and screams of men and women pierced her ears, and she buried her face deeper into her mother's warm body.

The flap to their home burst open and she glanced up thinking it was her father, but quickly realised she was wrong when soldiers with red tunics and golden armour streamed inside. Everything happened at once—she and Umar were violently torn from her mother's arms as they dragged them outside.

She would never forget her mother's face in that moment, tears streaming down her cheeks as she lunged for them both, calling out their names. After that she would never see her mother again—two soldiers dragged her away, deep into the shadows.

In a way she was grateful they'd taken her mother first so she did not have to witness the death of her son, as Lamia was forced to, right before her eyes. A soldier had simply slit Umar's throat with his dagger and left him there to die. Later she would understand that Umar had been too young to be a useful slave. He was still a baby and needed care, but she was old enough to work, old enough to be useful. But at the time she hadn't known that, she'd thought they would kill her too. So as soon as the soldier who held her relaxed his grip, she snatched her arm away and ran as fast as her legs would carry her.

He shouted after her, and for a few moments she heard his footsteps as he raced behind her, but something distracted him from her or someone called his name. She never knew what it was that caused him to stop, because not once did she look back.

Yet, even though she'd never looked back, the events that eve, the things she'd witnessed, would forever remain tattooed upon her mind and buried deep in her heart. Caught by surprise, most of the men fought bravely, but they were no match for the Roman army who easily struck them down, while terrified children rushed for safety only to be chased down and trampled beneath the hooves of soldiers' horses.

The women fared no better. Many were slain as they huddled over their children, trying to shield them from danger, while others were simply raped in the midst of the violent turmoil.

The last sound Lamia heard as she ran away, fleeing towards the fire lights of the city of Carthage, was the wail of a horn. The piercing sound reverberating off her ears caught her unawares, causing her to stumble. The sound came again. It was her tribe's warning horn, telling her people that there was danger, that they were under attack.

But it had come far too late.

* * * *

The Outskirts of Athens – The Port of Piraeus

Situated on the Saronic Gulf, about ten kilometres south of the main city of Athens, was the Port of Piraeus – the only gateway to Athens from the sea.

Thanos and his army of six thousand men were camped along the sandy banks of the port with over one hundred Theban warships dotting the choppy blue waters of the gulf. With the nearly eight thousand men from Athens, the combined Greek forces boasted more than twenty thousand soldiers. The rival hegemony of the Greek peninsula had united for a single purpose and that was to protect their homeland from the ambitious Romans.

The sound of hushed footsteps captured his attention and Thanos turned his pensive gaze away from the murky waters of the gulf. Adonis strode towards him, hopefully returning with the information he'd sent him off to Athens to gather.

"What did you learn?" he asked as soon as the young *hoplite* halted before him.

"Not much." A dark grimace marred his handsome face. "Spies report seeing around seventy ships in the Adriatic, but we already knew that. And the numbers are not consistent. One moment it is seventy, the next it's nearly two hundred."

Thanos frowned at the sudden tingling of his skin, unease crawling along his flesh like the slithering of a serpent. Something was amiss.

"The Romans should have made it into the Ionian by now."

"I know," agreed Adonis.

"I need you to return to Athens," he said firmly. "And I need you to stay there for four sun risings and work on gathering information. I want you to remain in the city long enough to gather as much information as possible, but come back immediately if you learn something that is vital. While you are there, also speak with Atallus. He may have more accurate accounts from more reliable sources."

Adonis nodded. "Yes, General." The young *hoplite* then spun on his heels to make the journey back to the city as commanded.

Thanos sighed as he watched Adonis disappear from sight. He absently traced the subtle imprint of the sheathed dagger he kept strapped against his chest beneath his *chamlys* – across his heart. He never thought he would envy Cleomenes, but for the first time in his life he wished he were back in Sparta and not on the battlefield. He'd been away from Lamia for little over a full moon and he missed her. He'd received one letter by messenger and from her account all was well in Sparta. The council was still furious with him and Cleomenes, but they had done nothing formally to demonstrate their anger, which he was relieved to hear. He did not relish the thought of fighting one war only to return home to fight another.

He let out another ragged breath, his gaze trained on the churning waters of the gulf, imagining that his emotions jostled about inside him much like the furious waves before him. He missed Lamia every waking moment and every restless eve. He loved her and even now wanted to be home with her, but he cursed himself for not giving voice to any of those feelings before he'd left. And now he couldn't. Now he had little time to do anything but train his soldiers, gather information and strategise for the battle that lay ahead.

He couldn't afford to succumb to thoughts of Lamia and he hated that he had to force himself *not* to think of her. In all his *annos*, he had never once put anyone or anything above his duty to Sparta as its king and military leader, but that was all before he'd met Lamia.

* * * *

Lamia burst into Cleomenes' courtyard, her entire body vibrating with fury.

"Did you see this?" She shook her fist in the air that held the crumpled parchment.

Cleomenes shot her a grim look as he stood to cross the distance between them. "I just received it—"

"They cannot do this. My husband is away fighting a war for *them*. To protect *them*. They cannot charge him with treason."

"And they won't." Cleomenes' handsome face was stern, his voice ringing with quiet authority, and she understood why, when he spoke, others instantly stood at attention. "That is just the council's futile attempt to get back at us, but they do not have the law to stand on."

She relaxed—somewhat—with Cleomenes' firm words. She'd been livid when she'd received a decree from the *gerousia* charging Thanos with tyranny and treason for taking Spartan troops to Athens. Cleomenes had also been charged and they both were now set to stand trial before the council within a fortnight. She thought it pathetic that they would try to charge and convict Thanos when he wasn't even present to defend himself. The cowards.

"I have to write to Thanos about this at once," she told Cleomenes. "He needs to know what they are plotting."

Cleomenes nodded and a tight smile pulled at the corners of his mouth. "He will know immediately that this is nothing but pomp, but I agree he should be kept abreast of the grumblings of the council. In the meantime, prepare yourself to stand before the *gerousia* in his absence."

She pursed her lips into a deep frown. She had no time for such nonsense but she did not argue. She knew that it was her duty and she'd promised Thanos she would be his eyes and ears while he was gone.

"I will, Cleomenes." She nodded, assuring him that she would stand in her husband's stead.

Their discussion soon turned to other matters and they made idle talk for a short while before she bade him farewell and headed for home.

She walked along the stone pathway, enjoying the balmy air that swept across the plain from Lakonikos Bay. The festival to honour the goddess Hera had heralded the beginning of summer in Sparta. The air was warm and clammy, so whenever the bay chose to send a breeze, she welcomed the cool air.

The homes of the two kings lay on opposite ends of the city, but despite the stifling heat she'd chosen to walk the distance, needing the time alone and the exercise.

With the sun now sweltering, Lamia decided she would stop to visit Basha and then continue her journey when it was closer to dusk and the city was cooler. She also had no desire to return to an empty home. With Armine at the *agoge* until dusk and Thanos gone, her home was eerily silent most of the dawn. She still had her work, but it had slowed some since the departure of the army. She smiled to herself. Despite all the ribbing she'd received, her designs were quite popular among a number of *hoplites* and now her most loyal patrons were away.

She turned down the street towards Basha's, her thoughts straying to Thanos. She wondered how he was faring. She knew her message had arrived with him and as soon as she was home she would send off another about the ridiculous actions of the council.

Lamia bit down on her cheek to keep the curse from forming as she thought of the stuffy old men who had nothing better to do than wreak havoc in Sparta because their egos had been wounded.

As if she could cast the thought from her mind, she shook her head. She refused to dwell on the actions of the *gerousia*. Like Thanos, she was not a politician. That was Cleomenes' job and she would let him do it.

Lamia neared Basha's home, looking forward to her visit, when a chill slithered down her spine and she stopped. She narrowed her gaze as she spun around, searching in all directions. Ever since Thanos had departed for Athens, she'd had the uneasy feeling that she was being stalked, but she'd pushed it aside, thinking it her own imagination, the result of her longing for Thanos. Now she wasn't so sure. She glanced around again, but saw nothing except streets full of Spartans hurrying to get inside their dwellings and out of the heat, just like her. She turned back around and quickened her pace, wondering if missing Thanos was driving her mad.

* * * *

Lamia knew something was wrong as soon as she stepped through the columns of Basha's home. She wandered into the courtyard, softly calling out Basha's name, when a shrill cry pierced her ears.

Rushing in the direction from which the harsh sound had come, she ran into the inner courtyard, nearly bowling over a young *helot* girl who stood there frozen in shock. Lamia glanced over the girl's shoulder, her heart tripping when she glimpsed Basha lying prostrate on the ground.

She turned to the girl, seized her shoulders and shook her hard.

"Send for a physician immediately. Say that it is an urgent matter concerning the king's sister within the law."

The girl nodded, quickly setting off.

Lamia rushed over to Basha and dropped to her knees, her hands brushing across her forehead.

She was warm—too warm. Lamia dipped her head just above Basha's face, her gaze fixed on her chest. Relief flooded her when Basha's faint breaths tickled her cheek to the rhythm of her chest rising and falling. Lamia relaxed, wagering that Basha had probably fainted from the intensity of the heat.

She looked up from Basha and searched the courtyard until her gaze landed on the small fountain in the centre. Tearing at her garments, she hurried to the fountain, plunged the cloth into the water and ran back to Basha's side. With gentle hands, she brushed the cool cloth against Basha's face, her neck, her shoulders — across every bit of skin that was exposed.

A smile eased across her face when Basha began to stir, but she pressed her hand firmly against her shoulder to keep her from sitting up.

"Do not move, do not try to speak." Lamia insisted. "The physician will be here shortly."

Almost as soon as she'd said the words, the *helot* girl barrelled inside with the midwife on her heels.

As if reading her confusion, the girl blurted out, "I could not find the physician so I asked her to come."

Lamia nodded. "You did well." She stood and pulled the girl aside again, instructing her to now find Callisto.

In the meantime, Lamia waited, silently watching while the midwife attended to Basha.

* * * *

Later that eve, Lamia sat on the edge of the bed, with Callisto in a chair behind her, as Basha began to stir awake. She'd floated in and out of consciousness for most of the eve. The midwife had said that was normal for a woman in her condition.

Before she'd left, she'd instructed Lamia to make sure Basha imbibed plenty of fluids, food, and some putrid herbs she'd left for her to drink as a tea. At Lamia's prodding, the midwife had agreed to return at dawn, although she'd sworn it really wasn't necessary. She was certain Basha would be fine by then. At the time, Lamia hadn't been convinced, but now, as she watched the colour return to Basha's cheeks, she began to relax.

When Lamia was certain that Basha was fully awake, she reached for a cup of water and lifted it to her lips, holding it there until the contents were gone.

"Are you hungry?"

"A little," she said quietly.

Lamia glanced over her shoulder to Callisto, who handed her a platter full of dates, bread and goat cheese, which she passed on to Basha.

"I know what you are going to say," Basha said after swallowing a mouthful of food.

Only then did Lamia realise that she must have been frowning, her expression as anxious as she felt.

"I am sorry. I never meant to frighten you."

"You have to take better care of yourself, Basha. The midwife said you fainted because of the heat and lack of food. What were you thinking? Do you not want this child?"

Basha's face paled, and Lamia experienced a twinge of guilt for frightening her. That had not been her intent, but hopefully the gentle reprimand would force Basha to take better care of herself.

"Of course I do. I just became so busy with orders for my pottery that I forgot to stop for a meal—"

"Well, you will just have to work harder to remember or else you will have a difficult time," she spoke quietly, voicing the concerns of the midwife.

Basha nodded. "I know."

Having suffered two miscarriages over the past three *annos*, Basha had never carried this long before. If the midwife was to be believed, Basha had passed one of the early hurdles.

"I have just been so busy that I did not even realise what was happening until just a few dawns ago."

Lamia figured that had been the case. The festival of Hera was a huge celebration and Basha's pottery designs, with their matronly depictions of the goddess, had been in high demand for the past several moons leading up to the festival. Lamia wagered she'd probably gone for several moons without realising she was with child.

"Do you plan to send word to Ulysseus?"

Basha sighed. "I haven't decided. I do not wish to disappoint him if..."

Her voice trailed off and Lamia reached out to clasp Basha's hand when she saw tears shimmer in her silver eyes.

"It is going to be all right," Lamia said soothingly, not wishing to upset her further. "Rest now. It will be all right."

Basha seemed to accept her words because she relaxed against the bed and once again succumbed to sleep.

As soon as she heard the sound of Basha's even breathing, she glanced over her shoulder to meet Callisto's gaze, finding her worry mirrored in her expression.

They both knew it was more than just Basha's fear of losing this child that kept her from telling Ulysseus. At the very mention of Ulysseus' name there had been genuine alarm in Basha's eyes, and it had not gone unnoticed by Callisto either. They were both aware of her desperation to have a child. She just hoped Basha had not done something so desperate, so foolish that Ulysseus would never be able to forgive her.

Chapter Twenty

Adonis returned the eve of the second dawn, his feet stirring up sand as he raced towards their camp.

Thanos, who'd been hunched over in the sand, outlining a number of strategies with Ulysseus and his commanders under him, shifted to his feet when he caught sight of Adonis.

It wasn't until the young *hoplite* drew closer and Thanos glimpsed his anxious expression that he knew whatever news Adonis brought with him did not bode well for him and his men.

"What is it?" Thanos demanded as soon as Adonis stood before him.

"You told me to return if I learned something vital. Well, as you commanded, I sought out the governor, but with no success. I looked for Atallus everywhere, General, but he is gone. His home is empty, his servants haven't seen him in several moons, not since around the time you were last here, they said."

Thanos froze, the meaning of Adonis' words chilling his blood. He'd received the summons for aid from Atallus and it had come from Athens...but, if his servants were to be believed, Atallus hadn't been in Athens for almost six moons...

"Adonis, I have one last task for you. I need you to go at once and ask Euripydes, the Admiral of the Theban navy, one thing—who issued the directive for them to assemble?"

Adonis wasted no time in carrying out Thanos' order.

Thanos was restless as he waited for Adonis to return. He had a gnawing feeling in his gut that Atallus had deceived them all, and when Adonis returned with an answer, Thanos discovered his instincts were right.

It was a trap.

* * * *

The eve before Lamia was to go before the *gerousia*, she was awakened from her sleep by the harsh sound of blaring horns.

Warning horns.

It took her a moment to stir because she thought she was dreaming—recounting that night so long ago when the Romans had come and destroyed all she'd ever known, all she'd ever loved...

The horn sounded again, forcing her fully awake.

This was no dream.

Her eyelids snapped open as she shot up from the couch at the foot of Basha's bed, where she'd fallen asleep. She stumbled, nearly tripping over Callisto, who'd passed out on the floor after overindulging in too much wine. Basha and Callisto had been trying to 'help' her prepare for her meeting with the council by plying her with spirits. Lamia had resisted most of the drink—but not Callisto, who now emitted a series of ear-singing curses as she swayed to her feet.

The only one of them who'd not indulged in wine, Basha reacted quickly. Rushing over to the window, her gaze searched through the dark eve sky.

"What is happening?" Lamia demanded.

Basha spun away from the window, her eyes darkening with alarm. "Sparta is under attack."

"What?" Lamia pushed past her to catch a glimpse outside, and the sight before her made her blood run cold. What seemed like hundreds of burning torches were moving steadily from the Taygetus in the west towards the valley that held the city of Sparta.

The Romans had never planned to attack Athens. It was Sparta they were after.

Spinning away from the window, she raced from Basha's chambers to the vestibule where Ulysseus kept his weapons. She wished she were at home to gather her swords that were familiar to her, but she didn't have time to go back.

She reached for a hunter's bow and arrows, shrugging the harness and case over her head. She then fastened a heavy straight sword at her waist and grabbed one of Ulysseus' shields.

From the corner of her eye she saw Callisto pull down a straight bow and a case full of arrows, along with a short sword. But when Basha moved to follow suit, she blocked her path.

"What are you doing?"

Basha's grey eyes turned molten silver as they flashed with impatience.

"I am getting weapons so that I can help defend my city, same as you."

"No, you're not—"

"Yes. I. Am," Basha gritted out impatiently.

Much like the first time they'd met, they locked angry gazes, neither one backing down. Lamia was not cowed — she simply worried how she was going to stop a woman with child if she could not touch her.

"We have no time for this," Callisto snapped, and Lamia nearly jumped out of her skin at the gruff edge to her friend's normally melodic voice.

"Basha, you are with child, and, unlike Lamia, I have no qualms about wrestling you to this ground to keep you here."

Lamia nearly choked on the laughter lodged in her throat when Basha's eyes widened and she stared down at Callisto as if she'd never seen her before. Lamia empathised with Basha wholeheartedly.

"If you want to help, go to Lamia's home, get Armine and find somewhere safe to hide."

Basha seemed to want to protest, but Callisto's fierce expression must have been enough of a warning.

Instead of arguing, Basha nodded stiffly and led the way out of her home.

As Lamia trailed behind both women, she actually felt pity for Basha. If Callisto had looked at her the way she'd just looked at Basha, Lamia would have been out the door and on her way to do whatever the little Spartan had commanded.

She'd never glimpsed that side of Callisto, and, as much as she admired Callisto's backbone in standing up to Basha, Lamia decided then that she would do whatever she could to make sure she never did again.

* * * *

Ten layers of the Spartan *phalanx* separated Sparta from its invaders, their iron shields reflecting the firelight from the torches of the advancing Roman army.

Joined by hundreds of male *helots*, every able-bodied Spartan woman stood high above the battlefield upon one of the many hills that made up Sparta. Together, Cleomenes and Lamia had chosen this position because it would allow the women and slaves to mount an attack, while remaining out of harm's way.

Lamia scanned the horizon, assessing the Roman forces. Much like the Spartan *phalanx*, the Roman legionnaires marched in the precise formation of the *tetsudo*, a name they'd earned because the protective formation was as impenetrable as the shell of a tortoise. They held their javelins in their hands, with their rectangular shields bearing the Roman seal fixed firmly in front of them, their footsteps steady as they descended the mountain.

As it stood, the Spartan army was grossly outnumbered. Still, from what she knew of the impressive size of the Roman army, they'd barely sent a quarter of their troops. This wasn't an invasion, she surmised. This was a weakening. They would take down Sparta with as few casualties as possible then send reinforcements to sweep through the rest of Greece. And, if they didn't succeed this time, they would keep sending soldiers until they did. Sparta was the key to securing Greece and everyone knew it.

She turned to signal the *helots* to load the bellies of the three catapults with the large stones weighing at least one hundred and fifty kilograms. Only in Sparta were catapults and artillery already assembled and ready to use. But then, war was their way of life.

She glanced over at the women who stood spread out across the hill, their bows at their sides. They all waited for Cleomenes' signal from below. When the

Romans were in range they would release the winches that held the catapults secure, sending massive stones smashing into their formation, breaking it apart so that the Spartan archers could pick them off. And when the catapults and arrows could no longer stop the advancing legionnaires, the Spartan army, the only barrier that stood between the city and the Romans, would advance to meet them.

She sent up a silent plea to the gods, praying for a miracle. The odds were against them. She could only hope that their plan would work.

* * * *

Thanos did not hesitate in withdrawing his army when Adonis reported back to him that Euripydes had received the directive to assemble from Thanos himself. He'd never issued any such directive, but he knew who had. *Atallus.* Atallus had been the one to forge his signature and his seal.

Somehow the governor had got into the pocket of the Romans and made sure that the two strongest militaries in Greece — the Spartans and the Thebans — were weakened by dividing their numbers between defending Athens and their own city-states.

He suspected that the Romans had planned to enter Greece through Sparta, move on to Thebes, and when the combined Greek armies finally received word of the invasion they would have had no choice but to move south along the peninsula to meet the Romans, leaving Athens vulnerable to an attack from the sea. He had to admire the brilliance of the plan, but it had taken treachery to execute, and, unfortunately for the Romans, they'd caught on to their ruse just in time. The Spartans and Thebans would return to their states and the Athenian navy and army would await any sign of the Romans.

The battle-ready Spartans made the journey home in four dawns, stopping only to rest their horses. They could not afford to eat or sleep. Every second wasted was a second the Romans got closer to Sparta.

It was almost midday when Thanos and his soldiers crossed over the Parnon from the east. Although he'd pressed his soldiers to make the journey at a punishing pace, he knew that the Romans had made it to Sparta before him and his men, so he had no idea what to expect when he rode over the mountains.

Chaos greeted him as hundreds of tiny fires burned across the landscape where catapults had sent their fiery stones hurling across the wide expanse to crush the Roman defences.

The soldier in him quickly assessed the casualties and he was relieved to see that the *phalanx* wall was holding with seven layers still intact, but he knew it could not hold forever with the steady barrage of Roman soldiers slowly wearing down the outer layers.

Nudging Zeus forward, he unsheathed his sword, released the Spartan war cry and led his soldiers across the plain to defend their city.

* * * *

Lamia pulled back the string of her bow and released another spray of arrows. She followed them with her eyes as two hit their mark, but the rest bounced off heavy metal shields. She was exhausted, her arms ached and all she wanted to do was curl up under a blanket and sleep, but she pushed her weariness aside.

Thanos had sent a messenger ahead of him and his army — *they were coming*. When she'd received the news at dawn, hope had flooded her, renewing her strength. All they had to do was hold the city until Thanos returned with his army.

Reaching down, she scrambled to gather another handful of arrows when she heard the wail of a horn in the distance. She shot to her feet, squinting against the midday rays as she stared across the battlefield.

The moment she saw him, her heart did a quick little flutter.

Dressed in his full armour, he rode astride Zeus, the white stallion standing out among the other warhorses. Much like the dawn they'd first met, she could not see his face with his helmet firmly in place, but, even had she not caught a glimpse of the scarlet crest, she would have known instantly that it was him. He rode with a steady confidence that called out to her, and, even if she'd closed her eyes, she still would have known that he was near.

Thanos.

She spun around to signal the archers and the *helots* manning the catapults to stop. They could not risk striking down the advancing men who, as she spoke, were caging in the Romans.

Relief rushed through her as the now vastly outnumbered Romans scrambled to push back the Spartans from both sides. As the dawn passed and the battle raged before her, Lamia realised that the Romans faced imminent defeat as Thanos and his *hoplites* slashed through their crumbling formation.

By dusk, the invaders were left with only two choices — surrender and live, or fight to the death.

Chapter Twenty-One

Captain Marcus Aurelius crept along the craggy rocks of the stoned path towards the centre of Sparta, already knowing that this plan was a mistake. General Scipio had ordered him to move a small band of two dozen soldiers along the southern trail into Sparta. Although the enemy spies had caught sight of their movement, Scipio believed the Spartan army would be far too busy defending the outskirts of the city to have time to react and flush out his men, whose main goal was to disable the catapults that were severely weakening the Roman troops then quickly return to their formation.

He knew Scipio hadn't expected such staunch resistance from the Greeks, but he thought it foolish on the older general's part to have underestimated the formidable Spartans. *His* foolishness was why Marcus was now being ordered to undertake an equally imprudent mission that he sensed would only end in disaster.

With stealthy steps he crept through the deserted and darkened city towards his destination until it was in sight. Three catapults sat atop a hill, along with hundreds of male slaves...and *women*. He grimaced. Scipio had not mentioned women. Marcus had strict principles when it came to killing women and children — he would not do it. He was a soldier, not a murderer, and killing innocent women and children was murder to him.

He turned to his men. "Our orders are to destroy the catapults but there are women up there so we will be quick about this. I do not want any innocent casualties, understood?"

"But, Captain, they're armed. Besides, they're *Spartan* women," a soldier spat out, his voice ringing with insolence.

Cornelius.

He'd never liked Cornelius — he was lazy and lacked discipline, and there was a sinister air that surrounded the younger man that had always unsettled him.

Marcus tamped down his rising temper so he did not succumb to the burning desire to smash his fist into the soldier's jaw. He did not wish to delay this task any longer than need be — and a fight between him and Cornelius promised just that.

"I do not care who they are, or that they're armed," he said sharply, his pointed gaze fixing on Cornelius. "If we cannot disarm them using brute force and our bare hands then we will retreat. Understood?"

"Yes, Sir," his men responded, all except Cornelius. His beady eyes were hard and cruel with blood lust, and Marcus swore that he felt his blood freeze as the air around him grew cold and ominous.

* * * *

The sun was waning in the sky, dusk giving way to a humid eve, as Lamia stood with the other women and *helots*, her attention riveted on the battle below. Never once did her eyes stray from the lone soldier atop a white stallion. Every time he lifted his sword to deflect an attack her breath hitched in her chest. She longed to be down there with him, not standing up here helpless and simply watching, but she knew Cleomenes would never allow her past the *phalanx* that stood like an impenetrable fortress before the imaginary gates of Sparta.

Cheers rang out as they watched Thanos' forces push the Romans deeper into the *phalanx* at their backs. Their Roman leader had yet to sound the horn and wave the white banner of surrender, so the Spartans pressed on. She had to admit that she was impressed by the fortitude of the Romans, but she knew the battle would be over by the time the pale silver moon shimmered in the black sky. And, from the looks of it, there wouldn't be many prisoners— most of the invading soldiers would be dead.

She was so engrossed in the battle before her that it took her a moment to notice the flickering flames of gold. She whipped her head around, her long braid flying over her shoulder, to watch in horror as seemingly dozens of soldiers scrambled about, setting torches to all three of the catapults.

"*Romans!*" she shouted at the same time that she lifted her bow, sending a stream of arrows hurling across the distance to catch four soldiers unawares. Cries of pain pierced her ears as they clutched at the long wooden darts now protruding from their flesh.

She reached for four more arrows to arm her bow, but then everything seemed to happen at once as they sent back their own fire and a whir of arrows buzzed around her head. She ducked and dodged flying arrows, desperately trying to grasp her shield, which lay at her feet, but she wasn't fast enough.

She heard her name at the same time a knot of pain exploded in her side.

With a sharp gasp, she dropped to her knees, curling her hand around the thin arrow.

"Do not pull it out. Do not move," Callisto barked as she helped her to the ground, laying her flat on her back. Fear flashed in the jade-coloured eyes of her friend, before she saw her push it away, replacing it with steely determination. It was a look Lamia wasn't used to seeing on Callisto's face, but one she'd grown accustomed to since the attack on Sparta.

She heard a deep male voice call out "*Retreat!*" and for a moment she thought it was Thanos, but then she found it difficult to form even the tiniest thought when a sharp pang ripped through her and more blood leaked from her wound.

"Go, Callisto. Push back the Romans. I will be fine."

She shook her head vehemently. "No."

If she'd had the strength she would have pushed her, but she didn't. She opened her mouth to *command* her to leave, but, before she could, a dark shadow fell across them. Terror filled her when a Roman soldier with sinister eyes lifted his sword high above her friend's back.

"Callisto, move!"

"*Cornelius, no!*" shouted that voice again, so much like Thanos', then she watched as, almost in slow motion, the soldier's eyes widened, his sword falling from his hand, and thick rivulets of blood gurgled from his mouth. Moments later he slumped over and collapsed to the ground.

Callisto whirled her head around at the same time that a handsome Roman soldier came into view, his piercing blue eyes filled with concern.

"Are you all right?"

She wanted to shout, *'Do I look all right?'* but the Roman's eyes were not on her.

His gaze was riveted upon Callisto as hers was upon him.

Her friend nodded slowly. "Thank you." And then she felt like an intruder when an invisible current of awareness arced between them. She felt it so she knew they must have as well. She wanted to shake them both and yell, *'Hello, I'm dying here!'*, but she didn't have the strength.

All of a sudden raucous shouts vibrated from around her and she struggled to make out the words. She swore she heard *'The king is coming'*. But that was impossible. Thanos had been on the battlefield only moments ago. She wondered why Cleomenes had moved his soldiers to the hill. Just before she'd fallen, they'd doused the fire from two of the catapults and were successfully pushing back the Romans. They didn't need reinforcements.

Callisto gasped at something over her shoulder at the same time that the Roman's eyes grew wide and he backed away from her, shouting *"Retreat!"* once again. He disappeared from her sight and, when Callisto stepped away from her, she finally understood why the Roman had been in such a hurry to leave.

* * * *

Thanos and his men had backed the Romans so tightly against Cleomenes' forces that it would be a blood bath if they continued, but that was their choice. Scipio had stubbornly refused to surrender, so Thanos was left with no other option but to completely destroy the Roman army. He almost admired the general, because, if the roles had been reversed, every Spartan would have died before they'd surrendered.

Still, he hoped that it didn't come to that, which was why he planned to crush the spirit of the Romans so brutally that the foot soldiers would simply give up, despite the word of their leader.

He urged Zeus forward to take up arms once again but halted his mount at the sight of angry red flames flickering against the black horizon along the hill above Pylos.

Anger knotted his belly. Somehow the Romans had managed to circumvent the *phalanx* to enter the city, probably through the tunnels just beneath the ground.

Narrowing his eyes, he scanned the distance. A little more than twenty soldiers stood on the hill battling the women and *helots*, who were succeeding in defending their position as they quickly doused the flames from the catapults.

His gaze snapped to Lamia, her long mane twisted into a braid that flopped against her back as she led the charge. Pride washed over him and he curled his lips into a small smile. He'd caught sight of her when he'd first ridden onto the battlefield and his gaze had periodically strayed to her, just to assure himself she remained unharmed.

Warmth settled around his heart as he watched her. He could not have asked for a better wife or queen to stand by his side. She was fearless, her bravery unmatched by any other woman he'd ever known.

He was just about to turn away from her, to rejoin the battle, when something he'd never felt before gripped him. He watched helplessly as a single arrow careened through the sky to lodge itself deep in her body.

"Lamia, no!"

Digging his heels into Zeus' flanks, he charged forward. The icy fingers of fear clenched tighter around his heart with each passing moment as he raced towards the hill, spurring his mount to go faster.

In all his *annos*, he'd never done this. He'd never broken formation, never once left the battlefield. He hadn't even stopped to transfer command to his second, Ulysseus, or even to Adonis who'd been close by. All thoughts of the Romans and the battle vanished from his head as he raced towards the city. None of it mattered. All he could think of was Lamia. That he loved her. That she was the most important person in his entire world and he'd not once told her this.

"Out of my way!" he called out before he reached the *phalanx*. The men were stunned to see their king charging forward, but they did as he commanded.

The six remaining layers all parted for him, immediately closing once again as soon as he'd passed through.

Zeus' hooves clapped along the cobbled streets as he navigated his way through the city until he reached the base of the hill.

"Up, Zeus," he commanded, pushing his treasured warhorse, who'd been with him since he was a colt, up the steep hill.

Zeus trudged forward, climbing steadily until they reached the top. He'd barely reined in Zeus to a stop before he leapt to the ground, ripped off his helmet and raced towards Lamia where she lay prostrate on the soft grass.

Nudging Callisto aside, he cupped the back of Lamia's head and pressed his hand against her bleeding wound. Her garments were stained red, and the angry circle had spread across her entire middle.

A cold sweat trickled down his forehead as fear gnawed at him. "Get a physician," he barked out as he held her. He'd seen enough wounds to know she needed to be attended to soon.

"Lamia." He called her name softly, stroking her warm brow, pushing back the tiny wisps of hair that had broken free from her braid.

"Thanos," she said breathlessly, a small smile lifting her lips.

"Shhh, do not speak. It will be all right," he said quietly, his voice cajoling as if she were a child. He ran his hand down her face to cup her chin. "I love you," he whispered, the words that had been locked inside him for so long tumbling forth effortlessly.

He *loved* her.

She tried to smile again, but this time the pain must have made it more difficult and her eyes watered. "I love you too, Thanos. My Spartan," she said weakly, and then it was as if his entire world stopped as he watched her lashes flutter shut and her body still.

* * * *

Ulysseus saw her as soon as his horse climbed over the ridge to his home. She stood there, her eyes anxious, although she did her best to hide her fear behind a brave mask.

Her face lit up as soon she saw him, and he urged his stallion forward until she was standing below him. Dropping down from his mount he dragged her into his arms, holding her close.

She clung to him, the warmth of her body seeping through his armour to heat his skin. He buried his face in her neck, inhaling her scent, which reminded him of wildflowers in springtime. He didn't want to let her go, not after so many moons spent without her, dreaming of her, hoping the last vision of her would not be one from his dreams that he carried with him to the Underworld.

"Ulysseus." Her touch was tender against his hair-roughened face, bringing him back to the present, reminding him that he was still very much alive.

He dipped his head to taste her lips. The kiss was gentle, just enough to tide him over until later when he'd explore her body more fully in the privacy of their bedchamber. Dragging his mouth from hers, he tucked her small hand in his and without a word they walked inside their home.

Ulysseus needed to visit the baths and cleanse himself before coming to her, but she gripped his hand tight, leading them towards their bedchamber, one of only two rooms in their home with a door. This was where they went when they needed complete privacy from the *helots* in their household.

He ushered her into the room before him and closed the door. Dawn was on the horizon, and tiny rays of shimmering gold streamed through the window, bathing their bed in their russet glow, fanning out behind Basha, casting her in their ethereal radiance. She looked like a goddess before him, her gauzy *chiton* almost completely sheer, which was why he soon noticed the changes in her.

They were subtle. Her breasts were fuller, her hips rounder, and there was just a gentle swell to her belly, but even with the slight changes, he *knew*. And it destroyed him.

He stilled, the pain of her betrayal threatening to buckle his knees. Ulysseus stood there completely helpless against the anguish that seared him, burning through his belly until it consumed his heart.

"Ulysseus—"

She took a step towards him, her hand outstretched, but when he drew away from her, pressing his back to the door, she stopped, letting her hand fall to her side.

It was as if a fist had closed around his heart and he felt as if he would die from the pain. He couldn't breathe—every single breath was painful, agonising. The air in the room had disappeared and now he was suffocating.

He'd known this dawn would come. He'd seen the signs, but he'd hoped he would be wrong. He'd convinced himself they were past this, and when she'd told him she loved him, he'd believed her, which was why he'd been certain she would not do what he'd asked her not to do, what he'd made her promise not to do.

"Ulysseus, let me explain—"

"What is there to explain, Basha? I asked you not to take another man into our bed, inside your body." His entire body shook as his voice climbed and he realised he was shouting, but he could not control himself long enough to temper his voice. "I asked you not to give another man what was mine, but you did not care. You claim you love me, but you don't. The only person you love is yourself."

"That is not t—"

"True?" A bitter laugh escaped his lips and he shook his head. To think he'd loved her since he was a young man, had spent his entire life trying to please her, trying to make her happy, but it had never been enough. Basha needed perfection. Driven by her own insecurities, she could not accept anything less.

"What is not true? That you took a lover? I know you made love with Zenos." He ignored her shocked gasp as he advanced forward, coming to a stop before her. "I saw you enter the baths with him, and I waited there for an hour until you both left."

She shook her head and opened her mouth to speak, but he didn't give her the chance. He didn't need to hear lies from her lips when he had eyes.

He had endured physical pain beyond what a normal man could stand and still live, and yet the pain of seeing his wife with another man, knowing she was a liar, had nearly killed him.

"I gave you many opportunities to tell me the truth, but you lied to me, to my face. Every time I asked you if you needed to discuss something, you said there was nothing to tell. Even when we stopped making love, you did not feel compelled to tell me the truth. Why do you think I would not touch you for so many moons? I knew if you would lie about taking a lover that you would not hesitate to get with child, then try to pass it off as mine and then lie about that too."

Tears spilled over her lids to stream down her face, which sent a jolt of lightning shooting through his entire body, and he stood there, completely frozen. Basha never cried. Never once had she shed a tear, not even after her miscarriages. His wife did not cry, she did not admit weakness, she did not show any emotion that would leave her open to attacks that she was not Spartan enough, not strong enough, not good enough.

"Are you done, Ulysseus?"

He narrowed his gaze at the almost imperious tone of her voice, as if he was the one who now carried another man's child, and not she.

"Because if you are done then maybe you will hear me when I say that I have never *once* taken a lover — *No!*" she said with the vehement shake of her head when he opened his mouth to deny what was an obvious lie. "You spoke, so now it is my turn. Zenos is a bit taken with me, and I used his obvious crush to draw him to me, but I have never once been intimate with him, not even so much as a kiss. Now, I will not deny that I went to the baths that day to do just as you believed, just as I will not pretend that I did not consider taking a lover, but I never went through with it, and the hour we spent at the baths... Well, we ended up bathing, *separately*, in the designated chambers for men and women. And yes, we came and left together, but that was all."

He snorted. "You expect me to believe that? Your obsession with having a child was so all-consuming that it became almost frightening. You once accused me of not wanting to talk to you about this matter, that I did not care as strongly as you did about having a child, but that was simply not true. It was your apparent lack of regard for me and my desires that I could not stomach. It was *you* who decided we should take lovers, it was *you* who thought this was for the best, but not once did you ask me how I felt. Not once did you even think to discuss this matter with *me*, your *husband*. "

"I was only trying to offer a solution that I thought was best," she said through her tears.

"That *you* thought was best. Not us. *You*."

His quiet words seemed to find purchase somewhere deep inside her and a fresh wave of tears poured from her eyes. He wanted to reach out and drag her into his arms, quiet the storm raging in her gaze, ease the pain etched across her face, but he couldn't. Maybe later, maybe when he'd calmed down, but in that moment all he could think of was that he loved a woman who was so selfish, so self-centred, that she would openly disregard his feelings.

"I am sorry, Ulysseus. Everything I've done, I've done for you, wanting to be the best wife for you —"

"Why can you not see? I never wanted you to be the *best* wife, the perfect wife. I simply wanted you to be you."

She nodded slowly, her voice so soft that he could barely hear it when she said, "I know that now. I began to realise that while you were gone."

She stepped towards him, but, just as before, he moved away from her, until she stopped. He could see the pain his withdrawal caused her, but he could not stomach the thought of her touching him. The closer she got, the harder it was to ignore the physical evidence that she was with child, that she'd lain with another man.

"I also realised I made a lot of mistakes," she continued. "But I swear to you that I do love you, Ulysseus. If you would just give us a chance, I know we could start over —"

"Whose child is it?" he blurted out abruptly. That was the question that had been burning in the back of his mind. If not Zenos, then who was it who had made love to his wife, who had given her the son or daughter that should have rightfully been his to give her?

She blinked as if she didn't understand the language he spoke before she said slowly, "Ulysseus, I told you I did not take a lover —"

"Truly, Basha, just tell me the truth. Maybe I could forgive you and we could start over as you want—"

"I *am* telling you the truth. The child that I carry is yours." She trembled before him, her hands clenching into fists, as her grey eyes turned silver with fury.

Her fury fed his. How dare she be upset for what was an obvious question, and now she had the audacity to lie again?

"I do not believe you."

Her nostrils flared. "Well then you can just get out."

"What?" he sputtered, his eyes widening.

"If you do not believe me then how could you stand to look at me, stand to share the same space with me, let alone a bed?" she mocked, the biting edge in her voice like ice to his ears. "I know you have no desire to be near me since I am such a liar, so get out of our home and do not come back until our son or daughter is born."

He lifted his brows, noticing for the first time that she had said *daughter*. Before, when Basha had talked of having a child, it had only been of having a son. He wanted a son too, but would have been just as happy with a girl, but Basha had been very clear that only sons would do—the perfect Spartan soldiers. The fact that she could bring herself to even say daughter told him some things had indeed changed in his absence, but her wilful stubbornness wasn't one of them.

"What do you mean get out and do not come back until our child is born?" He swept his gaze over her. "That does not appear to be for another four moons—"

"Five. Five moons," she corrected.

He scowled. Four, five—it was still too long to be living outside his home. "Where am I supposed to live?"

She shrugged. "Don't know. Don't particularly care. Go stay with Thanos. He owes you a favour since we took him in. Then there's always the barracks."

He blanched. *The barracks?* He hadn't stayed in those for many *annos* and he'd promised himself he never would unless he absolutely had to. He stared at his wife, with her rigid stance and unyielding glare, thinking that maybe this was to be one of those times.

"Basha, this is ridi —"

"I am also asking that you do not take a lover while you are gone." Her voice was quiet, and her eyes had softened but only just a small measure. She seemed almost embarrassed as her gaze darted around the room, landing on every other thing in there but him. "I—I know what you *think* I did, and that the thought of touching me makes you cringe, but I am begging you not to take a lover while I carry your child."

Cringe? Not exactly. He was furious with her, but he was starting to believe that she was telling the truth. Even if he discovered she wasn't, Basha had to know that there was nothing about her that made him cringe. Their issues had always been ones of communication and trust. His desire for her had never waned, and he reasoned that it never would.

"I agree not to take a lover," he said softly as he stepped towards her.

She was kicking him out to punish him for the insult he'd delivered her. He understood that. But for how long did she plan to punish him — punish herself?

"But I have needs, Basha, needs I expect my *wife* to see to." He was so close he could almost touch her, and he knew she felt the heat of his body when she shivered, desire darkening her eyes.

"I-if you have need of me, then I shall see to you. I am still your wife. Just as this is still your home and you are free to come and go at will…"

"But?"

"But I do not want you spending your eves here. You have insulted me, even after I swore I was telling the truth, even after I said I was sorry and begged you to forgive me. There are many things wrong between us, and most of our troubles are my fault, but I have never once doubted the truth of your words, and yet you doubt mine."

Her words sliced through his heart and he stilled, realising then just how wrong he'd been. He'd never once confronted her with anything and had her lie to him. No, she hadn't volunteered the truth, but he could understand why. To her way of thinking, she had not truly committed an act against him—why upset him over something that had never happened? No, she had never once lied to him in the past, so why should he think she was lying now?

"This child is yours," she said quietly, when he dipped his gaze to her rounded belly, voicing what he now knew to be true, but it was too late. Basha did not wish to hear about his moment of revelation.

"And when he or she is born you will know this for a fact. For you shall see yourself reflected in the face of our child and you will know."

But until the birth of their child, he would have to humble himself before his wife, just as she had done before him. Maybe their eves apart would be good for them as they learned how to trust again, how to communicate again. He certainly knew he would spend the time working to repair their broken relationship and restore her faith in him.

"Lysistrata," he said softly as he reached out to cup her cheek.

"What?"

Lysistrata.

The woman who led the strike of thousands of Spartan women to withhold the pleasures of their flesh from their husbands until they ended the Peloponnesian War. Yes, Basha was now his Lysistrata.

He repeated the name, but Basha shook her head. "You will still have the pleasures of my body," she whispered, and he didn't miss how her eyes clouded with lust.

Basha was stubborn, so he knew not to underestimate her, but he did wonder how long it would be before she caved and let him back into their bed for an entire eve.

He thought of the sleepless eves he would spend on the straw bed mats at the barracks that were so uncomfortable they had no right to even be called beds. No matter how long it took, it would still be too long.

"Well, let's be thankful you've agreed to allow me the pleasures of your body, because I believe that is the only way I shall endure the discomforts of those barrack beds."

Her eyes twinkled with laughter and he knew then she had no heart. He read it right there in her smug gaze. She was going to enjoy watching him suffer. And for what he'd accused her of, he would deserve every moment of it.

Chapter Twenty-Two

"For your own good, I wish I could lock you up for the rest of your dawns."

Lamia smiled at the sound of Thanos' gruff voice as his strong arms locked around her waist from behind.

"My first sun rising back on my feet and this is how you greet me?"

Thanos groaned against her hair before he released her and spun her around to face him.

"I thought I told you not to get out of bed unless I was here."

"Thanos, I am fine, really. The physician even said so. You have much to do with the prisoners and the meeting of the council. You do not have time to attend to me any longer—"

His expression was stern. "*You* are the most important person to me, not the council, not the prisoners. *You*. Do you understand that?"

Warmth settled around her heart as she stared up into his face, love shining in the depths of his gaze. She wanted to protest again that she was fine, but she knew her words would only fall upon deaf ears.

Thanos watched her like a hawk. Even now, with all of his duties, and despite the physician's assurances, he was reluctant to leave her side.

She reached up on her toes to place a gentle peck on his lips, careful not to wince when a sharp pain shot up her side where the arrow had stabbed through her flesh. If Thanos glimpsed even the tiniest bit of discomfort on her face it would be impossible to prise him from their bedchamber. "I am fine," she said again, her voice soothing as she stroked her hand across the frown lines that creased his face.

"You lost so much blood. I do not want you to be alone if you find yourself dizzy. You could fall and hurt yourself, or worse, reopen your wound —"

"Basha and Armine are here and Callisto will be here shortly. You have left me with three overbearing nurses but I doubt I will need any of them. My wound is healing nicely and I'm almost back to full strength."

A dark glower crossed his face. "I do not think you understand just how truly lucky you are, Lamia, that the arrow went clear through without damaging anything vital."

"I do, Thanos," she said softly. "I promise you, I do." And she did.

Thanos didn't believe she was taking her near-death as seriously as he was, but he was wrong. She knew just how fortunate she was that she *and* Thanos had come through this ordeal alive. She clasped her arms behind his neck, pulling him close until their lips touched. His strong hands fell to her hips, careful not to touch her wound, as he brought her mound against his hard cock trapped inside the confines of his *pyterges*.

"I should leave…" Thanos groaned against her lips. "Before I cannot stop myself." His hands roaming over her body were a testament to his words.

With the shake of her head, Lamia clutched him to her. "Thanos, please. It has been so many moons since we were together like this, and then the dawns while I healed…" She slid her hands across his chest, teasing lower to the bulge below his waist. "I need you," she whispered.

"We cannot make love with you not fully healed—"

"But we can do other things." She grinned, her eyes twinkling as she cupped his face between her hands and kissed him again.

He sighed against her lips, his body already weakening, and she knew he was caving in when he deepened the kiss.

Flames licked her skin at the urgency of his mouth pressed to hers, at his body pressed to hers. She embraced him, biting back a groan when her aching nipples scraped across his chest. Her channel clenched, the juices of her arousal filling her sheath. Thanos backed her to their bed, his movements gentle as he laid her across it, but he did not cover her with his body.

She reached for him, but he shook his head, his eyes lighting with mischief as he made his way down the length of her, slowly pushing her *peplos* up past her legs until it bunched at her hips.

She gasped at the first kiss against her thigh, heat curling in her belly, radiating outward until she was a quivering mass of need and warmth. Her cunt was sticky and wet, aching for his attention, and she grabbed his head, arching, drawing him to the core of her.

"I take it you missed me," he chuckled, making light of her urgency, her desperate need to have him touch her, taste her in her most intimate place.

"Thanos, please," she begged, the words barely escaping her lips before he latched his mouth to her tiny nub, sucking hard. She cried out, jerking towards him when he thrust two fingers into her dripping heat.

"Oh gods." She shivered, her cunt tight from the long absence of him inside her, but welcoming as she took his fingers deep within her. He moaned against her mound, his tongue, his lips feasting upon her flesh, lapping up her juices.

Every centimetre of her tingled, her nipples throbbed, and she cupped her breasts, stroking them, heightening her pleasure.

She quivered against him, her body just at the precipice of fulfilment, but she clenched her eyes shut, fighting the onslaught of pleasure that raged through her. She did not want it to end — not so soon.

"Do not fight it, Lamia," Thanos whispered against her tender flesh. "Come for me, *agapetos*. Come against my face," he demanded, and she screamed out as she surrendered to the erotic caress of his heated words. Her channel tightened around the pounding length of his fingers and she exploded into tiny pieces.

"Thanos," she gasped, digging her nails deeper into the supple flesh of her breasts as she arched her body like a bow, tremors rocking her through the endless waves of her climax.

Thanos held her to him, anchoring her through the storm, his mouth devouring her, licking up every bit of her juices until her breathing quieted and she relaxed against the bed.

He settled her *peplos* over her legs as he stood, and she sat up, reaching for him. He bent down to take her lips in a sweet kiss, full of love, tenderness. As she twined her tongue with his, she let her hands roam down to the bulge inside his *pyterges*, cupping the heavy weight.

He seized her hand as he tugged his lips from hers. "There is no time—"

"But I want to please you, Thanos. It has been so long for you too."

He smiled. "Your pleasure is my pleasure, *agapetos*." He caressed her cheek. "But when I am done at the barracks, I will return to my wife's bed for my reward."

She stood, wrapping her arms around him. "And you shall have it, my love," she whispered, her lips joining his in a tender kiss.

"She just got on her feet and already you are trying to put her flat on her back."

Lamia grinned against Thanos' lips when he swore softly. She dragged her gaze towards the door as Basha entered with Armine in tow.

"Shouldn't you be at the barracks with Cleomenes?" Basha questioned Thanos. "Ulysseus left over an hour ago."

Lamia held back a snort. That was because Ulysseus now *lived* there, but she kept that to herself.

Thanos looked between her and Basha, his eyes filling with concern. "I don't think my leaving is such a good idea. Lamia is just getting—"

"Have you forgotten your duties, Thanos?" Basha's eyes widened as if she did not recognise him. "The questioning of the prisoners cannot begin without you. Lamia is fine. We will be here to see that she stays that way," she said impatiently.

He stared at his sister within the law with hard eyes as if he wanted to argue further, but the matching determination in Basha's gaze must have discouraged him, especially since they all knew she was right…and with child. Everyone was also careful not to upset her these dawns, especially not after what she'd done to Ulysseus, no matter that he'd deserved it.

His gaze snapped back to Lamia. "I only have to remain at the barracks until the interrogations are done. It is simply for convenience sake and it will allow the process to go by faster. It should take only a few dawns and I will return the moment they conclude," he assured her, dragging her into his arms with one last lingering kiss.

She knew he did not want to go, that he wanted to remain by her side, and she felt the tension in his body as he reluctantly released her. With stilted steps, he turned away and marched towards the door, stopping only to nod curtly to Basha and lovingly kiss Armine's brow.

As soon as he departed, they all breathed a sigh of relief.

"That man is worse than a mother hen," quipped Basha, and Lamia laughed heartily because she could only agree.

* * * *

Marcus Aurelius stirred awake at the sound of soft footsteps along the stairs leading down into the prison. He stood up from where he'd been napping atop the thin straw mat that crawled with fleas and curled his hands around the iron bars. Peering through the rusty rods, his gaze searched through the darkness.

From thousands of men, to just a few hundred. The Spartans had crushed the Roman army and taken the rest as prisoners. He would likely be turned into a slave or, if he was lucky, executed.

When the Spartan king had learned it was Marcus who'd kept Cornelius from striking down his wife and her friend, he'd been placed into solitary quarters. The king considered it a small tribute, since they both knew he would have been murdered in his sleep if he were put in a cell with the rest of the prisoners. The punishment for treason, for killing one of your own soldiers — no matter that Cornelius had been a bloodthirsty barbarian — was death.

He appreciated the king's gesture of goodwill, but he could not have cared less if he'd lived or died. His rising career in the Roman military was over, and his home, his lands and his title would all be stripped from him if he dared to return to Rome... That was if he wasn't first charged and executed for treason as soon as he set foot on Roman territory.

"I — I brought you some things," a small voice called, interrupting his dark thoughts. "I know it isn't much but it was the least I could do."

Marcus squinted, straining to get a glimpse of the woman with the soft, husky voice. She stepped forward, the embers of the torchlight casting a warm glow across her face.

He recognised her immediately. The woman from the battle. The woman whose life he'd saved. The woman who was the very reason why he no longer had a home to return to.

He glared at her, the bitterness inside him driving him to snarl out, "The *least* you could do? I would think so." He sneered at her comely face, a fresh wave of anger hitting him. He'd thrown his entire life away for a woman who wasn't even a great beauty.

He swept her with his disdainful gaze. *And* she was *plump* — though pleasantly so. His ideal woman had always been tall and toned, not short and lush, but he found the petite Spartan's voluptuous figure quite enticing as her ripe breasts and wide hips strained against her obscenely thin *peplos*, which did little to hide her supple figure. He decided then that she wasn't plump at all, just abundantly endowed. But apparently she *was* simple-minded because she failed to heed the warning in his angry gaze and continued to walk forward, stopping just within his arm's length on the other side of the bars.

"Again, I know it is not much. But I wanted to thank you in person for saving my life." She held out a bed roll, a jug of water and a small sack of food to him, which he begrudgingly took and set aside. "My father is a wealthy man, a member of the *gerousia*. I-if you are released, he has promised to reward you in kind, but this is all I could do for now to show my gratitude since you are still a prisoner."

He arched one brow. She was wealthy. *Interesting.* Maybe the gods had chosen to smile down upon him after all.

"Thank you," he said gruffly.

"You're welcome."

With the slight bow of her head, she turned and prepared to leave. But before she could take a step, he lunged for her and a sharp cry fell from her lips as he gripped the back of her *peplos* to drag her against the bars. He reached both arms through the bars, one at her neck and the other around her waist, trapping her against the sturdy metal poles.

He held her tightly, his lips within inches of her ear.

"I have lost everything because of you and a few measly coins from your father will not be enough to satisfy me."

She gasped. "What is it that you want then? Land, a home — he can give you that —"

He curled his lips into a sardonic smile, his mouth against her ear. "And I shall gladly accept his gracious gesture if he should offer." He dipped his head lower so that his breath fanned out across her neck. He smiled when goosebumps broke out across her skin. "But what I truly want is *you*."

"Me?" She now struggled to wrench herself from his grasp, but he held fast.

"Yes, *you*," he whispered hotly. "When they are done torturing me. Done flogging me because I won't give them the information they seek, they will release me and I will come for you." She shivered against the iron rods and he smiled triumphantly. He affected her. That was good.

"And when I find you, I shall take your lush and supple body to my bed as my just reward. I fully intend to mount you, to spend myself so deeply inside you until I have had my fill of you — and then I shall take you all over again." He slid the arm around her waist upward to brush against the swells of her heavy breasts, and he had to bite back a groan as blood rushed to his cock. "I have no doubt that, after my torture, your tempting flesh will be more than enough to soothe *all* of my aches."

He moved his hand to cup her breast, delighting in her sharp intake of breath when he stroked her pebbled nipple with his thumb.

"You have beautiful breasts," he murmured close to her ear, his cock hardening some more as he gently fondled her. "I will spend my eves behind these bars dreaming of how wondrous it will be when I finally have you beneath me, my cock tunnelling between your supple tits—"

The press of a blade against his groin stilled his roaming hand, and he instantly released her from his grasp.

She pulled the dagger from between the bars and spun around, her emerald eyes shooting fire.

"There are many things my father can give you as a reward, but I am not one of them," she gritted out between clenched teeth before she spun back around and stormed off.

He gripped the bars and a smug grin curled his lips as he stared after her until she disappeared from sight. "But you shall be, my lovely Spartan spitfire," he promised, thinking she was the *only* thing he wanted as his reward.

And Marcus would not rest until he had her.

Callisto tripped up the stairs as she rushed from the prison, slipping her dagger back inside the small pocket at the side of her *peplos.* She nodded to the guard and waited for him to unlock the gates, silently fuming. She should have never gone down there, never should have visited him.

"Thank you," she said, flashing the guard a weak smile as she stepped outside onto the street.

It had been a mistake to take that prisoner anything. He was arrogant and cruel and not deserving of it, but she felt it was the least she could do for the man who'd saved her life.

"Do not lie to yourself," she muttered angrily. "You *wanted* to see him."

Ever since that eve on the hill she had been unable to get his handsome face out of her head. She gulped deeply, hating that even in her anger her nipples were hard and tight and the folds at the centre of her womanhood dripped with liquid heat. He'd touched her — groped her — and she groaned at her body's traitorous response as she hurried through the streets towards her father's home.

A frown crossed her face when she thought of her beloved father, Pericles. This was all his fault. Her father was possessed of far too much honour to allow the Roman's actions to go unrewarded. But Pericles had now placed her in a difficult position. If the Roman was released — and she knew, for also saving Lamia's life, that was Thanos' intent — by the Spartan code of honour her father was obligated to give him *anything* he wanted — lands, a home, coins...*anything*. But Callisto knew he would refuse it all.

The Roman didn't desire lands and coins — he wanted the one thing that had cost him all he held dear, and that one thing was *her*.

* * * *

There was nothing luxurious or comfortable about the barracks where the army of *hoplites* under thirty *annos* lived. Simple structures made of wood, there were no couches, no beds, or even tables. The earthen ground was bare and hard. The only luxury the young soldiers were afforded was the warmth of the fire that burned in the communal hearth.

The food was disgusting, and gods only knew what was ever in the muddy broth they ate. Thanos had come to appreciate the crude conditions of the barracks, enjoying the camaraderie of his fellow *hoplites*, but he would readily admit that he would never willingly trade his lavish home and comfortable bed for even the softest mat of hay in the barracks. He was a Spartan solider, and he could deal with anything and do with nothing if he had to, but he'd be lying if he didn't admit that, ever since Lamia had come into his home and taken up residence in his bed, there was no other place he'd rather be.

"Your foreign wife has made you weak."

Thanos stiffened at the familiar voice baiting him. Turning slowly, he met Cleomenes' wizened gaze with a tight smile. With measured steps, he moved towards the older man, who enjoyed taunting him.

As Thanos now mentored Adonis, Cleomenes had played a central role in his upbringing and training, along with his own father, Icolos. That was why Thanos was slow to anger when it came to Cleomenes' words. The older king would poke and prod until he reacted, and when he did, Cleomenes would always know his weakness, the one thing that galled him, and he would use it to bait him, trap him. Thanos was no longer the hotheaded youth he'd once been, quick to anger and easily defeated by Cleomenes' cunning.

He knew what Cleomenes was doing, making subtle references to his actions on the battlefield when he'd raced to Lamia's side. He taunted him so that he would react and admit how foolish he'd been, but Thanos knew his actions were neither weak nor foolish so he tempered his emotions, his expression as blank as an empty piece of parchment.

"You think Lamia makes me weak, but you are wrong. My wife has made me stronger. Far stronger than my father, even stronger than you."

The older man's eyebrows lifted, and a small smirk crossed his face, telling Thanos that he recognised his own strategy being used against him.

"Really? And how is that? How does forgetting all of your training, abandoning command, breaking the *phalanx* and leaving your soldiers and your city vulnerable for one woman make you strong?"

Thanos shrugged, as if he had no care in the world, and truthfully he didn't, at least not when it came to his feelings for his wife, and his actions. He'd acted on impulse, but he'd do it all again in a heartbeat, without question and without hesitation.

"No, I never said doing all of *that* made me strong — just Lamia."

His impudence must have annoyed Cleomenes because the older man's cheeks reddened, but other than that, the elder king showed no other signs he was frustrated with Thanos.

"Your love for that woman will one dawn cost you. It will make you do things you would otherwise not do and, because of it, you will become careless, leaving yourself vulnerable."

Thanos' smile was slow. "That is what *you* believe, although what you say may be true. Maybe it will cost me one dawn, but I care not. Yes, our love for one another makes us vulnerable...but to each other, no one else. She is my strength, just as I am hers. And had it not been for Lamia and her leadership, *you* would never have been able to hold back the Romans. What she gives to me, she gives to all of Sparta, and we are all blessed to have her as our queen."

Cleomenes' lips twitched and he was sure the old man thought him a love-besotted fool. Thanos did not care. He was not ashamed to revel in his admiration and love for his wife, not anymore. Lamia was his partner, the keeper of his heart and soul, his equal in every way. Sparta owed her queen her life, and she deserved every measure of praise he heaped upon her.

"I can see you are determined to be stubborn about your wife, but I simply caution you, because when I am gone you will be expected to lead, along with Adonis." Cleomenes sighed, his expression darkening, and Thanos knew then what troubled him.

"I am a hothead and now a lovesick fool," Thanos acknowledged. "And Adonis is impulsive, sometimes acting *too* swiftly. No, we are not perfect, just as the kings before us have not been, just as you and my father weren't. We will make mistakes, but our duty to Sparta will always be foremost in our hearts and minds."

"Foremost in your minds, maybe." Cleomenes' grin was knowing. "But we know who is foremost in your heart."

Thanos couldn't argue with that, but he had nothing to prove to anyone. He would die for Sparta, just as he would die for Lamia, but, unlike Cleomenes, he saw nothing wrong with the fact that his heart belonged both to his wife and to Sparta. Thanos thought a man should only be so lucky to find a wife whom he would willingly die for, one who also wouldn't hesitate to sacrifice her own life for him.

Thinking of his vow to Lamia and all he would do for her reminded him of why he'd asked Cleomenes to meet with him in the first place—the promise he'd made to her before he'd left for Athens.

"I need to ask a favour of you, Cleomenes."

He nodded. "Go on."

"I want to put out a warrant for Atallus' arrest."

"For treason, I take it?"

That and one personal offence, but Thanos kept that to himself. "Yes. He drew the forces of Greece into a trap and betrayed us all. He should be arrested and tried for treason."

"You don't have to convince me, but you are already too late."

Thanos froze. Too late? Had someone already got to the snivelling coward? If Lamia hadn't made a promise to him, he wouldn't have been surprised if she'd somehow slipped out of Sparta and managed to get to him before anyone else could.

She did not yet know that Atallus was the one behind the Roman attack—he'd not had a moment to tell her as he'd watched over her while she healed. Thanos also had not wanted to upset her in her condition, for if she'd discovered Atallus' treachery she would have redoubled her efforts for vengeance. Atallus had almost cost them both their lives and the life of every Spartan—death almost seemed too kind for the monster Atallus was.

"What do you mean I am too late?"

"Euripydes has already issued a warrant for Atallus' arrest. There is no city-state in Greece where he is safe. As soon as he comes out of hiding, we will find him, and he will be tried for all of his misdeeds against Greece."

Good.

Every city-state in Greece was eager to convict Atallus of treason, and with that conviction came the punishment of death. Lamia would have her revenge as he'd promised, and he wanted to be the first to tell her.

Chapter Twenty-Three

It had been two dawns since Thanos' departure to the barracks and Lamia was now mostly back to full strength. The wound, which had seemed so large at first, was now just a tiny speck marring the otherwise smooth skin along her waist. She barely even noticed it — only when she moved too quickly would her side twinge with pain. Thus far, she was fine, mainly because she'd kept her promise to Thanos and the physician to not burden herself physically.

She still could not remain idle, however, so she'd taken to menial tasks, mostly bookkeeping duties, to keep herself occupied until the physician allowed her to return to her swordsmithing. Lamia had spent most of this dawn poring over the ledger. Not an arduous task, at least not physically, but her mind, now swimming in a pool of numbers, was thoroughly exhausted.

"Mother?"

Glancing up from the parchment before her, Lamia sighed, grateful for the interruption. Lifting from her stool, she marched towards Armine, smiling warmly.

Armine had begun using the title ever since her official adoption—and it had been so natural, so seamless, as if she'd given birth to the child from her own body.

"Yes, Armine?"

The girl wrinkled her pretty face into a frown. "A Governor Atallus is here to see you?"

Lamia froze.

She had not expected to hear that name ever again, at least not coming from the lips of her daughter, within the walls of her home. What could he possibly be doing in Sparta? She nodded to Armine who had been left in charge of 'watching' her while Basha returned to her home to gather some fresh garments for herself.

"Thank you, Armine. I will go to meet him."

When the child did not make any move to let her out of her chambers, Lamia sighed. "I will be fine," she insisted.

Thanos was bad enough. Not her too.

"Armine," she said firmly. The little girl pursed her lips into a sullen frown, but she finally stepped aside. "I will just be a moment," Lamia said, her voice softer now and she gently stroked Armine's smooth cheek before she turned to leave.

Straightening her *peplos*, she lifted her chin as she headed towards the open vestibule in the centre of her home where she knew Atallus waited.

"Governor Atallus. What a surprise," she said dryly, her voice as devoid of warmth as a frigid mountain pass.

Disgust rose inside her when he turned to face her, his beady eyes roaming over her figure. He was a thin man, almost frail-looking, but she knew he was surprisingly strong. She schooled her features into a stoic mask, praising herself for not stepping back when he stalked towards her, just as she admired her fortitude for not openly wincing when he smiled, revealing mangled, rotten teeth. He was as hideous on the outside as she knew him to be on the inside.

"Ah, I see you have done quite well for yourself here," he cooed.

His voice grated on her ears, the high-pitched squeal sounding more like it belonged to a small girl than the twisted monster who stood before her.

"What do you want, Atallus?"

His gaze dropped to her breasts and she swallowed the rising bile as she forced herself not to slap his face.

He shrugged. "I simply came to pay you a visit since I am in Sparta for —"

"Yes, and why is that, seeing as my husband just left from Athens under the apparent guise of defending your feeble little city?"

Like most Greeks, the Athenians were very proud of the state they'd built, and his sinister eyes instantly darkened at the insult to his city. "How dare you speak to me with such disrespect? You would never have dared as my slave —"

"Well, seeing as I am *not* your slave, I can dare all I like. Either state your business or get out."

Malevolence crossed his face, but she did not flinch. He did not have the power to frighten her. He was a coward.

"Thanos has let you run wild. You are nothing but a stupid cunt," he spat out angrily, his eyes bloodshot red. "I would have broken you, Lamia. I would have broken you until all you did was crave my cock like the whore you are —"

Inside, she recoiled at the vehemence of his malicious words, but her fury was all she allowed him to see as she exploded. "Get out of my home! Get out *now*!"

"Thanos will not be able to save you this time, Lamia," he said coldly, his voice dripping with malice before he spun on his heels and stalked out.

She trembled with rage long after he'd left, certain that Atallus' presence in Sparta was for nothing but nefarious purposes, and she shivered suddenly when a chill crept along her spine at the thought, for Atallus was a deranged and demented soul who thrived on cruelty.

She knew, whatever business he had in Sparta, that with his ego he had not been able to resist paying her a visit just to have the sheer pleasure of upsetting her. Atallus could not accept that he had 'lost' her to Thanos, never realising that one did not gain someone's affection using cruelty and force, but rather with kindness and respect. Atallus' twisted mind could not comprehend that Thanos did not *have* her simply because he was strong enough to control her — as Attalus himself had tried to do. Instead she was with Thanos because he respected her, cherished her, and treated her as his equal.

She needed to speak with Thanos immediately. Something just did not seem right about Atallus' presence in Sparta so soon after the debacle in Athens.

As she readied herself to leave, Lamia could not silence the voice deep inside that urged her to follow Atallus, to go after him alone and not involve Thanos. That voice inside her came from a place within that screamed with rage, with vengeance — softly cajoling her to snuff out his life the way he'd snuffed out Darius' with no regard for anyone else. The urge to do just that was so strong it pounded through her until she was trembling.

She'd promised Thanos.
Thanos.

His handsome, smiling face flickered before her, his eyes trusting as they shimmered with love. Instantly, she quieted the vengeful thoughts, for she understood now what was truly important—the life she'd built with Thanos and their future together. Almost dying had made her realise that. And clamouring for Atallus' death only threatened that future, yet it did not change the past. Darius was gone—Atallus' death would never change that.

Her obsession with vengeance—it was destructive, unhealthy, and, if she let it, it would destroy her and the love she now shared with Thanos.

She was determined to never let that happen.

She'd promised Thanos she would give him the chance to bring Atallus to justice through the proper channels, and she would give him that chance, which was why she needed to speak with him at once.

With deft movements she crept through their home, careful not to alert Armine. If she didn't leave before Basha returned then she would never be able to leave, and she just didn't have the time to wait for a messenger.

So, before either Basha or Armine could catch her and stop her, Lamia quickly slipped from their home, careful not to make a sound.

* * * *

Thanos dragged in a long breath as he spurred Zeus towards home, trapping the crisp, balmy air deep within his lungs. They were finally done with the interrogations. Of the remaining Romans, those who were the strongest and brightest would become *helots*, while others, mostly those who were just young boys, would be sent to Thebes and Athens as slaves. Those who did not become *helots* or slaves would be executed. He did not relish the thought of executing hundreds of men, but such was the way of war. He knew that, if the roles were reversed and he'd been captured in Rome, he would be suffering the same fate.

He gripped the reins tighter, brushing aside all thoughts of war. He was going home. The council had dropped their ridiculous charges against him and Cleomenes, leaving him with a few sun risings of peace from the grumblings of politicians.

Now all he wanted to do was return to his lovely wife and spend what few moments he had reacquainting himself with her pleasurable body and collecting his just reward.

* * * *

The streets of Sparta were eerily quiet this eve as Lamia hurried towards the centre of the city, where the barracks and prison were located. She'd forgone a horse, knowing it would quickly draw attention to her, as she did not wish to alert Armine or anyone else who might stop her. She also wasn't allowed to ride until the skin at her side had completely healed itself back together — another promise to Thanos and the physician that she now kept.

With nothing but silence all around her, her sandals clicked noisily against the stoned streets as she hastily walked along the path, darting her eyes about. Clenching the dagger at her side tighter, she picked up her pace. She could see the torches blazing outside the barracks. She was almost there.

The sound of footsteps trailing behind her made her stop and she whirled around, searching the darkness, while at the same time a sense of foreboding trembled through her.

She withdrew her dagger but was already too late.

The crushing blow knocked the air out of her, sending her sprawling backwards. With a moan, she shook her head as she struggled to see against the heavy shadows. Her side ached and bile clogged her throat, but still she tried to gain her footing, only to falter and stumble, her knees scraping the ground.

When another blow struck the back of her head, her face slamming against the stones, she closed her eyes, hovering just beyond the veil of awareness as pain thundered in her head, until finally she lost her battle and succumbed to unconsciousness, slipping away into oblivion.

* * * *

"What do you mean she is *gone?*" Thanos bellowed. The last thing he'd expected was to return home to find his wife missing.

Basha's eyes were gentle. "Thanos, please try to calm yourself."

Clenching his fist, he bit out, "Who would want to kidnap her?"

Callisto's blonde tresses bounced against her cheek as she shook her head. "We do not know, Thanos. All we know is that a servant recovered her dagger, a-and there was blood." Her eyes lowered to the ground. "Thanos, I am so sorry."

Spinning away from them, he slammed his fist into the table, sending dishes and pottery shattering to the floor when the table splintered in two.

Startled, the women took a step back. Ulysseus nodded to his wife, who quickly grabbed Callisto's hand and together they hurried from the room.

Ulysseus inched towards Thanos but did not touch him. "I will assemble a band of men. Together we shall find your wife and bring her safely home," he assured.

Thanos nodded stiffly but said nothing. His anger was too great to form words at the moment, but more than that his fear crippled him. He knew not who would take her, who would harm her, and that was truly what terrified him. His wife now faced an unknown enemy, and he was helpless and ignorant, emotions Thanos despised.

He could only hope his brother was right—that they would find Lamia and bring her safely home.

* * * *

Lamia groaned as she struggled to turn over, a sharp hiss rising out of her when needles of pain shot from her head straight down her spine. She closed her eyes to keep from losing consciousness again. When her head finally stopped spinning, she opened her eyes, blinking until her vision eventually adjusted to the darkness of the room.

The space was unfamiliar and her nostrils flared at the foul stench of heavy musk and urine. The rancid odours swamped her, and she held her breath, struggling to tamp down the rising bile in her throat.

When she could finally take a breath without choking on her own vomit, she tried to stand, but stopped, or rather was forced to, when she almost tipped over. Her hands were tied behind her back, her ankles bound together. But that wasn't why she now shook with fury.

It took her only a moment to realise that she was also naked. Anger surged through her and she struggled against her bonds, trying to squirm free. There was only one who would dare to kidnap her, and then leave her bound and naked, and she wasn't about to wait around to find out what he planned to do with her.

* * * *

Thanos paced back and forth in the outer courtyard of his home waiting impatiently for Ulysseus to return with more men. He wished he would hurry up. The longer they waited, the longer it would take for him to follow the trail of Lamia's kidnapper—

"Father?"

He turned at the sound of the soft voice, quickly masking his fury as he gave his adopted daughter a weak smile. Armine adored Lamia. He did not want his own fears for Lamia to frighten her.

"Yes, Armine?"

She walked slowly towards him, her eyes fearful.

He stooped down to her height and gathered her into his arms, his heart lurching at her forlorn expression. "All is well, Armine. We are going to find her," he said gently.

"I-it is all my fault," she whispered.

He frowned when tears poured from her eyes. "None of this is your fault—"

"Y-yes it is," she choked out. "I—I tried to stop her from meeting with the governor but she was determined. I—I heard him threaten her and then she disappeared before I could stop her."

The governor.

Thanos stiffened with rage even as dread coiled in the pit of his stomach. There was only one who would come for Lamia, who would even dare to set foot inside Thanos' home when he was a wanted man, and then threaten his wife.

Atallus.

"You said she met with a governor? Do you remember his name?"

She nodded quickly. "Yes, I shall never forget it. He was so scary and mean-looking. His eyes were—"

"His name, Armine?" he prompted gently, trying to keep her from succumbing to one of her frequent ramblings.

"Atallus. His name was Governor Atallus."

* * * *

Whack!

Blood flew from her bruised lip as he struck her again.

"You will learn to treat me with respect, you stupid whore!" Atallus screamed, spittle dripping from his mouth.

Lamia's eyes burned with hatred. "You do not scare me, Atallus. When Thanos finds you, he will rip you into tiny pieces—that is, if I do not do it first."

His hand whipped across her face again, sending her head spinning. She ignored the bite of pain, focusing instead on the ropes that bound her wrists. They were almost loose.

His maniacal laugh echoed off the walls, forcing her gaze to his demented face, but she did not stop twisting and turning her wrists.

"By the time Thanos finds you, you will be dead and I will be long gone." His high-pitched laugher took on a frenzied pitch. "He will be devastated when he finds your broken and used body, not knowing whom to exact his revenge upon."

She stared at him. He was clearly mad.

"Why are you doing this?" she asked when he started towards her, hoping to purchase herself more time to loosen the ropes.

Her question gave him pause and, thankfully, he stopped.

"I have been here for several moons, watching you both, biding my time until I could punish Thanos for taking you away from me," he said with a smirk as if he thought himself clever that he'd stalked them without their knowledge.

She wanted to rail at him that Thanos had not taken her, that it was Attalus who had sold her, but she knew it was futile to try to reason with him. He was insane. And she realised then that he was also obsessed with her. Atallus was one used to getting everything he desired, so, to his addled mind, he'd lost while she and Thanos had won. That she was now Thanos' wife, and obviously happy with him, had snapped what little sanity Atallus had possessed.

"And with Thanos out of the way," he continued, "you would have no choice but to turn to me."

She was incredulous. He truly believed she would turn to him if somehow Thanos were gone. She shuddered at the gleam in his eyes, realising then that he was more deranged than she'd first thought.

"I had plans for you, Lamia, because you were the key. After I got my fill of you, I was all set to pawn you off for a hefty sum. You'd be surprised how few advantages come with the position of governor, but I have always fared well, given my long-time friendship with Rome. So, when they approached me, I was happy to aid them. And it was the perfect plan, too. I relished the thought of seeing Thanos' face when he discovered it was *I* who had brought about the destruction of Sparta. Thanos would lose everything, including you, with the fall of the city. It was *perfect*." His eyes clouded with fury. "But Thanos, always thinking himself so clever, had to ruin everything.

"He was supposed to remain in Athens until the Romans had defeated Sparta and Thebes, but he didn't, and now the Romans refuse to continue filling my coffers. They think I've betrayed them, so I cannot go to Rome, and now I cannot even go back to Athens. Euripydes and Thanos know the truth and have issued a warrant for my arrest across all of Greece." His eyes turned colder as he stalked towards her, froth foaming on his lips.

"The Romans would have given me a hefty payment for you as a prisoner, the *queen* of Sparta," he mocked. "But the fools lost, so there is no one to pay me. I have nothing and it is all your husband's fault. Thanos has taken everything from me, so now I shall take everything from him."

Lamia did not know what he was talking about. His words of treason were probably just the ramblings of a demented mind...but if they weren't, and he'd actually betrayed the Greek city-states to Rome, then he had every reason to be desperate, because there was no place he could go without being brought to justice.

Atallus stooping down beside her reminded Lamia that no matter what she thought he may have done, she *knew* what he planned to do now. So, when his filthy hand reached out to grasp her bound ankles, she thrashed wildly against him until he trapped her legs down with the weight of his body. Dagger in hand, he sawed effortlessly through the ropes, but as soon as the ropes fell from her ankles, he slipped from his position of bearing down on her legs, and she kicked at him violently, striking him in his chest, across his face, anywhere she could.

Triumph surged through her when squeals of pain erupted from him as he fought against her flailing legs. But her joy was short-lived when he finally managed to grasp her ankles again, wrenching her legs apart. Without the use of her hands, she could not keep him from seizing her, and her stomach churned as he stared between her thighs.

She struggled violently when he leant forward to rub his body against hers, the foul stench of him stinging her eyes.

She worked frantically at the ropes, her shoulders burning from the effort as pain ripped through her wounded side, yet Lamia did not stop. Not even when vomit rose to the back of her throat, when she felt him fumbling with the layers of his *chlamys* and he released his slimy erection to rub it against her skin, did she stop.

But when his eyes glazed over with lust and he fisted his tiny cock to point it at her entrance, she halted her struggles just long enough to butt him in the head with her own. The blow stung, but she ignored the pain. He shrieked loudly as he clutched at his forehead and she used that moment of distraction to buck him off her as the ropes finally loosened around her wrists.

Shucking her bindings aside, she scrambled to her feet, only to sway when a wave of dizziness struck her.

Grasping her head with one hand, she placed the other against the wall, using it to steady her. She took a few hesitant steps towards the door. She needed to get out of there. She was still too weak to fight Atallus in her condition. If she could just get out of there, she could get to Thanos and then he could come back and arrest Atallus—

Pain shot up her spine as her head violently snapped back and she screamed. Twisting around, she wrenched her hair from Atallus' gnarled fingers, wincing when clumps from her mane remained in his tight fist. She swung around again, racing towards the door. She was almost there, but then he grasped her ankle, sending her sprawling to the ground on her hands and knees.

She delivered several mule kicks trying to shake him off, but he wouldn't budge. Wrestling over onto her back she ignored the pain in her leg as her body went one way while her foot remained pointed in the other direction, her ankle still imprisoned in his grasp. Rearing back, she lifted her free leg and rammed her foot into his face as hard as she could. The sharp snap of shattering bones reverberated in the small room as his head flew back at an unnatural angle, but she didn't waste time to see if he was alive or dead as she shook free of his grasp and limped to her feet.

She reached for the door at the same time that it crashed inward, sending her jumping back with a tiny yelp. Her heart skipped a beat at the first sight of him—an enraged Thanos charging through the doorway with Ulysseus and Adonis on his heels.

Once they'd ascertained she was no longer in danger, the latter two men quickly ducked back outside, their faces red with embarrassment at her naked state.

Her attention returned to Thanos. He called her name as he rushed towards her. Dragging her into his arms, he held her close. Every breath he took was ragged, each one of them shuddering through her. When he finally did release her, his hands shook as he cupped her cheeks, his gaze roaming across her face.

"D-did he hurt you?" he choked out.

She sensed the depth of his question, knowing what he was truly asking when his eyes raked her badly bruised face and naked body.

"No." She shook her head. "I am fine," she said shakily, circling him with her arms, holding him tight. "How did you find me?" she asked when he finally drew away from her to wrap her tattered *peplos* around her body.

"Armine was the key. She was the one who provided the clue that it was Atallus who'd kidnapped you. But you also left hints. You dropped your dagger where he grabbed you. And we followed the trail of blood from that spot until it stopped. We then traced a circle of the area. I wanted to check every shop and house nearby, but Ulysseus was adamant that Atallus was staying at a boarding home. This was the only boarding home close by, and the owner gave us the room number of a man who fit Atallus' description. Thankfully, Ulysseus was right and I listened to him."

She could only agree.

Closing her eyes, she nestled deeper into the warmth of Thanos' embrace, holding him just as tightly as he now gripped her.

Several soundless minutes passed before Lamia lifted her head from Thanos' chest. "I think I killed him," she said quietly, glancing over at Atallus' limp form, which hadn't stirred once.

Thanos followed her gaze with eyes smouldering with barely leashed rage. He gave Atallus' broken and prostrate body a dismissive glance. "Only because I did not get to him first."

* * * *

That eve, Thanos held Lamia in his arms, gently stroking her smooth skin as they lay in their bed, listening to the crackling of the fire in the hearth.

He'd almost lost her not once, but twice, and it humbled him to realise just how important this woman was to him, to his happiness, his very existence. Should she not walk this earth, Thanos knew Lamia would take with her his heart and soul until he joined her in the afterlife.

As if she knew his thoughts were of her, she stirred against him.

Lifting her head from his torso, her unbound locks cascaded over her shoulder, tickling the hairs along his chest. He tangled his hand in her hair, cupping the back of her head, his body tensing when he glimpsed the disquiet in her eyes.

"What is it, *agapetos*?"

She smiled, her fingers lightly touching his stubbled jaw. "When I left Athens, I never thought I would want anything more than Atallus' death by my hands." Her fingers stilled against his cheek. "But then I fell in love. I almost cannot believe I risked my love for you, was prepared to throw it away and abandon you, all for the emptiness of revenge. The day of the battle, the day I was injured, as I lay there in your arms, not knowing if I would die, all I felt was an overwhelming sadness." Her expression grew sombre, and his heart hammered in his chest at the pain in her eyes. "All those moons spent plotting my revenge, wasted, when they could have been filled with happiness and joy and my love for you." Her gaze held his, unwavering as she said softly, "My last thoughts before I passed out were of you, Thanos — not Darius, not Atallus, not revenge. When I thought I would die, all I felt was regret that I had wasted these last moons on my destructive need for revenge instead of showing you how much I love you, how much you mean to me."

"But all is well now," Thanos said soothingly. "In the end, the gods allowed you your revenge. Atallus is dead, and he died by your hands."

She shook her head. "But that wasn't what I wanted, not anymore, and, in the end, the completion I thought I would feel was not there. I thought killing Atallus would make me feel whole again, but I was already whole long before this night. I thought I would experience a feeling of triumph when he was dead, but instead I feel nothing. Had Atallus not come after me, I could have lived the end of my dawns knowing he would be brought to justice in the afterlife."

She tightened her arms around him, and in that moment he knew what she was trying to convey, and it made that fist clench around his heart again. He knew that he had her love above all else — that she loved him, as he loved her, more than life itself — but to hear her admit she was free of her need for vengeance, that she'd abandoned it long ago out of her love for *him*…

She settled her hand over his heart, her warm breath feathering across his skin. "Your love was what made me whole, Thanos, not revenge. I realised that when I awoke from my injuries in your arms. I accepted that I no longer needed to seek vengeance because truly all I need in this world is *you*."

Epilogue

Callisto did not want to leave Sparta, her family, her friends, the only home she'd ever known, but the expression on her father's face told her she would have no choice.

"Come in, Father," she said, stepping aside to allow him inside her modest home. "Would you like some wine?"

He shook his head. "You know why I am here," he said softly.

Her father was a handsome man. His position on the *gerousia*, his distinguished good looks and vast wealth made women flock to him. Pericles was one of the few in Sparta who'd maintained a single union, remaining true to it, even after her mother's death. But he'd genuinely loved her mother, and when she'd died, he'd refused to take another wife. At first Callisto had agreed with his position, unable to accept another woman entering into their lives, attempting to tarnish the memory of their mother, but of late she'd come to terms with the realisation that her father was lonely, that he needed companionship.

That was the foremost thought she still struggled with as she plotted her escape. She didn't want to leave her father alone. He was getting older, and there would come a time when he would be called to the Underworld, and she knew that she would hate herself if she was not there for him in his final hours. She did not want this to be the last time she saw her father alive because she was somewhere in the far reaches of the world, hiding from a man she could not bear to give herself to.

"You cannot give me to him a-as some reward. I am not an object to be bartered and traded." She'd been outraged that her father had even entertained the Roman's request. How could Pericles let him have her — a filthy Roman, of all people?

"He saved your life, Callisto, and I promised him anything he wanted in return, and he wants — "

"Me," she spat.

"He comes from a distinguished Roman family, and he is far stronger than most of his comrades. He wears the scars of many hours of torture and not once did he break, not once did he speak. Many others died, but your saviour wasn't one of them. He may not be Spartan, but his spirit, his resolve is strong. I would argue, unbreakable. At least you know your sons will have his strength of will."

Sons? She fought back a strangled sob. Did her father not hear himself? How he sounded? Did he not understand that she did not want to bear this man's sons — she didn't even want him touching her?

That single thought was a lie and her body proved her false when her nipples tightened against her *peplos*, her legs trembling as she clamped them together, struggling to ignore the warmth flooding her passage.

That was why she had to leave. Her body was far too eager for him, and it was that eagerness that terrified her. He knew she wanted him, and he would not hesitate to make her a slave to her own desires, where he would use her body to humiliate her…after he'd finished using it for himself.

Just the thought of him angered her. He was a stranger, an arrogant Roman who had been raised to despise the Greeks, to look down upon them. He thought himself superior to her and the ways of her people, she'd seen it in his eyes. How could she possibly wed him and hope for harmony in their union?

"Father, I refuse to wed him."

Pericles was slow to anger, especially when it came to her—his oldest child, his first born, his only daughter. Ordinarily, she could wrap him around her little finger, but this dawn she wasn't quite so successful.

"Callisto, you have no choice. I have given my word, and my word is my honour. Tomorrow he will be released and you will meet him at that prison where you will stand by his side and wed him in a simple ceremony. Then you will return here until I can gift you with a home as my present to you and your new husband."

She was going to be ill. He'd saved her life—but to what end? Did that mean he now owned her body and soul? Apparently so.

She gave Pericles a small smile as she fell into his arms, absorbing his strength, memorising every single detail that was unique to him, resigning herself to the fact that this would probably be the last time she saw her father.

Pericles would be furious with her, but he'd left her no other choice. By dawn tomorrow she would be long gone, and when they realised she was not attending her own wedding, it would already be too late.

* * * *

"Out, Adonis!" growled Thanos as he stalked towards the young *hoplite*.

Adonis lifted his hands in mock surrender as he stepped backwards. "I am just asking you to think about it." He grinned mischievously before he turned and ran from their home.

"And do not come back!" Thanos shouted after Adonis' retreating back, scowling when the boy laughed all the way through the courtyard.

Lamia gently prised Thanos' fingers from the door to their *oikos*, closing it softly.

"He admires you, Thanos. That is why he enjoys taunting you so." She smiled. "It is because he wants to be like you some dawn."

"I *bet* he wants to be like me." Thanos grimaced. "More like he wants to *be* me."

She sighed. "He only flirts with me to anger you. And it always works."

"So requesting a threesome with my wife is your idea of *flirting*?"

"All right, so I admit Adonis can be a bit outrageous at times, but honestly, Thanos, he means no harm." She wrapped her arms around his neck to press her body against his.

"He is half in love with you, Lamia," he argued as he wound his arms around her waist.

"I disagree. He is young and infatuated. He simply wants a woman *like* me, not me exactly."

"Well, he is just going to have to go to Carthage and find some other woman, because you are mine, *agapetos*," he growled.

"Oh, I do not think he is going to have to go all the way to Carthage to find her."

"No?"

She grinned. "Oh, no. Much to Adonis' horror, when he was visiting here a fortnight ago, Armine proclaimed that she would become his wife when she was old enough to wed, since she knew no other woman would ever be up to the task." Lamia could not stop the laughter from bubbling out of her. "Armine even went so far as to tell him she would do him this *one* favour after the kindness he'd shown her by dealing with those bullies at the *agoge*."

Coughs racked Thanos as he choked on his tongue. "W-what was his reaction? He better not have let her down cruelly or said something to upset her or I will wring his neck."

"Oh no, he was not mean, just far from agreeable. But at least Armine has a thick skin. He told her that, as much as he appreciated her offer, he never planned to wed, to which Armine replied that he would change his mind and one dawn he would very much *want* to wed her—" She chuckled, unable to get her next words out.

"What is so funny?"

"When Adonis tried to tell her she was mistaken and that he thought otherwise, she kicked him. *Hard.* In the shin. You should have seen his face."

"That is my girl. I have to purchase her another present," Thanos said, joining her in her laughter.

Wind rustled through the bushes then and their soft laughter floated outside, through the open window until it slowly died.

She had never felt this way before. She had never felt such contentment, such happiness as she stood there locked in Thanos' arms. The threat of war with the Romans had not yet passed and she knew Thanos would be called to defend Sparta again, but she pushed those fears aside for the moment. For now, Thanos was home and they were together and that was all that mattered.

She nestled deeper into his embrace, enjoying the warmth of his firm body enveloping hers. She'd never dreamed that she would ever find a man such as him—fierce and passionate, full of honour and willing to die for those he loved. She had never known a better man and she knew she never would. She didn't know what she'd done to deserve his love, but she thanked the gods every sun rising that she had it, and that she was his.

She then thought of her parents, her brother, the street kids who had been her family after the Romans attacked her home, and of Darius, who'd rescued her and loved her as his own. She rarely thought of all of them at once—the pain that accompanied the totality of her loss was far too much to bear in a single moment—but she found she could do it this time, even though it still hurt...and she knew it always would. Yet this time, as the memories washed over her, she found herself able to endure the pain of their absence, because for the first time in her entire life she knew she did not have to hurt alone, that she did not have to carry the weight of her burden alone. Thanos was there to lean on if she needed him, just as she would be there for him, and that knowledge gave her strength, but more than that it gave her something she'd never had before — it gave her peace.

She smiled as she stroked her hands through the thick curls at the nape of his neck, certain that her eyes shone with everything she felt in her heart for her husband — her Spartan.

"I love you," she said simply.

He dipped his head to kiss her lips. "And I you, *agapetos*," he whispered when he lifted his mouth from hers.

She furrowed her brow, remembering then the question she'd longed to ask of him, but which she'd kept forgetting.

"What is it?" he asked, his blue eyes swirling with concern.

"You call me that often, almost from the dawn we met, but I do not know what it means?"

"*Agapetos*?"

She nodded.

His gaze burned with such deep emotion that she swore she felt it sear a path straight to her heart.

"It is a term of endearment. It means '*my heart*' or '*my love*'," he said softly.

Her heart swelled with love for him and she tightened her arms around him, holding him closer.

"And am I your heart, your love?"

"Always, *agapetos*." Thanos cupped her cheek, his eyes never leaving hers. "Always and forever."

About the Author

Nadia Aidan lives, works and writes on the West Coast in the United States. Under her real name, Nadia holds a PhD in Political Science and Public Policy and by day she works as an Assistant Professor.

She writes across all genres, from historical, to fantasy/sci-fi to contemporary. In addition to writing erotic romances Nadia enjoys reading other authors, playing flag football, studying muay thai, working out, listening to music, scuba diving, and target shooting.

Her other interests include collecting Top Cow comics, especially Witchblade and Tomb Raider. She loves professional football and soccer. Her favorite teams are the Washington Redskins and Manchester United, respectively.

Nadia loves watching, reading about, and writing about strong, assertive heroines which is why she is an enduring fan of Fight Girls, Xena, Buffy, American Gladiators—New and Old, and La Femme Nikita!

Nadia Aidan loves to hear from readers. You can find her contact information, website details and author profile page at http://www.total-e-bound.com.

Total-E-Bound Publishing

www.total-e-bound.com

Take a look at our exciting range of literagasmic™
erotic romance titles and discover pure quality
at Total-E-Bound.

www.ingramcontent.com/pod-product-compliance
Lightning Source LLC
Chambersburg PA
CBHW030918260626
47169CB00002B/308